PRAISE FOR LIBBY FISCHER HELLMANN

The Ellie Foreman Series

"A powerful tale... Foreman's pluck and grit married to Hellmann's solid storytelling should win a growing audience..."
—*Publishers Weekly*

"Libby Fischer Hellmann has already joined an elite club: Chicago mystery writers who not only inhabit the environment but also give it a unique flavor."
—*Chicago Tribune*

"A traditional mystery with a modern edge... the author's confidence shows from beginning to end... refreshing as soft serve ice cream on a hot summer night."
—*Crimespree Magazine*

The Georgia Davis Series

"There's a new no-nonsense female private detective in town: Georgia Davis, a former cop who is tough and smart enough to give even the legendary V.I. Warshawski a run for her money."
—*Chicago Tribune*

"Georgia Davis works the affluent suburbs north of Chicago, fertile territory for crime that's lain fallow far too long. Davis' arrival on the mean streets is long overdue."
—Sara Paretsky, author of the V.I. Warshawski Mysteries

Set the Night on Fire

"A top-rate standalone thriller that taps into the antiwar protests of the 1960s and 70s."
—*Publishers Weekly*

"Haunting... Rarely have history, mystery, and political philosophy blended so beautifully... could easily end up on the required reading list in college-level American History classes."
—*Mystery Scene Magazine*

A Bitter Veil

"The Iranian revolution provides the backdrop for this meticulously researched, fast-paced stand-alone... A significant departure from the author's Chicago-based Ellie Foreman and Georgia Davis mystery series, this political thriller will please established fans and newcomers alike."
—*Publishers Weekly*

"Hellmann crafts a tragically beautiful story... both subtle and vibrant... never sacrificing the quality of her storytelling. Instead, the message drives the psychological and emotional conflict painting a bleak and heart wrenching tale that will stick with the reader long after they finish the book."
—*Crimespree Magazine*

Havana Lost

"A riveting historical thriller... This multigenerational page- turner is packed with intrigue and shocking plot twists."
—*Booklist*

A Bend in the River

"Gripping...Hellmann smoothly integrates into her harrowing narrative such aspects of the conflict as guerrilla warfare, spying, Agent Orange, reeducation camps, and boat people. This passionate story of survival has staying power."
—*Publishers Weekly*

"Sisters Mai and Tam's very different paths to survival in war-torn Vietnam provide a compelling, page turning story. Hellmann brings history to visceral, tangible life."
—Amy Alessio, *Book Reporter*

"Hellmann's simple but elegant prose offers interesting nuance and added depth to a war we thought we knew but maybe did not entirely understand."
—*BookTrib*

ALSO BY LIBBY FISCHER HELLMANN:

THE REVOLUTION SAGAS: HISTORICAL FICTION

A Bend in the River

War, Spies and Bobby Sox

Havana Lost

A Bitter Veil

Set the Night on Fire

THE GEORGIA DAVIS SERIES

DoubleBlind

High Crimes

Nobody's Child

ToxiCity

Doubleback

Easy Innocence

THE ELLIE FOREMAN SERIES

Virtually Undetectable

Jump Cut

A Shot to Die For

An Image of Death

A Picture of Guilt

An Eye for Murder

NOVELLAS

The Incidental Spy

P.O.W.

The Last Page

Nice Girl Does Noir (short stories)

Chicago Blues (editor)

MAX'S WAR

THE STORY OF A RITCHIE BOY

LIBBY FISCHER HELLMANN

THE RED HERRINGS PRESS
CHICAGO, IL

ISBN (Print): 979-8-989253-01-2
ISBN (Ebook): 979-8-989253-00-5
ISBN (Audiobook): 979-8-989253-02-9

Subjects: World War II—Fiction. Historical Fiction. Historical Thriller.

To the Hellmann family,
in memory of Fred

To secure peace is to prepare for war.
—Carl von Clausewitz

PROLOGUE

December 1942
Camp Ritchie, Maryland

Max Steiner wanted to kill Nazis. He had reasons. The Nazis had killed the people he loved. They'd forced him to flee Germany, then, a few years later, Holland as well. Hitler had stolen his life. He was not—and would never be—like other twenty-two-year-old men.

It wasn't always that way. He'd been a good-natured, bright, carefree boy. A boy who respected his parents, enjoyed his friends, and loved sports. Because of Hitler, however, he grew into a man who was plagued by uncertainty and fear. He anticipated the worst. He carried a rage he couldn't tamp down.

But now everything would change. He was about to take control —control he'd wanted for years. He stood outside the gates of Camp Ritchie, tucked away in rural Maryland near the Pennsylvania border. After months of running, marching, doing push-ups, and learning to shoot in basic, someone realized his fluency in German and pulled him out of the group. He wasn't quite sure why he was here or what he would be doing, but he hoped to take revenge on the Nazis.

If he looked toward the horizon, he had a view of Catoctin Mountain, part of the Blue Ridge and Appalachian chain. Snow dusted the evergreens and edged bare branches with thin ribbons of white. Max closed his eyes and breathed in deeply. He could almost imagine he was in the Black Forest. In the years since his family had fled Germany, Max had lived in urban settings: Amsterdam and Chicago. Now the chilled air was scented with a whiff of pine. It awakened a sense of longing for the greenery and thick forests of home. But that was not an option. He swallowed.

An MP checked his transit papers, opened the gate, and directed him to the main headquarters building, which resembled a small stone castle with symmetrical towers and parapets on each side. Unusual for a military base or camp, he thought. Max turned around to get his bearings. Although it was winter, active construction sites dotted the campsite. He wondered what they were building. He turned back to the main door and pulled it open.

He walked into a large room and gave his name to a clerk behind a counter, who picked up a phone and mumbled to someone. A moment later a uniformed man who looked older than Max came toward him from a row of offices at the back of the room.

"Private Steiner, I'm Lieutenant Bob Townsend. Welcome to Camp Ritchie. How was your trip?" Townsend was tall and skinny and wore reading glasses. His dark hair was wiry, and although it was morning, a five-o'clock shadow on his cheeks was visible. He extended his hand.

Max saluted. As a private first class, he did not expect to be greeted by an officer. "Good morning, sir."

Townsend held up his palm. "You can dispense with that. We're pretty informal around here."

"Yes, sir." Max lowered his hand.

"In fact, I think you'll find this place is not like other military institutions."

"Yes, sir," Max replied without thinking. He stopped himself.

Townsend laughed, as if he knew exactly what Max was thinking. "I know. It takes some getting used to."

Max felt his cheeks get hot. He wasn't used someone reading his thoughts. Then the lieutenant did something that startled Max, once he realized what it was.

"We may not have been here a long time, but we think it's a special place, and we expect you will too. Today you'll meet our commander, General Charles Banfield, and his top officers."

The general of the camp? What was this place? Officers didn't associate with NCOs like Max. Was this some kind of test? But when Max heard Townsend switch to the American pronunciation of "Banfield" he realized something else, perhaps more important. The lieutenant had switched from English to German. With an accent Max hadn't heard since he left Germany.

Max couldn't help it—he gaped. He spoke German with his Chicago cousins, but when he heard a stranger in an official US military setting use his native language, with a local dialect no less, the emotional door he thought he'd nailed shut started to crack open.

Townsend smiled as if he knew the effect he was having on Max. "You'll also meet Lieutenant Colonel Walter Benway, our second-in-command. And Colonel Davis, our director of training, maybe even Major Theodore Gresham, who created the program. Where in Germany did you grow up, Private?"

"Regensburg," Max said in German, still off-balance.

Townsend nodded. "I know it well. I'm from Munich myself."

"Practically around the corner," Max said.

"You'll find plenty of Germans here. Austrians too." He paused. "You Jewish?"

Max nodded.

"Most of the Germans here are. It's not home, but it's—"

He was cut off by a shout in English from a nearby office with a closed door. "Get the fuck in here, Lieutenant."

Max raised his eyebrows. Townsend grinned, went to the office, and opened the door.

"I've got Private Steiner here." He ushered Max inside, then stepped out and closed the door.

Max gazed at the man behind the desk. He had a solid frame, beady eyes, a ruddy complexion, and ears that were too big for his face. His manner made Max think he was used to talking long and loud, and anyone who disagreed with him could go to hell. An open folder lay on his desk, and as the door closed, he looked up from it and studied Max.

"General Banfield, soldier. Good to meet you."

Max saluted. Banfield nodded.

"Pull up that chair in the corner," Banfield ordered.

Max complied.

Banfield opened a drawer behind his desk, withdrew a box of cigars, and took his time selecting, rolling, and lighting one. The pungent acrid smoke wafted over Max. "You smoke?"

He pointed his cigar at Max.

"No, sir." He repressed the urge to clear his throat. His father had always told him to say he wasn't "partial" to things he didn't like. Cigar smoke was one of them.

"Don't know what you're missing." Banfield puffed. "Probably for the best. More for me." He chuckled. "How much do you know about Camp Ritchie, Private?"

"Practically nothing, General."

Banfield nodded as though he'd expected Max to say that. "Good." He puffed again on his cigar. "You have been selected to join the first ever US Army Intelligence training program. You are inside the Military Intelligence Training Center. MITC. But that's classified. You can never divulge the name or where we are. Never. Got that?" A stern look came into his eyes.

Max nodded.

Banfield's expression relaxed. "Over the next couple of months you'll undergo intense training in a number of areas that will prepare you to go back to Europe and help end this goddamned war." He cleared his throat. "Ostensibly your job will be to interrogate German POWs, pry out German troop movements and as much intel as possible about their military strategy. Which you will then summarize in a report and send up the line of command."

Banfield exhaled, dispatching a cloud of smoke and the odor that went with it. "But that's only part of your mission. You will also be trained in counterintelligence by our friends in the OSS. What you learn will equip you to be flexible, to improvise if need be, but to succeed in whatever you are tasked with. Wherever you are." He paused again. "You get what I'm saying?"

Max's pulse quickened. Banfield was keeping the conversation intentionally vague, but Max guessed he would be sent on specific missions to prevent German advances. Or keep them from getting Allied intel. A mix of pride, excitement, and fear washed over Max. It was as if his life to date had pointed him to this place. This time. This was exactly what he was supposed to do.

PART I

TEN YEARS EARLIER: REGENSBURG, GERMANY

1932–1935

CHAPTER 1

December 1932
Regensburg, Germany

Opa Steiner used to say that animals had a sixth sense that helped them predict the future. Opa would have known; he'd been a successful racehorse breeder. Now, as Max Steiner hurried out of his father's shop into the frosty winter air, his pony, Klara, whinnied and tossed her head. Was she impatient because Max had kept her waiting in the cold? Or did she know some significant event or change was about to occur? Max checked his wristwatch and groaned. He'd have to ponder Klara's foresight later. He was late for Shabbos. Max scrambled up to the carriage bench, lithe and agile as only a twelve-year-old boy could be.

"Sorry, old girl." He grabbed the reins. The horse was turning fifteen, but that wasn't old for ponies, especially Morgans originally an America breed. Although she was older than Max, he liked to mimic his father, who called every mare "old girl," even if she was a filly. "But there's good news for you, Klara. My bicycle will be ready next week. Papa wasn't there, but Jonas promised. Which means you can look forward to a good long rest."

Max clucked and tightened the reins. A birthday gift to Max two years earlier, Klara snorted, lowered her head, and began to trot. They made their way from the center of Regensburg past the brewery, the theater, and a church, toward the Old Stone Bridge. The Bavarian town, which sprawled on both sides of the Danube River, dated back to Roman times. During the Middle Ages, as part of the Holy Roman Empire, it was an important city, hosting religious assemblies and events. Once the bridge was built in the twelfth century, the city became even more important for trade. Its residents considered themselves worldly, sophisticated people.

Halfway across the cobblestone bridge, Max heard church bells tolling the hour. Most people here would probably consider the Gothic cathedral with its twin spires the city's most beautiful landmark, but Max loved the bridge. Not because it was a century older, but because the atmosphere pleased him. Klara's clip-clops seemed to land precisely on the chimes of the bells, producing a rhythm that was unexpected but satisfying. Max gave Klara her head, and she seemed to enjoy the duet she was part of.

Shadows lengthened and twilight settled. Without the sun, the river turned purple and the clouds pale gray. When they reached Stadtamhof, a smart neighborhood on the other side of the bridge, Klara picked up her pace. She was on familiar ground and home was just around the corner. That meant warmth, hay, and rest. For Max it meant washing up, clean clothes, and a hearty dinner.

He stabled Klara behind their home, an attractive stone-tiled house with a mansard roof, then ran up to his room and changed into a fresh white shirt and his favorite green sweater. His mother always told him the sweater made his blue eyes appear green. With his light brown hair, rosy complexion, and nimble body, she would say he would fight off girls when he grew up. Max was still too young to appreciate her predictions; he'd rather be the star of the school's track-and-field team.

After Max's mother lit candles and welcomed in the Sabbath, Max recited the hamotzi, the blessing over the bread. His father made the blessing over the wine. They skipped the ritual of washing their hands. They were Reform, more liberal than

Orthodox Jews, although their synagogue still used traditional prayer books.

Max's mother, a graceful middle-aged woman with silver hair and bright blue eyes that Max had inherited, rang a small silver bell on the table. Their cook, Ivona, emerged from the kitchen with steaming bowls of vegetable soup. Originally from Poland, Ivona had been with them as long as Max could remember. He considered the plump, flaxen-haired cook part of the family, a source of maternal comfort when his mother wasn't home, as well as sustenance.

"Thank you, Ivona," Max's mother said. "It smells wonderful."

Ivona beamed. "I was able to get fresh beans and onions."

His mother ladled a portion into her bowl and picked up a soup-spoon. She smiled after tasting it. "Delicious."

Ivona retired into the kitchen. For a moment, the only sound was the clink of spoons against delicately flowered porcelain. Then: "So, what did you do with your day, son?" Max's father asked.

Max laid his spoon on the saucer as he'd been taught. "I went to the store to look at the new Mercedes-Benz that came in, but you'd already gone." In addition to a dozen racehorses Max's father had inherited, he'd opened a bicycle shop that, as more and more Germans bought cars, expanded into an automobile repair shop. He had hired a mechanic and invested in the required equipment. Max loved the smell of diesel and gasoline fuel, brake fluid, even oil. He also loved to ask Hartman, the mechanic, questions about chassis, gasoline lines, brakes, carburetors, and how they all worked together.

"We should call you Junior Mechanic." Hartman would laugh. "Soon you'll know more than me."

Today, though, Max had been talking to Jonas, who managed the bicycle repair side of the business.

"Jonas promised to have my bicycle fixed by next week," Max said.

"Ach!" his father exclaimed. With his steel-gray hair, at least what was left of it—Papa was in his fifties—his military bearing, and his weathered face with a bristle mustache, Moritz Steiner inspired respect and not a little apprehension from Max. "I am not certain you should be riding it."

Max stiffened. "Why not? I can ride to school in half the time it takes to walk."

"There is something we need to discuss," his father said. He glanced at Max's mother and raised his eyebrows. "You told me the flat tire was due to a nail you must have picked up, is that right?"

Max licked his lips. "I did." He looked down at his bowl.

"And the bent frame occurred when you fell, and the bicycle crashed on the concrete of the schoolyard."

Max nodded without looking at his father.

His father cleared his throat. "Jonas came to me the day after you dropped it off. He said you weren't telling the truth."

"How can you say that? How would he know?"

"Because Jonas could not find the nail. But he did discover that the tire was slashed on the rim."

Max kept his mouth shut.

"And as far as the bicycle frame is concerned, it seems that someone smashed it with a hammer."

Max ran his tongue around his lips.

"So, here is what I think. I believe you are trying to hide the fact that you were picked on by some Hitler Youth bullies."

Max didn't reply.

"That's how it starts," Mutti said. "Today a bully, tomorrow a Nazi."

His father waved a hand to silence his mother. She bit her lip.

"Maximillian . . ."

"Yes, Papa?"

"Isn't that closer to the truth?"

The tinkle of the silver bell interrupted his father, and Max had to wait while Ivona cleared the bowls and served roast chicken with stuffing, baby potatoes, and broccoli. While Ivona was serving, Max squirmed. His mother had temporarily rescued him from his father's questions, but his cheeks were on fire. He couldn't lie to his parents.

After Ivona had returned to the kitchen, Max said, "I didn't want you to worry. I had to stay after school for a few minutes. When I got to the bicycle, no one was there. Just the slashed tire and bent frame."

He decided not to mention the hushed jeers and chortles of several uniformed Hitler Youths huddled a short distance away. Boys who, in the past, had been his school friends. Who had come to his house, and he to theirs. He wasn't as angry as he was confused. Why had they turned on him?

His parents exchanged glances. Papa looped his thumbs behind his suspenders and ran his hands up and down the elastic. For the first time, his mother cut in.

"Moritz, it wasn't his fault."

"That is true. Still, he lied about the circumstances." He glanced at Max. "Did you not?"

Before Max could speak, his mother spoke again. "He was only trying to save us from worry, weren't you, darling?"

Max wasn't sure what to say. He gazed first at his father then at his mother. His father might be stern, but he wasn't cruel.

Indeed, this time his father rescued him. "You are absolutely right, my dear Hannah."

Mutti's expression said she might be on the verge of tears. To be honest, Max was as well. His throat closed up. He scolded himself. This was no way to act like a man.

"Maximillian," his father said, "you do not have to protect us. We are your parents. It's our duty to worry about you."

"Darling, it is no one's fault," Mutti repeated. "Except that madman from Austria."

"Hannah, keep your voice down." Papa gestured toward the kitchen and lowered his voice. "I've said it before. It is not so much Hitler and his thugs. It is the economy. The Weimar Republic suffered after the Great War. Then the crash on Wall Street. We are in the middle of a worldwide depression. With unremitting inflation. People from America to Europe and even Asia feel it. The German people are looking for a solution. They think they've found it with these National Socialists, but you can't take them seriously. We are a republic. Once Germany recovers and jobs return, the Nazis and little Mustache Man will fade away."

"Yes, but what about their antisemitism?" Mama said. "Ever since the National Socialists became the largest party in the Reichstag, a noose has been flung around our necks. And every day someone, somewhere tugs it, and it grows a bit tighter."

Papa was seven years older than Mutti, and sometimes he lectured both Mutti and Max. "Hannah, don't be melodramatic. Antisemitism has been with us for centuries. It will never disappear completely. We'll do what we always do: deal with it one day at a time. You'll see. This time next year, it will be different."

"So you believe we are safe here in Germany?" Max asked.

His father hesitated. Then: "Yes. I believe we are. And we are fortunate to be in a position where the economy will not affect us."

If his father believed they were safe, Max thought, he would too.

"What about Hitler?" Mutti asked.

Papa looked from Max to Mutti. "We must pray that Hindenburg is sensible and Hitler does not become chancellor."

CHAPTER 2

B ut he did.

A month later, at the end of January 1933, President Hindenburg appointed Adolf Hitler chancellor, head of the German parliament. For the first time the Nazis had majority control of the government. It seemed to Max they wasted no time. Every month brought a fresh assault on the rights of the German people.

At the end of February, barely a month after Hitler became chancellor, a suspicious fire burned down the Reichstag, the parliament building. The next day, the Nazis blamed the Communist Party for the arson and banned them from government. Hitler went to President Hindenburg and persuaded him to suspend individual rights and due process of law.

In March Hitler asked the Nazi-controlled Reichstag to pass the Enabling Act, which they did. From that day forward Hitler alone had the power to make laws. The government also opened its first prison camp to house political opponents, homosexuals, Jehovah's Witnesses, and others classified as "dangerous." The camp was located in Dachau. Dachau was just an hour's drive from Regensburg.

In April a flood of educational edicts caused major upheavals not only in the German school curriculum but in the schools themselves. Max was in the second year of secondary school and was looking forward to gymnasium in a few years. After that he would pursue studies at university. He was a good student and enjoyed learning. However, the changes dictated by the Hitler government did not augur well for Jewish students.

Classes in physical education were now required for all pupils. Max didn't mind. He wasn't tall, but he was fast and agile and was on the track-and-field team. However, as the spring season neared, the coach, with whom Max had a friendly relationship, failed to put him on the roster. When Max asked why, the coach replied that he had been forced to cut Max. Other students had been given preferential treatment.

"What does that mean . . . preferential treatment?" Max asked.

"It means that they are not as smart as you. The only thing they are good at is athletics. You are smart. You have other opportunities. They don't."

Max stared at the coach. "But I'm good at track."

The coach let out a breath. "I'm sorry, Max."

Max glared at the coach. "Is it because I'm Jewish?"

The coach turned and walked away without a word. They never spoke again.

A new course was added to the curriculum: Racial Science. In the lower grades, students were to learn about "worthy" and "unworthy" races, with the not-so-subtle conclusion that Aryans were the "master race." They were to check their eye color and texture of their hair against charts of Aryan or Nordic types, and create family trees to establish their biological ancestry. In math, stereotypes about Jews began to surface along with square roots and algebra. Students were urged to wear their Hitler Youth and German Girls League uniforms to school. Nazi propaganda posters and slogans began to cover school bulletin boards, and a few teachers began to read antisemitic articles out loud.

April also brought other mandates for Jews. Jewish teachers were told they could no longer teach at German schools and universities. Overnight they were banned from the education system. At the same time, the government issued the Law Against Overcrowding in Schools, which limited the number of Jewish students in a school to no more than 5 percent of the school population.

Regensburg's Jewish population was 427 out of a city of 81,000, barely half of 1 percent, so the Steiners didn't worry that Max would be barred, and he wasn't. But some Jewish families in other parts of the country were forced to pull their children out of public school.

The Nazi government also encouraged a boycott of Jewish shops and businesses. Despite the economy, Moritz Steiner's businesses flourished. His bicycle and auto repair shops were the only shops of their kind in Regensburg, so his customers had nowhere else to go. But other businesses in Regensburg didn't fare as well. At L. Josephsohn's store downtown, an SA Brownshirt with a rifle stood guard at the door to keep shoppers from entering. Still more Jewish businesses in the marketplace of central Regensburg were shunned. Some were attacked, probably by Hitler Youths, Max thought, and their wares destroyed.

In April the Nazis passed a decree that defined a non-Aryan. Any individual who was descended from a Jewish parent or grandparent was automatically a non-Aryan.

On a dazzling spring day when sunshine kissed the ground, robins chirped, and violets bloomed, Max's best friend, Günter, hurried out to Max in the schoolyard after lunch. Günter, one of the few Jewish boys left in school, was pale.

"What's wrong, Günter?" Max asked worriedly. "Are you ill?"

Günter shook his head. "What was the name of the book about Jews that was exposed as a fraud?"

"What are you talking about?" Max said

Günter was tall and had a sturdy build, and he looked like he could throw a solid punch. Because of that most of the other boys left him alone. Now, though, Max thought he might start trembling any second. "The one with the word 'Zion' in it," Günter added.

Max raised his brows. "Do you mean *The Protocols of the Elders of Zion*?"

Günter nodded. "That's the one."

"What about it?"

"Herr Schröder and Frau Brandt were at the lunch table reading through it and taking notes." The history and social studies teachers.

Max frowned. "But it's full of lies. They know that."

"It didn't sound like they did."

Max's pulse sped up. He pushed back a thatch of hair that fell across his forehead. "What did it sound like?"

"Like they were preparing a lesson."

Max stared at Günter, then spun around as if he was looking for the teachers. His stomach knotted. He didn't understand. Everyone knew the book was a fraud; it had been exposed as such.

Günter's face filled with fear. "What are we going to do if they bring it up in class?"

Max didn't have an answer.

Max was riding his bicycle home from school worrying about *The Protocols of the Elders of Zion* when he spotted one of the students whose parents had transferred her to the synagogue school. Renée Herskowitz was reading a book on the steps outside her house. A year or two younger than Max, Renée was a tall—taller than Max—slim girl with dark wavy hair, blue eyes, and pale skin. She just missed being beautiful; her nose was too big for her face. But Max liked that about her; she looked different from other girls. Like Max, she lived in Stadtamhof, just two streets away from the Steiners. Her family had come to Regensburg from Czechoslovakia after the Great War. Her father was a jeweler.

Max slowed as he approached. "Guten Tag, Renée," he said.

She looked up from her book. "Guten Tag, Max. How are you?"

Max braked, swung himself off the bicycle, and pushed down the kickstand. "Were you in school today?" When she nodded, he said, "How is it at the synagogue? Are there many students?"

"Maybe a dozen. They are hiring teachers."

"What do you think?"

"I miss our old school," she said. "It's not the same."

There was such a sad look in her eyes that Max searched for something to cheer her up. "Perhaps this will not last. Perhaps your parents will change their minds. You could come back to school, you know? There are—"

She cut him off. "My parents say this is just the beginning. They are already talking about leaving."

"No!" The word slipped out, louder and more forceful than he'd intended. "I mean, why? Where will you go? Back to Czechoslovakia?"

"I don't think so. Papa says it will be just as dangerous there." She shrugged. "I suppose my parents are used to moving. But I'm not." She closed her book with a thump and held it up. "I wish I could run away. Like Tom Sawyer and Huckleberry Finn in this book."

Max tilted his head. "What is that?"

"*The Adventures of Tom Sawyer.*" A smile crept across her face. "From America. My mutti bought it for me."

"What's it about?"

"It's a wonderful story about two boys—they're not children but not adults either. And their adventures are almost impossible to believe. They're practically hoodlums. There are Indians, thieves, gold, grave robbers . . . and a young girl named Becky. I'm almost finished. It's very exciting."

Max repeated the title. "I haven't heard of it. Tell me more."

Renée started into an explanation of the story, but after a minute, she shook her head. "It is complicated. I can't tell you everything." Her eyes twinkled with pleasure. "But it's a wonderful story. If you want, I will lend it to you when I finish."

"I would like that, Renée." He returned her smile.

By the last week of April, the Nazis had banned Jews from holding civil service, university, and state positions. They forbade Jewish lawyers admission to the bar. And they established the Gestapo, Hitler's secret police. Another productive legislative season concluded.

CHAPTER 3

Spring–Summer 1933
Regensburg

As the days lengthened and grew warmer, Max looked forward to summer. He would be working at the auto repair shop helping Hartman fix the Daimlers, Mercedes, and other cars that came in. Learning the complexity of an automobile, which he could study firsthand at his leisure, would be fascinating. When he wasn't at the shop, he planned to spend as much time outdoors as he could.

The Steiners usually made two summer trips: one to see his mother's parents in Alsace near Strasbourg, the other to the Swiss Riviera and Lake Geneva. He was an only child, and visits to his grandparents were a treat. His mother had a brother and a sister-in-law who visited from Berlin at the same time, and he had three boisterous first cousins to play with. They made him long for his own brother or sister, but it wasn't a subject he raised with his parents. He sensed it wasn't something a son did. But he did learn a bit of French when he was with his grandparents. And Mutti liked to reinforce it by chatting in French back in Germany.

Max loved the Switzerland trip as well for different reasons: It was the only time he had his father's complete attention. They would explore Lausanne's museums, then climb the steps of the Gothic cathedral to the bell tower for a vista of the lake. They would discuss architecture and history, a pet hobby of his father's; go to the beach, his mother's favorite activity; and eat far too many sweets. His father had discovered a small antiques shop tucked away on a street near the university. They would drop in every summer to see the new arrivals. Like his admiration for well-made automobiles, Max appreciated a carefully constructed piece of furniture, even an intricate clock.

The Steiners were just finishing dinner one evening in early May, and Max was planning to take his bicycle out for a short ride before dark, when his father said, "Son, we have something to discuss with you."

Max looked over. "Yes, Papa?"

"We won't be going away this summer."

Max stopped eating, his fork in midair. "Why not?"

His father glanced at his mother, then back at Max. "It's for a good reason."

Max laid his fork down.

"You will be turning thirteen in September. You must study for your Bar Mitzvah."

"I'm going to be a Bar Mitzvah?" He stole a glance at Mutti, whose expression seemed to indicate she wasn't altogether happy with the decision. Max hadn't given his Bar Mitzvah any thought. In Reform Judaism, it wasn't compulsory. Some families celebrated the event, but others, increasingly, didn't. "I thought you said it wasn't important."

"We changed our minds. I spoke to the rabbi today. He is going to schedule it for the middle of September. Perhaps on your thirteenth birthday."

Max folded his arms like his father often did. "What made you change your mind? Hitler?"

"Not really," his father said.

Max was bewildered. He attended Hebrew school one afternoon a week and on weekends, but nobody, even Bar Mitzvah boys, took their religious education too seriously. For most German Reform Jews, the goal was to assimilate as much as possible. To become "more German than the Germans."

"Moritz, tell him the truth," his mother said. His parents exchanged a glance.

His father hesitated. Then: "The hotel managers told us there were no rooms for us at either of the hotels we usually stay at in Lake Geneva. And the ones that do have rooms, we don't want. Plus, your grandmother insists you be a Bar Mitzvah. Apparently your three male cousins are planning theirs."

Max blew out a breath. "But Lake Geneva and Lausanne are in Switzerland."

His father shrugged.

"It is because of Hitler, isn't it?"

His father began, "The Germans and the Swiss have been—"

His mother cut in. "The truth is that Hitler and his hooligans have unleashed a poisonous brand of antisemitism that isn't confined to Germany's borders, son. Ces sont des monstres."

Max pushed his plate away. Angry tears stung his eyes. In his twelve-year-old mind, he felt entitled to a summer on the lake. The sun dancing on his skin. Spending time with his father. He hadn't done anything wrong, but he was being punished all the same.

His parents had drilled into him how fortunate he was to live in a large house, own his own pony, and have everything he needed. Hashem had blessed them. He shouldn't complain. Max tried to remember that when he was with others who weren't as comfortable and secure as his family. But this wasn't fair. To spend the summer in a stifling, airless room memorizing his Torah and haftorah while his cousins in Alsace played ball, swam, and rode their bicycles was an insult. Why couldn't the Nazis disappear? They were ruining his life.

In the back of his mind, however, and what kept him from complaining to his parents about his Bar Mitzvah preparation, was a sense that was bigger and more consequential than childish tantrums. It wasn't much more than a vague feeling at the time, but years later he would understand it fully. In the face of vicious antisemitism, his parents chose to use his Bar Mitzvah to defy the Nazis. To celebrate who they were—Hitler be damned.

~

On the tenth of May, students in Berlin burned more than twenty-five thousand books considered "un-German" in a massive bonfire. The move was encouraged by Joseph Goebbels, the Reich's head of propaganda, who declared, "The era of extreme Jewish intellectualism is now at an end." That night students in other parts of Germany marched in torchlit parades against the same un-German "spirit." Max thought back to *The Protocols of the Elders of Zion*. His mother had gone to his school the next day to register a complaint after he told her what Günter had seen. So far, the books had not come up in his classes.

The Elders of Zion wouldn't be on the list of books that were burned. But the book that Renée Herskowitz said she would lend him might well be. He bicycled to her house the next day after school. She wasn't outside, so he rang the bell.

She opened the door. A smile lit her face. "Hello, Max."

An unexpected rush of self-consciousness made Max's nerves tingle and his body feel awkward. "Hello, Renée."

"Please come in," she said. To Max's relief, she either didn't notice or pretended not to notice his unease. "Would you like some tea? Or something cool?"

"Something cool, please."

She nodded, still smiling. "Mutti made lemonade this morning. I'll get some." She led him into their front hall. This was Max's first time in the Herskowitz house. He glimpsed dark furniture, oriental carpets, and heavy drapes. He sat in an upholstered chair. He heard her in the kitchen opening and closing cabinet doors, pouring liquid into glasses. She was back a moment later carrying a tray with two large glasses of lemonade and a plate of biscuits. "Let's go out on the stoop," she said. "It's cooler there."

Max, still slightly embarrassed, recovered just in time. "Let me carry something."

"Why don't you take the biscuits?"

He took the plate. The scent of cinnamon, vanilla, and fresh-baked dough drifted up. "They smell wonderful."

"I just made them."

He wasn't sure what to say, and that bothered Max. He was rarely at a loss for words.

Outside, late afternoon sun shimmered rosy against blue sky. A soft breeze rustled the leaves. They settled themselves, and she handed him a glass. Max tipped it up, gulped down a few swallows, then abruptly stopped. Where were his manners? She would think he was a heathen. But she seemed absorbed in watching a bird peck at the ground beside the stoop.

Why did he feel so awkward? For the first time he was aware of how Renée moved, the expression on her face, even the way she waved her hands.

He tore his gaze away and looked at the biscuits. "May I?"

She giggled. "Of course."

He took one and bit into it. It was still slightly soft on top. As he chewed, cinnamon filled his mouth. But it was not too much. He sighed. "Perfection."

If a smile could become more dazzling, Max had never seen it until Renée's. "Thank you," she replied. "Have another. I can make more next week."

He picked up another biscuit. Vanilla this time. Equally good.

"So, how is school?" Renée asked.

"Only one more week."

"The same with us."

"Did they hire more teachers at the synagogue?"

"They did. They're not allowed to teach in public school, as you know. My father says they probably aren't making as much money."

"That's not right," Max said.

"At least they have a job."

"True." He took a third biscuit. "Have you read any of the books that were burned the other day?"

She shook her head. "But my parents did." She paused. "They banned Freud, Einstein, even Jack London. Oh, and H.G. Wells. Most of the authors live or lived in America."

Max hadn't known the authors were banned. "Do you think your book about the two American ruffians would be banned?"

"*The Adventures of Tom Sawyer*?" She tipped her head to the side. She was thinking. Max noticed her tongue jut out for a scant second. "Two young boys who take matters into in their own hands? Who do not follow rules? Absolutely. It would be considered highly provocative. Even subversive."

He grinned. "If you still have it, I'm ready to read it."

She grinned too. "You might have to hide it from your family. Certainly from any visitors to your home."

"Don't worry." He took another biscuit. He was beginning to feel like himself again.

"Which do you like more, the cinnamon or the vanilla?"

"I couldn't possibly decide. Can't I say both?"

She laughed.

They talked for another hour about their families—Renée had a younger brother, Wolf, whom she described as a "little menace"; their plans for the summer; their fear of the future; even the latest movies from Hollywood. As the sun dipped toward the horizon and the temperature cooled, she went inside and came back with the book and a package wrapped in paper with a string tied around it.

"These are for you, Max. Along with the book."

He took the biscuits, his cheeks once again flaming. Why? It was just Renée.

CHAPTER 4

Summer 1933
Regensburg

I n the middle of July the Nazis banned all political parties except themselves. On the same day, the Reichstag passed a law that permitted the forced sterilization of any German with a physical or mental handicap. A third law passed the same day stripped Jewish immigrants from Poland of their German citizenship. The Steiners had been in Germany for three generations; Max was the fourth. They weren't from Poland, and their Polish maid, Ivona, wasn't Jewish. Still, Max felt the anxiety, especially from his mother.

He was supposed to be studying his Torah portion for his Bar Mitzvah one night after dark, but he couldn't concentrate. He'd invited Renée on a carriage ride around Regensburg earlier that evening, and they'd followed the Danube as it curled around the city. Klara trotted briskly, but Max slowed as they approached Herzogs Park to watch the sun set. Purple clouds edged with gold glinted for a final burst of light before the sun slowly sank behind the trees.

Neither of them spoke. The sunset, like a perfect symphony, Max thought, had been too splendid for words. When he finally looked over, Renée was staring at him. In the encroaching twilight the color of her eyes had deepened to dark blue, as rich and royal as his mother's sapphire ring. He swallowed. An awkward sensation swept over him. He was supposed to do something, wasn't he? But what?

Renée broke the spell. "You know, Max, you have one of the final parashah of the year."

Max didn't expect the sudden conversational shift. Renée had to be the most intelligent girl he knew. Perhaps the smartest person in the world. Besides his father.

"That's what the rabbi said." He bent his head. "But how did you know?"

"The last Torah portion of the year, V'Zot HaBerachah, is always read on Simchas Torah, and that falls on October twelfth this year. Your Bar Mitzvah is barely a month before. So your Torah portion is the one right before it."

"It's the week before Rosh Hashanah. It's odd. I always thought we restarted the Torah on the new year. But we don't."

"There are theories about that. The one I like"—she smiled— "says that we hold off to 'trick Satan' about the exact day Rosh Hashanah falls on. And once we delay, we delay more, until the first Shabbos *after* the High Holidays so that we won't interrupt the Torah cycle with holiday readings."

He shot her an admiring smile. "Renée, how do you know all these things?"

She reddened as if a bit embarrassed. "I don't have much to read these days except the books at the synagogue."

Had she specifically looked for information about his parshah? "What about your American runaways?"

"I'm waiting for the next book. "It's called *The Adventures of Huckleberry Finn*. I hear it's quite popular, so it might take time to arrive. If it's not banned."

"Do you think it might be?"

She bit her lip. "It should be. But perhaps the Nazis don't know about Mark Twain."

Now in his bedroom, Max was thinking how special Renée was to take an interest in his studies. None of his other Jewish friends did.

When they got back to Stadtamhof, furthermore, she'd fished out another small package tied with string and dropped it in his lap.

"How did you know?" he said. "These are now my favorite sweets."

"I'm so glad." She squeezed his forearm. "Sweet dreams, Max."

~

Sweet dreams indeed, he thought now. He'd already wolfed down three biscuits. He turned his attention back to the Bar Mitzvah passage. He was determined to memorize a few verses but stopped when he overheard his parents talking quietly in their bedroom. It was almost ten. Usually their door was closed by now. He crept out of his room. The door was ajar.

"You know that Ivona is an immigrant, correct?" Mutti's voice was barely above a whisper.

"But she's not Jewish, and she's been here for years. How many? Ten? Fifteen?" His father.

"Yes, but—"

"But what, my dear?"

"What if she decides it's too risky to work for a Jewish family?"

"Then we'll find someone else."

His mother's voice rose. "Who will work for us?"

"Hush, Hannah," his father said. "Maybe the synagogue can find us a Jewish cook."

There was silence. Then: "My brother Willie is making plans to emigrate to America. His wife's father, Leo Bendheim, lives in New York and is sponsoring them. I will ask Willie if Rosa's father will sponsor us as well."

"But we are not leaving, my dear. We do not need to move. What else can they do to us?"

Max heard his mother sigh. "You know the rumors."

"Don't pay them any attention."

She persisted. "They say they plan to kill Jews who don't leave the Reich."

"Hannah—"

"And you said the other day that business has fallen off."

"There is a vast difference between losing money and losing your life."

"What if we lose all our money? Or it is taken from us?"

There was silence. Then Moritz whispered. Max could only make out a phrase or two. ". . . taking precautions . . . cash every week . . . under the mattress." He cleared his throat.

"Are you sure that's enough?" His mother's voice was fearful.

His father stopped whispering. "I believe so. And I will sell a few horses if I must. That should give us enough for Max's Bar Mitzvah. And more."

"But what if the secret police—the Gestapo—raid us? There is a camp an hour away in Dachau. What if they put us in prison in one of those—camps?"

"For what crimes?"

"Being Jewish."

"Hannah, my grandfather settled here three generations ago. I am a veteran of the Great War. We have ties. Allies. I am confident the mayor, for one, will vouch for us."

"I'm not. Hitler has destroyed the covenant between Jews and the world. I am afraid every time someone comes to the door."

Max heard swishing, as if his father had moved to embrace his mother. "Oh, Hannah, my dear. Do not be afraid. We will be fine."

"That may be. But I will still write my brother."

CHAPTER 5

Summer 1933
Regensburg

Max dutifully practiced for his Bar Mitzvah that summer. His mother, who came from a more observant family than Papa, had studied Hebrew as a child. She helped him with pronunciation. But his favorite person to practice with was Renée. She'd read a translation of his Torah parshah at the synagogue and was able to add to the rabbi's interpretation of the passages.

They studied at the synagogue in the library so they could pull information from other sources. It was well stocked and had been expanded once secular subjects were added to the curriculum. Max pulled out an old copy of the Talmud. The yellowing pages gave off the dusty smell of paper. Max found the smell comforting.

"So, you already know your parshah is from Deuteronomy," Renée said.

"Chapter twenty-six, verses one through twenty-nine," Max said. "My part begins with the words 'Ki tavo,' which means 'When you come.' It's part of Moses's last speech to the people he led through the desert. He dies soon after that."

"Right," Renée said. "From what I gather, he's instructing them on what blessings to say, what rules to follow, and what will happen if they don't."

"You looked it up?" Max asked.

She shrugged as if to make light of it, but Max was grateful. She *was* a special girl. She made him feel important. As if he mattered. He scanned his assigned pages from the Talmud. "Moses warns them they'll be cursed if they don't follow the rules. More than once, actually."

"Yes, he does. And then he—"

"Renée," Max interrupted her. "Do you believe Hashem is that rigid?"

"Rigid? In what way?"

"He doesn't seem to be very forgiving. At least Moses makes it sound that way. One tiny slip, and people are cursed. I'd like to believe Hashem gives us a second chance. Maybe even a third."

Renée folded her hands on the table. "I've never thought of it that way."

Max sat up straighter. Renée was curious about his thoughts and ideas. His parents weren't. At least not in the same way.

"You could bring it up in your talk after you read," she said.

"But what if the audience doesn't agree?"

"Why wouldn't they?"

"Because of all the 'punishing' laws and restrictions. If Hashem is so benevolent, why isn't He doing more to protect us?"

"Perhaps He is testing our faith," she said.

Max wasn't sure he believed that. "Why would a forgiving God do that?"

"That I don't know, Max," she said after a pause. "Perhaps you should ask the rabbi."

Max doubted the rabbi would provide a satisfying answer. He let it go. "The rabbi is teaching me trope so I can chant the parshah and my haftorah."

"That's impressive," she said. "Do you want to practice it now?"

Max considered it. He was reluctant to practice in front of Renée, not because he didn't know the proper inflections and intonation. But his voice had started to change earlier that summer, and he worried that a high-pitched squeak might burst out between his deepening, more resonant tones. "Um, perhaps later?"

"Of course." She smiled and changed the subject. "Have you started *Tom Sawyer*?"

"I did. I love it, so I'm reading slowly. I make it my reward for studying. I don't want it to end."

"I felt the same way."

"The freedom they felt when they were rafting down the river is . . . well, I was envious."

"Yes!"

Silence again. Max wondered if she was asking herself why *they* couldn't run away from rules and restrictions like Tom and Huck. He was. But he kept the conversation light. "Could you see yourself rafting down the Danube?"

She giggled. "It's not wide enough. At least in Regensburg. People would spot us."

"What would you take with you if you had the chance?"

"Hmm." She started to list items, using her fingers to count. "A change of clothes. My hairbrush. Sweet biscuits—"

"Agreed." He chimed in. "I would take a fishing pole. A hat. And some money."

"If we still have any." She hesitated. "And books. I would take a few books."

Were they talking about things they would take on a raft? Or things they would take someplace else? "*Tom Sawyer*?"

"And *Huckleberry Finn*. If it arrives in time." An uncertain look came across her face.

Now Max knew they were talking about someplace else. He spoke his next words carefully. "Suppose we were rafting down the Mississippi River . . ."

"Oh my. In that case we would have to learn English."

"That would be a problem. At least for me. I only know a few words. 'Hello.' 'Goodbye.' 'Hot dog.'"

She burst out laughing. It lifted his spirits. He laughed too. There wasn't much laughter at his house. If they could both laugh, how bad could things be? He wanted to hear that laugh more often.

On a perfect sun-dappled September day, it seemed as if the entire Jewish population of Regensburg had turned out for Max's Bar Mitzvah. The sanctuary was so crowded they had to bring more chairs. Max, wearing a new navy blue suit, sat in the first row with his parents during shacharit morning prayers. He and his father moved to the bima during the Torah service. In their synagogue, the bima looked more like a stage than a simple raised platform, but the rabbi claimed that was becoming more common.

It wasn't until they were seated behind the rabbi on the bima that Max grew nervous. A scan of the audience filled him with dismay. His mother was in the first row. Two rows back was Renée and her family. His uncle Willie, Mutti's brother, and Aunt Rosa had come down from Berlin with their family, his cousins. He spotted Günter and his father, as well as most of the Jewish boys and girls he knew from synagogue. And there was Jonas, his father's shop manager, and Hartman, the mechanic, in the back of the sanctuary.

The rest of the crowd were his parents' friends, and Max didn't know them. Or at least not well. He swallowed. His throat felt thick. He would give anything for a glass of water. He saw few non-Jews in the pews. Two years ago, he'd gone to one of his friend's Bar Mitzvahs and saw at least a dozen Gentile boys and girls from school. Boys who had been friends. Those same boys now shunned him.

He'd thought it wouldn't happen to him. Wilhelm, perhaps his best Gentile friend, had told him at the beginning of the school year that Max was different from those "other" Jews. "You're my friend, Max, and you'll always be my friend. I promise."

Although Max wondered who those "other" Jews were, he was happy to have at least one non-Jewish friend. But over the school year their friendship cooled. Wilhelm always had an excuse when Max invited him over, and Max noticed there were no invitations from Wilhelm.

It had something to do with race, he knew. The Nazis kept talking about Aryans: the purest, superior race. And this master race, as his teachers called it, with their blue eyes and blond hair, was largely German. Jews were not Aryans. They were an inferior race.

The rabbi cut short Max's thoughts and gestured him up to the podium.

Aside from the squeak in his inflection when he began the prayers over the Torah, his voice behaved, and Max got through the parshah smoothly. He chanted his haftorah as well; it was a passage from Prophets, the book of Isaiah. The passage focused on images of light "to remind us that though we may be in dark times," Max summarized from his reading, "God's light will eventually return."

He added what he and Renée had discussed earlier about the nature of Hashem. "Many Jews, much wiser than I, talk about the curses we will suffer if we do not follow Hashem's rules. But I do not believe in a punishing God. That said, I cannot explain why we face so many challenges today. Still, I cling to the notion of a benevolent presence, a loving God, whose will for us is to find joy and purpose. I will search for Him, and I pray that you find Him as well."

As Max sat down he heard rustling and whispers from the crowd. A wave of fear buzzed his nerves. Had he made a mistake? Should he not have been so optimistic? He jerked his head up and made eye contact with Renée. Her eyes were shining, and there was a huge smile on her lips. He felt better.

After the service the crowd moved to a large room where a kiddush buffet lunch waited for them. Although many families no longer kept kosher, the synagogue did. The dairy spread included several kinds of fish, salads, bread, and kugel. Max, too excited to eat, fielded compliments on his readings. Many said they loved his description of Hashem as a forgiving, benevolent force for good. Max had given them hope, they said.

Nevertheless, the rabbi tempered Max's words at the conclusion of the kiddush. He mentioned several Jewish families who had already left Germany during the past six months and predicted more would follow. And while he praised Max for his "youthful idealism," he warned congregants that they were facing a long, dark night before the morning light dawned. As the Steiners posed for what would be their last family photographs, Max desperately hoped the rabbi was wrong.

CHAPTER 6

1934
Regensburg

A ntisemitism in Regensburg, which had been smoldering for
months, erupted into a fiery blaze after the new year. When a
Jewish trader was arrested on suspicion of murdering a Christian boy,
Regensburg's Nazi press accused the Jews of committing the crime.
The trader was ultimately released when the perpetrators turned out
to be Gentiles, but truth didn't matter. The Nazis never corrected
their error, and denizens of the city allowed their bigotry to fester.

Jewish students were evicted from Regensburg's high schools.
Although Max would not be attending gymnasium yet, the only
schools open to him now would be private. And expensive. Meanwhile, students in his current school snickered and whispered about
him, not even bothering to wait until he had left the room. Most of
the boys were now members of the Hitler Youth and wore their
uniforms every day. The symbolism wasn't lost on Max.

Even worse, history teacher Herr Schröder assigned the class one
of the most popular antisemitic books published in Germany. *The
Handbook of the Jewish Question* was written by a virulent antisemitic
political scientist, Theodore Fritsch. Fritsch, who'd become second

only to Adolf Hitler in popularity, was referred to as "the father of antisemitism." By 1934 millions of Germans had read the book, and it became an indispensable propaganda tool for the Nazis.

One day Schröder called on each student to stand up and read a paragraph out loud from the book. When Schröder called on Max, he said, "Steiner, read the first paragraph on page 204."

Max stood and started to read. "It is impossible to accept the Jew as a human being, because I can find no trace of any real human trait in him. I accept to some extent the theological Weltanschauung: God creates vermin as a challenge to man. Where—where . . ." Max forced himself to keep reading. He didn't want to give Schröder the satisfaction of losing his composure. "Where dirt piles up, vermin multiply, and . . . and to get rid of the tormenting vermin we have to remove the dirt and try to keep them away." Max stumbled, each grotesque word seeming to inflate like a giant balloon. "The average—average Jew is sharp at business and glib at tongue, greedy for money, cunning and addicted to dishonesty—"

Max stopped short, suffused with anger. He couldn't go on. "This is trash!" He threw the book down on his desk, narrowed his eyes, and gazed around the classroom. Someone scoffed. Max's eyes narrowed as he studied the students to see who it was. One or two seemed like they agreed with Max, but most wouldn't look at him.

Herr Schröder was indignant. "So you disagree with the words of Theodor Fritsch?"

Max couldn't bear the teacher's arrogance—and stupidity—a moment longer. "Of course I do. This is garbage. And you know it." He whipped around to face his classmates. "This is an antisemitic screed. You can't possibly believe it. What if Jesus . . . and Christians were labeled vermin? What would you do?" He stared at the boys wearing their Hitler Youth uniforms. "You'd beat up anyone who spreads filth like this." He turned back to Schröder. "Like our teacher."

Everyone in the classroom froze. A blanket of silence covered the students. Then Herr Schröder's eyebrows arched to the ceiling, and his face grew as red as a rotten tomato. "Steiner," he roared. "Out of my class. Principal's office. Now."

That evening at dinner Max begged his father for a transfer to the synagogue school. His father demurred. "I don't know, Max. It's expensive, and my business, as you know, has slowed. One of the goyim is planning to open a second auto repair shop. They are trying to drive me out of business. I'm going to have to sell the horses."

"Papa." Max laid down his knife and fork. "Last year you said things would be different by now. Well, they are. They're worse."

His father and mother exchanged glances. Mutti's eyes bored into Papa's as if to say, *When will you realize we are powerless against these thugs?*

His father looked at his plate. "Yes. Things are changing. But going to the synagogue school will make you more of a target."

"What do you mean?"

"Think about it. If someone wanted to really wreak havoc, they could set fire to the synagogue or set off an explosion. That would wipe out half the young Jews in Regensburg."

"Moritz," his mother cut in, a terrified expression on her face. "Stop it. You're scaring Max. And me." She turned to Max. "No one is going to do that."

"You're probably right, Hannah. Still, I'd rather Max deal with a few insults than worry whether he is going to come home in one piece."

"Papa, there is no 'dealing with insults' at school. If I ignore them, they get worse. If I fight back, I end up in the principal's office. I can't accept this—this . . ." His voice trailed off. He didn't have the words.

"I know it's hard, son. Try to give it a little more time. We'll discuss it in a week or two."

By February Max was one of only three Jewish students left at his public school. Günter had left last semester, Renée a year earlier.

Max didn't want to call attention to himself, so he didn't mingle much with the other two still there.

It didn't matter.

Every morning when he walked into school he found a nasty note taped to his desk. Sometimes it was a cartoon that illustrated Jews with huge noses or money falling out of their pockets. Or the body of a devil. Other times, it was swastikas or Nazi slogans. Occasionally there were slurs about his father. The notes were never signed.

Max was furious and vowed to get even with the perpetrators. But first he needed to find out who they were. He decided to show up at school early one morning. Perhaps he could catch them in the act. On a dark, frigid morning he hauled himself out of bed, dressed, and slipped out of the house before his parents were up.

When he arrived at school—he was more than an hour early—he found the door open. That was a good sign. Someone else was there. He went in as quietly as he could and snuck down the hall to his homeroom. A supply closet in the back of the room was the perfect place to hide. He stepped in, angling the door so only a crack remained open, and settled on the floor to wait.

He was half dozing when he heard footsteps slap the floor. The steps grew closer. Someone was entering the room. Max became instantly alert. If he shifted just an inch or two he could see through the crack. He peered out as a man took a piece of paper out of a brief-case and moved toward Max's desk. To his shock, it was Herr Schröder.

Max sprang out of the closet. "So it's you!"

Schröder stepped back in alarm. His face paled. "Who—what are you doing here?"

Max, who had shot up several inches since his Bar Mitzvah, now stood taller than the teacher. He closed in on the man until their bodies were barely a foot apart. He drew himself up, his voice laced with fury. "Why are you doing this?"

"Because you are a dirty Jew, and you don't belong in Germany. You need to get out while you still can. Unless you want your family to end up in a concentration camp."

The only thing Max saw was a red mist of rage. He fisted his hands and raised them in front of his chest.

Schröder backed away. "If you hit me, I will say you attacked me without provocation. You will be expelled."

"If I'm to be expelled, it will be for a good reason." Max drew his fist back and belted Schröder in the face as hard as he could. The blow landed with a satisfying crunch on the teacher's cheek below his eye.

Blood started to run. Schröder staggered out of the room, cupping his hand against his eye. Thirty minutes later he still wasn't back for the beginning of school, and Frau Brandt substituted for him. Thirty minutes after that the principal sent for Max.

When Max arrived in the office, the principal was surprisingly calm. "Well, Max, we seem to have a problem. Did you hit Schröder with your fist this morning?"

Max explained what Schröder was doing and how he had caught the teacher.

The principal folded his hands on the desk. "I am not as stupid as you may think." His voice sounded sad. "Schröder has swallowed the Nazis' garbage in one huge bite. I wager it makes him feel like a big man."

Max almost smiled, but under the circumstances, he knew it wasn't the right response.

The principal went on. "I respect your family. They've been here for decades. Your grandparents and parents helped make Regensburg what it is today. But I cannot control what's happening now. The Nazis are experts at propaganda. You've seen it yourself. The sad fact is that you do not belong here anymore. If I try to protect you, I will be fired, perhaps thrown into prison myself. Please tell your parents how sorry I am. But you are lucky in one respect. You have an alternative. Take it."

When Max returned home before lunch, his face was streaked with dirt. His pants were torn at the knees, and his right eye was swollen almost shut.

His mother covered her mouth with one hand and bit her finger. "Max, darling, what happened?"

"I was expelled, and while I was gathering my things, a couple of Hitler Youth attacked me. I fought back." He started to give her the details but she cut him off.

"Enough! We need to leave Germany," she said. "I will talk to your father tonight."

"I doubt he will agree."

She shook her head. "Then we will leave without him."

CHAPTER 7

Summer 1934
Regensburg

At the end of June the Nazis ate some of their own. During the Night of the Long Knives, more than 150 high-ranking officials of the SA, the Stormtroopers, or Brownshirts, as they were called, were executed. The Nazis claimed it was to root out an imminent coup by the SA leader, Ernst Röhm. But the hidden objective of the "Röhm purge" was apparent to anyone with an ounce of intelligence, Max thought.

Hitler wanted to consolidate his power and reassure the German military, who feared and despised the SA, that they would not be a threat to the armed forces. Hitler was spending millions to rearm the military; he needed their total allegiance. This event was intended to achieve that.

So hundreds of Brownshirts were assassinated or arrested by the SS and the Gestapo. The purge neatly solved a second problem for Hitler. As the leader of the SA, *Röhm* had demanded that Nazi policy embrace socialist goals through a redistribution of wealth. Indeed, the word "socialist" was embedded in the name of the party. But socialism was not a direction the Nazis wanted to pursue any longer, so the SA were eliminated.

~

Barely a month later, on August 2, President Hindenburg died. Two weeks after that, Hitler combined the posts of president and chancellor and gave himself the name Führer. The military swore their allegiance to Hitler. Civil servants, including teachers, government workers, and professionals, were forced to do the same.

Max paid attention to events, but his heart was elsewhere. The summer of 1934 would be the last summer he would recall as happy. In March he'd transferred to the synagogue school to finish the year. He joined youth groups and participated in meetings, outings, and Jewish sports events. The International Maccabiah Games had begun two years earlier. While the synagogue didn't participate, they held smaller events in Regensburg. Max took home track-and-field honors.

The Jewish community was the glue that held young Jews together by keeping them happy and busy. There were no antisemitic attacks. Max felt protected. Between his work at the auto repair shop and the synagogue's social events, he belonged.

But the magical part of that summer wasn't at the synagogue. Max's hair lightened and highlighted his blue-green eyes. That, plus his growth over the year—four inches—and a summer tan, made him a good-looking young man, who, his friends said, could pass for an Aryan.

Renée had also matured. No longer gangly, she moved gracefully, the curves of her body quite apparent. She cut her hair and wore an attractive bob with one side falling over her cheek. Her features had caught up to her nose, and it seemed to Max it was just the right size. Like her, noble and dignified. And very pretty.

The two spent as much time together as they could. She was always the first person with whom he shared his thoughts. She brought out the best in him. They analyzed Germany's problems and dreamed of a future without Hitler. They traced the change in their status over the past two years. Renée was convinced their citizenship would be revoked soon; Max disagreed. Renée told him her father had learned that Shanghai, China, allowed Jews in and that her parents might emigrate if life got worse.

Max was distraught. "You can't leave. What will I do without you?"

Renée bit her lip. "Do you believe you are safe here?"

"No."

"Then you must convince your family to leave. Soon."

"My father will not go."

Renée sighed. "The clock is ticking."

Their time together was not always gloomy. They tried to spend afternoons together, especially since sunset was so late in the day. Sometimes Max harnessed Klara and they took long carriage rides. Other times they went for jaunts on their bicycles. One summer afternoon, they took Max's carriage back to Herzogs Park.

"Do you remember when Klara and you were the same height?" Renée said, an amused smile on her face. Max climbed down and stood beside the pony. He was at least three inches taller than Klara now. And two inches taller than Renée.

"You see?" Renée clapped her hands.

Max grinned and secured Klara around a tree. Renée had brought a picnic basket, Max a blanket. They found a secluded grassy area set back from the walkways. Renée set out cold chicken, early tomatoes, potato salad, and, of course, sweet biscuits for dessert. When they had finished, they both lay down on the blanket. The smell of the wool crept up Max's nose. He gazed at a perfect blue sky that cheerful white clouds scudded across. He raised himself on one elbow and glanced at Renée. Her eyes were closed.

At the caw of a crow her eyes fluttered open. She looked at Max with an expression Max had not seen before. A slight smile, welcoming him, but something else as well. His breath skipped. What was it? Before he could stop himself, he reached over and ran his fingers down her cheek. Her chest suddenly heaved. He did it again. She moved closer to him, stretched out her arms, and drew him close. He leaned over and kissed her. Not the sweet chaste kisses they'd shared in the past. This was something altogether different. His shadow fell over her face as he gathered her in his arms and kissed her again. And again.

CHAPTER 8

December 1934
Regensburg

More edicts came down from the Nazis. By the end of the year, Jews had been excluded from the arts and the newspaper business. Hotel and restaurant owners could no longer serve Jews. In some areas Jewish children were no longer allowed to go to public school. Jews had been barred from the legal profession, the civil service, and from teaching in schools and universities. Books considered un-German, including those by Jewish authors, had been burned. Jewish citizens were harassed and subjected to violent attacks.

What Hannah Steiner feared had come to pass. German Jews had been pushed out of society. Non-Jews stopped socializing with Jews and avoided shopping in Jewish-owned stores. Max spotted a banner in downtown Regensburg that said "Whoever buys from Jews is a traitor to the nation." They were outcasts. Unwanted. Pariahs.

This time Moritz couldn't ignore the signs. But waiting until the sword of damocles fell had consequences. To leave Germany he would need to pay up to 90 percent of his wealth in an emigration tax, and that didn't include the cash needed to bribe officials for short-term visas. He would need to sell the shop, the horses, and his house, all at a loss.

Another issue was the problem of finding a country willing to take them. While Hannah had been prescient about getting her sister-in-law's family to sponsor them in America, visas from the State Department could take years. The US government was known to be quite stingy in doling them out.

"I have horse-racing associates in Holland," Moritz said a few days later as he picked up his coffee cup. "That's where we'll go when it's time. And if we can't find living arrangements in Amsterdam, we may need to send Max to America by himself."

Max went rigid. "No!"

"Darling," his mother said, "we have no future here."

Max folded his arms. "I will never leave Germany without you and Papa."

Moritz drained his coffee and placed the cup carefully on its saucer. "I understand, son. I don't want that to happen either. Let's see what happens."

"Moritz, time is running short," Mutti said. "Les jeux sont faits."

The Steiners' cook, Ivona, appeared in the dining room while the family was eating dessert. She was wearing her coat. She ran a hand through her graying hair, and an anguished expression came over her.

"Herr Steiner, Frau Hannah, and Max," she said slowly. "My husband says I can no longer work for you. I am so sorry. I want you to know this is not my decision."

Max wasn't surprised. He glanced at his parents. They didn't seem shocked either. As if they were expecting it.

His father confirmed it. "We understand, Ivona. You have given us ten years of dedicated service. We are grateful. Do you have anything lined up?"

Her cheeks reddened. She nodded briefly.

"Tell us who you'll be working for."

"Herr and Frau Sigmond Baer. He is a party member."

"Ah . . ." was all Max's father said. "In that case, best not to tell them that your former employers were Jews."

Her face grew even more flushed. "I have not, sir." She glanced over at Max. "My dear Maximillian, I have known you since you were a little boy. You are almost all grown up now. I wish you nothing but success. I hope you will not forget me."

Max remembered the times she'd bandaged his skinned knees, applied ice to sore muscles, slipped him extra biscuits or cheese. His throat thickened, and his words were tight and wheezy. "That will never happen, Ivona."

His father rose, dug in his pocket, and pulled out some cash. He handed it to Ivona. "Here, use this to buy yourself something frivolous. You've worked hard for us."

Ivona's face crumpled, and tears rimmed her eyes. She hugged his father. His mother rose from her chair, and Ivona hugged her too. Max saw his mother's eyes were wet. Then she came around to Max. He stood up to receive her hug. "Take care of your lovely friend."

Max knew she meant Renée. He swallowed. "I'll try."

CHAPTER 9

1935
Regensburg

With a calm start to the new year, Max dared to hope the worst was over for the Jews. Renée wasn't sure. Support for Hitler seemed to be at a fever pitch. His economic plans were yielding jobs through massive public works and construction programs. Inflation was stabilizing. And Hitler's key goal, to rebuild Germany's military, was thriving with investments in weapons, tanks, and airplanes that overshadowed civilian spending.

The German people approved. Their shame at losing the Great War was eclipsed by adulation, even worship, of the Führer. Germans told themselves that Hitler would lead the way to a new European prosperity.

Jews were not a part of the recovery. Max's father clung to a brief moment of hope when he heard that one of the largest public works programs would be the expansion of the autobahn. With a modern-day highway linking the country, his auto repair business would profit from a burgeoning industry. All he had to do was hold on.

That never materialized. Gentiles no longer came to his shop, and Moritz realized the end was near. One or two Jewish customers weren't enough to justify Hartman's salary. He raised the issue as they drove to the synagogue one morning.

"Ever since the boycott, the pressure for Jews to sell our businesses to Gentiles—far below market value, I might add—has mounted. I thought we could weather the downturn. And I have been taking precautions . . ." He paused. Max recalled the conversation he'd overheard the night he eavesdropped on his parents. Something about hiding money under the mattress. His father continued. ". . . Now I'm not sure it will be enough."

"Will we have to sell Klara?" Max asked.

Moritz flashed a sad smile. "I don't know yet. I will try not to."

"Please. I'll—I'll buy her from you."

His mother cut in. "Darling, you don't have the money. Moritz, I got a letter from Willie. Rosa's father, Leo, is willing to sponsor us."

His father stroked his mustache. "That's generous of him, but how can we move across the ocean? My roots are here. In Regensburg and Germany. So are yours."

"Whether we go or not, you know how valuable it is to have papers. Many German Jews would sell their souls to emigrate to America. And we will have them. How can we not use them? What else needs to happen for you to open your eyes to the truth?"

His father looked like he wanted to say something, but his mother wasn't finished.

"If you will not go, I will. And take Max with me. As soon as Leo Bendheim sends the affidavits to the State Department and we get our visas."

Another spring, another season of uncertainty. The assaults, vandalism, and boycotts, which the Nazi government had temporarily curbed the previous year, resumed, more frequent and violent this time. The propaganda machine directed by Joseph Goebbels claimed that the Jews themselves were responsible. Superior races either must battle inferior races, the Nazis said, or be corrupted by them. Aryans were superior. Jews were inferior. It was that simple.

Goebbels's shrewd use of radio, newspapers, and staged events was so successful that many average Germans came to support stronger antisemitic laws. Leni Riefenstahl's new propaganda film, commissioned by Hitler himself, helped. The film recounted the Nazi Party Congress at Nuremberg in 1934. Its clever use of camera shots, editing, and sound track appealed to Germans and reinforced the perception that Germany, with Hitler at the helm, had returned as a great power.

The Jews of Regensburg wore the worry and anxiety on their faces. They were living in a hostile world. Max and Renée tried to focus on happy thoughts, but the atmosphere, soured by official hype, grew oppressive.

They were walking home from the synagogue school one afternoon when they heard a commotion on the block ahead of them. They jogged over. Three SS officers and two local policemen were beating a middle-age man on the sidewalk with whips. The man was bent over and was trying to protect his head with his hands. The two policemen managed the crowd of people who'd gathered to watch, keeping them a safe distance away from the man.

"Oh my God!" Renée cried out. "They need to stop!" She stiffened, then started to move to the man. Max grabbed her before she could take off and pulled her toward him.

"Stop, Max," she cried. "This is wrong! Let me go!"

Max pulled her into his body. "No!" he whispered. "They will kill you if you interfere! Stay here!"

Renée twisted around so they were face-to-face. She gazed at Max with horror. Max tried to soothe her. "Come, Renée, let's go the other way."

"No!" She twisted back to watch the SS men but made no effort to go over. The SS men stopped beating the man but stripped off his pants and his shoes. Someone printed a primitive sign, which they hung around his neck. The sign said "I am a racial defiler and a traitor to the German people." The men dragged him down the block by his barefoot heels and disappeared around a corner.

Renée sagged against Max, all her outrage and fury seemingly sapped. When she turned back to Max, she was crying. Max tenderly wiped her tears away.

That night at dinner he told his parents about the incident. "I didn't tell Renée, but I knew the man."

"Baruch Hashem," his mother said. "Who was it?"

"Remember Günter, my friend from school?"

His mother nodded. /

"It was Günter's father. He is married to a Gentile woman but she converted. It's crazy."

The end of May brought another blow. Jews were barred from serving in the German armed forces. A few months earlier, Hitler had defied the Treaty of Versailles by reinstating the draft and expanding the army. It was clear he was preparing for war. A secret law reorganized the army into the Wehrmacht, making Hitler its commander-in-chief. Had it been three years earlier, there would have been no question of Max's loyalty, indeed his eagerness to serve, his country. But now? Truthfully, he was relieved at the ban.

In September, on Max's birthday, in fact, the situation exploded just as Max's mother had predicted. At a political rally in the city of Nuremberg, the Nazis announced two new laws. The Law for the Protection of German Blood and German Honor was the first. It defined who was a "pure" German, a Jew, and an individual with mixed blood, and went on to ban interracial marriages. The Jews, it said, were guilty of "racial defilement" where Aryans were concerned. The second law, the Reich Citizenship Law, stripped German Jews of their citizenship.

Max and Renée were in the Steiners' sitting room listening to a Bach concerto on the radio. Halfway through the first movement, a breathless announcer interrupted to report the events at the rally. As Max listened, his stomach pitched. Renée's face went ashen. She clapped a hand on her mouth.

"Did you hear that?" she whispered.

"I don't believe it," Max said. "It can't be true."

"Of course it is." She took a long, shuddering breath. "Max, what are we going to do? We are now stateless. Just like the Jews in the desert with Moses."

He moved closer and took her in his arms. "They can't do that."

"They just did."

"It won't last."

She disentangled from him and moved to the other end of the settee. "Max, how can you keep repeating these bromides? You're postponing the inevitable. Pretending things aren't so bad. It's over. If we are no longer citizens, if we can't vote, we are useless. And that is precisely the Nazis' intention. Aryans are the master race. Jews are unworthy."

The concerto returned, but neither of them listened. What was wrong with him? It wasn't his nature to be passive. He was a fighter. But here he was, acting as if he could brush away reality like a speck of dust. He realized he was trying to comfort Renée, and in another rush of understanding, he understood that was exactly what his father was doing by delaying a decision to leave. Downplaying the situation in the hope it was just temporary. But that hadn't changed anything. In fact, things had deteriorated. Renée had known it before him.

"You're right, Renée."

"I wish I wasn't." Her eyes were wet.

"So. We cannot marry Aryans or have relations with 'real' Germans."

Renée drew back as if he surprised her again. "Why would you want to?"

Max tried to smile. "I don't. You know I only want you."

Renée burst into tears.

"Stop, Renée, dearest love. Don't cry. We have each other."

She shook her head. "No. We don't."

"What do you mean?"

"My parents almost left after your Bar Mitzvah, but I begged them to hang on. I was trying to be optimistic. Like you. 'How could it get any worse?' I said. 'Germans aren't racist. It's just the Nazis who are.' I tried to convince them that at least we're not slaves, like the Negroes in America were." She wiped her nose with her sleeve. "My father said I sounded willfully ignorant . . ." She sobbed. "And that anyone who believed the Nazis weren't going to kill Jews isn't seeing reality. We are out of time, Max. My family will be going to Shanghai soon."

Max jumped up and started to pace. "Shanghai? Why must you go halfway around the world?"

"So we can live our lives without being persecuted. There are already Jews there. Even a synagogue. Ohel Rachel."

Max's eyes narrowed as he paced.

"What? What are you thinking?

"Maybe I can persuade my parents to go to Shanghai, too."

"Really?" Despite the tears her eyes shone.

Fundamentally Max knew there was little hope. He was doing it again. Trying to cushion the blow. His mother was set on emigrating to America. Renée deserved the truth, but he didn't want to let her down. "Let me talk to them." He sat back down and brushed a tear from her cheek. "In the meantime, let's try to enjoy the time we have left. You won't be leaving right away, will you?"

She leaned her head against his shoulder, fresh tears trickling down. "My father wants to sail before the end of the year."

More bad news. That was less than three months away. Max would remember his fifteenth birthday as the second worst day in his life.

CHAPTER 10

Autumn 1935
Regensburg

The worst day of Max's life began on a crisp October morning. It was Saturday, and Hannah Steiner had made pancakes for breakfast. One of Max's favorites, the pancakes were actually thin golden crepes rolled up and served with preserves on top. His mother brewed strong coffee to temper the sweetness, and Max wolfed down as many crepes as she allowed. It was one of the only times he noticed her smile with the same joy she used to.

His father wiped his mouth with a napkin and rose from the table. "I'll look in on the shop. Jonas and Hartman are working until noon." Neither man was Jewish, so they could work on the Sabbath. Both were happy for the extra hours. Then again, the Steiners didn't observe Shabbos either.

"I'll go with you, Papa," Max said. "Hartman's working on a Daimler and I want to see what he's doing."

Moritz nodded. "Be quick. I'd like to be back by lunchtime."

"Take a jacket, Max," his mother said. "It's chilly out."

Just as they were about to leave, they heard a determined knock on the door. Hannah's eyes widened. "Who can that be? On the Sabbath, no less?"

Max reached for the door.

"No!" his mother cried out. "Don't answer it!"

"Mama," Max tried to reason with her. "It's probably just the postman with a package for us."

"Don't! Max, please."

The knock came again. Louder. Longer.

His father took charge. "Hannah, don't worry. I will deal with this." He stepped in front of Max and opened the door.

A man in a black overcoat and hat stood on the flagstone porch. Two uniformed Regensburg police officers were behind him. Papa knew many police officers in town and he nodded pleasantly. Max could tell he and one of the officers recognized each other.

"Guten Tag," his father said.

The policeman he nodded to wouldn't meet his father's eyes. Max studied the man in the overcoat. The flaps were open, and underneath he was wearing a suit. Gestapo.

"Herr Steiner?"

"Yes?"

"We have reason to believe you have committed treason against the new Germany. You are a traitor, and you must come with us."

"What? That is ridiculous. What is this treason? Who is accusing me?"

"I am not at liberty to say. But you must come with us. We are putting you in protective custody."

"What is 'protective custody'? And who are you? Your identification, please."

The man fished something out of his pocket. A card. Max looked over his father's shoulder. It confirmed he was Gestapo.

His father stared at the card. "There is no name on your card. Why should I believe you?"

"Do not worry about me. Worry about your crimes."

"I have committed no crimes. I am not an enemy of the state.

What are the charges? And for the second time, what is 'protective custody'?"

Max heard the irritation in his father's voice and saw it on his face.

"For your own safety, you must be kept away from good Germans who wish you harm."

"Who would want to harm me?" Moritz turned to the police officers. "You know me. I have lived in Regensburg my entire life. My family helped build this city. I fought in the Great War. Tell this Gestapo man I am no traitor."

The officers kept their mouths shut.

"You are an enemy of the National Socialist government," the Gestapo man went on. "And you have flagrantly disobeyed the law."

"What law?"

"You, a noncitizen of Germany, have associated with and employed Aryans in your business."

"What exactly are you suggesting?"

"The Law for the Protection of German Blood and Honor forbids you from working with or associating with Aryans. Not only have you attempted to enslave them but you have paid them bribes to prevent them from reporting you. You have also bred horses for the purposes of gambling, which is strictly prohibited by the government."

"This is rubbish. Hannah, call our lawyer."

"If they are Jewish, they will not do you any good. Jews are no longer permitted to practice law. Come with us." The Gestapo man gestured to Moritz and stepped back. Under his breath he told the officers, "If he resists, subdue him."

His father tried to slam the door in their faces. But the officers anticipated it and one shoved himself against the door, forcing it wider. The second officer, the one who recognized Papa, Max thought, grabbed his arms from the back and held him fast. The first officer slammed his fist into his father's face.

Hannah screamed. Max shouted, "Stop! He has done nothing wrong!"

Did the policeman clutching his father wince at the violence?

Whether he did or not, the blow squeezed all the fight out of Max's father. He sagged against the officer and would have fallen if the officer who grabbed him didn't prop him up. When he seemed steady, they half guided, half dragged him to their car. His father had trouble catching his breath.

They opened the back door of the police car, pushed his head down, and threw him inside.

He was gone.

Mutti ran upstairs to her bedroom and slammed the door. Max could hear her sobbing. Of course she was upset. So was he. Still, he hoped she'd stop soon. Otherwise, Max would need to handle the situation. He tried to think what he should do. Just in case. Before he was taken by the Gestapo, Papa had told Mutti to call their lawyer. Gerald Katz, whose son was a year younger than Max, was their family lawyer. He was an observant Jew and would be at synagogue. Max went upstairs, knocked on the door, and gently asked, "Mutti, can I get you anything?"

A muffled voice replied, "No, darling." Then a sniff. "I'll be out in a moment." Relief washed over Max. He rocked on one foot, then the other. He knocked again and told her he was going to the synagogue to talk to Katz and would be back soon. She didn't reply. He took that as approval.

Outside he jumped on his bicycle and raced to the synagogue. By the time he got there, shacharis, the morning service, was just ending. He peeked into the sanctuary, spotted Katz, a sixtyish, round man, bald except for a white fringe around his head, in the minyan. Max crept inside and pulled him out.

After Max explained that his father had been arrested, Katz blinked several times and shook his head. "Oh, Max, I wish there was something I could do. But I am no longer allowed to practice law. All I can do is advise you."

"Fine, advise me. Mutti and I need to find him and bring him home."

Katz took a breath. "These—incidents have been accelerating. It's almost as if the Nazis are playing with different forms of imprisonment and punishment to see which are the most grievous and humiliating."

"So what should we do?" Max said impatiently.

"Go to the police station. Find out exactly what the charges are and what punishment is intended. If it's a fine, ask them if they'll accept cash. If they say you're trying to bribe them, say that's the farthest thing from your minds. You're just trying to pay the fine. If they still don't accept the money, try to find out if he's being held at the station or somewhere else."

"Where else would he be?"

Katz held up his index finger. "Tell them you want to see him. Sometimes it works. Sometimes it doesn't. Meanwhile, I will try to find you and your mother a Gentile lawyer. It won't be easy. Most don't want to stick their neck out for Jews."

"But what if the Gestapo says we can't see him, can't pay the fine, and won't tell us where he is? What do I do then?"

Katz shook his head. "Take the names of the officers you talk to, their badge numbers, write down dates and times. We'll write an appeal."

"But Papa hasn't done anything wrong. They're trumped-up charges, and you know it."

"Max, I know that. You know. Your mother knows. Even they know. But this is what we must do. We are no longer considered citizens of the Reich."

Max left the synagogue. He wanted to smash his fist through something. A window. A wall. A Nazi. His rage was just as powerful as his mother's tears, and he didn't know how to manage either. He finally understood his mother's metaphor about a balloon waiting to explode. He was exploding now. He swung himself onto his bicycle with no idea where to go, except that he needed to ride as fast and as far as he could.

As he peddled off, someone from the synagogue called out his name. He circled around and looked back. Renée. She was running toward him.

"Max, I just heard. I want to help! Make room on your bicycle for me."

He braked sharply. He was relieved to see her. They could work together to find Papa. He made room for her on the bar in front, and they started off slowly, one of his arms on the handlebar and the other around her. He could smell her perfume. It calmed him.

CHAPTER 11

Autumn 1935
Regensburg

Max's mother was in the kitchen by the time Max got home. After he told Mutti what Katz had told them to do, Renée volunteered to stay at the house while they went to the police station, in case someone called or his father returned.

The police station turned out to be a wasted trip. A man at a desk in the front told Mutti to come back Monday. The weekend staff was limited in what they could do. Mutti asked the name of the Gestapo officer. The desk man wouldn't give it to her. Max realized that having their citizenship stripped meant, among other things, not being given any worthwhile information. The worst part was that it was public information, news that would eventually be printed in the Regensburg newspaper. But as disenfranchised Jews, they got nothing.

Max ran a frustrated hand through his hair. They left and went back home. Renée had made soup and was frying potatoes in a pan.

"What happened?" she asked.

Mutti hugged her and said, "You are the best part of this day, my dear. I am grateful."

"It's nothing," Renée said, but her cheeks flushed.

"I'll finish making lunch, and then we decide what to do next, Max."

Mutti had to be as frightened, unsettled, and angry as he was, but she was still making lunch. Max wasn't hungry, but he'd never admit it.

"Well, if you're both all right," Renée said, "I'll go now."

Max wanted her to stay, but Mutti shooed her out. "I'm fine. Just fine. But you are a godsend. Thank you."

Max walked her to the door and drew her close.

She threw her arms around his neck. "I'm so sorry," she breathed.

Max allowed himself to hold her. But only for a moment. "The Gestapo man kept bringing up protective custody. How they had to take him in for his own good. That ordinary Germans might hurt him if they knew his crimes."

"You don't believe that, do you?"

"Of course not, but I need to know more about it. This is all new to me."

Renée thought for a minute. "I can ask my father. I can ask him to come here, if you think it will help."

Max didn't think Mutti would mind. "Yes. Tell him he's welcome." He kissed her lightly and nodded. The knot in his stomach loosened just a bit.

Julius Herskowitz was a slender man. A full head of handsomely graying hair gave him an elegant, dignified air. His steely dark eyes and aquiline nose—that's where Renée inherited hers, Max knew—contributed to his bearing. He wore a tailored suit, tie, and shirt with gold cuff links. Of course. He was a jeweler.

"Thank you for coming, Mr. Herskowitz," Max said.

"Julius." Mutti came out of the kitchen wiping her hands on a towel. "How generous of you to give us some time. You have a very special daughter."

The man smiled. "Thank you, Hannah. She is so special I often find myself in awe of her."

Renée colored again.

"Would you like some tea?" Mutti asked.

"That would be lovely."

"Please. Come into the kitchen. We'll keep it informal. I hope you have some advice for us. I—I must admit, I feel powerless."

Max knew exactly how she felt.

Herskowitz cleared his throat. "Several of my clients have had—run-ins—with the authorities," Julius said after a sip of tea. "And, as you know, people at the synagogue talk." He settled himself at the table. "I have picked up a thing or two about 'protective custody.'"

"So, what is it?" Max sat next to him at the kitchen table, leaning his elbows on his knees. "And how do we get him released?"

"Before we get to that, why do you think he was arrested?"

"We have no idea," Mutti replied.

"Did he have any enemies you know of?"

"Of course not," Mutti said firmly. "You know what an upstanding, honest, straightforward gentleman he is." She looked Julius in the eye. "That was why he opted not to sell automobiles. Repairs were one thing, but sales were another. Prices ran the gamut from reasonable to exorbitant, but my Moritz wanted to be fair. It was the same with the horse-racing business. He was happy to breed horses and, yes, sell them to the right owner. But he never gambled. Or went to the racetrack to stand in the winner's circle. That just wasn't Moritz Steiner. His customers repaid his honesty and straight dealings with respect."

"I think you may be mistaken," Julius said.

Mutti frowned. A swell of unease came over Max. "In what way?"

"If he is as honest and decent as you say, Hannah, and I don't doubt it, someone must have set him up. Reported him to the Gestapo. Which means he does indeed have an enemy."

"But who? And why?"

"I don't know who, but as for why, someone probably wanted what he has. Or thinks they can get it from him."

"A Nazi? A Gentile?"

Herskowitz shrugged. "Perhaps, perhaps not."

"So what is this 'protective custody' and how does it help?"

"It doesn't. It is a euphemism for arrests and imprisonment. It's supposed to intimidate Jews and other enemies of the Reich to leave Germany."

Max felt his stomach pitch. "Is there a central prison for those arrested?"

"From what I understand, some sites have been repurposed from other activities. But I do know a man who was sent to Dachau."

His mother went ashen. Max stifled a shiver. Dachau had been one of the first German concentration camps built to house Hitler's political opponents. He'd heard the rumors about Dachau. Many men went in. Few came out.

"But Moritz isn't political," Mutti said.

Herskowitz said, "As I said, it's been repurposed. And wherever the prisons are, the treatment of prisoners is harsh. The Nazis make sure everyone understands that Jews are enemies of the state, dangerous to associate with, and fair game for acts of violence."

"Harsh? What happens to them?" she asked.

Herskowitz sighed and took another sip of tea. "Nothing good. They shave prisoners' heads, give away their clothing, and force them to wear rags. They starve them, feed them rancid food, perhaps withhold water. The main goal is to isolate and terrorize them, even from each other." He paused and glanced over at Max. "Are you sure you want me to go on?"

Max swallowed. He felt nauseous and wondered if he was going to vomit. He suppressed the urge. Then he nodded.

Herskowitz continued. "Physical violence is common. Prisoners suffer broken arms, legs, cuts and bruises. And, of course, humiliation. The Gestapo are in charge, but the guards are SS. They go to great lengths to embarrass the prisoners and break their spirit."

"Are they're doing that to Papa?" He and Mutti exchanged horrified glances.

Julius tightened his lips. He didn't answer directly. "I heard of one prisoner who was chained up and forced to bark like a dog. Another was forced to clean toilets with his bare hands. Up north in the villages I hear the Nazis stage processions of open trucks with prisoners standing in the beds of the trucks. Villagers are encouraged to throw things at them."

"Papa will never stand for this treatment." Max fumed.

Herskowitz's voice softened. "He doesn't have a choice, Max. Some men have tried to assert their rights, but it did them no good. They were beaten and further isolated. We should pray that your father has the sense to keep quiet."

Max blinked.

"He will," Mutti said. Max wasn't certain if she believed it or simply hoped that would be the case.

"The only good news is that 'ordinary' Jews are released after a period of time."

"Really? So he will be coming home?" Mutti asked.

"Theoretically, yes," Julius said. "If he agrees to leave Germany as soon as possible after his release. When he will be released depends on the 'crimes' the Gestapo says he's committed. If he was a left-wing journalist or a Communist, it wouldn't be for months, maybe years. The same may be true for lawyers and judges. There are even rumors that assassination is not out of the question. Naturally, they would label it as a suicide. But I don't know about businessmen like your father."

"My father has never been political," Max repeated.

"I understand. The problem is that once it's known your father was imprisoned, his livelihood is over. Former prisoners are forbidden to tell anyone, but you know how people talk. No one will buy his horses. Or have their automobiles repaired at his shop. He will be considered a dangerous person to associate with. Even among Jews."

Mutti let out a breath. "They said he broke the law by employing Aryans. They accused him of enslaving and bribing them."

"That might fall under the crime of 'racial defiler' now that we're considered an inferior race," Julius said sarcastically. "It's used mostly for Jews who have had relations with Aryan women. But I suppose they could make a racial defilement case against him. Let us hope that, whatever the charges, he will be released so you can leave Germany."

Max fisted his hands, trying to assimilate what Renée's father said. He didn't know what to do with his rage. And, if he was honest, his fear. His father assassinated? The Nazis forcing them to flee? Hadn't they done enough? How could Katz and Mr. Herskowitz talk about these subjects so—so calmly? As if they were talking about some trivial event, not their very survival? Who allowed the Nazis to decide whether his family lived or died? For Max it was raw. Unfair.

He struggled to keep his composure. "So if someone did report Papa, how do I find out who? The German horse-racing community is huge."

"Then start small. At the auto shop."

"Is that what you would do?" Max asked. He and Mutti had a dual mission now. Not only to rescue his father, but to identify who had set him up. Max didn't know what he would do when he found the bastard, but he did know it wouldn't be pleasant.

Herskowitz cleared his throat. "What I am doing, son, is taking my family to Shanghai. Hannah, you and Moritz should make a similar decision as soon as possible."

CHAPTER 12

Autumn 1935
Regensburg

Two days later Papa still wasn't home. Max hadn't slept more than a few hours. Although exhausted, he was determined to help find out who had betrayed his father and rescue him. He wasn't afraid of a fight. He had to do something. He was his father's son. Sons were loyal to their parents.

It stood to reason that whoever reported his father had to be a Nazi Party member. Renée suggested they start combing lists of Regensburg residents. They rode their bicycles to the public library just across the Danube. The librarian told them there were no such lists but that it was an excellent idea. She did tell them about the Golden Party Badge, a special award given to all Nazi Party members with unbroken party membership since 1933 or who showed outstanding service to the Reich. Max tried to forget what she said. They left the library empty-handed.

"We aren't being specific enough." Renée mounted her bicycle. "There must be people who know which party members are reporting Jews. We just need to find those people."

Max stared at her for a long moment. Suddenly it came to him. "Oh my God. I've been so stupid."

"What is it, Max?"

"I'll tell you when I get back."

His father's shop was a one-story warehouse with concrete floors that served as an interior garage. A tiny office attached to the garage sat on the side of the building. Papa had built it outside the Old Town and Stadtamhof during a flurry of industrial activity in the 1920s. Max parked his bike near the office and hurried inside. The smell of gasoline mingled with that of industrial oil. Max had loved the combination since he was a little boy. It centered him.

Jonas was there as usual, working on a bicycle. He looked up as Max came through. "Max, I heard about your father. I am so sorry. Is there anything I can do?"

Max shook his head. "I am trying to find him. No one seems to know where he is, or at least, they're not revealing it." He gazed around. "Where's Hartman?"

Jonas frowned. "He hasn't been in since Friday." Today was Monday.

"Is that so?" Max looked around again. "What about the Daimler? It belongs to Johann Mendelsohn. Where is it?"

"It was gone when I came in on Saturday. I figured Hartman finished the repairs and Mr. Mendelsohn picked it up."

Jonas didn't know the first thing about automobiles and didn't want to. That's why his father had hired Hartman. And kept Jonas too, although bicycle repairs were only a fraction of the business.

"Did Hartman tell you the repairs were done?"

"No. I haven't talked to him."

An idea slowly took shape in Max's head. "Jonas, you know in all the time Hartman has been here, I don't know his first name. What is it?"

"Reinhard."

"Did he ever express any . . . any hostility about working for us?"

Jonas looked away.

"Jonas . . ." Max waited. He tried to be patient. His father would have been.

Jonas swallowed, then looked back at Max. "Not until the past few months."

Blood rushed into Max's ears. His pulse started to race. "Tell me exactly what happened."

"He threatened me. If I told you or your father, he said he would make trouble."

"Told us what?"

"It didn't happen until the work prohibitions started. He said he could turn this place around if he owned it. I don't think he hates Jews. It was more that he saw an opportunity to make money." Jonas stopped.

"To your knowledge, did he do anything to make that happen?"

Jonas didn't say anything for a while. He ran his tongue around his lips.

"What did he do?" Max repeated.

"He showed me his party card. Made me swear not to tell anyone. Said he'd know it was me if word got around."

"He joined the Nazi Party?"

Jonas nodded again.

"Did he steal the Daimler?" Max said.

Jonas shrugged.

Max stood in front of Jonas for a long minute.

"Thank you, Jonas. I don't know how long the shop will stay open. When Papa gets home, we'll likely be moving. But you have been a trusted, loyal employee, and we will compensate you for that loyalty."

"I don't want your money, Max. All I care about is that your father is safe. I will pray for him."

Hartman. On his way home Max berated himself. He should have known. The man had been so friendly. And, ironically, had taught Max so much about cars. Still, even if he had figured it out earlier, what steps could a fifteen-year-old Jewish boy take? Who would believe him? A Nazi Party member had more influence in his little finger than Max had in his entire body.

~

When he got home Mutti was cooking again. Omelets, buttered toast, and salad. He realized that must be what she did when she was upset. Cooking for her family brought her a sense of order. And peace. He washed up and forced himself to have an appetite.

"Mutti." He gave her a hug. "This looks wonderful."

His mother poured coffee for Max and carried a plate with a cheese omelet and toast into the dining room. "Come sit. Eat your lunch. Manges." She sat at the table with him and stirred a cup of coffee. "I think we need to take more aggressive steps to get your father back home. We cannot allow ourselves to become victims."

"I agree." Max dug into his eggs. "And I have news. I think I know who set up Papa."

"What did you learn? How?"

Max explained what Jonas had told him about Reinhard Hartman, the mechanic. When Max got to the part where he admitted he'd joined the Nazi Party, his mother rose, walked into the kitchen, and spat in the sink. "That piece of shit. I never trusted him."

"It doesn't matter," Max said. "He and the Nazis have the power. Even if we try to bring him to justice, we probably would lose. Unless someone with a very high rank is a friend of yours."

His mother frowned. Then she turned to him. "Of course. You are a genius, my son! Why didn't I think of that?"

"Who do you know?"

"It doesn't matter." Which Max knew was her way of telling him it was none of his business.

~

His mother spent most of the next morning on the telephone. First she called the American consulate in Munich to check on the progress of their visas. She was told it would take at least another year.

"What if instead of three visas, we only need one?"

It would take the same amount of time, she was told. "Is it legal for someone to come to the US through Canada or Mexico?"

Max could tell from her frown she'd been told no. When she disconnected, Max said, "Mutti, I told you before. I won't go anywhere without you or Papa."

"That's what you say now, my darling. But we don't know what the future will bring. There's no way we could have predicted what's happened so far."

Max decided this might be a good time to raise the idea of going to Shanghai. He told his mother the Herskowitz family would be emigrating to China. "You don't need visas to get into Shanghai," he said. "There seems to be an absence of immigration officers. The Chinese are more concerned with the Japanese invasion than they are with refugees. We could all go there."

She smiled. "I know you are very fond of Renée, Max, but going to Shanghai would thrust us into the middle of a war zone. The Japanese are an aggressive people. They want to destroy China, if they haven't already. You belong in America, my darling, and your father is set on emigrating to Holland if necessary until the papers come through."

But he's not here, Max thought. He kept his mouth shut.

She went on. "The Japanese have their eye on Shanghai. I wouldn't be surprised if they invade again. Holland isn't so bad. We can make it work. Afterward, who knows?"

"We can't go anywhere until Papa comes home."

"I know, my dear. But I still have a Gentile friend or two. I will make inquiries."

Max left the room without further conversation. Suspicion had become second nature. Who were these Gentiles his mother called friends? And what was her relationship with them?

CHAPTER 13

December 1935
Regensburg

M ax never discovered whom Mutti called or whether those
calls made a difference, but ten days later, two weeks after
his father had been taken away, the same black police car pulled up
to the house. Max heard the horn blast and ran to the front door. A
moment later his father carefully climbed out of the back.

Papa looked like he'd aged ten years. His face was pale and
haggard. His body looked frail. His head and mustache had been
shaved, but stubble flecked the top of his head and cheeks. When he
walked, he favored one leg.

"Mutti, come quickly!" Max cried. His mother looked through the
window, raced outside, and threw her arms around his father. Max
did too, and the three of them stood locked in a tight embrace on the
lawn. Max was so relieved he said nothing about his father's condi-
tion. The family was reunited. That was what mattered.

Except for their decision to leave Germany. At dinner that night
Mutti said, "Moritz, do you remember I told you that when it was
time to leave, I would take Max if you were still reluctant to go?" Papa

raised his hand. "No, don't cut me off. It is time. And I won't take no for an answer."

"I was just going to tell you that I agree," Papa said. "It is time. I will contact my racehorse-breeding friends tomorrow."

"How long will it take until we leave?" Max asked apprehensively. He didn't want to go.

"A few weeks," Papa said. "Luckily, we—mostly your mother—put some of it in motion months ago."

Over the next three weeks the Steiners packed up their lives. His father sold the auto repair shop—at a loss—to a Gentile. It wasn't Hartman. The house was sold at an even steeper loss. The horses, including Klara, went to a breeder near the Black Forest.

Coincidentally, the Herskowitz family planned to leave the day after the Steiners. Every time Max thought about losing Renée, the hole in his heart expanded. Their last conversation, mercifully brief, took place on the porch of the Herskowitz house an hour before the Steiners boarded their train for Holland.

"Don't forget me, Max," she whispered, tears edging down her cheeks.

"Never." He wrapped her in his arms. "I will find you when this is over."

She tried to smile. "I believe you. Until then the name of the synagogue is Ohel Rachel. As soon as you get to Holland, write me where you are living and post it there. I will keep asking for letters. Once I get yours I will write you back."

"Perhaps I will jump on a ship and join you in Shanghai."

"Perhaps you will." But they both knew it would never happen. She dug into her bag and pulled out a small oblong package tied with string. "Here," she said. "A parting gift."

"What is it?"

She tried to smile but the corners of her lips didn't turn up. "You'll see. Open it when you're alone."

Max took the package, then slipped his arms around her. "Renée, I love you."

"And I have always loved you, Max. I always will."

His throat closed up. He couldn't speak. He had to tear himself away.

PART II

HOLLAND

1936–1940

CHAPTER 14

Winter 1936
Amsterdam

I t took months for the Steiners to feel safe in Amsterdam.

Holland's economy was still depressed. The wild inflation and joblessness that caused the collapse of the Weimar Republic had belatedly spread to the Netherlands. Hitler was digging Germany out of the economic morass by public works programs and rearming the military. But Max's father was unsure his auto repair business would flourish in a stagnant economy like the Netherlands.

What redeemed the situation, at least for German Jews like the Steiners, was the Dutch aversion to Hitler. Nazis were not accepted in Holland. The Dutch were a tolerant people, and relations between Jews and non-Jews were good. Jews were attracted to the social and liberal aspects of Dutch culture. Intermarriage wasn't unusual, and most Jews assimilated into Dutch society. In fact, Amsterdam was known as "Jerusalem of the West" by its Jewish residents. Sephardic Jews from Spain, Portugal, or the Middle East, as well as Ashkenazi Jews from Eastern and Central Europe were a vital presence.

Thanks to a contact in the horse-racing business, the Steiners were able to rent a corner apartment on the second floor of a building just outside the Jewish Quarter. One of several charming structures, it boasted white multipaned framed windows with cheerful curtains behind them. Compared to their home in Regensburg, it was small and modest, but by Amsterdam standards it was spacious, with two bedrooms, a sunny living room, a kitchen, and a view in two directions.

Because so much of the Netherlands was below sea level, Amsterdam was a city of canals, which added to the city's beauty. In front of the Steiners' apartment building a small footbridge arched over a canal, and the sidewalk was edged with trees and grassy areas. Although the grass and trees were now stiff with frost, Max knew Holland was known for gaily colored tulips that bloomed early.

Max couldn't wait to explore his new neighborhood. An hour after they arrived, he went out after promising he would unpack that night. The Jewish Quarter stretched from Central Amsterdam at Waterloo Square—where markets offered fish, fruits and vegetables, clothing, and more—west to the Plantage neighborhood, a greener and more spacious area compared to other parts of the city.

With each breath of the chilly winter air, Max breathed in both sorrow and hope. This was a new start to his life, but it was a life he never wanted. If only Renée could share it. She'd been his only friend at the end in Germany. He thought about the book she had wrapped and given to him before he left. It was a German translation of Mark Twain's *The Adventures of Huckleberry Finn*, the sequel to *Tom Sawyer*. Brave of her to hang on to it, he thought. Max read half the book on the train to Amsterdam. He refused to admit he was tearing up.

When he passed a secondhand bookshop in the quarter, an idea occurred to him. He ducked inside. He would buy a dictionary with some of his leftover Bar Mitzvah money and teach himself Dutch. How hard could it be? After all, he'd learned how to read Hebrew, and that required an entirely new alphabet. Dutch was, reputedly, quite similar to German.

The shop was small, dusty, and smelled like paper that had been deteriorating for decades. A weak afternoon sun seeped through the front window but didn't do much to brighten the shop's interior.

Behind the counter was a young man who looked to be the same age as Max, but taller and skinnier. His face was pleasant, with a strong chin and dark, almost black hair. A pair of glasses perched on his nose.

Max approached and asked in German whether they had any bilingual dictionaries. The boy—was he the son of the owner? Max wondered—frowned and pushed his glasses further up his nose.

Max repeated the word. "Wörterbuch?"

The boy stared at Max. A second later recognition dawned, and he grinned. "Ahh . . . Woordenboek!" His accent was quite different from Max's.

Max nodded eagerly. "Ja, das ist es!"

The clerk came out from behind the counter, beckoned to Max, and hurried down a crowded narrow aisle. On a bottom shelf was a row of dictionaries. He turned toward Max and flipped up his hands.

Max nodded. He was asking what kind of dictionary Max wanted. Max bent over to examine the books. "Deutsch und Holländisch."

The clerk leaned over and studied the dictionaries too. "Aha!"

He pulled out a volume from the stack. Max looked it over. It was a bilingual dictionary that translated from Dutch to German. Gently used, it sported a leather cover. Almost perfect. Max would have preferred German to Dutch, but this might be the only Dutch-German bilingual dictionary in the quarter. He nodded to the clerk.

The clerk said in German, "Das ist gut!"

Max stared at the clerk. "You speak German?"

The clerk continued in German. "Most Netherlanders speak a second language. German is the most common. Many people consider Dutch a dialect of German, anyway. English is second."

"I see," Max said. He followed the clerk to the front. "We just arrived from Germany."

The young man grunted as he slipped back behind the counter. "I'm sorry for your misfortune. But you're safe here."

"I hope so." Max picked up the dictionary and turned it over in his hands. "Thank you for this. I will start studying."

"What is your name?" the clerk asked.

"Max. Max Steiner. You?"

"Carl Weber."

"You're Jewish?"

Carl spread his hands. "Almost everyone in the quarter is."

"Of course. I didn't live in the Jewish Quarter back home. I apologize."

"Where are you from?"

"Regensburg."

"Ja. I've heard of it. When did you arrive?"

"Today."

Carl's eyes widened. "And you're shopping already?"

Max shrugged. "I wanted to explore." He tapped the book. "How much?"

Carl didn't answer for an instant. "It's a welcome gift."

"No," Max replied. "I can't let you do that."

"It's my family's shop." Carl looked aggrieved. "I can do whatever I want."

"Still . . . this is not right. I want to buy it."

Carl pushed his glasses further up the bridge of his nose. His brow furrowed. Then: "I'll tell you what. You learn Dutch in a year, then bring it back so someone else can use it."

Max grinned. "It's a deal. Thank you, Carl. You are a mensch." He slipped the book into his coat and turned toward the door. Then he stopped and turned back. "You wouldn't happen to know of a second-hand bicycle I could buy, would you?"

While the Steiners were able to rent a decent apartment in Amsterdam, they had to be careful with their money. In Regensburg Moritz had literally hidden some of their cash under their bed. But the house, shop, and horses had not brought in the revenue he wanted. Between the exorbitant emigration taxes, the bribes to get speedy exit papers, passports, and visas, plus limitations on how much they could withdraw from German banks, for the first time the family's assets were precarious.

When Max asked for numbers, his father said, "You don't need to know the numbers. But you don't have to worry where your next meal is coming from."

"What about school?"

"You will be in the public school, as you were in Regensburg," his father said. "There is no need for you to go to a synagogue school here."

Max nodded. His father planned to open a secondhand bicycle and repair shop. While he wouldn't expand to repairing autos, it wasn't a bad idea. Everyone in Amsterdam biked, and he hadn't seen a bike shop in the Jewish Quarter.

"Where did you get your bicycle, Max?" his mother asked a few nights later when they were arranging furniture in the parlor.

"A fellow in the bookstore had a friend who was moving to America and wanted to sell it," he said.

"Look at that, Moritz," his mother said happily. "He's already making new friends."

His father ignored the comment. "Here, Max, help me move the sofa."

"Of course, Papa." Max easily lifted his end of the couch. His father struggled with the weight. His father's arrest and incarceration might be over, but the repercussions were apparent. He was physically weaker, and he walked stooped over like an old man. He hadn't regained his confidence either, and while he didn't seem depressed, he was muted. At times taciturn. But he wouldn't talk about it, at least to Max.

Mutti, on the other hand, surprised him. In Regensburg she had never been the type to shop or spend money frivolously. She always had a "project" underway, whether it was for the synagogue, Max's school, or a civic organization. Now she threw herself into her role as cook and housekeeper. Her priority, she confided to Max, was caring for Papa, but she was eager to join a new synagogue and meet new people. She would even join the synagogue's sisterhood.

"I think the settee looks perfect there," she said after Max and Papa had moved it several times. We'll mount the painting on the wall behind it." She turned to his father. "What do you think, darling?"

"Whatever you want, Hannah," Papa replied disinterestedly.

Despite his mother's cheerfulness, which Max thought might have been somewhat forced, he knew that of the three, he was the youngest and most able to adapt to change, however temporary. But from the way Papa and Mutti were talking, neither of them seemed to admit that moving to Holland was temporary. Max thought they'd be there a few months, a year at most. But Mutti wanted to join the synagogue's sisterhood, and Papa was setting up a new business. Not something one did during a six-month stay. How long would they be staying in Holland? They hadn't brought their furniture. They'd sold the house and the shop. Did they want to build up their assets so they could go to America? What was the plan?

He recalled conversations he'd shared with Renée's father. Julius Herskowitz had told him that Amsterdam was an international center for diamonds. Julius himself would visit once a year to take a look at new stones from Africa or Russia. A diamond was an ugly stone, he said. If you didn't know what to look for, you'd miss it. The beauty was in the cutting and polishing. There were several reputable Jewish diamond dealers in Amsterdam, Julius said. Max decided to search them out to see if anyone had a part-time job for him. Not only would he learn new skills, but it would help him feel closer to Renée.

His hopes were dashed when his father said, "You should plan to work with me in the bicycle shop after school, Max. I will need help."

"But—" Max stifled his dismay. He was an only child. He was obligated to help the family. It was the right thing to do. He swallowed and hoped his voice didn't reveal his disappointment. "Of course, Papa."

CHAPTER 15

Spring 1936
Amsterdam

Renée's first letter arrived on a bright April day, almost four months after they left Germany. Max had sent her a card at the Ohel Rachel synagogue in Shanghai when they moved; at the time he hoped she received it. When he finally saw an envelope with her tiny, precise handwriting, he grabbed it, hurried to his room, and tore it open.

Dearest Max,

Thank you for sending the card to Ohel Rachel with your new address. I asked about mail for me when we first arrived at the synagogue, and the woman who gave me the card winked as if we shared a secret. But I will get to that later.

First, I want to catch you up on the past few months. It's still strange that it's been that long since we were together. Back in Germany, I felt anxious when a week had passed without word from you. I suppose we must accommodate ourselves to this extended way to measure time.

After you boarded the train for Amsterdam, I felt lost. I had a right to be. I had just lost my best friend in the world. So I cried. I continue to miss you terribly.

We left the next day and boarded a train from Regensburg bound for the Italian border. The Gestapo checked our papers and passports. Once we started to move again everyone cheered because we had made it out of Germany! The ship, which we boarded in Naples, was a luxury liner with four or five decks and a staff so large that each family was assigned a stewardess to take care of them. Ours was a lovely young woman, Gretchen, who spoke enough German to be helpful. There were at least five other Jewish families on the ship, perhaps more, all bound for Shanghai. One family included a girl about my age, Henrietta, from Vienna. We spent time together.

Luckily I did not get seasick, although Wolf did. That was lucky because everyone on the ship, including Gretchen, Mutti, and the other families, encouraged us to eat, eat, eat. We didn't know what was in store for us in Shanghai, so we should fatten up in advance. I kept thinking we were cows or pigs being prepared for slaughter. I kept that to myself, of course. To be honest, it wasn't difficult to do what they said—the food was very good.

The voyage lasted 4 weeks. Can you imagine? It felt endless, especially when sun, sky, water, and fish are the only elements one sees and smells. Once in a while, a whale or family of dolphins would surface. The little ones were delighted and were sure they had come to amuse them. Finally, the night before we landed, they told us to prepare to disembark after breakfast the next morning.

Oh, Max, Shanghai is not at all what I expected! At least the downtown near the wharf, which they call the Bund. (Not the German word— it's Hindu.) There are tall skyscrapers everywhere, and the harbor lies directly in front of them. Once you get ashore, there are hordes of people packed into small spaces. There are rickshaws, with young men pulling people all over town. You can see the veins on their legs popping out. There is also a glut of bicycles which do the same, but only a few autos. From a distance, it looks very Western, with electric signs and buildings and trolley cars. But up close, I noticed that the streets are not well maintained, and the odor is insufferable. I gather there is little indoor plumbing unless one lives in an affluent neighborhood. There are a proliferation of stalls selling food and drink, but we wouldn't think of eating anything off the street.

Even so, they tell me Shanghai is truly an international city, the largest in China. It is responsible for over half of the imports and exports, and everyone is in the business of making money. They call Shanghai the "Paris of the East, the New York of the West" because aside from legitimate trading, Shanghai is somewhat notorious as the center of criminal activity in China.

Fortunately, Papa had been corresponding with his gem contacts here, and he was able to rent us an apartment in a western district called Jessfield Park, which is quite nice. Away from the tumult of the city, I see trees, birds, and grass outside our windows. The zoo is not far away. We are lucky, you and I, to have emigrated from Germany when we did—at least our families were able to bring some of their assets. My father is quite excited about opening a jewelry store.

A few weeks ago we were invited to Shabbos dinner by the Sassoons, who are probably the most prominent Jewish family here. They are Baghdadi Jews, a branch of Judaism I confess is new to me. They come mostly from Iraq, Basra, and Aleppo, and other Arabic-speaking parts of the Middle East. They've been in Shanghai for decades, and are extremely wealthy. The family does most of their trading with Britain, and they all speak English. They are so central to Shanghai's wealth that no one would dare to impose any antisemitic decrees. So different than Germany. I often squeeze my eyes shut and pretend the Nazis are nothing but a bad dream. They are friends with the Kalash family and introduced them to us. They have two children. The oldest is Tomas, their eighteen year old son. He seems nice.

The only problem here is the Japanese. Did you know they bombed Shanghai in 1932? They occupied Manchuria but Chinese students protested (as they should), so the Japanese broke up the protests with bombs. They are so aggressive they almost make the Nazis look pacifist. Although why anyone would want to occupy Manchuria, I do not know.

Now, the part of the letter I find hardest to write. Max, I hope you *know how much I love you. And I believe you love me too. But realistically, we both know we will not see each other for a very long time, if ever. I want you to know that if you meet someone else and are feeling conflicted because of us, I release you from any obligation to me. There never was one to begin with, but I know you, and I suspect you will feel one. Try not to. Love her with all your heart. If she loves you back, I will be happy. Truly. Of course, I will follow the same path. I doubt I will meet anyone "suitable," as my mother calls it, in Shanghai. But if I do, I will weigh his prospects. Max, this is not to say goodbye. It is simply acknowledging where we find ourselves in time. We both know war is inevitable. My dearest wish is to find you after the Nazis are defeated.*

Now, write me a long letter that I can read over and over, as I hope you will mine.

All my love,
Renée

PS I hope you enjoyed my parting gift. You must have finished it by now. I wish we could talk about it together. I read it before I gave it to you. I'm certain that if Huckleberry Finn lived in Germany, he would join the Resistance.

When Max finished her letter, he wanted to smash his fist into the wall. Renée's absence had blasted his heart into pieces. She had called him her "best friend in the world," but they were so much more. They were friends whose transition to lovers had been stolen by Hitler. He felt cheated, as if the cards in his hand were marked. From her letter he was sure she felt the same.

He agreed with her about Huckleberry Finn. He'd heard rumors about Germans and others in Europe who were resolutely opposed to the Nazis, Hitler, and fascism. Apparently, resistance groups were secretly banding together to destroy the Nazis any way they could. Max smiled. Huckleberry Finn would likely be in the forefront of that fight. Was Renée suggesting he should do the same? Perhaps the war that Hitler wanted would be short. Other nations, ones with democratic governments, would surely come to their rescue, wouldn't they? In the meantime, he would try to adapt. And if he couldn't, he'd have to find a way to reclaim his power.

He wrote her back that night.

CHAPTER 16

Spring 1936
Amsterdam

U nlike Regensburg, Amsterdam, a much larger city, was home to several synagogues. Sephardic Jews had their own temple, and the Ashkenazi Jews had theirs. The Ashkenazi community was building a new synagogue in the Lekstraat, which would be open to all Jews within the year.

Because the Sephardic Portuguese synagogue was one of the largest in Europe, the Steiners first went to services there. Lit entirely by candlelight on ornate, low-hanging chandeliers and tall candelabras, the sanctuary seemed to project its own spirituality. The rabbi and cantor wore white robes and tall black headdresses that reminded Max of oversized berets. Congregants wore hats: caps, bowlers, and fedoras, rather than the kippahs Max wore in Germany. A full choir, hidden in the balcony, chanted some of the prayers.

When worship was underway, most of it was in Hebrew, not Dutch. It didn't matter where in the world a Jew landed. Whether Amsterdam or Shanghai, whether there was a choir, or whether they covered their heads, Jews recited the same prayers in the same language in the same order. The Steiners had not been Orthodox, or even very observant. But the stability, the unbroken chain of sacra-ments through the centuries—despite discrimination and oppression —was a heritage to be proud of. Max should go to synagogue more often, he thought.

In March, Hitler sent German troops to reoccupy the Rhineland, a chunk of western Germany that hugged the far side of the Rhine River. After the Great War, the Treaty of Versailles stipulated that German troops were banned from the land west of the Rhine. Hitler marched twenty thousand Wehrmacht soldiers in and retook the area anyway. Neither the British nor the French government did much about it. Whether they were unwilling or, more likely, unprepared to face another war, the Nazis interpreted their inaction as weakness. In addition to running roughshod over domestic law and order, it was clear Hitler had no intention of respecting the international order either.

Max and Carl Weber became fast friends. Both were curious about everything and dogged about pursuing answers. They were both bookworms. And Carl had a sly sense of humor that Max found appealing. After Carl helped him buy his bicycle, Max began to meet Carl following his shifts at the bookshop. Carl's father Jacob Weber, middle-aged, his body turning soft, was friendly too. While Jacob's penetrating blue eyes belied the jovial disposition he displayed when people came into the shop, everyone received a hearty welcome.

It was through Carl that Max met two other Jewish youths, Tony Asscher and Pieter Cohen, both Amsterdam natives. Max was the first refugee from Germany they'd met, and all four boys had nonstop questions for one another. Max was guarded at first. Boys he'd been friends with for years in Germany had turned cruel. How much should he reveal? Then again, these lads were Jewish. They would be different.

Max met Carl outside the bookstore on a balmy spring Saturday afternoon. They were to meet up with Tony and Pieter. "We want to show you some of our special places." Carl grinned.

Max cocked his head. "Why are you grinning? You look like the fox that's just cornered the hare."

"You'll see." Carl mounted his bike and took off.

Max wasn't working that day—his father's shop wouldn't open until their work permits were approved—so he hopped on his bike and followed Carl.

The Jewish Quarter, or Jodenbuurt, as it was called, occupied a large district in eastern Amsterdam, although the Steiners lived outside the quarter in a neighborhood of well-to-do streets and canals. While this neighborhood did include the narrow alleys and crowded streets Max had seen before, the quarter also included comfortably wide avenues that ended at squares. Every so often a canal intersected the streets, which were linked by short bridges.

Carl pedaled down one of the broader avenues toward the Portuguese synagogue. As they approached the building, Carl twisted around and gestured. "There they are!"

Tony leaned against a building while Pieter straddled his bicycle, making enthusiastic arm circles. They were clearly in the midst of an intense conversation.

Carl called out. "Hey, kameraads!"

They turned around.

"What was that about?" Carl teased. "Pieter, your arms were pumping so fast it looked like you might fly away!"

Max could almost understand Carl's Dutch. Carl was right. The Dutch language included plenty of German words, although almost all the inflections and pronunciations were different.

Pieter said, "I was talking about the Tramp's new movie, *Modern Times*. A new starlet named Paulette Goddard stars in it with Chaplin, by the way. I was trying to explain that Chaplin is a socialist at heart.

But Tony says I take everything too seriously and should just stop searching for a deeper meaning." He threw Tony an injured look.

Tony fired back. "Well, you do. Who cares if he's a socialist? He's a great actor and his movies are fun."

Carl, always the peacemaker, rolled his eyes at Max. "Why don't we discuss that later? We have a schedule. Let's go."

Max was surprised that boys his age could get so emotional about trivial matters. For the past three years the Nazis' persecution, coupled with his dread of what was coming next, was at the forefront of his mind. He and Renée had talked about books just to keep their sanity. The boys' chatter reminded him he wasn't in Germany anymore. Normal people loved to chat—even argue—about movie stars, restaurants, art, and other diversions.

With the boys all back on their bicycles, Carl turned off the avenue and wound through a warren of narrower streets. When they passed a diamond factory with a retail shop next door, Max made a note of it. They emerged from the Jewish Quarter in the Plantage district and pedaled to the botanical garden, where they parked their bicycles and walked through a few of the gardens.

"It's one of the oldest gardens of its kind in the world," Tony said. Max was blank until he looked up the Dutch words "oudste" and "wereld" in his dictionary. He smiled. "Ja?"

Pieter spoke slowly. "Did you know that one coffee plant here in Amsterdam was the source for all the coffee that now grows in South America?"

Max recognized "coffee" and "plant." He deduced from the word "Zuid," which Pieter had said before the word "Amerika," that he must mean South America. Or a place close to it. Max arched his eyebrows.

From the gardens they rode to the Artis Zoo, which housed an assortment of animals, most spending a sunny day in outdoor cages. Monkeys chirred, lions roared, elephants trumpeted. Their meaty odors filled the air. Throngs of small children giggled and screamed their delight. Big ones too. There was no zoo in Regensburg, and Max was fascinated to see live creatures, some of which he'd only seen in photos.

After the zoo they stopped in at a small café to share a plate of biscuits and cakes. The tantalizing aroma of sugar, vanilla, and cinnamon reminded Max of Renée's biscuits. A shadow passed over him, and he was suddenly sad. He hoped the boys didn't notice. He didn't think so, because they were joking and laughing, each trying to outdo the other with the memory of some exploit they'd shared.

Carl tried to translate here and there, but their conversation was too fast-paced for Max to pick up much. It didn't matter. His own memories washed over him, and for the first time since arriving in Holland, he longed to be back in Regensburg. To what he thought of as the Before. Life then was predictable, comfortable. His biggest worry was whether Klara would behave or if he'd win another blue first-place track ribbon. No Nazis. No fights. No restrictions. He glanced enviously at Carl, Tony, and Pieter. They didn't have the Before. Though they were all roughly the same age, Max felt years older.

Mutti kept assuring him the good days were back. They were safe. Still, this seemed to be the After. Could life return to what it had been? He had escaped Germany and was now living in a new home and country, meeting new friends. The traditions that had anchored him in Germany were in the past, and who knew if they would return? Everything was different, and Max feared that the Before could happen again. The only reliable constants were the services at synagogue.

He decided to concentrate on the boys' banter about school. All three went to the same school, the one Max would be attending in September. Not knowing Dutch well would probably bring his grades down, and that would affect his academic standing. In the Before Max had entertained thoughts of becoming a lawyer or a professor. Perhaps a track-and-field coach. Now, though, in the After, would any of those be possible?

Tony interrupted his thoughts. "Max, now we will show you the best part of the afternoon."

Max understood. "Wat is dat?"

Tony smirked as he mounted his bike. "Follow us." Volg ons. "But it is a secret. You cannot tell anyone what you see. Can we trust you?"

Max shook his head. "Wat is vertrouwen?" he asked.

Carl translated into German. "Vertrauen. He's asking if we can trust you."

Max nodded. "Ja. Ja. Natuurlijk." Of course.

The other three nodded. With Tony in the lead, the four youths biked through the Plantage district and turned at a busy intersection. On a quiet side street, they came abreast of a building with a sign on the front that read "Ballet Studio."

Max read the sign, frowned, and called out to Carl in German. "What are we doing here?"

Carl's cheeks reddened. He put a finger to his lips. "We dismount, hide our bikes, and watch. Discreetly."

Clearly confused, Max glanced at the other boys. Once their bikes were parked in a nearby alley, they crossed the street to a small playground for children that was bordered by several benches. The three boys sat on the benches that faced the ballet studio. Carl tapped the space on the bench next to him. Max sat.

"It should only be another minute or two."

"Yes, but why are we here?" Max asked again.

"You'll see."

A moment later, the door to the ballet studio opened, and about a dozen young girls exited. Most looked to be fifteen or sixteen, close in age to the youths. The girls wore dance leotards and short skirts, which left quite a bit of their legs showing. Several of the girls released long hair from the chignons they'd pinned up while dancing. Even from a distance, many seemed attractive, and their laughter and smiles added a radiance that made their faces glow.

When the girls spotted the four youths, some of them waved, as though they'd seen the boys before.

Suddenly Max understood. He grinned, made himself comfortable, and waved back.

CHAPTER 17

Summer 1936
Amsterdam

On a cloudy but humid end-of-summer day just before school began, Max biked to the diamond factory he'd passed on the afternoon he spent with the Four Musketeers, as they'd begun calling themselves. Sandwiched on a narrow street in the Jewish Quarter, DeCastro Diamonds occupied a shabby two-story building where taller, four-story structures blocked out the sun. A small retail shop faced the street and a window display illustrated gemstones, in addition to diamonds, that were available. Photographs of dazzling rings, bracelets, and necklaces showed off the finished products.

Max dismounted and locked his bicycle around a lamppost. DeCastro must be a Sephardic Jewish family; he'd never heard the name in Germany. He studied the eye-catching sign in the window. He'd visited Julius Herskowitz's workplace in Regensburg, but it looked like a normal office in a building shared with lawyers, doctors, and other professionals. A small notation below his name declared he was a "Registered Purveyor of Fine Diamonds."

The front door of DeCastro's was locked. Max was just about to press a buzzer on the side of the door. Suddenly he hesitated. He wasn't sure what to say if and when they opened the door. Why was he here? Did he really want to work in a diamond factory? Or did he miss Renée so much that anything that reminded him of her would give him solace? And what if taking a job in a diamond factory did not ease his grief?

Perhaps he should wait until he was more certain of his motives. Although they'd been corresponding faithfully, he had to face the fact that he hadn't seen Renée in nine months. It was quite possible he would never see her again. Max stood at the door for a long moment, then went back to his bicycle. He took one last look at DeCastro Diamonds, unlocked the bicycle, and boosted himself onto the seat. As he rode away, he gripped the handlebar palm down. With his other hand he brushed away something wet on his cheek.

After his trip to DeCastro's, the acceptance Max allowed himself to feel in Amsterdam helped restore his faith in humanity. Between helping his father set up the new shop, and spending time with his new friends, the anxiety and fear of the past three years started to loosen like a necktie that had been too tightly knotted.

In August the 1936 Berlin Olympics began, with the American Negro track-and-field star Jessie Owens the star competitor. Although Max would have loved to watch Owens perform in person, he consoled himself with the fact that as a Jew, he would never have been allowed to buy a ticket or be admitted to the Games. He was delighted when Owens metaphorically spat in Hitler's face by winning four gold medals.

The other Musketeers helped Max with his Dutch. By talking slowly, correcting his pronunciation, and above all, having the patience of sixty-year-old men rather than youths of sixteen, the Musketeers helped Max enough that he was able to start the school year in the same grade with them. He'd taken a test prior to beginning the semester, and while Dutch was his weakest grade, his math and social studies aptitude more than compensated.

In addition to Dutch and German, Max began to study English, the second-most popular language in the Netherlands. The relationship between the three languages never failed to frustrate him. Just when he thought he could transpose a German word or expression into Dutch or English, he discovered he was wrong. English, especially, he concluded, was a language of exceptions.

His parents joined the Ashkenazi Neue Shul in the Jewish Quarter just before the High Holidays. His mother became a member of the sisterhood and was soon gossiping about the women she'd met. Three new families had come from Germany, she said: two from Berlin and one from Munich, which was practically next door to Regensburg. Max and his father patiently listened to her accounts of Jewish geography: who knew whom, how the cousin in one family married another, whose children had already left for even safer countries. Listening to Mutti, Max was convinced every Jewish person in the world was related to the others through some branch of their family tree.

His father, too, seemed to have jettisoned some of his burdens. Thanks to the Committee for Jewish Refugees, a Dutch charity that, since 1933, had helped immigrants settle in Holland, he'd received a work permit and opened his shop in July. When he wasn't trying to build business, he drank strong coffee and smoked cigars after morning minyan with his new synagogue friends. At dinner he would report the latest news and rumors about the situation in Europe.

By his sixteenth birthday in September, Max was nearly six feet tall. With his stature, sandy hair, and green eyes, he was the epitome of an Aryan. The other boys teased that he must be a foundling, or worse, a Nazi spy. Max tried to take it with grace and good humor. Sometimes he could.

It wasn't home, but it was peace.

CHAPTER 18

Winter 1937
Amsterdam

The red-light district of Amsterdam occupied a neighborhood called De Wallen, not far from the Jewish Quarter. Max thought it fitting that the area, now rife with men and women engaged in the world's oldest profession, was once home to several monasteries. Over the past few years, a new practice called "window prostitution" had emerged. Women sat behind a window with the curtains mostly closed. Customers could peek through a gap and decide whether to buy time with the lady, who was illuminated by a red light.

Shortly after the new year on a chilly January night, the Four Musketeers trudged through the snow to De Wallen. At sixteen, all four had decided that ogling young ballet dancers was no longer satisfying and was, in fact, immature. They were young men now. It was time. Fortified with testosterone, they started down the main street, which was flanked on both sides by a canal. With glowing red lights emanating from dozens of windows, Max thought it looked picturesque.

Tony, unsurprisingly, was the first Musketeer to peel off. His choice of a black-haired beauty with pale white skin reminded Max of Snow White. The others chuckled when he remarked on it.

"Well, you must be waiting for Sleeping Beauty," Tony shot back. "She won't give you any problem if she's dead asleep."

Carl let out a low whistle. "I sense a competition in the works."

Max shrugged. Pieter chortled. Tony pretended to bow with a flourish and turned into a doorway.

"Have fun," Max called out.

More laughter.

Eventually Carl and Pieter found girls, and Max was alone. He strolled down the street. He wasn't sure what he wanted. He hoped he'd know when he saw her. The women behind the curtains did their best to lure him in with low-cut dresses, knowing smiles, and smoky, come-hither poses, but Max kept walking, covering most of the main street and an alley.

He was starting to doubt the wisdom of coming to De Wallen. Why wasn't he attracted to any of the women? Was there something wrong with him? Yes, it would be his first time, but this wasn't a life-and-death decision. He wouldn't see the woman after tonight, and she certainly wouldn't remember him. He frowned, turned around, and started back up the street. He was determined to choose someone. If he didn't, Tony would be finished before Max had begun.

Halfway up the street he came to a window he'd peeked in before. This time, though, a woman he hadn't seen now sat behind the curtain. He slowed. She had pale blond hair that fell to her shoulders. Her skin was a rosy hue, probably because of the red light, he thought cynically, and a lot of that skin was showing.

She wasn't in a tawdry dress like the other prostitutes. She wore a lacy white lingerie bodice that stretched from her breasts down to her thighs. Silk stockings completed the outfit. Most of the women wore heavy makeup, their eyes kohled, their lips a gash of red. Except for her eyes, she didn't appear to wear any paint. It made her look younger. Almost waiflike. She couldn't be older than eighteen, could she?

Max stopped and peered into the window. The girl looked

straight at him. Something in those eyes made Max catch his breath. What was it? She was appraising *him*. Not the other way around. Her eyes gave off a cool intensity from which Max couldn't look away. He froze, feeling light-headed. Her lips parted. What was she doing? After what seemed like a timeless moment, a slight smile lit her eyes. He didn't wait to see the smile reach her lips. She was ravishing. He forced himself to move, hurried to the door, and went inside.

~

Two months later, on a chilly March evening, the Steiners came home from the movies. They'd seen *Modern Times*, which had been released six months earlier but was still playing. His parents discussed the movie while sipping tea. Max peeled an orange.

"It's apparent Mr. Chaplin has some strong ideas about modern society," Papa said.

"All the rumors say he's a Communist," Mutti said.

Papa smiled. "I doubt it's a rumor. Or a secret, after a film like this."

His mother glanced over at Max. "What do you think, dear?"

Max looked up, startled. "I'm sorry. What did you say?"

"Where have you been?" she asked. "We're talking about the movie."

"Oh." Max studied his orange. "It was fine." He finished peeling and separated it into two sections.

"Your head is in the clouds tonight. What are you thinking about?"

He shook his head. "Nothing."

His parents exchanged a glance. His father cleared his throat. "There is bad news from Germany."

Max watched his mother's expression tighten. The familiar look of fear—no, more than fear; terror—shot across her face. "What?"

Max braced himself.

"Don't worry, darling. It doesn't affect us. Anymore. It seems as if the Nazi Kripo, together with the Gestapo, rounded up more than two thousand convicted offenders and threw them into concentration camps."

"What's new about that?" his mother asked. "This isn't the first time. You, of all people, should know."

"This is the first mass roundup of so-called criminals, not political opponents."

His father went on to explain how the Kripo, the police organization that had expanded into a national detective force in Germany after Hitler came to power, now had the power to arrest any racial or social enemies of the Reich, not just criminals, and incarcerate them in the camps. Hitler and Himmler were thinking of merging the Kripo with the Gestapo. Which would make an already formidable police force even more intimidating.

Max listened halfheartedly. Over the past eighteen months he'd lived in Amsterdam, events in Germany had taken on a remote quality, as if thick armor was shielding him from the brunt of developments. He lived in Holland now. His life was here. He wasn't the same person he had been in Germany. After eighteen months of living here, the younger Max, the Before Max, seemed far away.

There was another reason that he wasn't focused on Germany. Her name was Annaliese Laine.

The first night felt like a dream, as if she'd cast a spell on him. Inside the brothel he paid a beefy-looking man who guarded a closed door. The man, with a perpetual scowl on his face, wore pants with a bulge in one pocket. Max spotted a black metal tip poking out. A pistol. The man counted the money, then opened a door. It wasn't the room with the curtained window. This was a small room with a smaller bed, sheets that appeared to be clean, and a towel. Annaliese sat on the bed wearing her lingerie. When Max entered, she rose.

Max had never seen such an alluring woman. Her hair loose and wavy. Her body, slim but lithe. Her face innocent and wanton at the same time. Without a word, she took two steps toward him and slipped her arms around his neck. Max wasn't sure what to do next. She knew. She leaned in and kissed him. Max had never tasted lips so soft and sweet. He savored the warm, wet touch.

She drew back before he'd had enough. Instinct took over and Max leaned in to kiss her again. This time her kiss was longer and more languid. When her tongue slowly made its way into Max's mouth, a wave of excitement spilled over him. His arms encircled her, and he pulled her close. She pressed up against him. They both felt how hard he was.

She led him over to the bed and made him sit. While he watched, she slowly took off her clothes. First the stockings. She rolled them up one at a time. Then her garter belt. She glanced at Max. He was having trouble breathing. She smiled and took off her lacy bodice. Then she knelt on the floor facing him, slid his hands into hers, and pressed them against her breasts. Another wave of desire washed over him. He pulled her up onto the bed.

It was over much too soon.

CHAPTER 19

They didn't talk much that first night, but they did exchange names, and Max asked for more time.

She nodded. "But you must pay."

She spoke Dutch with a slight accent. Then again, so did he. He wondered where she was from. He got up, pulled on his pants, and paid the man more guilders. They went more slowly the second time, and Max had more control. She showed him things he'd never thought of, and when he did them to her, her back arched and he heard a soft cry of pleasure. He forgot about time. About Germany. About the boys who were likely looking for him. The only world he cared about was that small room in De Wallen and the young woman on the bed.

Afterward Max asked when he could see her again. She said two nights later. He spent those two days in a private world reliving the past and imagining the future. When the night finally arrived, it was better than the first time. The curves of her body were more familiar, and when he ran his hands around them he wanted those curves to belong to him. The same with her lips, her breasts, and her legs, especially when they clasped him tightly around his waist. He even wanted her smell.

He'd never felt so complete. So satisfied. So invincible. She made him want—no, need—to possess her. To have her for himself. No other man should touch her. In the back of his mind he wasn't sure that his thoughts were respectful or even decent, but the maleness, the passion she'd roused in him, blinded him to any needs but his own. And hers.

This time, after they made love, Max plied her with questions. Where was she from? Where was her family? What did she want to do in the world? They lay in the impossibly small bed facing each other. He propped his head on his elbow.

"I am from Finland. Helsinki," she said. "It is very dark and cold in winter. My mother moved us here two years ago."

"What about your father?" Max asked.

"We ran away from him. He drank all the time. He beat us."

"Us?"

"My mother, sister, and brother. We borrowed all the money we could, mostly from my grandparents, and took the train here."

"Does your mother work?"

"She cleans houses. I help."

"What about school?"

"The little ones go."

"But you don't?"

"We need to put food on the table. The last I heard, school doesn't do that." Her voice was neutral, but Max couldn't help thinking she was reprimanding him for not understanding her situation. Perhaps she had similar thoughts, because she changed the subject. "Tell me about you."

He told her about his family, their escape to Holland, and why.

"You are Jew?"

The old familiar fear welled up. "Is that a problem?"

She ran the back of her fingers down his cheek. "Not for me. But I hear stories."

"I'm sure you do. But you see, we know better than to believe them."

"What do you mean?"

"You and I, we are both outsiders. We are making a life here because of the tolerance of the Dutch people. But even tolerant and kind people can make outsiders feel—inferior. They make up stories or believe certain things about us because we are not natives and they are. We try to fit in—you know—be like them. But our accents, sometimes our clothes or our behavior, give us away. Do you see?"

A flick of her eyebrows indicated she did. "You and I . . ." she whispered, as if she was trying out words in a new language.

"Yes," Max said. "You and I. And our families. We will always be outsiders, tolerated but at the fringes of their society."

She inclined her head as if thinking about it. Then she shifted her weight and pulled him toward her. She forced him to roll over on top of her.

"Again?" He stroked her hair.

She held a finger to his lips. "But don't tell Guillermo."

Two weeks later Max's Bar Mitzvah money was practically gone. He didn't care. Somehow he would find more. He needed to be with Annaliese. They understood each other. They talked. They laughed. They made love. She dazzled him. He fascinated her. Yes, their worlds were sharply different. His parents would have sacrificed anything for Max. Annaliese came from a world where there was nothing left to sacrifice. Where the pain of just enduring was sacrifice enough. He was in love. He would rescue her.

He visited De Wallen three or four times a week. He couldn't get enough of her. Her hair, her body, her lips, her scent. He looked up her name. It meant "grace of God." He had to smile. God had indeed graced him with Annaliese. But he wanted her for himself. He didn't want her to see other men. He invited her to go to the movies, to have dinner with him, even to meet his parents, but each time, she refused.

"Why won't you let me take you out?"

"I am not from your world, Max. It would never work."

"How do you know? You haven't tried. Come to dinner with me. You will see."

"No. Better to cut it off now. I cannot—"

Max cut her off. "No. Annaliese, please. Give us a chance."

"You are a stubborn boy. Do you not realize I need the money I make here? And it still isn't enough? I work all night then clean houses with my mother all day. I have no time for you."

He was quiet for a moment. Then: "What if I could help find you a job where you could make the same money but not"—he waved a hand around the room—"have to do this? I can't bear the thought of you with other men."

A sad look came across her face. "You said it yourself. I am a foreigner. I barely know the language. I do not go to school. Where could I make this much money? What would I do? This money feeds my family."

"But if I could . . . If you had a different job that pays the same . . . would you leave De Wallen? And give this up?"

"Oh, Max. How can you be so young and yet so sure of yourself?"

"Because—because I am in love with you."

She was quiet for a moment. Then: "You must fall out of love as quickly as you fell in. You know I cannot be faithful to you."

"Yet." He smiled. "I can wait."

She shook her head, but a small smile remained on her face.

Max took that as tacit approval "So. If you could do anything in the world, what would it be?"

She bit her lip. "You really want to know?"

"Of course."

"I want to design clothes for women."

"Fashion," he said. His mother often bought fashion magazines and thumbed through them. "Why?"

"The clothes that women wear are dowdy. Full of bows and buttons and lace collars that make them look like doddering old ladies. My mother and I laugh about it. We make our own clothes. We design clothing that young women would love. Simple. Soft fabrics. Pastel colors. Oh, and black. Lots of black."

"So you can sew?"

"Of course."

"I do not notice women's clothes. Perhaps I should."

"You noticed I was not wearing a dress the first time we . . . met."

"That is true. You captivated me with your choice of—of—" He couldn't think of the right word.

"Lingerie, Max. With lots of lace and bows. You see, they belong on lingerie. They are intimate objects for intimate encounters. Not on a dress that is worn on the street."

"How clever you are."

"Just because I am not in school does not make me stupid."

"I never thought you were." He cupped her chin and kissed her gently. "So. If I could help you find a job in fashion, would you leave this place?"

"It must pay as much as I earn here," she said, a skeptical note in her voice. "But without an education, that will not happen."

"But if it could, would you consider it?"

He couldn't tell if she was exasperated or amused. "Oh, all right Max. Yes. Yes I would."

The Musketeers didn't like Max's obsession. Tony, in fact, delivered a stern warning. "It could be a trap."

"What do you mean?" Max asked.

"She's a prostitute. Not the best example of strong moral values."

Carl tried to defend Max. "Perhaps she's a prostitute with a sharp brain and a heart of gold."

Tony shot him a mocking look. "Then why is she a prostitute?"

Pieter cut in. "What if she tells you she's pregnant and it's yours? You won't be able to prove that it's not. And then demands that you marry her? I agree with Tony. You are in a dangerous place."

"You are all simply jealous." Max knew he sounded defensive, but he hadn't expected so much resistance from his friends.

"Yes. You're getting laid," Tony said. "And yes. We are jealous about that. But what about your girlfriend in China? Have you forgotten her?"

Max didn't want to think about Renée. She was from the Before. Annaliese needed him now. And he needed her. He was going to change her life.

"There's one other thing," Carl said slowly.

"What's that?" Max said, his voice tight.

"She's not Jewish."

"She's an immigrant. Like me."

"Max. Stop dodging the issue. What would your parents say?"

"Isn't it more important what I say? We are both outsiders. We share the same journey."

Carl frowned. "You can't really believe that, Max."

"I do." Max folded his arms.

"And you call that love?"

"What would you call it?"

Carl didn't answer. He shrugged and threw up his hands.

Over the spring and summer Max started tutoring Dutch students in German. It wasn't a lot of money, but it was enough for liaisons with Annaliese. Between school, working in the bicycle shop, tutoring students, and Annaliese, he was rarely home. He left the apartment shortly after dawn and didn't come home until late at night.

His mother grew worried. "Why are you so busy? Where do you go at night? At least come home earlier. It isn't healthy, the hours you keep."

"Don't worry. I'm fine."

"Where do you go?"

"I have appointments." His reply was almost curt.

His mother planted her hands on her hips. "Max . . . don't be disrespectful." She was about to go on, but his father touched her shoulder and shook his head.

CHAPTER 20

August 1937
Amsterdam

Near the end of August, a letter arrived from Renée.

Dearest Max,

I haven't heard from you in a long time. I suspect you must be very busy. The same is true for us. Shanghai continues to receive more Jewish refugees every day. They are coming from Germany, Austria, Poland, Russia, and the Balkan countries. The increase, in large part, is due to a diplomat from the Chinese legation to Vienna. His name is Ho Feng Shan. He is fluent in German and has many Jewish friends. He understands the persecution that has become a daily trial for Jewish people, as well as Hitler's dictate that they leave the Reich. So he has proposed they come to Shanghai, where, because of the Japanese occupation of the city, there is (and has been since we arrived) no immigration or passport control system. Which means no need for an entrance visa, although Ho is supplying them. Apparently people listen and take his advice because ships filled with refugees arrive almost every week.

Unfortunately, most of them have little more than one suitcase for their entire family. As I understand it, the amount of money that Jews can with-

draw from European banks has been sharply reduced. However, the Bagh-dadi Jews I told you about are proving to be quite generous toward these poor souls, supplying them with food, clothing, and housing. Most are living in a neighborhood called Hongkou. It is crowded and considered to be a slum, but it is free. The Baghdadis have even inspired some Ashkenazi Jews (like my father) to contribute to the immigrants' welfare.

As it happens, one prominent Baghdadi family, Herr and Frau Kalash, have become friends of my parents. They live nearby, and they have two children. Tomas is two years older than I, and his sister, Maria, is just my age. We spend quite a lot of time together. Herr Kalash calls himself a busi-nessman, but my parents say he is heavily involved in the opium trade. Of course, we never mention that when they're around. Remember how alone and isolated we felt in Regensburg? Those days are behind me. I certainly don't miss them.

Summer in Shanghai is hot and humid. We caught the tail end of a typhoon last week, and all the streets flooded. That was not altogether a bad thing. The stench on Shanghai streets, the result of goats, pigs, rats, unwashed people, and their waste, can be odious. Especially in the Bund (downtown near the wharf.) It is much less pronounced where we live, and the trees and foliage help cool us. But fans are definitely de rigueur.

In addition to events in Germany, we are carefully following what the Japanese are doing. They attacked Beijing last month and now occupy the city. This means they now control large swaths of China. Next, it is rumored, they will head south toward Shanghai and Nanking. We are very nervous, even though they already control part of the city. You see, it is now a full-blown war. They say Japan will plunder raw materials from China to produce the weapons and equipment they need to conquer more of Asia. I shiver to think about it. We came here to get away from a warlike country. And have landed in the midst of another.

As a result some of us have decided to keep an eye on the Japanese so that we know what they're doing and when. As you may know, there is talk they will sign a military pact with Germany. That would be a disaster. So we must discover as much as possible about that and their other plans. We may be on the other side of the world, but we are not isolated from world events.

I am so glad you have such good friends in Holland. It must be a relief to be in a free, welcoming country. Although I miss you terribly, it warms my heart to know you are safe.

I wish you a wonderful year on your 17th birthday, Max. How could we have imagined four years ago how much our lives would change? Sometimes your Bar Mitzvah seems like yesterday. Other times, it's a lifetime ago. I hope life has become less of a struggle and that your dreams might soon be reality.

With love,
Renée

The last line in her letter sounded as if this could be the last one she'd ever write to him. She was pulling away. Putting distance between them. He should have expected it. They had both moved on. Still, if he was honest, he felt a trace of annoyance that Renée was moving on without him. He knew he was being selfish. He'd moved on with Annaliese. He was more involved with her than he'd been with Renée. But a part of him felt justified in holding on to Renée. The Nazis had stolen his life in Germany. Why shouldn't he keep everything he could now? Including Renée?

The aroma of roast chicken woke him after a nap, and he went into the kitchen. It was late afternoon, and Papa was still at the shop. Mutti, taking a break from cooking, paged through a magazine in the living room. She looked up when he came in. "Well, well, look who's here. Do I know you? What did you say your name was?"

He grinned and dropped a kiss on her cheek. "How are you, Mutti?"

"I'm cooking supper. Will you have some roast chicken with us?"

"I think that can be arranged. It smells wonderful." He sat next to her on the settee and glanced around the room. "You were right, you know."

"About what?" She canted her head.

"The settee does look best here. And the painting above it on the wall brings out its blue."

"It does look nice, doesn't it?" She smiled. "How are you doing? How is school? Have you made a decision about university?"

"Not yet. I'm considering a few ideas."

"Such as?"

Such as I want to live with my lover from Finland and make love to her every night, he thought. To his mother, he said, "I'll tell you when it's sorted out. But I might take exams to see if I can place at university next year, instead of wasting another year in gymnasium."

"You have always been a good student. What courses are you considering?"

"I don't know yet." He glanced at her magazine. "What are you reading?"

"It's a fashion magazine. From France. I'm just looking at the photos."

He thought about Annaliese and how far away Germany was in his thoughts. "There was a time when I didn't think we'd ever be able to relax with a magazine again."

"We have been lucky, Max. Never forget it. N'oublies pas."

He smiled. His mother was dropping French phrases again. She was definitely cheerier. "May I see?"

His mother handed him the magazine and he started paging through it. Photos of beautiful young women appeared on every page in different clothing. Every few pages the same women turned up again in a different fashion. An idea struck him.

"Do these women make good money modeling?"

"I would think so."

"How do they get this kind of job?"

"I'm not altogether sure, but they must be photogenic. And have a pretty face. I suspect some are actresses. Why do you ask?"

Max shrugged. "Just curious."

"Ahh." His mother arched her brows. She changed the subject. "Have you been keeping up with events in Germany?"

"I try not to, actually. But I hear bits from the radio you and Papa listen to every night."

"Then you may have heard that the Nazis opened a concentration camp near Weimar in July. They call it Buchenwald. By the end of the month there were already a thousand inmates, most of them Jews." She shifted. "And Hitler is about to withdraw from the Treaty of Versailles."

"I heard. But you and Papa keep reminding me we are no longer in Germany, Mutti. We are safe."

"For now." She folded her hands and laid them in her lap. "There is something important you need to know. I've been meaning to tell you for some time."

Max looked over.

"You know those visas from the State Department in America we've been waiting for since—well, for years?"

Max nodded.

"They arrived."

"When? Why didn't you say anything? Why aren't we on a ship to New York?"

"They came after we arrived. About six months ago. I gathered all the papers and went to the US consulate for an interview. I didn't tell your father."

"Papa."

His mother tightened her lips. "He refuses to go. He is confident Holland will protect us."

"What do you think?"

"I disagree. Which is why I'm confiding in you. The papers are in a safe-deposit box at Amsterdamsche Bank. Along with exit visas and some cash. If and when the situation—"

"Mutti, stop. If Papa thinks—"

"Your father has not been the same since they arrested him, Max. He isn't thinking the same way. It's almost as if—" She cleared her throat. "Well, the point is that I haven't told him about the visas. I considered selling them to a family that is more desperate than we are. I could have named my price. But I want you to keep the key to that box. If you ever need what's inside, you will have it. You will need to buy a ticket for the journey to New York on your own. And you will need to alter the exit visas so the dates line up. Don't worry. Many people do it, I'm told. There is some cash in the safe-deposit box. Enough for the ticket."

"Mutti, no! I will not leave if you and Papa cannot come too."

His mother was silent for a long moment. Then: "Max, I don't ask much from you. I know you are growing up. Becoming a man. You need your independence. But there is one thing I want you to promise. You must do everything in your power to survive. For yourself. For us. For our people. If times become desperate again, take this key, grab the papers, and get the hell out of Europe. Do you understand?"

She stared at Max with such intensity that Max was temporarily frozen. His mother had never talked like this to him. He stared back. A bit dazed, he rose and walked slowly around the parlor. In the back of his mind, he'd always known there would be a time when his parents wouldn't be there. He'd wondered where he would be and what he'd be doing when they passed. But he'd never seriously considered that his parents would be taken before their time. Before he had begun to live his own life.

They were safe here in Holland. But what, if one day, they weren't? It happened in Germany. His mother was preparing him for that possibility. She had made it clear that Max *must* survive. Hitler would not annihilate *their* family. Max's survival would be the proof. He made a second circuit of the room, then faced her. With a slight dip of his head, he agreed.

On the way to De Wallen that night, Max stopped at a newsstand and bought a copy of the same magazine his mother had been skimming. He waved to Guillermo on the way in; he came so often that he now paid by the week; Guillermo was a "friend." Max made sure to notice what Annaliese was wearing. A dark green robe edged with a lighter shade of green. Elegant but not fussy. It made her cheeks paler and her blond hair almost white.

"Hello, dear Max." She embraced him. "Let me help you take off your clothes."

"You look beautiful. But wait. I want you to see something."

Max took out the magazine. "Tell me what you see."

Annaliese thumbed through a few pages and smiled wryly. "You are shopping for a new dress for yourself?"

He laughed and peered at the magazine over her shoulder. "Seriously, what do you think about the women posing for the camera?"

"The models?"

"Yes."

"What about them?"

"What are they doing?"

She scooted closer to him and pointed. "They are wearing the clothing and accessories the stores want to sell." She frowned. "You know that."

"What else are they doing?"

She studied the page, then shrugged. "Not much."

"Exactly! They are doing nothing except that they are very attractive."

"So?"

"How do you suppose these women got those jobs?"

"I have no idea. Why do you ask?"

"Do you think you can stand around and look beautiful?"

An aggrieved look flashed in her eyes. "I can do more than that."

"Yes, you have proven that." He gazed at her. "But for the world of business we need to start someplace."

Annaliese glanced down at the magazine, up at Max, then brushed her fingers through his hair. "No one has ever cared about me as much as you, Max." She kissed him tenderly. "You might make me fall in love with you yet."

CHAPTER 21

Winter 1937–1938
Amsterdam

As the autumn leaves swirled, there was bad news from the East. In December the Japanese army landed in Nanking, where they launched a fierce massacre that lasted six weeks. During those six weeks the Japanese committed widespread war crimes: the cold-blooded murder of three hundred thousand innocent Chinese; hundreds of arsons and looting. But the worst atrocity was the mass rape of more than twenty thousand women. Few women from the age of nine to ninety were spared.

Renée had written Max that the Japanese were cruel and aggressive. Would they now extend that brutality to Shanghai? Would Renée be safe? He tightened his lips. What could he do? Sending a letter wouldn't shield her from danger. It was a feeble attempt at concern. Nevertheless, Max wrote her that day.

Closer to home, a disturbing event, in itself not that important, nevertheless became one of the first warning signs for Jews in Holland. The National Socialist Women's Organization had been part of the National Socialist Party. The National Socialists had lurched toward respectability during the 1930s, even accepting Jewish members. Gradually, though, it had become more radical, anti-semitic, and Nazi-like. The women's branch was designed for social activities like sewing circles, walking tours, and informal gatherings, but they began each meeting by pledging allegiance to Hitler.

Max wasn't paying attention to current events. He was swept up in his master plan. He would take Annaliese out of the brothel and help her find a job in the world of fashion. They would become betrothed. He would continue school at night at the University of Amsterdam and work during the day. He wasn't sure where; he was tempted to work in an auto shop, but he knew his parents expected more from him. He would choose his university classes with an eye toward becoming an attorney, perhaps. Or a business executive. He and Annaliese would marry and raise their own family.

He kept his plans to himself. He didn't want face more skepticism or outright antagonism from the three other Musketeers, and he knew his parents would be shocked. But he would be eighteen on his next birthday. He was no longer a child. He could make his own decisions.

When the winter break was over and school started again, Max intercepted a schoolmate, Simon Metz. Simon's family had founded Metz & Co. in the 1700s. Today it was biggest department store in Amsterdam. Simon's ancestors had been Jewish, but intermarriage over the decades had made them secular at best.

"Hey, Simon." Max buttonholed him during a break.

"Hallo, Max." They weren't close but friendly.

"I hope your holidays were grand."

Simon, a tall, lanky boy with dark hair and ice-blue eyes, nodded. "And yours?"

"Quite interesting." He took a breath. "I have a friend. A young woman. Actually she is my girlfriend. Her dream is to become a fashion designer, but I know we must start small. I was thinking she might start as an assistant to someone. Or, perhaps, a model. She is exceptionally beautiful. I know there must be stiff competition for a job like that, but I promised I would ask how she might apply for a job at Metz. What the requirements are. Who to contact. Do you think you could help us out?"

"I don't have much to do with the store, but my father is there. I'll ask him." Simon held up a finger. "It might make sense to start with the advertising director. He would hire the girls. Or at least he'd know better than I who knows."

"Whatever you think."

"No worries, Steiner. I'll get it sorted. Give me a few days."

CHAPTER 22

January 1938
Amsterdam

Two weeks later on a blustery overcast January morning, Max skipped school to meet Annaliese in front of Metz & Co. The store had become such a well-known institution that it had the right to display on its door the Dutch royal coat of arms as a "Royal Warrant Purveyor." Over the years the store had expanded and relocated several times. It now occupied the corner of the Leidsestraat, Amsterdam's busiest shopping street, and the Keizersgracht, one of the three largest and widest canals in Amsterdam. The six-story stone building was impressive, with gargoyles on the facade and an ornate clock tower with a cupola on the roof.

Max was beginning to notice what Annaliese wore, and she looked beautiful in a simple navy-blue dress with strips of white around the collar. She called it "piping." Her hair was pulled back in a twist, which made her look older and her face more angular, something he'd noticed in the fashion magazines. Max himself wore a tie and a suit his parents had bought him for the High Holidays. Together they took the elevator to the executive offices on the fourth floor. At the end of a hall, a sign on a polished wood door announced they had arrived at the director of advertising's office. Underneath the sign was a placard with the name Jan Van der Berg.

Annaliese rarely showed fear, but this morning she clutched Max's arm. He understood. He recalled their first assignation. She'd been the expert. Proficient and skillful, yet willing to teach a new pupil. This, though, was alien territory. She'd never worked in the professional business world. Max covered her hand with his and gave it a squeeze. She smiled nervously. Max opened the door to a reception area where an attractive woman sat behind a desk.

"Good morning. I'm Max Steiner. We have an appointment with Mr. Van der Berg."

The receptionist picked up her phone and spoke in a quiet voice. A moment later she smiled and rose from her desk. "Follow me, please."

She led them down a short hall to a corner office and knocked on the door.

"Come."

They entered a large room with a picture window that gave onto a splendid view of the Keizersgracht. The office was furnished with an oriental carpet, a polished mahogany desk, a round table, and matching chairs. A royal coat of arms with the words "Royal Purveyor" hung on the wall. Max smelled furniture wax.

Jan Van der Berg was nothing like Max expected. He'd prepared himself for a younger man, perhaps in his thirties, well-groomed and a snappy dresser, but this man was middle-aged and soft with iron-gray hair. He wore an ill-fitting suit, and a round belly became more pronounced when he rose to shake Max's hand.

"I understand you're a chum of Simon Metz."

"We—we were in school together, sir."

"Oh, you're not in school anymore?"

"No, sir," Max lied. He wanted Van der Berg to think he was in business.

"And your friend?"

"Annaliese Laine." Max had told Annaliese to shake Van der Berg's hand if he offered, which he did. Max saw him examine

Annaliese as she extended her hand. The man's expression didn't change. Max couldn't figure out what his reaction was.

"Please, sit." Van der Berg motioned to the round table. They sat facing the window. He pulled up a chair and sat across from them. "How can I help you?"

"We have been researching fashion magazines, and I believe my friend Annaliese would be an excellent addition to your roster of models for upcoming fashion shows and ads."

"I see." He looked her over again. Annaliese gave him an innocent smile. "She is very attractive. But she is too young." He addressed Annaliese. "What are you? Eighteen?"

"Nineteen next summer," she replied.

"Ahh. You see, my dear, our models are older. They are women who look like our customers. And they are in their thirties or forties."

"Exactly, sir," Max cut into Van der Berg's patronizing comment. "And you've been extremely successful doing that. But we believe there is an untapped pool of customers who could add to your success."

"And that would be?"

"Younger women who want stylish fashions at a reasonable price. Fashions that would not be available for your current customers but for new, modern customers. Many of those young women see moving pictures from Hollywood, and they love the style and fashions they see on actresses like Jean Harlow or Carol Lombard. Annaliese has studied their costumes and could easily adapt them for the young modern Dutch woman."

Van der Berg cleared his throat. He did not look pleased. "So you think our advertising strategy is what—obsolete? Out of date?"

"Forgive me, sir," Max said in what he hoped was a conciliatory tone. "You and your staff are clearly the experts in this field. We are amateurs, but it occurred to us the clothing you manufacture—if adapted and worn on models who are a bit younger—could result in a wave of new customers."

"Hmmm," Van der Berg interjected. "Your audacity is—how should I put it—courageous for someone without any experience in retail or a large organization. But it is an untested theory. We would need significant research and persuasive data to move forward. I'm sorry. I do not authorize changes in direction based on the whim of two inexperienced young people."

Max's earlier confidence waned. This man didn't want to change. Didn't want new customers. Max had made a terrible mistake. Annaliese would be shattered. He didn't know what to say, so he said nothing.

To Max's surprise Annaliese spoke up. "Mr. Van der Berg, I have said to Max many times how I wish that high fashion extended to young women like myself. It's not that I dislike what you sell now. I love it, and in a few years I will probably be one of your biggest customers."

Max's eyes widened. Where had this burst of bravery come from? He'd expected Annaliese to remain paralyzed with fear.

"For now, though, I could do without the bows and bustles and frilly lace collars on the dresses. I prefer simpler clothing. Costumes that are appropriate both for work and evening wear. So many of the fashions I see are . . . forgive me, sir, but I do not want to look like my mother. Or my aunt. I want silky, sophisticated material, smooth lines, and something that is comfortable and easy to get in and out of."

Van der Berg was listening. Max suppressed a smile. The man inspected Annaliese as if for the first time. Max could see him taking in her hair, the deep green of her eyes, her angelic face, her slim build. Was there a lascivious cast to his expression? Or was he taking her seriously? It was difficult to tell.

"And you would like to model those clothes?"

"I would." She smiled. "I would also like to help design them. Or procure them for young women."

"Oh, really?" Was Van der Berg mocking them? "We call that position a buyer. Someone who buys from other dressmakers what we don't manufacture ourselves."

"Yes. I would like to be a buyer. And, perhaps, designer. I make my own clothes. I can show you."

Max was astonished. Annaliese had never been so assertive. She clearly had an eye for style—her navy dress, for example—but this was the first time she sounded so confident about making it a career.

Van der Berg templed his fingers. "You have big ideas, Miss Laine." Max let out a relieved breath. "Do you have a résumé? And references from your previous employers?"

Annaliese nodded and glanced over at Max.

She had nothing at the moment, Max knew, but they would produce them.

Van der Berg nodded. "Send them to me as soon as you can." He turned to Max. "I am not sanguine about finding a role for this young lady, but because you are a friend of Simon Metz, I will consider it. I will admit that you two are a breath of fresh air. As the head of a department in a large organization, we sometimes settle with what we know works. And fail to move forward. I will raise the idea with my colleagues. Call me in two weeks."

Max knew it was time to leave. "We are grateful, sir. Thank you for seeing us." Given his rapt attention to Annaliese, Max wasn't convinced Van der Berg's motives were honorable, but that was a matter for another day.

Annaliese rose too, and extended her hand. Van der Berg rose, shook both of their hands, and led them to the door.

～

"Was that a dream?" Annaliese asked breathlessly when they were back on the street. They headed down the Leidsestraat, one of the busiest streets in Amsterdam. The look on her face was ecstatic. "I can't believe it."

Max slid his arm around her. "Come. Let's get some hot chocolate and a sweet."

She giggled. "I will need to stop eating treats. I cannot get fat."

"Even if you did, it wouldn't detract from your beauty. But, Annaliese, let's be realistic. There is a good chance this will not work out."

But Annaliese wasn't having any of it. "Oh, Max, if it does, how will I ever thank you?"

"You already know the answer. If you get a position there, you will leave De Wallen. And you will not 'entertain' any other men except me."

She smiled. "You drive a difficult bargain."

"And you'll save some of your salary. Perhaps eventually you'll buy a house or apartment for your mother."

"But how will I live? I'll need to spend most of it just to make do."

They reached a café that said they made the best stroopwafel in Europe. Since the cookies were invented in Holland, Max figured there might be some truth to it. Max guided her to the entrance. He grinned. "No, you won't. You will be married to me and caring for our children."

"Really?" She stopped and turned around. "Are you asking me to marry you?"

He took a breath. "Will you?" he asked softly.

She looked up at him. "You know the old folk tale about Cinderella?" When he nodded, she said, "You are turning me into a princess."

Max took that as a "yes."

CHAPTER 23

Spring 1938
Amsterdam

The walls Max had constructed between his Before and After began to crumble during the second week of March 1938. Hitler sent the German Army into Vienna to annex Austria. The word "Anschluss," or "union," as Hitler called it, was chosen to persuade the world that Austria's acceptance of Hitler's move was not coerced. It was true that Austria had once wanted to unite with Germany, but most people knew Hitler was the driving force behind what was essentially an occupation designed to strengthen Germany's fighting power.

The Germans integrated the Austrian army into the Wehrmacht, giving Hitler millions more soldiers. The SS and Gestapo moved in, and all the antisemitic laws in Germany became law in Austria. Jewish Austrians were stripped of their citizenship overnight and risked being sent to concentration camps. Rumors filtered back that Austrian Nazis, who seemed to have proliferated overnight, forced Jewish men and women to scrub the streets with small brushes and women's fur coats.

Like the Rhineland invasion, the lack of denunciation from

England and France helped fan Nazi flames in other countries. Over the next month, anti-Jewish pogroms spread across Poland. In April Jews in Vienna were rounded up on the <u>Sabbath</u> and forced to eat grass at the Prater, a local amusement park. Sweden restricted Jewish immigration, and Romania stripped some Jews of their citizenship. In May Hungary adopted a law restricting the rights of Jews.

Max could no longer pretend the Nazis were remote and distant. Their poison was spreading. Infecting the whole of Europe.

The one bright spot for him in the darkening sky was Annaliese. She and Max had spent two weeks assembling a portfolio that included photos of the clothing she'd made for herself and her siblings. She also sketched out some of her fashion ideas for young women. After a second interview and an additional three weeks of nervous waiting, she was offered a position at Metz. She would be an assistant in the department, learning the advertising business and working with the fashion buyers. She would also model some of their apparel when needed.

They celebrated with dinner at Blauwe Theehuis, the Blue Tea House, which had opened a year earlier. A popular restaurant nestled in the middle of Vondel Park, where Max and Annaliese loved to spend time, its menu concentrated on hearty fare. Over a glass of wine, Annaliese said, "Here's to our new life together, Max. How will I repay you?"

"Stop asking me that. When I see the sparkle in your eyes, it's payment enough." They clinked glasses and sipped. "Tell me," Max asked. "How did your mother react?"

Annaliese giggled. She was doing that more often, he thought. Wearing a simple black dress—he was forcing himself to notice what she wore—and her blond hair in a fancy updo, she looked radiant.

"She was shocked. In the best possible way. She wants to meet you." Annaliese carefully set her glass on the table. "But she is worried this is all a dream, and we will wake up to find out it never happened and you have disappeared."

Max slid his hand over hers. "I will never leave you."

How could he? She filled him with purpose. He had ended her

life where she was nothing more than an object to be exploited. He'd helped her find a life where she would be valued. Respected. He had rescued her. Annaliese made him feel powerful in a world where he felt increasingly powerless. Nothing in his life thus far could equal that. Not Klara. Not his athletic ability. Not even Renée, whom he often felt had rescued *him* when life in Germany became intolerable. In a small way it was his turn to balance the scales of the universe.

Annaliese prattled on. "And the money is better too. Working in De Wallen was unfair. The costs were outrageous."

"Really? I thought you made good money."

She scoffed and counted on her fingers. "At first. But then there was rent for the room. Paying Guillermo for protection. The sheets, towels, even the pillow rental. And the tips I left each morning. Some nights I had nothing left over."

Max frowned. "You never told me any of this."

She shrugged.

He squeezed her hand. "Thank God that's over now. You will have enough for yourself and your family."

The waiter came to take their order. After he left, Max said, "I want you to meet my parents, Annaliese."

She took another sip of wine. "That makes me nervous. What if they don't accept me? What if they want to know how we met?"

"We'll tell them we met at a party. Given by a school friend. It isn't far from the truth."

"You will give me names and places?"

"Of course. Don't worry. My father will love you. And as for Mutti, well..."

"Well?" she said.

"She will too," he said.

"And what will you be doing when I start at Metz?"

"I can only tell you what I won't be doing. I won't be working at the bicycle shop." He didn't talk about what was on his mind. The fact that Hitler seemed poised to wage war or invade every country in Europe, and that it was time for Max to do something to stop him.

But he and Annaliese never talked current events. He couldn't dwell on a darkening reality during their limited time together.

"I have one question," she said with a sly smile.

"What is that?"

"Where will we make love now that I'm not at De Wallen?"

Max cocked his head. They hadn't had sex in weeks. He'd been too busy helping her get a job, and now he was worrying about a possible Nazi invasion. He made himself think. Then he grinned. "There is a room above the bicycle shop. No one uses it. I will make sure it's in good shape for us."

"But what about your father?"

"He closes the shop at six every day. And I have a key."

"Perfect." She drew imaginary lines on his hand with her finger. He'd told her before how sensual it felt when she touched him. "Can we go there tonight?"

CHAPTER 24

Spring 1938
Amsterdam

"What do you mean Czechoslovakia's next?" Carl asked.

"It was on the wireless yesterday," Max said.

It was the end of May, and he was helping Carl shelve books at the bookshop. They were talking softly so as not to be overheard. Although the shop was in the Jewish Quarter, plenty of Gentiles shopped there, and Max knew to be careful. A woman turned into the aisle where they were talking. Max abruptly stopped talking. The woman asked if they had any books on Sweden and Norway. Her family was planning a summer holiday.

Carl smiled. "Follow me." He signaled for Max to wait and led the woman two aisles over. Max heard them chat about how lovely the Scandinavian countries were and to be sure to take a jacket. It was so much cooler.

The woman laughed. "I'm even taking gloves."

Carl helped the woman find a travel book and rejoined Max. "So what were you saying about Czechoslovakia?"

Max heard a rustle and shook his head. Jacob, Carl's father, appeared at the end of the aisle. Usually a cheerful, likable man, Jacob wore a serious expression. He crooked his finger at the boys and gestured for them to follow him into a small office behind the counter. Carl and Max exchanged worried looks. What was going on? Had their voices carried farther than they thought? Was Carl's father angry at them?

Jacob closed the door and faced the boys. "We need to talk." He rubbed his chin as if trying to think of the right words. Max braced himself.

"Tell me something, boys. Have you felt a coolness from your Gentile friends at school? Have they become more distant?"

Max didn't have to think about it, but Carl apparently did. "Tony mentioned something like that just the other day," Carl said. "And Pieter agreed. I guess I have."

"What about you, Max?"

"That's what happened in Regensburg. It was my first clue that something wasn't right. My best friend, who was Protestant, told me we'd always be friends, but that didn't happen. I was never invited to his house again. And then the teachers got involved. I got into fights. Eventually I had to switch schools."

Jacob scowled. "That is the first step. The goyim distance themselves from us. Then come other actions. They no longer shop at Jewish shops. No longer invite our children to their homes. I could go on, but you know what I mean."

"My mother said the same thing in Germany. How Hitler slowly tightened a rope around our necks until we were suffocating but didn't realize it."

"I'm afraid that process has begun for us," Jacob said.

Carl frowned and interrupted. "But the Dutch want to remain neutral."

"That won't happen this time." Jacob shifted. "It's clear Hitler intends to invade every country in Europe. Become the dictator of the continent. I'm sure the Netherlands is on his list. Marching the Wehrmacht through Holland and Belgium is the best way to get to

France, and possibly Spain." He paused. "That's why what I'm about to share with you two can never leave this room. You cannot tell your friends, even Tony and Pieter. Or your parents, Max." He looked at them in turn. "Do you understand?"

Max swallowed. He nodded. So did Carl.

"Some of my friends and I want to be prepared. We need to know exactly what Hitler's designs are in the Netherlands, as well as in adjoining countries. We will fight. Clean, dirty, or both. We will do anything and everything to stop our country from being overrun by the Nazis."

"Are you talking about a resistance movement?" Max asked.

"That's too formal for what we're doing. But I suppose that may the best way to describe us. We're calling ourselves the Dutch Jews and Refugees for Liberty, DJRL for short." He looked from Carl to Max. "This is where you come in, Max. You are fluent in German. Most of us, while we speak passable German, don't have your proficiency. We would like you to monitor the Reich radio stations and write down what they say about Hitler's plans for the future.

"If you hear anything about the Wehrmacht, SS, or Gestapo—how many, how they're organized, and what roles they play, that would be helpful. Any mention of other countries and the plans to 'deepen the friendship' between them and Germany. And any deviation in the tone of the broadcasts. For example, any change in the nature or subject of the propaganda might indicate a change in Nazi fortunes, one way or the other. We need to know. Understand?"

Max nodded.

"Write everything down in a report and give it to Carl. You and he are school chums, so nobody will suspect if you give him school paper with notes on it. They'll simply think you're helping him with his homework."

The boys exchanged surprised glances.

"Carl, you will bring that report to me. I will see it gets into the right hands."

"You are sure you want us involved?" Carl asked.

"Of course. Max was the first person I thought of for this task. The others agree. You're going to be eighteen in a few months, correct?"

"That's correct."

"Old enough . . ." Jacob's voice trailed off. "You won't be in any physical danger. It's just, well . . . we need information. We realize most of the broadcasts will be nothing more than Nazi-sanctioned propaganda, but we'll still have an idea of the direction they're moving. Yes?"

"What about Germans who oppose Hitler?" Max asked. "Will you be making contact with them?"

"That's an entirely different issue. Once we know who they are, I'm sure we'll discuss whether to reach out. The problem is we won't be sure they're genuine. They may be plants or moles, designed to mislead us. Perhaps do us harm. By the way, we also will have people who speak English monitoring the BBC as well as radio stations here in Holland and Belgium."

Max's pulse raced. Here was a chance, finally, to do something. It was a small task, but it was real. He would no longer be a victim, subject to Hitler's malevolent whims and Nazi oppression. He would be involved in something that would not be dangerous and might even help. This was what he had longed for. Prayed for.

There was only one problem. He'd decided not to finish his final year at gymnasium. His test scores the previous summer were high enough to guarantee him acceptance into university, and he planned to find a good-paying job so he could help support Annaliese. He would attend night school instead. But Jacob's "assignment" depended on his being in school with Carl. He had to tell Jacob the truth.

"Sir, there's a chance I won't be back at school next fall," Max explained.

"First off, it's Jacob, not 'sir.'" And second, we'll deal with that when it happens, if it does." Jacob shot an intense look at both boys. "What do you think? Will you help us?"

Max took a minute to frame his response. "I would be honored, Jacob."

"Good. Good." Jacob rubbed his hands together and turned to Carl. "And you, son?"

"Of course, Papa. Anything."

Jacob nodded. "Excellent. We'll get those bastards." He paused. "But not a word to anyone. Ever."

CHAPTER 25

Germany's state-owned radio network was the Reich Broadcasting Company. It had been on the air since 1925, but the Nazis took it over in 1933. From that point on it became one of the most valuable tools of Joseph Goebbels's propaganda efforts. Technically a consortium of regional German broadcasters offering local programming, RRG's broadcasts were dictated mostly by Berlin.

Because the RRG's signal was powerful, its programs were heard not just in Germany but in other European countries as well, including Holland. The Steiners' only luxury purchase since they'd come to Holland was a Philips radio. It was a boxy cube of polished wood and a dial that marked both AM and short-wave frequencies. Max's parents listened to the Netherlands station in the morning before Moritz left for work and then again after dinner when they would settle in the parlor. They even tuned in to the German station when they could bear it. Max usually walked out of the room.

But now, if Max wanted to eavesdrop on German broadcasts, he would have to find a time his parents weren't listening. The safest time would be after they went to bed, but that cut into his time with Annaliese, and he wasn't sure there were overnight radio broadcasts. The next best alternative was probably midday, but he was often in the shop with his father at that hour. Still, the thought that he was doing something substantial made the decision easier.

So Max took time during lunch to run home and catch the RRG noon broadcast. It usually began with the latest news, which focused on the Führer and what he was doing that day, as well as stories that made Germany seem like a world power. Carefully orchestrated propaganda followed. Today's programming began with a repeat of Goebbels's annual speech the previous month on the eve of Hitler's birthday, April 20.

Max listened.

THE FÜHRER HAS PROBABLY NEVER HAD SO MANY HAPPY PEOPLE GATH- ERED ABOUT HIM FOR HIS BIRTHDAY AS IN THIS YEAR. ALL THE 75 MILLION PEOPLE OF THE GREATER GERMAN REICH STAND BEFORE HIM TO EXPRESS THEIR HEARTFELT BEST WISHES AND DEEPEST THANKS TO HIM. IN THE TRUEST SENSE OF THE WORD, THIS IS A HOLIDAY FOR THE ENTIRE NATION.

LONG COLUMNS OF PEOPLE STOOD OUTSIDE THE BERGHOF [HITLER'S MOUNTAIN HOME], WAITING TO MARCH PAST. THEY CAME FROM ALL PARTS OF OUR GREAT REICH, BRINGING FLOWERS AND MEMENTOS, AND WERE HEARTENED BY BEING ABLE TO LOOK INTO THE BELOVED FACE OF THE MAN WHOM THEY SAW AS THE EMBODIMENT OF ALL OUR NATIONAL HOPE.

The florid language, praising Hitler as if he were Hashem, went on forever. Max thought he might vomit. He turned the volume down, slapped together a sandwich, and waited for the slavish speech to end. When it was over, he fished out paper and pen to prepare for the next segment.

Since the Anschluss_with Austria in March, Hitler had turned his attention to Czechoslovakia. The program now focused on Heim ins

Reich, the "Back to the Reich" foreign policy through which Germany was trying to convince all ethnic Germans who lived outside Germany either to "come home" or build a "Greater Germany" where they were. In either case the result would be to expand Hitler's power.

Max recalled his father twisting the radio dial one evening before Austria was annexed. He'd randomly stopped the dial on a radio program from Munich aimed at Austrians. The broadcast bombarded listeners with what Hitler had already done for Germany, and the wonderful feats he would accomplish for his native country. All in the name of German brotherhood.

Now, at the end of May, Hitler was aiming the same message at the Sudetenland, a C-shaped slice of Czechoslovakia's eastern regions populated largely by ethnic Germans. It wasn't a small number; the Sudetenland made up nearly 25 percent of the entire Czech population. The Nazis were trying to persuade the people of Czechoslovakia that they'd be much better off as part of greater Germany.

Max listened to a report proclaiming that when Hitler visited a sports festival in Breslau, the Sudeten team passed the VIP stand and shouted, "'Back home to the Reich!' People yelled, cheered, and cried," the announcer said. "The Führer was deeply moved."

The Nazis were using the velvet glove rather than the iron fist to soften the Czech people. But anyone who studied Hitler knew the fist wouldn't be far behind. Max made notes. Didn't people know this was all hype? And that the Nazis, including Goebbels, knew it? That was the ultimate shonda—shame—as his parents would say. They knew they were spreading lies.

Disgusted by the hypocrisy, Max turned to the BBC for some "real" news. According to their reporting, Hitler told his inner circle he wanted to "destroy" Czechoslovakia. It was an irrevocable decision, he'd fumed. What held him back—at least temporarily—was opposition from chief of staff General Ludwig Beck, who, apparently, was resisting Hitler's aggression and even lobbying other top brass to join him.

Max was cheered by Beck's position. At last someone in Germany was unafraid to speak out against Hitler. Maybe . . . just maybe . . . the monster could be stopped. Max made more notes between bites of his sandwich. He would submit a detailed report to Carl for Jacob Weber's DJRL.

~

School was over by the first week in June, and Max had more time to devote to Annaliese. He'd set up the room above the shop for the two of them with cushions, pillows, and a small rug. If his father knew what was going on upstairs, he didn't mention it.

After working at Metz for a few months, Annaliese seemed like a different person. Back when she worked in De Wallen, Max had noticed a coolness, an impassive attitude that tamped down her emotions. It was as if she wore an invisible cloak that kept her from feeling pure joy. He wasn't sure where it came from. Was it an underlying shame for being a prostitute? Or was it baked into her psyche because of the poverty and abuse she'd suffered?

Whatever the origin, that indifference had now dissipated, and Annaliese had turned into a vivacious, animated young woman. Yes, she was on the lowest rung of Metz's career ladder, but she'd already designed an outfit for young women that had been approved by the Design Department, and she was caught up in developing specs, colors, and materials for the fabricators. Max couldn't have been prouder or more excited, and despite recent events, the time they spent together took on a celebratory, festive air.

A few weeks later Annaliese invited Max to dinner and introduced him to her mother. They lived in a cramped apartment on the blue-collar western side of Amsterdam. As he climbed the stairs to the third floor, the scent of cabbage cooking, the slightly musty smell of the carpet, and as he got closer to their apartment, the perfume that Annaliese wore, wafted over him.

Kaarina was an older, paler imitation of Annaliese. The same blond hair, fair complexion, and slim body, but her forehead was lined, and she wore a perpetually anxious expression even when she smiled, as if she knew trouble was waiting to pounce.

Max sat down to a dinner that included grilled whitefish, potatoes, tomato salad, and a strawberry meringue pie. Annaliese's flaxen-haired younger siblings, boisterous and full of energy, plied Max with questions about Germany and what children there were like. Max didn't mind; he imagined his life one day with Annaliese and their own children clamoring for attention.

After dinner Annaliese hopped on her bicycle and followed Max to the shop. They crept upstairs to the attic room. Max was ready and couldn't wait to have sex, but Annaliese forced him to watch as she slowly took off her clothes. Max grew so aroused that he pulled her to him before she was finished and pushed her down on the pillows. He made love to her with so much passion it bordered on ferocity.

A week later Max came home for lunch. His mother was there. He listened to the RRG, took a few notes, then went into the kitchen. Hannah was getting a roast ready for the oven.

"Why are you listening to that treif?" She sniffed, using the word for "not kosher" to disparage the propaganda spewing from the German radio broadcast.

He smiled. "That treif is interesting."

"What are you talking about?"

"What's the expression—keep your friends close but your enemies closer?"

His mother nodded.

"Hitler is becoming more aggressive. If we know what he's planning—and it's easy to read between the lines when you listen to this Scheisse—we stay one step ahead of him."

His mother nodded. "Your father thought we didn't need to concern ourselves with Hitler anymore. I wanted to believe him. We were both wrong."

"He's going to start a war," Max said. "Everybody thinks so."

Before she could reply, he said, "But that's not what I came in to talk to you about, Mutti." He grinned. "I want to tell you something."

She opened the oven door, took the roast from the counter, and slid it into the oven. "Of course."

Now that he was going to tell her about Annaliese, he felt suddenly shy. How would she and Papa react to his Gentile girl-friend? He cleared his throat. Best to spit it all out at once. "Mutti, I have a girlfriend. Her name is Annaliese Laine. She works at Metz's Department Store. We've been together two years, and I want to invite her for Shabbos dinner so you can meet her."

His mother straightened up and turned around. Her eyebrows were sky high. "Two years? And you're just telling me now?"

He shrugged. "It was never the right time."

"Well, never let it be said you can't keep a secret." His mother frowned. "Well, what is her family name? What synagogue does she go to?"

He let out a breath. "She's not Jewish. She comes from Finland."

Hannah planted her hands on her hips. "Finland? You're joking."

Max felt a chill. "No."

"How did you ever meet a girl from Finland?"

He was quiet for a few seconds. Then: "A friend from school had a party, and I met her there."

"I see."

Max could tell from her pinched face that his mother was angry but trying not to lose her temper. "Mutti, I can imagine what you're thinking, and I understand. But she's special. I want to marry her."

"Max," his mother exploded. "After everything that's happened, how could you fall in love with a goy"

"She's an immigrant to Holland. Like us. She's had a hard life. Doesn't she deserve a chance?"

"A chance for what? She doesn't understand our suffering. Our culture. Our values. She's from Finland, God forbid."

"She's had her own suffering, Mutti. She was abused by her father. That's why they fled."

"Oh, Max." Her voice was half fury, half sorrow.

"Mutti, this is the woman I want to spend the rest of my life with. Please. Just give her a chance. Please."

His mother didn't say anything for a long while. Then: "Have her come next Friday night." She untied the apron around her waist and walked out of the kitchen.

CHAPTER 26

Spring–Summer 1938
Amsterdam

The following Friday evening was especially warm for late spring, and Max opened all the windows in the apartment to catch the breeze. Max and Annaliese sat across the table from each other; Hannah and Moritz in their traditional spots. Annaliese wore the dress she'd worn to her interview at Metz. It was her most conservative outfit, she said. Her blond hair was pulled back off her face. Max wore a tie with his shirt and pants.

When Max introduced her to his parents, he saw approval in his father's eyes but wariness in his mother's. If he could see it, so could Annaliese. That wasn't fair, he thought. Mutti should give her a chance. But Hannah barely looked at Annaliese after taking her hand. Annaliese's smile froze.

Hannah lit a match and recited the blessing over the candles, waving her hands in small circles as she spoke. Moritz said kiddush, sipped the wine, and made the blessing over the challah. He broke off three pieces, sprinkled salt on them, and passed them down the table. Everyone took a bite.

The rituals over, Hannah ladled soup into bowls and passed them around. Max waited until everyone was served and watched Annaliese dip her spoon in the soup and swallow. "This is delicious," she said.

Hannah didn't reply. A long beat of silence ensued. Finally Moritz said, "No one makes soup as well as Hannah."

Hannah rose again and went into the kitchen. Annaliese and Max exchanged glances. Annaliese looked worried. She knew something wasn't right. Anger at his mother's behavior rippled through Max. She was going out of her way to be impolite. His mother returned, carrying a platter of brisket with small potatoes, carrots, and onions. When everyone was served, she helped herself and said, "The recipe for this has been handed down for over a century, did you know that Max?" She looked over. "Your cousins in Alsace eat the same dish. With the same vegetables. I believe your great-grandmother created it."

Max dug into his dinner. "Annaliese is in the fashion industry, Mother," he said after a bite. "You know all those magazines you thumb through? She's going to be responsible for some of the outfits you'll see in them."

Annaliese's cheeks reddened.

"That's quite a coup for a young woman like you," Moritz said kindly. "Have you always wanted to do this?"

"All my life, sir."

"Please, don't call me sir." Moritz ran a finger across his upper lip. "It's much too formal."

Max hadn't seen his father this talkative in years. He seemed to like Annaliese. Max held on to a sliver of hope.

"My mother taught me to sew. I make all my own clothes as well as my younger brother's and sister's."

"Oh, you have siblings? How jolly for you."

Annaliese laughed. "I'm not sure I'd call them 'jolly.' They're a lot younger and always underfoot."

"Are they in school?" Moritz asked.

"Oh yes. Mama makes sure of that."

"And does your mother work?" Hannah cut in.

"She does. She—she is a seamstress, among other things."

"I see." Hannah turned toward Papa. "Moritz, did you hear what happened to Simon Kirschenbaum?"

Max frowned. What was she doing?

"Kirschenbaum from the synagogue?"

She nodded. "His family's papers came through, and they're off to Palestine." She cut a sliver of meat and glanced at Max. "You met their son, Avi, during the High Holidays last year. They sailed last week."

Annaliese shifted uncomfortably. Max scowled at his mother. She'd deny it, but the fact was she did exclude non-Jews from any but the most superficial relationships. Moreover, she made a point of letting a non-Jew know she was doing it. Talking about people and events that Max knew about but Annaliese didn't was how she kept her on the other side. *You can listen, but you'll never be a part of our life, our history, our pain. You're just our son's shiksa.*

By the time Max and Annaliese left the apartment, Annaliese was in tears. "She hated me!" she sobbed.

"I am so sorry, sweetheart." Max tried to comfort her. "She had no right to treat you the way she did. If it makes you feel any better, I'm furious at her."

Tears streamed down her cheeks. She shook her head. "It's—it's like I was an insect crawling on the sidewalk and she stomped me into the concrete."

"She needs to apologize to you."

"No, Max. She's your mother. She can do and say whatever she wants. But it's clear she—"

Max cut in. "It's because you're not Jewish."

"What?"

Max tried to explain how they were treated in Germany before they moved to Holland.

"But shouldn't that make her sensitive to others who've left their homeland? It's as if she blames me for your troubles."

"I felt it too. I wanted to pick you up and take you away from it all."

"I wish you had."

Max slipped his arm around her. "Please don't hold my mother's behavior against me. I love you so much, Annaliese. I want to marry you. Have children with you. Don't let her bitterness get in the way. My father adores you. He hasn't been this charming in years. And Mother will change her mind. When she does she'll love you as much as I do. Well . . ." He gently wiped away a tear on her cheek. ". . . almost as much."

Annaliese sniffed. "I think I want to go home."

"What about the bicycle shop?"

She bit her lip. "Not tonight."

"Are you sure?" When she didn't reply, he said, "Annaliese, promise me you won't let tonight affect us."

"I love you, Max. Ever since you walked into De Wallen. I couldn't help it. I tried not to. But you wouldn't give up. You were—what my mother calls you—the prince with the glass slipper."

He heard the past tense. "And you are my princess."

She smiled, but he saw sorrow in her eyes. Max hailed a taxi and took her home. A queasy sensation lodged in the pit of his stomach. He decided to walk the two miles back to the apartment.

CHAPTER 27

August–December 1938
Amsterdam

By August events accelerated, one after another, as if time was hurtling toward an unknown but ominous future. In Germany the Great Synagogue of Nuremberg was destroyed on orders of the city's mayor. The founder of the antisemitic weekly *Der Stürmer* claimed it "disfigured the beautiful German townscape."

A decree ordered that all Jews in the Reich must add to their identity papers the name "Israel" if they were male, or "Sara" if they were female. It was a transparent ploy to further identify and persecute Jews by anyone, official or not, who demanded to see Jews' papers.

Unfortunately, August also brought the resignation of Hitler's chief of staff General Ludwig Beck. He'd failed to persuade Hitler to leave Czechoslovakia intact. The Führer maintained that there were solid economic reasons, as well as political, to occupy the country. When Max heard the news on the radio, he slammed his fist against the wall. Max cared about the Czechs and the Slovaks. But he worried more where Hitler would turn his attention after Czechoslovakia.

September was no better. Max celebrated his eighteenth birthday on September 15. For the first time since they'd met, Annaliese didn't spend it with him. She said she was ill, but Max didn't believe her. The Three Musketeers took Max to a beer hall, where they all got drunk. Despite copious steins of Dunkel, Schwarzbier, and Bock, Max remained sullen and despondent.

"She's fine. I know it. She's pulling away from me," he said. "It started when my mother humiliated her. I could see it in her eyes. Now she watches me with this cool, distant expression. I don't know what she's thinking anymore."

Tony tried to joke. "You're probably better off not knowing."

Max shot daggers at Tony, who raised his hands in a submissive gesture. "Sorry, Max. Why don't you ask her?"

"I did. She denies anything's wrong."

"Well then, it's just your paranoia."

Carl and Max exchanged quick glances. It was true the broadcasts from Germany were souring his attitude. The fear and helplessness that scraped his gut before his family fled Germany had returned, but thinking it might only be his imagination didn't relieve it. Annaliese had been the only bright spot in his life. Now that light appeared to have dimmed. It felt like someone had sawed off one of his arms.

The pace of events gathered steam. On Max's birthday England's prime minister, Neville Chamberlain, met Hitler in his summer home, where he and Hitler agreed on a timetable for Czechoslovakia to cede the Sudetenland territory to Germany.

A few days after that meeting, however, Hitler changed his demands. He wanted the territory immediately. Britain said no, so on September 18 and 19, Germany attacked Czechoslovakia. The Czechs resisted, but German forces moved into some of the border areas with artillery, tanks, and armored vehicles.

Events had come to a crossroads. The situation everyone in Europe feared was materializing. For the next few days the world teetered on the brink of war. Then, in a meeting hurriedly arranged in Munich, Chamberlain and Hitler met again. Hitler promised not to invade any more European countries, and Chamberlain agreed to cede the Sudetenland to Hitler by October rather than the extended timetable they'd originally planned.

A weight settled on Max's shoulders. For Chamberlain to appease Hitler, metaphorically falling on his sword to give Hitler precisely what he wanted, was horrifying. Hitler had forced Chamberlain's hand and won. But the rest of the world was celebrating because war had been avoided. For how long?

He learned years later that a conspiracy, led by none other than General Ludwig Beck and the deputy head of the Abwehr, had been in the planning stages at that time. Troops were to storm the Reich chancellery, kill Hitler, and overthrow the Nazis if Hitler invaded Czechoslovakia. But the coup depended on strong support from Britain, which Chamberlain's appeasement in Munich made impossible. The conspiracy dissolved.

On November 7, Herschel Grynszpan, a seventeen-year-old Jew, walked into the German embassy in Paris and fatally shot a German diplomat because Grynszpan's family had been deported to Poland. A day later Goebbels made sure German newspapers and radio stations published headlines like "The Shots in Paris Will Not Go Unpunished!" and "From This Vile Deed Arises the Imperative Demand for Immediate Action Against the Jews, with the Most Severe Consequences."

From November 9 at midnight through the next day and night, the German people, whipped to a frenzy by the publicity, demolished Jewish businesses and homes all over the country. Synagogues were set on fire. One hundred people lost their lives. The police were ordered not to interfere or stop the carnage. Thirty thousand Jews were subsequently arrested and sent to concentration camps. The events of Kristallnacht, "the Night of Broken Glass," as it came to be called, were labeled "spontaneous outbursts," but everyone knew those "outbursts" had been orchestrated by the Nazis.

Over the next few months in a stunning German reversal worthy of Houdini, the Jews themselves were blamed for the uprising, and a slew of draconian edicts followed. Jews were banned from receiving government services. They now had curfews. Orders went out for them to relinquish their driver's licenses and, for some reason, their radios. Jewish businesses that had managed to stay open were forcibly closed; homes were ransacked and pilfered. Children could no longer attend public school. Movies, concerts, and other cultural events were off-limits. The government even forced Jews to pay for the damage of Kristallnacht.

By the end of the year Max alternated between rage and despair. The bullies were multiplying. Austria, Hungary, and Poland had either already restricted or planned to limit the rights of Jews. Britain, whom everyone thought would have courage, was led by a mealymouthed bureaucrat. Even America's president, Franklin Roosevelt, was keeping his distance.

The Steiners had fled to the Netherlands because Max's father assured them they would be safe here. But all the news from Germany reinforced the belief that Hitler wasn't finished. What could possibly be happy about the new year?

CHAPTER 28

January 1939
Amsterdam

Max did return to gymnasium for the fall semester but decided not to continue after winter break. The repercussions from Kristallnacht were still news, and inflammatory broadcasts from Germany kept running. Max needed to allocate several hours a day to monitor the RRG, transcribe, translate, and deliver what he heard to Carl who would then give them to Jacob. Jacob then circulated his reports to the Dutch Jews and Refugees for Liberty. Max still worked at the bicycle shop too. In fact, his father came in less and less, preferring to spend time with his friends at the synagogue. With so much time devoted to the shop and the news from Germany, it was no wonder Max felt the distance between himself and Annaliese.

That, at least, he could do something about. On a frigid evening at the end of the month, Max rode his bicycle to Annaliese's home. It had snowed earlier, and each breath of cold, crystalline air felt as sharp as a blade. With the wheels of his bicycle crunching on the newly fallen snow, Max rehearsed what he would say.

They had been together two years; two years in which both their lives had changed dramatically. They had helped each other grow, and she had been the source of the happiest moments of his life. The past few months were the first time they'd had problems. But both of them were under stress: Max from the existential threat of Hitler, Annaliese from the demands of her new job. Fundamentally, he knew they loved each other. They could weather this rough patch.

Max locked his bicycle around a lamppost outside her apartment, climbed the steps to the third floor, and knocked. From inside he heard a loud complaint in Dutch from Annaliese's younger brother, who apparently did not want to go to bed. Then the quieter but firm voice of Annaliese's mother in Finnish. Her voice got louder as she approached the door.

Her surprised expression when she opened the door indicated she had not expected Max. He rubbed his gloved hands together.

"Good evening, dear Max. Please, come in. You look so cold. It's warm in here."

Max took a step in and shoved his hands in his pockets. "Hello, Kaarina. Could you please tell Annaliese I'm here?"

Kaarina hesitated. Max's gut clenched. Something was wrong. In a soft voice, almost a whisper, she said, "She's not here, Max."

Max frowned. "Is she working late? Will she be home soon?"

"I do not know."

"But she's okay?"

"She's fine, Max. She's just . . . out."

"So she's not working late?"

Kaarina shook her head.

Max went rigid. "And you don't know where she is."

She kept her mouth shut.

He paused. Then: "Is she with another man?"

She whispered, "Someone from work."

Max couldn't breathe.

"I'm so sorry."

Somehow Max managed to nod. He wheeled around and clattered back down the stairs into the cold.

❧

On his way home Max swore he would never forgive Mutti. Two years together, ripped to shreds, because of his mother's refusal to accept that Annaliese was not Jewish. Jews were persecuted all over Europe, yet his mother refused to acknowledge Annaliese wasn't one of the persecutors. Was this his mother's idea of revenge? If so, why was she taking it out on him?

CHAPTER 29

February–May 1939
Amsterdam

In February Italy passed anti-Jewish legislation. In March Nazi troops entered Lithuania. In April Germany issued a secret order to seize Danzig, a port city in Poland, even though Germany and Poland had signed a nonaggression agreement. Chamberlain announced that the UK and France would guarantee Poland's sovereignty in the event of a German attack. At the end of the month Hitler canceled the nonaggression pact. In May Hungary passed discrimination laws against Jews.

The most tragic event involved the USS *St. Louis*, a ship with a thousand Jewish refugees from Germany. It sailed from Hamburg on May 13 and arrived in Cuba en route to America. However, after a combination of misinformation and nefarious attempts at extortion, the Cuban government refused to allow the ship to anchor. The ship sailed up the East Coast of the United States. Despite impassioned pleas from multiple sources, Roosevelt also denied the passengers entrance to the US. He anticipated a tough reelection campaign; accepting a thousand Jewish immigrants would exacerbate the American public's isolationist leanings. The USS *St. Louis* was forced to sail back to Europe with the passengers still on board. They hurriedly settled in Belgium, France, the UK, and the Netherlands. It would turn out to be a temporary arrangement.

Max sensed the edgy anxiety from the other three Musketeers when they met at the beer hall two days later on a Saturday afternoon. It was Tony's birthday, but no one was in a festive mood. On the twenty-second of May Germany and Italy had signed what they called a Pact of Steel. Mussolini was a second-rate leader, but he aspired to the same reverence from the Italians as Hitler had achieved in Germany, and he was doing all he could to emulate his mentor's cruel tactics.

"Makes me sick. And I love Italy," Tony said. We vacationed in Naples every summer."

Max nodded. "It's a beautiful country. The Italians don't deserve Mussolini's incompetence."

Pieter downed most of his stein and burped. The others laughed. "I have a question for you." He shook his head. "But it's not funny."

"Neither was that, heathen," Tony cracked.

"Tell me, why is the antisemitism unleashed by Hitler so virulent? There have always been those who despise us. They have their reasons, mostly bullshit of course, but they try to explain it. The Führer's version is different. It's malignant. It slithers through their soul, leaving venom in its wake. And people allow themselves to be infected by its poison. They fall into a fever dream of hatred. Violent hate. Their thinking becomes distorted. They now have only one goal in mind: to destroy us.

"It's insanity," Carl agreed. "He's exposed the basest level human beings can sink to, and it's festering across the entire continent. We are insects who must be exterminated. The world will be purified when we no longer exist."

"We've been a convenient scapegoat," Pieter said. "Why should today be different?"

"It's never been this bad," Tony said.

"They say he has a Jewish grandfather," Carl said. "That could explain it."

"If people blame the 'undesirable' Jews for a conspiracy to ruin their lives," Max said, "then they don't pay attention when they lose their freedom and rights as citizens." He picked up his stein and took a long pull. "The Nazis are just fine with that."

"Do you think there are any good Nazis?" Pieter asked.

Max thought about it. "The Germans who tried to assassinate Hitler—"

"They failed," Pieter said.

Max nodded. "True. Then there are the Germans who help Jews escape—"

"They have no power," Tony said. "You're right about one thing, Pieter. The Nazis have inspired the fear of a painful death if you cross them. It's like God has been replaced with Hitler."

They were quiet for a moment. Then Max said, "The war that's coming? It's not going to be like any war we've known. It will include the mass movement and possible murders of millions of 'undesirables.' And we are at the top of that list."

Carl, always the optimist, tried to lighten the mood. "Don't look now, Undesirable, but you have a visitor."

Max looked up. Annaliese! How had she found him here?

As if she knew what he was thinking she said, "I stopped at the bookstore. Carl's father told me where you were."

He rose from the table. "Did you ride your bicycle?"

She nodded.

Contrary to his anguish when he discovered she was seeing someone else, he didn't confront her about it. The truth was, he couldn't bear to lose her. They continued to see each other sporadically. She never raised the issue either. It was as if nothing had changed. Did she learn that working as a prostitute? Max wondered. Had she been faking her feelings for him over the past three years? Playing him for a fool? And if she was, what did it say about him that he still wanted her?

They left the beer hall and pedaled to the bicycle shop. It was closed for Shabbos, but Max had a key. Max guided her upstairs. She slipped into his arms and took the lead when they made love. It felt like old times, times when they couldn't keep their hands off each other. He grinned afterward. "Where did that come from?"

"I've missed you," she said. "You're always so busy."

"It's a difficult time. Hitler is on the move. There will be war."

She nodded.

"And what about you?" he went on. "You barely have time for *me*." He hesitated. Was this the time to clear the air? To tell her he knew she was seeing other men? He decided to go at it sideways. "It must be going well at Metz & Co."

Annaliese didn't answer.

Max frowned. He propped his head up on his elbow. Annaliese stroked his cheek, her expression slowly changing from pleasure to sorrow. "What's wrong?"

Annaliese's lips stretched into a thin hard line.

"Annaliese? What's happened?"

Her face crumpled, and she started to cry. "I was fired yesterday."

Max wasn't sure he'd heard her correctly. "Fired? Why? Didn't they just approve one of your designs for young women?"

She swallowed. Tears rolled down her cheeks.

"I don't understand."

"They—they told me they didn't need me anymore," she stammered. "'My—my presence was no longer required' was the way they put it."

"Go on."

"That was all. They never got more specific."

"They must have given you a reason."

The afternoon sun streaming through a window made her tears glisten. She turned away.

"Did someone there become an enemy?"

She shrugged.

"Who was it? Why? Did you fight back? At least try to explain?"

Still no response.

Max was flummoxed. Clearly she knew more than she was telling him. She was either too hurt, embarrassed, or afraid. He needed to be gentle if he wanted the truth.

He lifted a finger to her cheek and tried to wipe away a tear. "Did you steal something?" he said quietly.

Her cheeks reddened in anger. "No! I would never do that."

"Did you do something to put someone in danger?"

She shook her head.

Now he was exasperated. "I can't help you if I don't know what the issue was."

Annaliese must have been wounded by his tone because she broke out in uncontrollable sobs. She curled up in a ball as though she was trying to make herself so small she'd disappear.

The next morning, although he would be late to the shop, Max went to the home of Simon Metz, the schoolmate who'd arranged Annaliese's introduction to the store. Simon lived on Herengracht in a large gabled home with a view of the canals. One of the wealthiest neighborhoods in the city, it wasn't far from Metz & Co.

Luckily Simon was home and answered the door himself.

"Good morning, Max. So good to see you," Simon said. They hadn't seen each other in nearly nine months, but Simon didn't look in the least surprised. "How are you faring at university?" Max had told his classmates he wouldn't be returning after winter break.

"I decided to wait until the fall semester to matriculate. I'm working in my father's shop. What are you doing this summer?"

"Worrying," Simon replied.

Max raised his eyebrows. "Ah. Aren't we all?"

"What will you do if Hitler invades?"

"I will fight. I will not let him chase me all over Europe." Simon nodded. "Simon, I'd be happy to talk about this with you, but I've come on a more urgent matter."

"I think I know what it is."

Max cocked his head. "Annaliese?"

Simon bit his lip. "Max, please come in." He guided Max into a spacious parlor where Max and he sat on comfortable sofas.

"Thanks to you, Simon, she got a job at Metz and, as I understand it, was very happy. But she told me yesterday she'd been fired, and she says she doesn't know why. I don't believe that, but she won't say anything else. I'm hoping you can tell me how to find out what happened."

"You are a loyal boyfriend, Max. She is lucky to have you."

Max was surprised. Wouldn't anyone want to help the person they loved most in the world?

"Let me get you some coffee."

With that Max knew Simon had a story to tell. "I would appreciate it."

Simon ducked into another room. A few moments later, he returned. He was followed by a woman in a black uniform with a white apron who brought a silver tray with coffee and pastries and lowered it onto the coffee table. Max hadn't had breakfast, so he tucked in.

"I may know why she wouldn't tell you the reason she was fired."

"Please."

Simon shifted. "There's no easy way to say this, Max. Do you know what she was doing before she started working at Metz?"

Max felt his stomach twist. "Go on."

"So you did."

Max set his coffee back down on the tray.

"Apparently, one of the executives—he wasn't in her department —knew her from her previous career. He wanted to resume the relationship, but your girlfriend—Anna, is it?"

"Annaliese."

"Right. Annaliese," Simon continued. "She didn't. Want to resume. So, basically, he said he'd tell management about her former 'career' unless she did restart relations. And she did."

That answered one question. Anger washed over Max. It wasn't her fault. He understood extortion. And Hobson's choices. He swallowed his fury. "How do you know this?"

"My father is senior vice president and on the board of directors.

The story came out in pieces. In fact, it's the biggest scandal ever to hit the store. Disgusting."

"Who was the man?" Max asked. He'd expected Jan Van der Berg, the director of advertising to be at the top of the list, but Simon had said the man wasn't in her department.

Simon held up a finger. "That wasn't the worst of it."

"What do you mean?"

Simon flushed. This was not easy for him either, Max realized. "I —I'll just tell you straight out, Max. He started 'loaning' her to other executives in the company."

Max's mouth dropped open. He was speechless.

"Again, she was told if she said a word, her employment at Metz would be over."

Max closed his mouth. He took a moment to compose himself. "And this—this situation reached the board of directors?"

"One of the executives—an honest man—was approached and reported it." Simon sipped his coffee. "Of course, the man who first approached her was fired. After a long discussion, they fired the other execs too. Then the board decided she had to go as well. Having her around would be too difficult. Distracting. Not something Metz & Co. could condone. We have values." He put his coffee cup down. "I'm so sorry, Max."

"So your father—?"

"Told me everything. He said to expect you to visit at some point. And here you are. Of course, we hope you will keep this to yourself."

"Of course. I am, frankly, shocked." Max paused. "So she was a victim. Blameless."

"That's right. It's unfortunate she had that prior—uh—profession."

"Tell me the man's name."

Simon fidgeted. "My father said not to."

"Well, tell me this. Was the man Jewish?"

A smile that wasn't a smile crossed Simon's lips. "No." He wiped his mouth with his napkin. "If I told you he has Nazi leanings, would you feel any better?"

Max wasn't surprised. "It makes my plan simpler." He leaned back. "Tell me, Simon. You're Jewish. Would you let him get away with it? I mean, haven't the Nazis taken enough from us already?"

Simon kept his mouth shut.

"Firing him was the least the board could do. He needs to be held accountable in a more—more substantive way, don't you think?"

"Look, Steiner. I can't tell you what to do. I just hope you're not planning anything violent."

Max looked him in the eye. "No violence. I swear it."

Simon didn't say anything for a long moment. Then: "You didn't hear this from me. I'll deny it."

Max nodded.

"The man was the director of accounting. His name is Heinrich Wagner," Simon whispered.

CHAPTER 30

The skies had never been so serene and placid that August. If Max ignored current events, he could delude himself into thinking the last full month of summer promised gentle breezes, lazy days, and starry nights. But Hitler had other plans.

In an August speech to his generals, Hitler proclaimed that Poland should be completely dissolved so that Germany could add Lebensraum (living space) for Germans. In other words, the Nazis did not care whom they displaced or what happened to them as long as the Reich could expand.

It was in August that the Molotov-Ribbentrop Pact was signed. The treaty guaranteed Hitler would not have an eastern-front war in addition to his other planned conquests in the West. Secretly Germany and Russia agreed to carve up Poland equally. They also threw in an equal division of Eastern Europe, including the Baltic states of Lithuania, Estonia, and Latvia, and parts of Romania.

Hitler promised to respect the neutrality of Belgium, Holland, Luxembourg, and Sweden. Dutch newspapers reported it with celebratory articles but failed to point out that his words were no guarantee of his behavior. In fact, Max thought, every time Hitler made such a promise, he did the opposite.

Max made sure to emphasize that point in his reports to Jacob and suggested the DJRL reach out to other resistance groups as soon as possible. Jacob took his advice, but the Dutch people as a whole did little to prepare. Didn't they know invasion was imminent? Were they naïve enough to believe their neutrality would be honored? Max was so frustrated he wondered if perhaps it was time to flee. He recalled the visas from the US State Department. Despite his anger at Mutti, he was grateful. They had a way out. But the thought that he might cut and run made him clench his teeth. That just wasn't his way. He would rather make a stand and fight.

On September 1, after what some believed were false flag operations launched by Hitler to inflame the public, German forces overran western Poland. On September 3, Great Britain and France declared war on Germany.

It had begun.

CHAPTER 31

October–November 1939
Amsterdam

Not much changed in Holland during the first few months of the war. That wasn't the case for Poland. Hitler kept his promise to Russia, and on September 17, the Soviet Union invaded eastern Poland, and the two nations split the country in two. During September the Nazis and the Wehrmacht made incremental but steady progress overtaking their half of Poland. The SS established ghettos and drove Jews into them. They herded thousands of other men and women into concentration camps and publicly humiliated them at every opportunity.

Rumors drifted back to Holland: Jews forced to urinate in the local synagogue and use their tallit (prayer shawls) to clean it up; starving Jews made to clean latrines with their bare hands; Jews deported during the High Holidays, the most sacred part of their year. Poland surrendered at the end of September.

In October Germany issued a decree that made slave labor mandatory for all men and women between fourteen and sixty in occupied Poland. Hitler made it clear to his generals that "Jews, Poles, and similar trash" must be removed from all corners of the Reich.

As the weather cooled in November and the leaves in Amsterdam began to shiver, Jacob Weber, his son, Carl, and Max met after dark at the bookshop. When he had the time, Max had begun to listen to news broadcasts from Poland, Austria, France, and the UK, as well as Germany, for updates.

"I think I've pieced together what the Wehrmacht might do," Max said.

"Go on," Jacob replied.

"Hitler knows that in order to take France and England, the Wehrmacht will need transit rights and bases in Holland and Belgium. But the army doesn't think they will be at peak force until next year, so they want to delay any attacks until then."

"So we have time to prepare?" Jacob asked.

"Perhaps. The problem is that the generals are not being told what Hitler's battle strategy is. They've had to find out through back-door channels."

"Is there's a rift?" Carl asked hopefully.

Max let out a disparaging laugh. "You could say that. There was another coup attempt. A group of generals in the Wehrmacht and the Abwehr wanted to overthrow Hitler at Zossen, Germany."

"Really? When?"

Max shook his head. "The plan fell apart. For the most ridiculous reason. One of the generals heard Hitler vow to destroy the 'spirit of Zossen' in a speech and thought they had been exposed."

"Were they?" Jacob said.

Max squeezed his eyes shut in exasperation. "The general was wrong. Hitler was just talking about the army headquarters building. But the conspirators panicked and shut down the entire plot."

It was Carl's turn to sigh. "So what does that mean for us?"

"On the positive side, it means the Wehrmacht hates Hitler and would kill him if they could," Jacob said.

"But, Papa, how does that help us?" Carl asked. "Or Holland?"

"That was the second assassination attempt, don't forget. In time there will be more," Jacob said.

"I agree, " Max said. "And there is one other piece of good news.

Hitler wanted to attack France this month. But he realized—or someone told him—the Luftwaffe and Wehrmacht aren't ready. So he's delayed it."

"When will it happen?" Carl asked.

Max shrugged. He turned to Jacob. "What's happening with the DJRL?"

Jacob sat up straighter. "I've been putting out feelers to potential resistance groups. The Communists have already said they'll resist, and there are some church groups who feel strongly too. I believe a military-style resistance group will also be forming. Word is out they plan to call themselves the Ordedienst"—the Order of Service. "And there's a fellow named IJzerdraat in Rotterdam. He's been involved in anti-fascist activities for a few years. He plans to continue if and when the Nazis invade. I'll be meeting with a few of them to see how we might work together."

"And then there's us," Carl added.

Jacob nodded.

"What do you see us doing, Jacob?" Max asked.

"Intelligence, mostly. But if the invasion is successful, we must be ready to help our Jewish brothers and sisters."

"How?"

"Hide them in the homes of sympathetic Gentiles. We need to identify those good souls and help them prepare their basements and attics."

"Excellent idea." Max rose. He started to pace to control his restlessness. "I want to do more than just listen to the radio."

"I know, Max. You want to fight. I see it in your eyes. The way you hold yourself. Coiled. Ready to spring. Look at you. You can't stay still."

Max forced himself to stop pacing. "Enough of this damn Dutch 'neutrality.' This isn't the Great War. This is pure evil. Holland must take a stand."

"Have patience. That day will come. Whether here or someplace else. For now, however, be on the lookout for Gentiles who might hide Jews."

Max started pacing again.

"For example, your girlfriend is in a perfect position at Metz. Plenty of Gentiles work for the company. And it's Jewish-owned. The employees must be open-minded folk. They could be useful."

Max stopped. "She's not there anymore."

"What? What happened?" Carl asked.

"They let her go." Max folded his arms, and the dark look on his face must have told the Webers he would brook no further conversation on the matter.

Max and Annaliese spent his nineteenth birthday in a quiet restaurant downtown. Over dessert he told her about his meeting with Simon Metz.

Annaliese squeezed her eyes shut. "I didn't want you to know. Now you will never forgive me."

Max covered her hand with his. "You were in over your head. With sleazy people who thought nothing of exploiting a woman with a reputation."

"I never cared much about what people thought of me. Before."

"You were young. You needed money more than you needed a good reputation. You—"

"Stop defending me, Max," she cut in. "I am ashamed. How can you—"

"Believe me, Annaliese. I do not take this lightly. I would like to rip out the balls of the man who exploited you and watch him beg for mercy. He's no better than the Russian soldiers who rape women in the territory they conquer." Indeed, rage had consumed Max ever since Simon Metz told him about Heinrich Wagner. Unlike the Russians, though, this was personal.

Annaliese looked alarmed. "You can't just beat him up."

"I understand. I hear he has Nazi leanings. They'd come after me. I would have to flee."

"No!" she cried. "What will I do without you?"

He squeezed her hand. "We'll get through this. We've been through worse. Are you working at all now?"

"I'm cleaning houses with my mother. She lets me do most of the work. So I have a little money." She smiled. "How is your mother reacting?"

"She doesn't know." He looked down.

"You see? You are ashamed of me."

"It's not that. I just don't want her to get the wrong idea." He looked her in the eye. "She's worried about the war, anyway."

"I understand. So is my mother."

He grinned. "I'd put our mothers up against Hitler any day. They'd probably win."

Annaliese giggled.

That night when they made love in the shop, they were tender with each other. As if they were both fragile and would shatter if either was too rough.

CHAPTER 32

April 1940
Amsterdam

Days turned into weeks, then into months, with no invasion. Anxiety became the norm. Most people believed the Germans would enter via the city of Maastricht in the south and sweep north with such a powerful army that a negotiated political solution would soon follow. By January 1940, however, reports surfaced that Hitler's plans had changed. He would invade Holland using blitzkrieg tactics. The Luftwaffe would bomb the urban population.

But when January, February, and March passed with no attack, even government officials were baffled. Max and Carl discussed it one morning at the bookshop.

"Now that he's started a world war," Carl said, "I wonder if he's unsure of the best way forward."

"I don't think so," Max said. "More likely he's listening to his generals. They know they're not at peak force and want him to delay until they are."

"So we're just sitting ducks, waiting for the Wehrmacht to get to full power?"

"We should take advantage of the lull. For example, I'd really like to get a two-way radio setup at the bicycle shop. I think I can locate German military conversations and eavesdrop on them. I'd be able to get more details on—"

"Never. That's crazy, Max!" Max's back was to the door, and he hadn't heard Jacob enter the shop. "It's much too dangerous."

Max whipped around. "Only if we're invaded. I've done some reading, and I think—"

Jacob strode over. "Even if we're not invaded, the Nazis could be next door in Belgium. And they already have informants all over the Netherlands. Your antenna would be a dead giveaway. So, too, the frequencies you'd use to receive and transmit. Anyone could triangulate your position within minutes and figure out where you are."

"But I could hide the antenna and limit my transmission time. That way I could report the most current updates—"

"No. And that's final," Jacob said. "I won't have your death on my hands. We won't need it anyway. We'll have plenty of intel. Many Dutch citizens are vowing to resist Hitler."

"Like the Germans did?" Max said sarcastically.

"It's true the Germans and the Dutch have been quite close over the years. But Holland has always been neutral during wars. Perhaps the delay is Germany realizing we will never take sides."

"I don't believe that for a minute," Max said.

"Just promise me you will not get a radio setup. If they trace you, they will come for us next."

Max should have thought of that earlier. He wasn't willing to put his friends in danger. He hesitated. Then: "I promise."

Max was surprisingly relieved that the man who extorted Annaliese at Metz & Co. wasn't her direct superior, Jan Van der Berg. Max probably had misconstrued the way the man eyed her during their interview. Van der Berg had turned out to be a gentleman. An honest broker, at least.

Heinrich Wagner was another matter. Max couldn't use a radio set to eavesdrop on Nazi military movements, but he might be able to deal with one Nazi up close and personal. Max ruminated over how he could hold Wagner accountable. He came up with a plan. Wagner losing his job at Metz & Co. would be just the beginning. Wagner would rue the day he first laid eyes on Annaliese. But first Max needed to do some research. Field reconnaissance, he labeled it.

CHAPTER 33

May 1940
Amsterdam

Hitler delayed the invasion of the Netherlands twenty-nine times between November 1939 and May 1940, often at the last minute. It wasn't a secret. German officials were quite open with their Dutch counterparts, informing the Dutch of their battle strategy and invasion points. In fact, some said afterward that Dutch officials had been overwarned and likely confused by all the delays. Others said the Dutch blundered because they didn't search out enough intelligence to prepare a solid defense strategy. Still others talked about personality conflicts among Dutch leaders. And although the government had issued an "alert" at the start of the war, no one quite knew what it meant. In the end, though, the whys didn't matter. Holland was woefully unprepared.

On Friday, May 10, in the early hours of the morning, Max woke to the roar of airplanes overhead. At first he thought it was a dream, but as he cracked his eyes open, he realized the rumble was still there. He'd seen and heard planes in the sky headed for the UK, but this was louder and closer. When he heard a whistle followed by the thunder of a distant explosion, he knew the German invasion was underway.

He scrambled out of bed, hurried to the radio, and turned it on. The announcer confirmed it. A moment later, his parents, disheveled and rubbing sleep from their eyes, joined him. His mother brewed coffee, and they sat around the radio in the parlor, silent and stunned. The radio broadcast was interrupted several times as news broke that a bridge was in flames, and a factory on the outskirts of Amsterdam near Schiphol Airport had been hit. They learned later that the airport had been the target. Aside from those incidents, Amsterdam was largely spared, but bombs were exploding in The Hague and Rotterdam. The German military was moving into Belgium and Luxembourg as well. So much for Hitler's promise of neutrality.

As dawn broke, knots of people gathered outside, scouring the sky. By then German paratroopers were dropping from planes all over the country, many of them disguised as Dutch army recruits, farmers, even women.

The next day, Saturday, May 11, the Netherlands high command said any German soldiers who were found wearing Dutch uniforms should be shot immediately. In the UK, Prime Minister Neville Chamberlain resigned. His successor, Winston Churchill, declared, "I felt as if all my past life had been but a preparation for this hour."

But for Max, the most disturbing event was a single German bomber that dropped four bombs on the Herengracht, a canal close to Simon Metz's home. The Metz family survived, but forty-four civilians died.

On Sunday, May 12, Max woke to a thick cloud layer over the city. Eight air-raid sirens screamed all day. The radio was rife with rumors of Dutch betrayals, pro-Nazi activities on the streets, and random shootings. Trucks full of German soldiers patrolled, their weapons in plain sight.

That afternoon his parents called him into the parlor.

"Invasion was always a possibility," his father began. "But we never thought it would come to pass. The Netherlands has maintained its neutrality for centuries. That's over now. And it's time that you leave Holland."

Max started to interrupt, but his father silenced him with a raised hand. "Our decision is final. Your mother told me you know about the visas and the cash in the bank. On Monday, assuming the bank is open, we will retrieve them."

His mother picked up the conversation. "I will write to your cousins. Your uncle Willie and aunt Rosa left last year and settled in Chicago. But Rosa's father, Leo Bendheim, is in New York. Once I know what ship you will be on, I will tell him to expect you. I agree with your father. It is time for you to go."

"You and Papa are coming with me, yes?"

His father replied. "We are not going anywhere."

"What are you saying? You must. They will deport you or you'll end up in a camp. If they don't kill you first."

"I've run for the last time," his father said. "I fought in the Great War. It's your turn now."

"No!" Max cried. "I'll find a place for you to hide from the Nazis. A lot of Gentiles are taking Jews into their homes. And Jacob says they're trying to save Jews in Bulgaria."

Papa and Mutti exchanged glances. "We are too old, son," his father said. "And we do not want to travel to yet another country. Nor do we want to be cooped up in someone's attic or basement. If the Nazis take over Holland, so be it."

Desperation washed over him. "Do you understand what you're saying? You're willing to die at the hands of Hitler!"

"Moritz," Mutti interrupted. "Tell him the truth." She didn't wait for a reply. She turned to Max. "The truth is that your father is sick. He has cancer of the stomach. The doctor won't say it, but I am convinced he was given something at Dachau that poisoned him. We don't have much time. And before you say anything, I will not leave him alone. He and I are in this together. You, on the other hand, have an entire life waiting for you."

His father picked up the conversation. "That's why we're sending you to America. We've made our choice. We do not fear death. You will survive. You will fight the Nazis."

"Assuming the Americans come to their senses and enter the war." His mother's voice dripped cynicism.

"The fact is I should have listened to your mother long ago," his father said. "We should have gone to America when the visas arrived." His father paused. "I made the wrong decision."

"How could you know?" Max automatically defended his father even though he'd been wrong. "You'd just returned from Dachau."

"I begged your mother to leave and take you with her. But she was stubborn. I gave up. She has a spine of steel."

"How can I allow him to fend for himself, sick as he is?" Mutti cut in. "As I've said before, you will be the proof that the Nazis did not win."

Max knew any more words were futile. He had to accept his parents' decision. He went quiet, but tears filled his eyes.

Despite the rumored patrols of German soldiers, Max rode his bicycle to the bookshop without trouble. Over the past few months the bookshop had become the central meeting place for Jacob's DJRL. The group now numbered more than a hundred, mostly Jewish men and women, all anxious to hear the latest news and rumors.

Jacob and Carl had removed a few aisles of books to carve out a small meeting space at the back of the store. They added a table and folding chairs, and half a dozen people were seated around the table. Although they kept their voices low, Max overheard snippets of conversation.

"So many rumors. Don't know what to believe."

"They're saying ordinary Dutch citizens have betrayed their countrymen."

"Germans who have lived here for decades are firing at Dutch soldiers."

"It's really bad in Rotterdam and The Hague."

Jacob was behind the counter, where he had a view of the front door as well as the space in the back.

"Everything under control here?" Max asked. He was learning to compartmentalize his feelings, assigning them to a corner of his mind where they wouldn't interfere with his working activities. He wasn't repressing his distress and anguish about his parents. Just choosing to deal with it another time.

"Nothing is under control. But it's quiet. Did you have any trouble getting here?"

Max shook his head. "Didn't see any soldiers. Maybe they're staying out of the Jewish Quarter."

Jacob snorted. "For now."

"What are you going to do?"

"I've arranged for my family to get the hell out of Amsterdam. Next week. They'll be staying on a farm with a Gentile family."

"And you?"

Jacob replied. "There's much work to be done here."

Max admired his courage. Jacob was almost a second father to Max. Max would have joined the Resistance to fight the Nazis with him. But. "My parents are pushing me to go to America right away."

"You should. There is nothing you can do here. Get out while you can."

"But what about—"

"Max, you have shown time and again your heart is in the right place. For now, though, do what your parents say. You can be more help to us in America than on the ground here. You have papers?"

Max wasn't expecting that from Jacob. In fact, he was shocked that Jacob agreed with his parents. What had changed? "I—I . . . do you really believe that I can do more good in America than here? They aren't even in the war. Roosevelt wants to stay out."

"I don't believe that, Max. He's just waiting for the right time. And yes, if you join the military you will make a fine soldier in America."

"I—I will need transportation to Rotterdam," Max said, still dazed. "And a ticket on a steamer." He licked his lips. "Oh, and my passport and my transit visa need to be updated."

"I can take care of those. When do you want to go?"

"Not for a few weeks. I want to see what happens here." How could he leave Annaliese?

"Don't wait that long. Your parents are right. Get out now. While I can still help you."

Max considered it. If Jacob wanted him to leave, he wasn't abandoning his friends and family. But Annaliese? Was there a way to bring her with him? He had to think about it.

The next afternoon, on May 14, a German air raid on Rotterdam destroyed a major part of that city. The Germans threatened to bomb The Hague, Amsterdam, and Utrecht too, unless the Netherlands surrendered. At seven o'clock in the evening, General Henri Winkelman, the commander in chief of the Dutch army, pledged to cease fighting. The surrender was signed the next day.

The queen and her cabinet fled to England and set up a government in exile. While Max was relieved the bombing was over, a dark cloud was settling over Holland, and its future was uncertain. Max felt as if there had been a death in his family. In a way, there had been.

CHAPTER 34

Summer 1940
Amsterdam

Arthur Seyss-Inquart, an Austrian lawyer turned politician, was named Reichskommissar of the Netherlands after Holland surrendered. He was an SS member and Nazi politician devoted to Hitler. At first, he seemed to be reasonable: he promised to leave the Dutch legal system intact. He also suggested that if Dutch Jews stepped back from public, professional, and academic activities, life would go on as usual.

Most Jews didn't believe him. The evidence from Germany, Austria, and Poland was clear; either Seyss-Inquart was lying or he had a secret plan. A bitter taste climbed up Max's throat when he thought about the future. Not satisfied with ruining his life in Germany, the Nazis were now preying on him in Holland. It was impossible not to take it personally. What country was next? France? England? Spain?

As if Max's prophecy was fulfilled, the Nazis stormed into Paris in June, barely a month after Holland was occupied. The City of Lights folded like an accordion hissing out air. In retrospect, the event seemed to be a tacit signal to step up persecution of Jews in Holland.

By November 1940, not even six months later, Jews had been fired from all government services and universities. When citizens protested, the Nazis closed the University of Leiden and several churches as well.

The final insult was that a staff of only twenty Nazis was needed to administer Jewish persecution in the Netherlands. The Dutch bureaucracy did the rest. When they finished, more than one hundred thousand Jews were deported to concentration camps.

Still, Max couldn't leave. Not yet. He had one more task to accomplish.

It took a week for his plan to go public. It started the third week of June when Annaliese showed up at the bicycle shop carrying a letter from a complete stranger.

"What is this, Max? What did you do?" She waved the letter. "Read it." Her cheeks were flushed, but her voice was all business. Max couldn't tell if she was pleased or dismayed. She handed it over.

It was from a Catholic priest. "My dear child, Annaliese, I have read of your suffering at the hand of Heinrich Wagner. His family prays at our church, but he rarely attends. Now I know why. The church does not support such cruel, manipulative behavior. I hope you will not think less of our church and Jesus Christ our Lord." The letter went on to invite her to talk to the priest anytime she wanted. "Together, we can cleanse this horrifying part of your life and return you to the pure vessel of innocence you once were. Father Hegel."

Max looked up. "I'm not surprised."

Annaliese seemed unsure how to respond. She took the letter back. "Who is this priest? Why is he writing me? How does he know everything that happened? Metz & Co. said they were going to lock this ugly scandal—that's what they called it—in a cupboard and never revisit it."

"That isn't going to happen. At least not yet."

"Max, what did you do?"

"I didn't lay a hand on Wagner. You know I wanted to. But that would have been too easy. He wouldn't suffer enough. So I decided to make sure no one would ever again accept him in society. I wrote an anonymous letter detailing everything he did to you and how he sullied the reputation of Metz and Co. I sent copies of it to his wife, his priest, his doctor, his business contacts, accounting firms, and Amsterdam companies who have their own bookkeeping departments. I also sent a copy to *De Telegraaf*. I wanted every potential employer to know the truth. I never identified you by name, however."

"Someone did," Annaliese said. Her voice was laced with anger. "He knows exactly who I am. How did he find out? If a priest knows, others will too. I will become an outcast along with Wagner. And a target for anyone who wants to retaliate."

"Perhaps the priest already suspected him of adultery. He probably wasn't discreet. And anyway—"

She cut him off. "Max, you aren't listening. If the Nazis support him, they will come after me. And my family."

"I've already talked to Jacob. He has arranged a hiding place where you can stay until I'm settled in America. It's a farm. About an hour from Amsterdam. Your family can go too. You will be safe there."

Annaliese kept her mouth shut, but her cheeks were red and her eyes narrowed.

Max persisted. "This will blow over. After all, there is a war to wage." He took a breath. "And you won't be here long enough for it to matter."

"What are you talking about? I live here."

"I want you to come to America as soon as I am settled."

"What?"

"You'll need to get your passport in order. And I will send you the fare for the ship."

Annaliese's mouth fell open. "How, exactly, do you plan to get a visa for me?"

He hesitated. "I already have it."

She threw him a dubious glance. "What? How?"

"It was intended for my mother," he said. "But Jacob knows someone who can 'revise' it. And create a transit visa."

"Your mother?" Annaliese folded her arms across her chest. "Why is she not using it?"

He bit his lip. "They are not coming."

Annaliese raised her eyebrows.

After they told him they would remain in Holland, Max thought about the other two visas. Using his mother's papers for Annaliese was, in a subtle way, payback for her shoddy treatment of her. His better soul rebelled against that idea. In light of recent events, his anger at his mother seemed misplaced, the tantrum of a petulant child who refused to acknowledge that life—and love—could be hard. So he'd made one more attempt to save his parents. They continued to say they would stay in Holland. Moritz was in his sixties now. He was too old—and too sick—to move to a new country, a new culture. They would defy the Nazis in their own way.

"It won't be long. A month at most. And then we can get married. How does that sound?" He pulled her close. In spite of her anger her body began to loosen.

"Are you sure?"

"What do you think?" He kissed her forehead. "I can't imagine life without you. We can finally begin our new lives together."

"Yes." It was a whisper. He released her. Tears rimmed her eyes. He gently wiped them away.

"Then I will leave the visa with Jacob. You and he can make arrangements once everything is in place."

She burrowed her face into Max's shoulder and took a deep breath. Her voice was muffled. "Yes."

"So. It is settled. Now. Will you come upstairs so we can have a proper goodbye?" Max reached for her hand.

"Wait. There is something I need to tell you."

"What?"

"Let's go upstairs," she said and followed him up.

"So, what is on your mind, Annaliese?" He sat on the cushions and blankets and pulled her down beside him.

"Max." Annaliese stumbled on her words. "I—I am pregnant."

Max blinked. "You are pregnant?" He repeated the words slowly. She nodded but didn't go on. He let out a breath. "Is it mine?"

She winced as if she was expecting a blow and he had indeed delivered it. "I think so."

"But you don't know for sure."

"I know it's not Wagner's. The timing doesn't work. I haven't been with him since—well since he started to . . ."

"Don't say it." Max was stunned. He didn't know what to say. Annaliese was pregnant. He was going to the US. If everything worked out on schedule, she would have the baby in America. "Weren't you using protection?"

"I was. Every time." She looked down.

"What?"

"Except with you."

He ran his hand over his mouth. He wanted to be cautious in the words he chose. "So there shouldn't be any problem, should there?"

"I don't think so, but you never know."

"You never got pregnant at De Wallen."

"No."

"So why are you worried now?"

"Because, because, it wasn't what I wanted. At De Wallen, I wanted to make money. With Wagner, it was a punishment."

"And you think it was your fault. That somehow you are guilty, immoral, and degenerate."

She nodded.

"Because you were exploited by a manipulative bastard."

She swallowed.

"Annaliese, I know you love me. And you know how much I love you. If you are sure, then so am I." Max brightened. "You have nothing to feel bad about. We are going to have a baby! I am thrilled. And you will give birth in America. He or she will be an American citizen years before we will. Think of it. We are going to be a real family!" He pulled her close. There would be something to salvage from this brutal war after all. Hashem was looking out for him.

"If you're sure . . ." She let her words trail off.

"Let me show you how sure I am." He gently took her in his arms.

CHAPTER 35

Summer 1940
Amsterdam

Annaliese fell asleep afterward. But Max was wide awake. Relief flooded through him, as if a valve inside his body had opened to release the pressure. He'd done what he set out to do. No one in Amsterdam would hire Wagner. Max had prevented Annaliese from becoming a public victim, and they'd made plans to reunite in the US. And he was going to have a baby with the woman he loved.

Now he could leave. He was already packed. Jacob had carefully made the necessary revisions on his passport and visa and arranged forged exit papers. Max bought a steamship ticket and would set sail from Rotterdam to New York in two days. All he needed was a ride to the ship.

He was just drifting off when someone pounded on the door to the bicycle shop. Max came alert at once. His breath went shallow, and his pulse started to race. Who would be here in the middle of the night? Max wasn't wearing his watch, but he guessed by the angle of moonlight through a window that it was midnight or later.

The banging continued. Max sensed an urgent undertone to it.

Bad news always arrived in the dark. Annaliese moved and asked sleepily, "What's going on?"

"I don't know. Stay here. Do not come downstairs." He threw on his pants, grabbed a steel pipe he kept near him, and descended the steps. He peered through the shop window and saw a form in the darkness, hands clutching a bicycle. He couldn't make out whether it was a man or woman. He couldn't tell if the figure was carrying a weapon.

He yelled through the window. "Who's there? What do you want?"

"Max, it's Kaarina." Annaliese's mother. "It's urgent."

He slid the door open. "Kaarina. What are you doing here? How did you know about this place?"

"That's not important. Max, you have to get out of here right away."

"What is it?"

"A group of Nazi thugs came to my door about thirty minutes ago. They wanted to know where to find you. I wouldn't tell them, but then one pulled out a pistol and aimed it at me. I had to tell them where you lived. I gave them the wrong address, but I'm sure they will figure that out. They may find out about this place. I know you two meet here when you . . . Please, Max. you need to go. I will take Annaliese to a safe place. But go. Now."

He spun around. Annaliese, half-dressed, was on the steps. "We must warn Max's parents," she said. "I'll ride over to his apartment."

Max refused. "No. The men may already be there." He looked around the shop and pointed to a bicycle. "Take that and go home with your mother. Help her pack so you can all get away. I'll deal with my parents."

Annaliese froze.

He went to her and folded her in a tight embrace. "Go. We will meet in New York."

She shook her head. "No. I want to be with you."

"It's not a good idea, Annaliese."

"I want to make sure you get away safely, Max. I won't change my mind."

He knew her well enough to know she wouldn't change her mind. She wasn't stubborn, but once she made a decision, she stuck to it. She had a point. If for some reason he did not make it onto the steamer, how would she know? How would anyone? He thought for a moment. He recalled the outrageous tips he'd left the security guard at De Wallen. It was time to collect. "I'll go to De Wallen and see Guillermo," he whispered. "He owes us."

Annaliese nodded. She put on the rest of her clothes and took the bike outside. She and her mother got on and raced up the street. Max watched them go. His stomach twisted with fear. He forced himself to ignore it, finished dressing, and took another bike. Outside, he headed in the opposite direction.

It was peaceful in front of his parents' apartment building. No men. No bicycles or cars. Where were the thugs? Did they figure out they'd been led to the wrong address? Or did they already know and were arming themselves with more firepower? Max took the steps two at a time. Inside all was quiet. He broke the peace by shouting.

"Wake up. Papa. Mutti. Right now! Wake up!"

He ran into his room, grabbed his backpack, which held several changes of clothes, his papers, and the cash his parents had given him. By the time he hoisted the bag on his back, his parents had shuffled into the parlor.

"What's going on, Max?" His mother tightened the sash of her bathrobe. "You're scaring me. It's the middle of the night."

He hurriedly explained. "You must go to Carl and Jacob Weber's home. Not the bookshop. Their home. Jacob will be the only one there. His family has gone. Here is the address." He scribbled it on the pad Mutti kept in the kitchen. "Tell them what I've just told you. Take your bicycles. You will be safe. You can come home in a few days."

"Why? I have a—" His father began.

"No, Papa. No weapons. They will kill you. Please. Do what I say. You will be safe."

"What about you?" Mutti said in a strangled voice. "Where will you be?"

"I will to go to Rotterdam and lie low until the ship leaves. It's only two days." He embraced his mother. "I love you both. Now, go!"

Max cycled to De Wallen, the only place he figured the Nazi brutes, who certainly had been sent by Heinrich Wagner, wouldn't bother to search. The red lights, painted ladies, and weak illumination seeping through closed curtains brought back memories. This was where it started. He locked his bike near the window where he'd first seen Annaliese and banged on the door.

Nearly three years had passed, but the man who opened the door was Guillermo. With deeper lines on his face. Grayer hair. And a bigger belly. He looked startled at first, but his expression relaxed when he recognized Max. It was almost a smile, Max thought.

"What do you want?"

"Guillermo, I am so happy to see you! I—we need you. Annaliese and I."

"Annaliese?" Guillermo stared at Max. "You and her—"

"Yes. We are still together."

Guillermo's almost smile turned serious. "And you—in trouble?"

"I need a safe place to hide." Max kept it short. The less said the better.

Guillermo frowned. "This is about war?"

Max knew what he meant. He gave the man a solemn nod. "It is."

"She is good girl."

"I love her, Guillermo. And she loves me."

Guillermo stared at his feet, as if making a decision. Max waited. Then he led Max to a door in the back of the brothel.

CHAPTER 36

June 1940
Amsterdam

Max hid in a dusty, dark basement that smelled of dead rats, stale urine, and sex. He tried to sleep but could only nap fitfully. He waited for Annaliese, but two hours later when dawn broke she hadn't shown up. Where was she? Where were the men? Was Wagner with them? The thought of what they could do to her—and their baby—made him furious. His fear turned to rage. He would find her.

When Guillermo opened the basement door, morning sun splashed down through the windows upstairs. "She no come." Guillermo spread his hands, palms up.

"I will find her."

Guillermo nodded and repeated, "She good girl."

Max tightened his lips and pumped the man's hand. This would probably be the last time he would see Guillermo.

Outside he unlocked the bike. He was just about to take off when he heard his name.

"Max, Max, wait!" Annaliese cycled toward him from the other end of the cobblestone street. Max let himself breathe. She pulled her bike up next to him and dismounted. She was smiling and her cheeks were flushed.

He threw his arms around her. "Where were you? I was so worried."

"I helped my mother pack the little ones, and then waited for a car to take them to the country. It took longer than I thought."

"You're going to meet them there?"

She pulled back and shrugged. "If I can't stay with you."

"Annaliese, I'm leaving. Go to the farm. You'll be safe there. I'll be in touch as soon as I can. Just make sure to stay in contact with Jacob."

"I will. And I will write down the address of the farm for you."

"What happened to the thugs?"

"They never showed up. I was scared they would come back, but they didn't."

"Do you think they gave up?"

"I don't know, and I don't care. I needed to see you one more time before you left."

Max leaned over and stroked her hair, her cheeks, and traced the outline of her lips as though committing her face to memory. "Come. Let's get some food that you can take with you. But then you must go."

"I want to say goodbye to Guillermo first. I'll never see him again."

She disappeared into the brothel. Max shifted his feet. She needed to hurry. When she finally came out, they mounted their bikes and rode in the direction of the bookshop. Max stopped at a nearby store to pick up bread and cheese but told Annaliese to head down to the bookshop. As he waited to pay for the food, Max grew wary. Every customer who came through the door was a potential threat. Any one of the thugs from last night could be on the lookout for him. Each minute he wasn't hiding was a risk. Max wouldn't feel safe until Annaliese was gone and he was on his way to Rotterdam.

When Jacob opened the bookshop door and saw Max, he shook his head. "You two shouldn't be here. It's not safe. Come in. Quickly." Max followed him in. Annaliese was already at the table in back. Jacob turned the "Open" sign to "Closed." "By the way, I had some visitors at home last night."

"My parents." At Jacob's nod, he said, "Are they still there?"

"I hope so. I practically had to tie them down to keep them from leaving. Well, your mother anyway," he said. "Are those men still after you?"

"We haven't seen them," Max said. "But we haven't been home."

"Good. Baruch Hashem."

Max's brows arched. Jacob was as secular as a Jew could be and still call himself a Jew. "Why the blessing?"

"Well . . ." Jacob rubbed his chin. He hadn't shaved in a week and his stubble was visible. "We've been ignoring Him while we analyzed and deliberated and came up with a plan to save our brothers and sisters. It's time to ask Him for help, don't you think?"

Were things that desperate, Max wondered, that even Jacob felt the need to pray? He wasn't sure he wanted to know the answer, so he kept his response light. "Well," Max said, "if He's inclined to, I know just the person he can experiment on . . ."

"Don't worry. I'll get you to Rotterdam if I have to drive you myself."

Max smiled. "You are a mensch, Jacob. I will always treasure our friendship."

"As will I." Jacob turned away and cleared his throat. Max felt his own throat thicken. He changed the subject. "Have you heard from Carl yet?"

"Not yet. They just left."

Max glanced around at the cramped space, the dusty shelves, the table in the back. It occurred to him that this would probably be the last time he would see the bookshop. And Jacob. He and Carl had said their farewells earlier and promised to find each other when the war ended. Tony and Pieter as well. He wanted to tell Jacob that

Annaliese was pregnant with his child but decided to wait until she was safe with him in the US.

Jacob came out from behind the counter. "You two stay here. I'm going out to confirm your ride to Rotterdam. I'll leave the "Closed" sign on the door. Do not open the door for anyone. I don't care if it's Adolf Hitler himself. You hide in there." He pointed to the small office behind him. "Swear to me, Max. You too, Annaliese."

"I swear," Max said. "We'll catch up on our sleep. We've been up all night."

Jacob gathered his things. "Stay in the office." He walked out.

Sometime around midmorning, the crash of glass shattering roused Max from a sound sleep. Annaliese and he were curled up on the floor of the tiny office. On the other side of the door men shouted in German and Dutch. Max came instantly awake, his pulse thundering in his ears. A second wave of glass smashed, shards tinkling as they fell. Had to be the shop windows.

"Where are you, Steiner?" a voice full of rage roared. "It's time to settle scores!"

Max scrambled to his feet and hurried to the door.

"No!" Annaliese whispered, fully awake now too. "It's him!"

"Wagner?"

"I know his voice."

Max blinked. Of course she did.

"Don't be a fool, Max. Don't open the door. Hide!"

Footsteps stomped across the floor. Wagner was furious. "I've got you, you Jewish pig! And you thought you would get away? Stupid, arrogant piece of shit."

Annaliese cringed at Wagner's words, but Max's eyes narrowed.

"We'll get a piece of you! And your whore!"

Max glanced at Annaliese. Her face was white, her eyes huge. Didn't she realize there was nowhere to hide? This was the time. This was the place. All accounts would be settled in the next few moments. If she wasn't so panicked, she'd realize that. Max took in a breath and threw his shoulders back. All he had to do was the next right thing. What he'd wanted to do so many times in the past. Hashem would want it that way. If it meant a fight, so be it. God would be on his side.

And with that recognition, Max's fear vanished. His pulse slowed and his breath steadied. "He's right about one thing. It is time for me to take a stand. But I don't want you to be in the middle. So when I open the door, I'll distract him. When I do, I want you to run as fast as you possibly can out of the shop."

"Max, you can't! He and his men will kill you!"

"I'm not afraid." These might be his last moments on earth, but Max felt eerily calm. He was ready. He grabbed his knapsack, threw it on his back, and glanced back at Annaliese. "I love you more than you'll ever know." Then he grasped the doorknob and twisted it open.

He stared into coldness. Eyes full of venom. Hatred. Dark hair, average build. If Wagner had been alone, Max could have taken him. But two other men loomed behind him, both with smug expressions.

Wagner belted Max in his stomach. Max doubled over. One of the men closed in on his back and yanked him upright, seized his arms, and pinned them behind his back. Wagner continued to pummel Max's chest, stomach, and intestines. Max went limp. The second man picked up a long shard of glass from the floor and started toward Max. Max glanced up. His vision was hazy, and pain rippled through his torso. He was about to die.

Suddenly he heard Annaliese cry out. "Stop! All of you. Right now!"

Wagner stopped battering Max and whipped around to face Annaliese. The man pinning Max's arms let go and faced her too. Max fell to the floor. He raised his head but Wagner blocked his view. Max craned his neck. Annaliese was holding a pistol! Where the hell did she get it? Her mother? No, she would have said something. Had it been in the office? He didn't think so. Then it came to him. De Wallen. Guillermo. He must have given her his gun when she went inside to say goodbye.

Wagner stepped sideways and gazed at Annaliese. "What are you going to do? Shoot me? In front of all these witnesses?" He sneered. "I dare you." He hocked up a ball of spit in her direction. "That's what you're worth to me. You're not good enough to shine my boots."

Annaliese returned his gaze. For an instant time stopped. No one moved. No one spoke. Then a half smile came across Annaliese's face, and Max knew she was at the same place he'd come to a moment earlier. He belly-crawled behind the counter to escape the line of fire. At the last possible moment he stuck his head out. He watched while Annaliese coolly aimed the pistol at Wagner and emptied three bullets into him.

Wagner lost his sneer. A look of astonishment came over him. He staggered back, fell to his knees, then to the floor on his back. A splotch of dark liquid oozed out from his stomach and slowly expanded across his shirt. He was dead.

"Max, get up," Annaliese said in an eerily serene voice. "Leave the store. Now."

Max hesitated. Annaliese turned the gun on him. "If you don't get out, I'll shoot *you*. Get the hell away from this place."

Max started to get to his feet. If he could wrest the gun away, he might be able to do some damage to the two men before they could react. But it was too late. Before he could reach her, one of the thugs lunged at Annaliese and grabbed the pistol. In a flash the man took a step back, aimed, and shot Annaliese in the chest. She crumpled to the floor.

Max rushed over and knelt down. He wanted to take her in his arms and tell her he loved her. Hear her say she loved him too. But the red blood spilling out of her chest told him she was dead.

He began to pick her up so he could hold her one last time when another bullet threw up splinters from the floor. He ducked down behind the counter. One bullet was left. Any second now the thug with the gun would lean over the counter and shoot. Max marshaled all his strength, sprinted to the front of the shop, and scrambled through the space where a window had been minutes earlier. The last bullet whizzed by close to his head. He didn't look back.

CHAPTER 37

June 1940
Amsterdam

The peal of church bells woke Max. For a moment he was in Regensburg, driving Klara and the carriage across the Old Stone Bridge. As he gained consciousness, he realized he was lying on grass that was shaded by trees. Stiff and uncomfortable, he opened his eyes to a setting sun, the clouds above it glittering with purple, gold, and pink. Max propped himself up on his elbows. Pain throbbed in his legs, and his abdomen felt like he had been knifed.

Where was he? He gazed around. Vondel Park, home of the Blue Tea House restaurant, where they'd celebrated Annaliese's job with Metz & Co. How did he get here? A flash of something violent and catastrophic flickered through his mind. He blinked, and the events of earlier that morning crashed through to consciousness. They'd been asleep in Jacob's office. Wagner and his men found them. Annaliese shot Wagner. Wagner's thug shot her. She was dead.

Max got to his feet unsteadily. With consciousness came the sickening realization that he was responsible for her death. His campaign to publicly shame Wagner had backfired. Wagner had retaliated.

What had made Max think it would succeed? It was as if Max himself had fired the bullet that killed Annaliese.

He took a few steps and stumbled on uneven ground. He had been full of hubris. So sure his plan to avenge Annaliese would succeed. Anguish shot through him. He had destroyed the one person he loved. No. He corrected himself. He had put his parents in jeopardy as well. Forced them to escape in the middle of the night. The people who had sacrificed everything, and quite possibly soon, their lives, to make sure he lived. How would he live with himself?

Nightfall was still a few hours off. He recalled Jacob leaving the shop that morning to pin down a ride to Rotterdam for him. He should go back. Decide what to do when he arrived. A block away Max inhaled the odor of smoke and fire residue. He quickened his pace. The odor intensified the closer he got. When the store came into view, he saw the charred remnants of furniture, broken glass, and debris.

The shop had been looted and ransacked. Windows were shattered, and glass shards were strewn all over what once was a cleanly swept floor. Books had been flung everywhere, most of them burned beyond recognition. The bookshelves on which they'd sat had been set on fire as well, the heat and flames twisting them into misshapen, unrecognizable objects. The table and chairs Jacob had added in the back were either burned or smashed into pieces. The cash register was open and empty. Jacob's tiny office was nothing more than scorched two-by-fours that had once supported walls.

Max's mouth went dry. As he got closer, he saw several people rummaging through the mess. For a moment he thought they might be Nazis looting what remained of the books. Then he recognized Pieter's father, Noah Cohen. He was a DJRL member. The man with him was as well.

Noah spotted Max and did a double take. "You're alive!"

Max was taken aback. "I—I was supposed to meet Jacob."

Noah shot Max a strange look. "He's not here. He may never be back."

"Where is he?"

"The Gestapo's got him in for interrogation."

A wave of panic poured over Max. "When?"

"Where the hell have you been?"

Max ran his tongue around his lips. "I was sleeping in Vondel Park. I just woke up."

"How did you get there?"

Max still wasn't sure. "I—I don't know."

The other man, Wilhelm Berg, who was listening to their conversation, placed his hand on Noah's arm. "Hold on. Max, are you saying you don't remember being here earlier today?"

Max looked from one man to the other. "I remember that Wagner showed up in the morning. His men beat me up. Annaliese shot him. Then one of his thugs shot her. Where is she? Is she—her body—"

"No, Max. They took her hours ago."

Max felt his heart break into pieces. It was hard to breathe.

"So you don't recall how you got to the park?" Berg asked.

Max shook his head. Why couldn't time go backward? Eight hours. That was all he wanted. He would put himself in the path of the thug's bullets instead of Annaliese.

Noah and Berg exchanged glances. Berg took a breath as though to steady himself. "Okay. We didn't know if they'd taken you or—"

"Let's get you some coffee and something to eat," Noah said.

Why were these men treating him so well? Max wondered. Didn't they know what he'd done?

The men led Max to a nearby café. Max asked, "When did Jacob come back?"

"Not long after you must have left. But the word was out. More Nazi thugs came to destroy the shop. There was arson. Looting. Then the Gestapo showed up and took him away."

Max bent his head to hide a tear. Jacob. His mentor. Teacher. Resistance fighter. Max mentally added him to the list of people he'd doomed.

Noah leaned forward. "Jacob was devastated when he discovered the shootings and saw the shop. But he was also upset about your ride. He didn't know who, when, or even if he could get you to Rotterdam."

"Why not?"

"He said the people he usually dealt with—mostly farmers who bring their goods to town—need advance notice so they can make room in the back of their trucks to hide—um—their cargo."

The waiter brought their coffee and sandwiches. Berg waited for him to leave, then said in a quiet voice, "There's another problem as well."

"What?" Max looked up.

"The Gestapo. They've taken over the roads and highways. They put up roadblocks and barricades, supposedly to check for papers. Now everyone is afraid to drive. Especially at night."

After what he'd done, Max wasn't sure he deserved to escape Holland.

"Jacob said his contacts are trying to find someone. But we—you —won't know until you know." Noah hesitated. "You must hope for the best. Stay close to the shop all night."

"In the meantime," Berg said, "eat."

Max gazed at the sandwich on his plate. He'd been ravenous, but his appetite disappeared. "What time is it?"

"About six," Noah said. "But don't expect anyone to show up before midnight. If they come at all."

It would serve Max right if no one came. But he went through the motions anyway. He pulled out a pencil and wrote on a napkin. "This is my relative's address in New York. He helped us get our visas. If Jacob makes it back, please make sure Jacob has it. He'll know how to reach me."

Noah nodded and tucked the paper into his pocket.

Max took a few bites of sandwich and thanked the men for their kindness. Outside there was no bookshop to wait in, but he found a bench close by with a view of the street next to the bookshop. He hunkered down to wait, still unsure whether he would be leaving.

Six hours later no one had come. The café closed and the owner exited, locking the door behind him. Max sat for another ninety minutes. He was about to give up when a vehicle turned into the street beside the shop and slowed. A pair of headlights flickered twice. Max waited until the vehicle's engine stopped and the driver jumped out. Max made his way toward the headlights.

The vehicle turned out to be a full-size truck. A hefty Dutch man with a beard went to the back of the truck and started unlocking the doors. Max wondered if the man would double-cross him. He approached gingerly. The driver wheeled around.

"Steiner?"

"That's me. You heading to the port?"

The driver grunted. "I'll get as close as I can. But I can't promise anything, understand? The Gestapo." He eyed Max. "You ride back here."

He flung open the doors. Max peered inside. When he saw the truck's contents, he gulped. "My God!"

The truck was filled with coffins. Most of them were closed. Still, the sight of them made Max freeze.

"They're mostly empty. Get into one. You'll be safe."

Max didn't move.

The driver shuffled his feet. "Go on. We don't have much time."

But Max's mind wasn't on the present. The events of the day kept spooling though his mind, like a scratched record. Wagner and his thugs. How they battered him. How Annaliese killed Wagner to save Max. How the thug grabbed her gun and killed her. And their baby. Max struggled to breathe. There wasn't enough air in the world.

The driver misunderstood. "Look, I know it stinks. I'll give you a rag to cover your nose. At this time of night it's only an hour or so to Rotterdam."

If he hadn't put his plan for revenge into motion, Annaliese would be alive. At the farm. Preparing to join him in America. She'd sacrificed her life for him. A sharp pain shot through his heart, and he let out an anguished cry of grief.

The driver's irritation surfaced. "Keep your mouth shut, damn it!

You're lucky to get a ride at all. Now, get in!" He pointed to a coffin farthest away from the doors. "That one's empty." The driver levered himself up, went to the coffin, and slid off the top.

Slowly Max obeyed. He levered himself up into the back of the truck and crept to the coffin. The stink was overwhelming. His eyes watered, whether from the stench or his grief, he didn't know. He climbed in. Someone had drilled holes for breathing. The driver handed him a rag to cover his nose, then replaced the top of the coffin. A moment later the truck's doors slammed shut.

The coffin was dark and suffocating. The corners of the box seemed to close in on him. He wanted to take a deep breath, but the rag over his nose and mouth prevented it. He had to get by with short puffs of air. Even with the rag, the sickly-sweet odor of decomposition was ripe.

It was a fitting end to Max's life in Europe. His thoughts were of Annaliese. How much he'd loved her. How brave she'd been. How ironic that, in the end, she had saved him from the Nazis, not the other way around. She'd sacrificed her life for him. Max had no choice going forward. He would fight until Hitler and his acolytes were wiped off the face of the earth.

PART III

CHICAGO

1940–1942

CHAPTER 38

June 1940
New York

M ax disembarked from the ship on a breezy summer day a week later and was quickly routed through Ellis Island. There was no trouble with his immigration status, although the customs official wanted to verify how long he'd lived in Holland. He dashed off a quick letter to Mutti letting her know he'd arrived safely and thanking her for her foresight and determination.

He barely recalled his trip across the Atlantic. Steeped in grief and misery over Annaliese, he didn't come out of his cabin often. He didn't remember eating a meal, although he must have. Images and memories of Annaliese had invaded his dreams and his waking hours. They all ended with the blossom of blood that dyed her blouse red. Or a dead baby. He woke screaming once or twice when, in nightmares, Wagner aimed at the baby and shot it. At the time Max didn't know or care what life had in store for him. He didn't expect his time in the US to be as heartbreaking as in Amsterdam. He wouldn't get involved with another woman. He'd already experienced the worst pain Hashem could deliver. If He existed at all.

~

Leo Bendheim, his uncle's father-in-law, was one of many waiting outside the main building, but Max knew who he was as soon as he saw him. An elegantly dressed elderly gentleman who looked to be in his sixties, he wore a suit and tie and carried a cane with a polished silver handle. His salt-and-pepper hair, which was still plentiful, was combed back from his face. No one else waiting for travelers looked as self-assured.

Max threaded his way through the crowd and approached the man. "Mr. Bendheim?"

Bendheim broke into a wide smile. "Exactly right," he said in a gravelly voice that sounded like he smoked a lot of cigarettes. "So good to meet you, Max." He shook Max's hand and clapped him on the back. "How was your journey, young man?"

"Uneventful," Max lied.

"Good. Welcome to America." He looked Max up and down. "Are your dear parents coming soon?"

Max swallowed and shook his head. "They chose to remain in Amsterdam."

Leo looked distraught, as if he knew what that meant. "I'm so sorry, Max."

Max nodded. "They didn't want to flee. Again. Papa thought he was too old. And he's ill. Cancer."

"Well." Leo was quiet for a moment. Then he spoke in a more cheerful tone. "Let's grab a cab. Dina can't wait to meet you. And please, call me Leo."

Max smiled. "Thank you so much, sir. I am so grateful for your hospitality. So are Mutti and Papa."

"Of course. You're family. I'm quite fond of your uncle Willie, you know. My daughter, Rosa, chose well."

"Thank you, sir."

"I'm only sorry they live in Chicago."

"I haven't seen them since my Bar Mitzvah. Almost ten years ago, now."

"I'll bet your cousins can't wait. By the way, your English is quite good." Leo switched to German. "But if you're more comfortable in German, that's fine."

"Danke. I'd prefer to speak English. I know my accent needs work."

~

Max stayed in New York almost a week before he took the train to Chicago. Leo and his wife, Dina, took him sightseeing. Max ascended to the top of the Empire State Building, the tallest building in the world; walked through Central Park; visited Wall Street; took in the dazzle of Times Square at night, ate in Chinatown, Katz's Delicatessen, Coney Island. He even went to Yankee Stadium with Leo's two sons for a baseball game. The Yankees won.

On the way back from the stadium he noticed all the small flimsy houses crowded together on one block after another. They looked like they'd been built with matchsticks and cardboard. Homes like this could never withstand German bombs. He wished he could shout out that the notion that Americans were an ocean away from a real war was an illusion. America should protect itself.

He was overwhelmed by the massive skyscrapers that created canyons between them; the people and automobiles clogging the streets; the whine and cacophony of traffic; even the Bronx Zoo. He was particularly impressed by the suspension bridge connecting Manhattan and Brooklyn. The department stores, Macy's and Gimbels, made Metz & Co. seem like an underprivileged stepchild. Max had never seen so many consumer products under one roof.

Leo explained that New York had become the world's largest manufacturing center, with forty thousand factories and more than a million factory workers.

"No wonder there are so many products in the stores."

While they were sightseeing, Leo and Dina told Max their story. Leo had come to the US from Alsace as a child but went back to Germany every few years to visit. On one visit he met and fell in love with Dina. Leo stayed in Alsace to marry her. They had three children.

Leo said, "We actually met you, Max, at one of your grandmother's summer reunions. You were a baby."

Max grinned. "I hope I didn't cry or drool."

Dina laughed. "You were perfect, of course."

After the Great War ended, Leo and Dina moved back to the US when his father, a successful furrier, died of a heart attack. Their two sons came with them, but Rosa married Willie and stayed in Berlin. A few years later Leo had the farsightedness to divest from the stock market before the crash.

"We were lucky," Leo said. "Business was poor, of course, but we survived." After staying in their spacious, beautifully furnished Upper West Side apartment, Max knew Leo was being modest.

"Then, as you know, the world changed. Willie, Rosa, and their family left Germany in 1935 and settled in Chicago." Leo tightened his lips. "I'm only sorry I didn't know your family needed visas earlier. As soon as your mother wrote, we began the process."

CHAPTER 39

June 1942, Two Years Later
Chicago

S ummers in Chicago were so hot Max could feel waves of heat radiating from the sidewalk. It was barely eight am and he was waiting for the bus. He sighed. The heat would make his shift at Goldsmith's Garage in Southeast Chicago a visit to the gates of hell. On days like this he regretted not buying a bicycle when he first arrived two years earlier. He missed the breeze that the wheels kicked up when they were in motion. At the time, though, he'd felt unsettled and wanted to wait until he knew what he'd be doing.

Two giant lethargic fans labored to cool the garage but barely stirred the hot air. Max and the two other mechanics usually took off their shirts before noon and worked shirtless in overalls. Despite the heat Max enjoyed the job. It was a welcome break from more cerebral activities. The satisfaction he got from analyzing, then fixing a machine or a part, giving it new life, was fulfilling. American cars weren't that different from German cars; Max had even worked on a Ford under Hartman's supervision in Germany. He figured he was using a part of his brain that otherwise would have lain dormant.

The two other men in the shop were the owner, Victor Goldsmith, and his adult son Ricky. They were members of the South Side Synagogue, the same German Jewish temple that Willie and Rosa attended. Max and Ricky had been introduced a week after Max arrived. They promptly started talking about cars. The following week they hired Max.

Now, two years later, Max started in on a Chevy with a suspicious carburetor. The owner, a doctor at Michael Reese Hospital, complained of black smoke spilling out of the exhaust pipe, backfires, and trouble starting the engine. The symptoms all pointed to a carburetor gone bad.

Max knew that the biggest problems with carburetors were that they got clogged up with dirt. When that happened, the correct mix of air and fuel became unstable and caused the problems the doctor described.

Max popped the hood and studied the carburetor. It was filthy. But he could take it apart and clean it. Then he looked more closely. "Looks like there might be a tiny crack."

Victor, a beefy guy, lumbered over. "Let's see." He peered at the part. "Yep. You could be right." He paused. "Too bad."

"Why?" Max asked.

Victor wiped the back of his hand across his nose and mouth and sighed. "The war's caused a run on Chevy parts. General Motors is building airplanes, diesel engines, trucks, and even Cadillac tanks, not to mention millions of shells. They're saying there won't be a single passenger car coming off the assembly plant at any GM factory until the war is over."

"Won't be cars from any American plant for that matter," Ricky added, limping over to take a look. He'd had polio as a child, and while he'd made an excellent recovery, he was left with a limp.

Max straightened up, crestfallen. "So what do I do with the good doctor's car?"

Victor flipped up his palms. "Improvise."

Ricky said, "We might be able to track down a Carter W-1 or a 569S W-1."

"Maybe a Stromberg BXV or a Zenith," Victor added. "But I doubt it."

"If manufacturing is gearing up for war, how do we find them?" Max asked.

Victor shook his head. "Hit or miss. Start with the manufacturers. Call other garages in the area."

"And if we 'miss'?"

"Like I said, improvise."

It was all Max could do not to roll his eyes.

After work Max took the bus up to Hyde Park and walked over to South Blackstone, a block or two away from the University of Chicago campus, Jackson Park, and the Fifty-Seventh Street Beach. He kept walking until he reached one of the mansions in Hyde Park. It had been built in the previous century by a rich businessman now deceased. The current owners, who apparently had come upon hard times, rented out the coach house behind the mansion. His uncle Willie and aunt Rosa had helped him find it when he arrived. Along with Leo Bendheim in New York, they were the ones who had written affidavits to the State Department years ago that made his legal entry possible. He owed it all to Mutti's foresight.

A stab of guilt sliced through him when he thought about Mutti and Papa. The visas and affidavits had been meant for them too. The three of them should have shown up at Ellis Island years ago. But after his father had been detained in Dachau, after they'd escaped to Amsterdam, and after his cancer materialized—everything changed.

Despite the fact that deportations of Jews were accelerating, they were still in their Amsterdam apartment, but the Nazi government had been stripping away their rights. His mother wrote him every month. It was Germany all over again, she said. Max begged them to come to America in every letter he wrote back. He would find them an apartment and help his father find a doctor here. Work too. Maybe he and Goldsmith could figure something out. It was a garage, after all. But his parents refused to consider it.

He couldn't think of his parents without also thinking of Annaliese. Sweet, innocent Annaliese. Who did nothing wrong except fall in love with him. And what had he done in return? Watched her die. Even after two years, he still mourned her death. And the baby's. He would never forgive himself—or the Nazis. They had been complicit, the Nazis and he. He was no better than they were when it came to the sanctity of human life.

Life had turned out to be a cheap commodity. Maybe that was why he didn't know what he wanted to do with it. He'd already experienced it, and he had failed. He wasn't sure a second chance was in the cards. He felt almost as if he were marking time these past two years, just trying to keep his head above water.

He opened his mailbox, expecting a letter from his mother. An envelope lay inside, but it wasn't from Holland. It was from Shanghai. Postmarked last month.

Renée.

Dear Max,

It has been some time since we have corresponded. I suppose that is the natural course of events when two people have not seen each other in seven years. We read with alarm how the Nazis invaded Holland along with Belgium and France. Of course, I thought about you and your parents. I ran across some refugees from Munich by way of Holland, and they said Shanghai is the end of the road for them. They have been displaced twice and cannot do it a third time. They did say that sympathetic Dutch families are hiding Jews in their basements and attics. I pray you have found a safe place.

We are still in Jessfield Park near the zoo, but now it seems we are on borrowed time. Ever since Pearl Harbor was bombed, the Japanese have become much more aggressive, and the rumor is that they will still order all the Jews to move to the ghetto in Hongkou, which is little more than a slum near downtown. It is only a one-mile square and is already desperately crowded. People live on top of each other. Imagine a family of six living in one room. There is no plumbing. No kitchen. Toilets are Benwayets which are spilled on the road every day. People cook outdoors on small stoves. And plenty of Chinese are already living there. Now ten thousand more people will be thrown into the area. However, I understand the Chinese are a compassionate people (compared to the Japanese) and will share what they have, although what they have is meager.

As you no doubt can imagine, we are very upset. Not at the lack of amenities or housing but the end of our freedom. It's ironic . . . the Baghdadi Jews bought up property in Hongkou for refugees who arrived over the years with nothing in their pockets. They financed soup kitchens, helped build a hospital and a school. But now, no one, even the rich Baghdadis (although some of them fled Shanghai), is exempt from the ghetto. We have no idea where we will be, how long we will be confined, or how we will live. The deadline to move is February 1943.

It seems as if the war has given us parallel lives. At least you still have your freedom. I should amend that to say I hope that's the case.

Nonetheless we are not sitting idle here. I think I mentioned in one of my letters the Kalash family. They are originally from Iraq but have lived here for decades. Their son, Tomas, and I are quite close. He is nothing like his father, who still imports opium. In fact, he feels strongly that his father is a criminal. He and I bonded when we realized we harbor the same hatred for the Japanese and their ruthless cruelty as you have toward the Nazis. There are others who feel the same way. We operate under the radar and make it a point to know who our friends are. And aren't. We have succeeded where others have failed. We will persist.

Along the way, Tomas and I fell in love. We became engaged a few months ago and plan to get married when the war ends, whenever that is. We plan to emigrate either to America or Palestine—there are pros and cons to each. But I wanted you to know. Max, you will always be my first love . . . the first boy who treated me with respect. I will never stop loving you for that. You made me feel beautiful and desirable when I thought I was neither. But the times have wrought their own reality, and I must meet the challenge. Tomas is a wonderful man; I think you would like him.

Who knows if or when we will ever meet again, Max. I hope we do, but life is so uncertain. Through it all, however, I will always be your

Renée

PS You can send mail to our Jessfield Park home; my parents will see that it is forwarded to us in Hongkou.

Max reread the last line of her letter. What did that mean? She had just told him she was going to marry another man. Was this her idea of a Dear John letter? If it was, it didn't sound like it. Then again, he clearly owed her one of his own. He'd never told her about Annaliese. Admittedly it was two years earlier. But something had prevented him from writing her. Was he afraid she'd judge him for wanting to marry a Gentile? Or was it something else? He folded her letter and slipped it into his pocket.

CHAPTER 40

August 1942
Chicago

Chicago's Blackhawk Restaurant on Wabash Avenue had a reputation for fine food and even finer entertainment. Big band and swing favorites from Glenn Miller's orchestra performed on the stage in the main room, and customers often danced between appetizers and entrées.

Max didn't plan on dancing, but he was there to celebrate. He and two of his pals had finished a summer semester of night school at the University of Chicago. Max was always amused that male friends in America were "pals," not "friends" or "colleagues." Everything in America was informal. Even relationships.

All three men had scrimped for a few weeks so they could afford to eat here. Max was an auto mechanic. Buddy—Arnold Gorham— was a hospital orderly, and Jimmy Esposito worked construction in the summer and as a security guard in winter. They'd met in an English literature class and became "pals" when they discovered that each of them aspired to something more.

Max arrived first and gazed around. Diners were packed elbow to elbow, and it wasn't yet seven o'clock. Beautiful murals separated by rich wood panels covered the walls of the six-hundred-seat dining room, and the ceiling boasted crystal chandeliers. Each table was set with white tablecloths and napkins, crystal glasses, and crested china. Men wore ties; women wore pearls. A cloud of cigarette smoke hovered near the ceiling. The noise, laughter, and clink of silverware on plates made it difficult to think.

In a place like this, it was hard to imagine a brutal war was under-way. The ability of Americans to compartmentalize was still jarring. So, too, was the contrast between American idealism and European realpolitik. Americans were dangerously optimistic. Always bragging that their culture, their heroes, even their ability to wage war was the "cat's meow."

A deep voice cut into his thoughts. "Well, Max, what do you think?"

Max wheeled around. Buddy. Tall and gangly with thick glasses and the remnants of teen acne on his cheeks. Tonight he was almost unrecognizable in a coat and tie.

"This place is"—Max hesitated—"swell." He spoke English with an accent, but he was working on it. He sometimes had trouble reaching for the right word. He still thought in German and occasion-ally Dutch. To make it worse, too many English words had similar meanings. Finding the precise word felt like trying to land a fish in an ocean of relentless waves.

"My mother said to enjoy it while we still can. We'll probably be drafted soon." Buddy grimaced. "You get anything in the mail?"

Max shook his head. "I don't think they've reached immigrants yet. But I don't think I'm going to wait."

"You're gonna enlist? Why? You're German. A good one, but, you know . . ."

"It's a long story. I'll tell you sometime." Max wasn't upset by Buddy's comment that he was a "good" German. Buddy didn't know Max was Jewish. Not that it mattered. The Japs had attacked Pearl Harbor eight months earlier. Nothing was the same. America was swept up in war fever.

Jimmy Esposito loved dramatic entrances, and tonight was no

exception. He sashayed into the dining room wearing a straw fedora tipped to the side, a pair of camel slacks, and a navy-blue blazer over a tie and shirt. His olive skin, straight black hair, and dark eyes always attracted sly glances from the ladies. Jimmy took it in stride. He'd elevated flirting to high art.

"Hey, guys. Did you see the hat-check girl?"

Max didn't notice women anymore. He shook his head.

"She's a real looker, that one," Jimmy said. "Right, Buddy?"

Buddy had a steady girl, Phyllis. They were "pinned," or as he explained, "engaged to be engaged." He shrugged.

Jimmy cast a reproachful glance their way. "How can you two not notice the best thing about being alive?" He shook his head too. Max laughed. "I'm telling you." Jimmy grinned. "You're missing out. Hold on. I'm going to check my hat and get her telephone number." He wheeled around and backtracked to the coat-check booth opposite the front door of the restaurant.

The maître d' approached just as Jimmy returned, slipping a scrap of paper into his breast pocket and patting the pocket. The maître d' led them to a table in the middle of the room. But the table next to them wasn't occupied, so their view of the stage was excellent. All three ordered a cocktail from a waiter who looked old enough to be Max's father. A Manhattan for Jimmy, a martini for Buddy, a daiquiri for Max. When the drinks came, they grinned at one another.

"We're high rolling tonight!" Jimmy took a long sip.

"Well, we probably should enjoy it while we can," Buddy repeated. He wasn't the most articulate person Max had ever known. "Especially you, Max."

Startled, Max looked over. Had Buddy read his mind?

"With that sugary drink," Buddy said.

Max relaxed.

"They just started rationing, and sugar is first on the list."

Max glanced at his stemmed cocktail glass, twirling it between his thumb and forefinger. "Somehow I have a feeling the Blackhawk will get all the sugar they need for their daiquiris."

"You betcha," Jimmy said. "So let's toast each other. We're a few months closer to graduation. Do you think we can squeeze in one more semester before we're drafted?"

"Steiner can't," Buddy said. "He says he's gonna enlist."

"Is that so?" Jimmy asked. "You came here two years ago, right? How come you didn't do it then?"

"It wasn't the right time," Max said. "If I did, I probably would have ended up in New Mexico. Or Utah. I want to fight in Europe. Now that we're 'officially' at war, I hope they'll let me." That was the truth. Well, part of it anyway.

"So, you wanna kill Nazis?" Jimmy said.

Max fell silent for a moment. He nodded.

"But you're from Germany, right? So are they."

"That doesn't make us 'pals.'" Max's expression must have been so intense that Buddy and Jimmy exchanged glances. Neither followed up.

"Well, I'm starving." Buddy picked up a menu. "Let's order."

After dinner they listened to the band that had been warming up while they ate. The singer, a pale imitation of Frank Sinatra, who Jimmy predicted would become the most popular singer in the country, probably the world, was passable. But the band's lively swing music was better than average. Jimmy excused himself and went up to a young woman sitting with an older couple who must have been her parents. When he asked her to dance, she looked at them for approval. Her mother smiled. Jimmy whisked her onto the dance floor, where they "cut a rug," as the Americans said. Yet another expression Max had to learn.

Buddy laughed. "Esposito's hopeless. Always the life of the party. I bet he ends up in show business. He'd make one hell of an entertainer."

Max smiled. "He would. And you want to be a doctor, right?"

Buddy nodded. "I hope the army makes me a medic. I hear if you already know what you want to do, you might get it if you enlist."

"I didn't know that."

"What about you? What do you want to do when Uncle Sam calls you?"

Max pondered it. "I haven't thought much about it."

CHAPTER 41

August 1942
Chicago

A light rain fell as Max climbed off the bus in Hyde Park that evening. The scent of fresh rain hitting the still warm sidewalk was comforting. He picked up his pace and trotted the four blocks to his apartment, still thinking about their conversation at the Blackhawk. He'd been honest when he told Buddy he didn't know what he wanted to do with his life. Since the age of twelve, his entire life, except for a brief time in Holland, had been entangled with the Nazis. Survival was the only goal. All he'd known was the immediate future. Sometimes that meant a few years, as it did in Holland; other times, a few months. Or days.

Here in America it was different. Young people—at least some—actually had the time and opportunity to plan a future unencumbered by external forces. In the States Max would have a chance to decide not only what he wanted to do in the army, but also what occupation or profession might be most suitable for him. It was a luxury he'd never explored. He turned it over, playing with the novel idea. Buddy knew he wanted to be a doctor. Jimmy was a people person and knew it. But Max? He knew something about automobiles, enough to work as a mechanic. Something about radio, broad-casting, and Nazi propaganda. Four languages, if you counted the rudimentary French he learned when he visited his Alsace relatives. What kind of future did that make?

~

After work the next day Max took the bus up to the Fifty-Seventh Street Beach. He couldn't wait to dip into Lake Michigan and cool off. He'd been to a few beaches in Chicago, but this was his favorite.

Situated just north of Jackson Park and directly across from the Museum of Science and Industry, which Max considered the best museum in the world, the beach curled around a concave stretch of land. Which meant bathers had a stunning view of Chicago's Loop across the water from several vantage points.

Max trotted across the rocky sand and scrambled onto concrete slabs at one end of the curve. He peeled off his shirt and dropped into the water. Its bracing shock slapped his skin, erasing his lethargy and fatigue. Lake Michigan was always freezing, much colder than the lakes of his childhood. But the sudden jolt helped him think about the carburetor from a new angle. He'd called around and discovered the chances of getting a new carburetor were slim. He might have to jerry-rig something. He swam away from the shore, then stood upright. The bottom of the lake felt smoother than the beach sand.

He noticed two young women giggling and splashing nearby, their hair hidden under knotted kerchiefs. They reminded Max of the "Rosie the Riveter" posters that were popping up all over Chicago. He wondered if they worked in a factory. A steel mill, perhaps. Or the Ford plant nearby. Would they know if an extra carburetor or two happened to be available?

Their chatter suddenly stopped. Max looked over. They'd noticed him and were checking him out. Despite the frigid water, his cheeks felt hot. He couldn't approach them. He ducked back down and swam away.

Back on the concrete slabs that edged the water, he swung himself up, grabbed his clothes, and headed back toward Hyde Park. But the late afternoon sun threw off such blazing rays that he squeezed his eyes shut. He turned to face the lake again.

When he'd first arrived in Chicago, he thought the sun set on the "wrong" side of Lake Michigan. There were no pastoral scenes of lake and water, the sun in a western sky tinging the clouds gold, the water violet. But that didn't matter. Compared to Lake Geneva and Lausanne, Lake Michigan was magnificent. It seemed as huge as an ocean. He couldn't see the opposite shore. It had its own tides. Before coming to Chicago, he thought of the city as a gray, dingy, industrial place. But parts of it, especially near the lake, were as beautiful and gracious as any European capital. Where else could he see a beach with skyscrapers close behind? And parks where people rode bikes, swam in icy water, and skimmed across the waves in boats? He smiled, turned back around, and hurried to his lodgings. He could imagine living here one day.

As he reached the mansion on South Blackstone, the owner's wife came outside to meet him. She was holding a yellow envelope. "Max, this telegram arrived at your uncle's about an hour ago. He brought it over. I've been waiting for you to get home." She handed it to Max.

Max took the envelope and tore it open. Inside was a yellow paper with "Western Union" at the top of the page. A paragraph of black type, all capitalized, followed. It was in German.

TO: Max Steiner, Chicago USA
FROM: Jacob Weber, Amsterdam, Netherlands

Jacob was still there! Alive! Max read the text.

Gestapo apprehended parents. STOP.
From Westerbork to the east. STOP.
Baruch Hashem. STOP.

CHAPTER 42

August 1942
Chicago

M ax never worked on another carburetor. The next morning he assembled all his immigration and travel papers, slid them into a knapsack, and rode the bus up to the Loop.

He stared out the bus window without seeing the streetscape. His parents were gone. It wasn't a surprise; they'd all known it was just a matter of time. His father was sick. Still, the fact it did happen had made him choke up. Max had compartmentalized his feelings so well that he'd convinced himself it wouldn't happen. Somehow they would be exempt. But he'd been wrong, and they weren't exempt. Once again his world was divided into Before and After. He blinked back tears. Perhaps it had always been After, a lonely, grim existence punctuated by snatches of happiness. The only salve to his heartbreak was that it clarified what he planned to do next.

The Federal Building, a Beaux Arts structure with stately columns, huge windows, and an eight-story gilt dome, occupied an entire block between Dearborn and Clark. It had been built for the US post office but also housed other offices, including an army recruiting branch on the first floor. Max arrived just after the office opened.

Inside, a middle-aged man in an army uniform was knotting his tie. He had a crew cut turning gray, no facial hair, and a patch with three triangular stripes on his jacket. When he saw Max he smiled in greeting.

"Well, good morning. You're up and around early. I'm Staff Sergeant Robert Dudley." He finished knotting his tie and adjusted it at the neck.

Max nodded. "I want to enlist."

"Is that so." It wasn't a question. Dudley went over to the coffee pot and lifted it up. The scent of coffee wafted over Max. "How about a cup of joe? Still have a little of the real stuff."

"Sure." It was a word he'd picked up along with "swell" for good, "joe" for coffee, and "chicken" for coward.

Dudley retrieved two cups and poured. "What's your name, son?"

"Maximillian Steiner. Max."

"Well, Max, take a seat over at that desk." Dudley pointed to a large desk with two chairs in front and brought the coffees over. "You take cream? I got some packets here." He went behind the desk, opened a drawer, and pulled out a few small packets.

Max settled in the chair with his knapsack on his lap. "No, thanks."

Dudley opened a packet and dropped its contents into his cup. The liquid turned from dark brown to a gray mud. "How old are you, Max?"

"Twenty-two next month."

"Very good." Dudley cocked his head. "Married?"

It took him a moment to answer. "No."

He paused. "I can tell by your accent you are not native-born."

"I was born in Germany. A town called Regensburg. Not far from Munich. I came here two years ago." Max eyed Dudley. "Legally." After he added the word, he realized he didn't need to.

"I see. Your family as well?"

Max clenched his fists so hard that his nails cut into his palms. "I was—am—an only child. I came alone. I heard yesterday my parents were taken from Holland to a concentration camp."

Dudley sipped his coffee and went quiet for a moment. Then: "So they're true . . . ?" It sounded to Max more like a declaration than a question. "The rumors about people disappearing all over Europe . . ."

"If you're talking about Jews, Communists, Poles, sometimes even Catholics, yes. They're true." He decided to spare Dudley the trouble of asking. "I am Jewish."

Dudley looked him in the eye as if he was trying to figure out if Max was truthful. Then he sighed. "I am sorry. I realize those are only words. You have my deepest sympathy."

Max nodded. "That's why I'm here today. I want to destroy the Nazis. And Hitler."

Dudley set his coffee down, reached into a drawer, and drew out a two-page form. "Let's get started." He scrawled on the form. "Did you bring your immigration papers?"

"Yes." Max slid them over.

Dudley scanned them. "You are not yet a citizen."

"I have a few more years. I hope to become one."

Dudley smiled. "You were lucky to get here."

Max bit his lip. "My mutti—mother made sure of it."

Dudley asked more questions, about his education—he seemed interested that Max spoke Dutch as well as German and English—his health, fitness, and what he was doing now.

When Max said he was a mechanic, Dudley perked up.

"Is that something you'd want to do in the army?"

Max thought about it. It was an option. He was skilled enough, he reckoned, and what he didn't know, he could learn. But learning or polishing his mechanical aptitude wasn't why he was here. He wanted to fight. He needed to fight. He wanted to see into the eyes of a Nazi up close. And then kill him. He shook his head. "No mechanic job."

Dudley didn't seem surprised. He asked more questions, taking notes when Max answered. Finally, he put down his pen and folded his hands.

"All right, son. I think I have all the information I need right now. My preliminary classification for you would be 1A. But that could change. You will need to take some tests and go through a physical exam. What I can tell you is that your timing is excellent. We are anticipating significant changes in recruitment numbers this fall. Because you're enlisting, you may have more say in your MOS—your military occupation specialty. By the end of the year, enlistees won't actually be entitled to any preference. Everyone, volunteer or not, will be considered a draftee."

"But I don't know what I want to do. All I know is I want to fight."

"Max, your language proficiency alone makes you a desirable candidate for a new intelligence program that just began. After basic, of course."

"What program is that?" Max asked.

Dudley didn't answer. "Tell you what. Come back here tomorrow. That's when we'll have staff give you a physical and a couple of other tests. After that, we'll see."

"I don't want to sit behind a desk, sir."

Dudley smiled. "I don't want you to either, Max." He rose. "And it's 'Sergeant.' Not 'sir.' See you tomorrow."

Max mulled over what he'd learned at the recruiting office. It was a huge step for any man to enlist. But the news about his parents was the trigger he needed. There had not been a time in his life after he turned twelve, with the exception of his time with Annaliese, that had not been woven through with fear or rage or misery. The deportation and certain death of his parents was his breaking point. No more waiting around. He was ready to attack, literally and figuratively.

During the two years he'd been in America—perhaps he should start using the words "US" or "the States" as the Americans did—

Max had been marking time. The first year he spent mourning Annaliese's death. He'd been full of self-loathing, assuming he was the cause of that death. The second year he started to build a life, but it wasn't a full-throated effort. The pain and self-hatred were less sharp, but they were still constant companions. Despite taking classes at the U of C at night, he was aware of being at loose ends, often wondering, "Why him?" Why had he survived?

Now he knew. Like a puzzle the pieces clicked into place. The time for ruminating and grief was over. He had a purpose. This was how he would even the score.

He wanted to tell someone about it, but there was no one to tell. He didn't know his uncle and aunt well enough. His parents were gone. So was Annaliese. He couldn't tell Jacob. Or Carl. Or even the other Musketeers. He didn't know if they were still alive.

The bus slowed and Max blinked. He was at his stop in Hyde Park. He climbed down the stairs and headed toward South Blackstone. There was perhaps one person who might understand. At least she would have if she'd stayed in Germany. He would write Renée that night.

CHAPTER 43

August 1942
Chicago

The next day Max arrived at the Federal Building by nine. The recruiting office was larger than it had appeared the day before. Behind the front room where Dudley had interviewed Max was a tiny hall that opened onto two additional rooms. A uniformed medic conducted a physical of Max in one; the second was a small office where Max filled out forms about his background, education, goals, and which military occupation specialties he found attractive. By the time he finished it was nearly five. Too late to go to work. Dudley told him to get a sandwich and come back in twenty minutes.

When Max returned, Dudley smiled and told him he had passed everything with flying colors. "I will be proud to call you a fellow soldier."

"Thank you, sir." Max let out a long breath. His life was about to dramatically change.

"I mentioned yesterday that your timing is good, remember?"

"I do."

"You'll have twenty-one days—three weeks—to get your affairs in order."

"What does that mean, 'get my affairs in order'?"

"It means you should wrap up any personal and business matters. You'll need to settle any current financial obligations, like taxes, loans, credit debt, mortgages. You might want to talk to a lawyer on a couple of issues——there is a Soldiers' and Sailors' Civil Relief Act." Dudley paused. "I'll give you a list of what's in it. For example, it allows you to arrange allotment checks for your dependents that will be deducted from your army paychecks. Life insurance too, and designating a power of attorney."

"As I said, I have no debts, just a job. A small savings account. No dependents. Or life insurance. I don't need three weeks."

Dudley smiled. "It's required whether you need it or not. By signing the forms," Dudley said, "you agreed to enter the United States Army. You will be formally inducted at Fort Sheridan, about twenty-five miles north of here. It's one of the army reception centers. You'll be there for a few days."

"And after that?"

"Hold your horses, son." Dudley grinned. "Consider it your final acceptance and orientation. There will be another physical, some aptitude tests, and more choices for your MOS. Of course, the army makes the final decision. There will be other new recruits, some enlistees, some draftees. You'll learn what the army expects of you and how to handle yourself. That's what I mean about good timing, by the way. We're speeding up the pace of recruiting. It used to be that potential recruits might wait a few months before getting their notice to report. Now, it's practically right away. After that you head to basic training."

"I see," Max said. "So what do I do with my last three weeks of civilian life?"

Dudley laughed. "You're not about to die, son. You're going into the army. Take your time. If I were you I'd figure out who is important to you. Spend some time with them. Have fun. Maybe draft a simple will and make them your beneficiaries."

"I told you. I have no money. No dependents. No close relatives. Give it to someone in need."

∽

Max spent a restless three weeks. He made a mental list of the tasks he needed to do before he went in. He went into Goldsmith's Garage for the last time and resigned. He made sure to thank Ricky and Victor for the opportunity to work there. He'd enjoyed every minute, he told them. He meant it.

He called Buddy and Jimmy to tell them he was going in. They met at a Loop tavern for beers a few nights later.

Max wrote a note to Leo Bendheim in New York, thanking him for his support and hospitality. He wrote that he hoped his service would be meaningful and promised to write.

He'd already replied to Renée with the news about his parents and his subsequent enlistment. He told her he'd send her the address to reach him and that he'd love to hear from her. He'd accrued enough credits in night school to enter college when the war was over. He was thinking he might even stay in America. He wished her well with Tomas and wondered whether to tell her about Annaliese. He chose not to.

Max spent the rest of his time buying essentials like underwear and socks and spent time with Willie and Rosa. He'd called to tell them about his parents the night he got the telegram. When he told them he'd enlisted, Rosa threw a dinner party and invited some of the folks he'd met at synagogue, including Victor and Ricky.

He made arrangements to give up the coach house and decided the few pieces of furniture he'd added weren't worth storing. He packed his clothes in a suitcase and took it to Rosa and Willie's for storage. Dudley had told him to travel light.

"No big suitcases or trunks. All you need is a small overnight bag with your razor, toothbrush, change of underwear, and extra hand-kerchiefs. The rest of your things will be sent home."

He put his overnight bag together. He was ready.

CHAPTER 44

September 1942
Fort Sheridan, Illinois

Max despised the symbols and rituals of patriotism. He'd seen how Goebbels and his henchmen had manipulated and fabricated patriotic activities to brainwash the German people. Even so, he couldn't help the tingle running down his skin when he was formally inducted into the army at Fort Sheridan the next morning. He and two dozen other young men stood in a group at one end of a large auditorium while a uniformed officer led them in the oath of enlistment.

"I, Maximillian Steiner, do solemnly swear that I will support and defend the Constitution of the United States against all enemies, foreign and domestic; that I will bear true faith and allegiance to the same; and that I will obey the orders of the President of the United States and the orders of the officers appointed over me, according to regulations and the Uniform Code of Military Justice. So help me God."

He glanced around after he finished. Some of the men were already in khaki uniforms or fatigues; others, like Max, were still in civilian clothes. Max wondered if they felt as energized as he did. He had just crossed over to a new world, one about which he knew practically nothing. Every day, every hour, every moment, from now on would be a direct consequence of his decision to join the army. In a way the slate of his life had been wiped clean overnight.

He lined up at a long table in the auditorium and was given a pile of clothes, a duffel bag and bedding, and a manual. He was assigned to barracks 42 and was told to report back to the auditorium at fifteen hundred hours for haircuts. When he asked where to find the barracks, a soldier told him to go outside and face the water tower. His barracks would be to the west.

He emerged into a sunny, crisp September afternoon, a fresh breeze cooling the sun-burned prairie. Since 1877 Fort Sheridan had occupied roughly six hundred acres taken from the villages of High-wood and Lake Forest. The focal point of the base was a giant half circle on the southern side of a parade ground that stretched over a thousand feet. In the center was a two-hundred-foot-high water tower flanked with dozens of two-story brick barracks on both sides. Officer quarters and post buildings, generally no more than two stories, filled in the rest of the semicircle. There was also a hospital, training grounds, and stables. To Max's delight, Lake Michigan was just a stone's throw away.

One of four recruiting centers in the country, Fort Sheridan also conducted basic training although there was no guarantee Max would be assigned here. In addition, the base had been designated as headquarters for prisoner of war camps in Illinois, Michigan, and Wisconsin. Now that American forces would soon be joining the British in North Africa, plans were underway to prepare, transport, and incarcerate captured German and Italian POWs back to America. POW camps in Europe were already crowded, and it was cheaper to feed and house prisoners in the US.

Max made his way to barracks 42. A neat two-story building with a sidewalk and a patch of grass in front, it looked more like an elon-gated Chicago bungalow than a military structure. Inside were two stories of no-frills dormitories. On the first floor he found a bare mattress on a cot and slung his duffel bag and clothes onto it.

Next to his bed was a young man with a crew cut and the

remnants of acne on his face. He couldn't have been more than eighteen, Max thought. He was lying on his back reading a Superman comic book. Max hadn't interacted much with younger Americans. He hadn't known any. To be honest, Max figured they didn't know how lucky they were to live in a country that wasn't threatened by invaders. The Japanese had tried to destroy the US military, but not with battalions of soldiers.

The young man watched Max as he made his bed. He closed the comic book, rolled it up, and propped himself on his elbow. "Hey, rookie," he said. "You just git here?"

The boy spoke with a broad Southern accent that included a twang, which made him hard to understand. "I took the train," Max replied. "I'm from Hyde Park on the South Side of Chicago."

The young man nodded. "I hail from the Ozarks."

Max knew little about that part of the US, but he must have read something about the area because corncob pipes, banjos, and bathtub moonshine came to mind. "Southern Missouri?"

"Yep," the boy said. "You git drafted?"

"I enlisted." Max extended his hand. "I'm Max. Max Steiner."

They shook. "Guy Brooks," the boy said. "So how come you got an accent?"

Max thought Guy's comment ironic, given the kid's rural drawl. "I was born in Germany. Been in Chicago two years."

"Well, sheee-it. You ain't one uh those Natcees we fightin', are you?"

"Not at all. My family fled Germany and escaped to Holland for a few years. Then I came here."

Guy scratched his chin and frowned, as if he was trying to put something together. He sat up. "That would make you a Jew, don't it?"

"That would be right." Max was suddenly on his guard.

Guy stared at him, then cocked his head. "Really?"

Max folded his arms. "I am."

"Well now, my granddaddy said all Jews got horns comin' out of their heads. But I don't see yours. Where's your horns, boy?"

Max's eyes widened. Was he really hearing this? From an American soldier? "Where are yours?" he replied.

Max knew antisemitism was on the rise in the US. Despite the promise of America, the country was no bastion of equality. Even Hitler supporters were allowed to voice their opinion. It was hard to ignore the weekly radio shows of Father Coughlin, who ranted that Jews controlled all the banks in the world and were spreading Communism far and wide. Which made Jews either greedy rich capitalists or impoverished political insurgents.

Why didn't anyone point out the hypocrisy? Jews couldn't be both rich and poor at the same time. Max recalled the posters that had appeared back in primary school showing Jews with huge noses and coins spilling out of their pockets. The truth was that most Jews Max knew were, like his parents, stripped of all their belongings, killed in concentration camps, or hiding in cramped attics. Only a lucky few managed to escape to America.

Max himself had been the butt of an antisemitic comment or two, and there were Gentiles here who would never invite him into their homes. But antisemitism was more subtle here; Americans generally didn't proclaim Jews inferior. Or, frankly, anything beyond just being Jewish. It was mostly a whisper here, a rumor there. A denial of an application to a country club. Or private school.

The German American Bund had operated in New York and Chicago from the late 1930s until 1939, when war was declared in Europe and its American leader was prosecuted for embezzling funds from the organization. At one point more than twenty thousand people had gathered to hear a Nazi try to persuade Americans to support them. It was gone now, thankfully, and most of its leaders were either in prison or had their American citizenship revoked.

The boy shrugged as if he realized Max was being sardonic. "Hey. You the first Jew I ever met. My daddy sez you caint trust a Jew."

An itch of irritation tickled Max's skin. Was this kid trying to pick a fight? Max was determined not to take the bait. "Well then, I guess you better watch yourself."

Guy frowned again and cocked his head. "How come they let you into the army?"

Max's irritation grew. He was starting to resent this kid's attitude. So what if it came from ignorance? Listening to Gentiles spew hatred for Jews was hard, no matter what the intent. He managed to restrain himself one more time. Then: "I enlisted. Remember?"

"Yeah, yeah. But how do we know yer fightin' for the right side?"

Max stiffened and squeezed his eyes shut. The kid was becoming unbearable. He wanted to belt the guy. Time to end the conversation. He sighed audibly. "Because maybe your daddy and granddaddy are wrong."

Guy kept staring at Max, but he didn't say anything.

Max bit his lip and turned his back on the kid. "Well, I'm going back to the reception center."

That afternoon in the reception room the number of men had doubled. They must have been swearing in recruits all day. He was directed to another building, where his hair was shaved and he underwent his third physical. This time they took blood and urine and gave him some shots. He spent the rest of the afternoon marching and standing with more than fifty other recruits in his company. A drill sergeant yelled at them to do better, and they repeated the same turns, starts, and stops so many times that Max wanted to scream. The day was capped by a lecture from the sergeant in charge of his platoon, which he learned was a group of sixteen to forty men, all from the same barracks.

"As you may have noticed," the sergeant began, "you are no longer in the civilian world. We like to say 'There's no privacy for the private.' You will eat and sleep, work and play, toilet and dress, right along with a whole bunch of other fellows who are doing the same thing. You are now a member of a team. Your squad, your platoon, your company. Those are your teams.

"You've already received your clothing and shoes. You've been given toiletries. Be sure to keep track of everything since from this point on you're responsible for maintaining your government issue. You pay for lost uniforms or boots."

More rules. Max wondered if he'd remember them all.

"During the next week you'll be taking aptitude and classification tests. You'll be interviewed again as well, after which army staff will weigh your skills against the military's needs and make an assignment for you when you finish basic. That will be where you go for advanced training. You are allowed to list your preferences but we make no promises you'll get them."

After dinner that night Max fell into his bunk, exhausted. He was about to drop off when he realized today had been his twenty-second birthday.

CHAPTER 45

October 1942
Fort Sheridan, Illinois

A week later Max was assigned to Fort Sheridan for basic training. He was pleased. Eventually he'd be able to visit his cousins on Sundays, go to the USO, even stop into a tavern in Highwood. The first day, though, a sergeant told him he'd have no free time for a while, he could not leave the post, and that the army owned his soul.

He wouldn't call it a routine, but the words of the sergeant proved true. As an only child, Max had lived not a solitary life, but one in which he was the sole child. He'd never shared a bedroom, a shower, a chest of drawers, or a locker. Now, a few days into basic training, he not only shared all those items and activities, but he had to adapt to new sounds, sights, and smells: naked bodies, men's sweat, body odor, an occasional whiff of aftershave. At night he had to deal with the rustles, mumbles, farts, coughs, and snoring of dozens of men in the same room.

The army's philosophy was to train a soldier to think less like an individual and more as part of a team, and it was reflected in every-

236 | LIBBY FISCHER HELLMANN

thing the recruits did. Not only did they eat, sleep, shower, and study together, but they spent hours every day together.

Max had been a track-and-field star as a teenager, but this was different. Army training didn't require skill as much as endurance. No one cared that Max could run a hundred-yard dash in twelve seconds. What they did care about was that recruits learn to march in perfect formation for hours, follow directions, handle their weapons properly, then do it all over again. The instructors commanding the soldiers were drill sergeants who insulted, picked on, and penalized anyone who made a mistake. And when a recruit made a mistake, the drill sergeant punished the entire group, not just the man who made the mistake.

Max learned that lesson the hard way. One particularly hot day in October he was marching in formation on the parade ground with his platoon. The previous night he had barely slept. He'd had a nightmare in which Annaliese was calling for him, but he couldn't reach her. When his five am wake-up arrived, he was still lingering in the dream. Later that day he turned right when he should have turned left and promptly marched into an adjacent row of soldiers. The drill sergeant, one of the harshest, yanked him out of line.

"Why the fuck were you thinking, soldier?"

Max kept his mouth shut.

"Don't have anything to say?"

"No, Drill Sergeant."

"No, Drill Sergeant? That's all you can muster? You got a hangover or something? That's no excuse for losing focus."

"Yes, sir."

"I should put a boot up your ass, trooper."

"I'm sorry, Sergeant." He idly wondered if that's where the military expression "boot camp" came from, then rebuked himself for losing concentration. Again.

"Well, let's see if six extra hours of marching for the entire platoon and sixteen hours of KP for you helps that hangover go away."

"Yes, sir." His fellow recruits made sure Max never missed another step.

Everything was regimented and highly disciplined. At the mess hall, recruits lined up and stood at parade rest until a spot opened up. Their beds had to be made according to military standards. They had to clean their barracks every morning until floors were buffed and latrines sparkled. Every man had to shave daily and make sure his boots were shined. Everything and everyone was part of a team. Max Steiner, the individual, disappeared. In his place was Soldier 35897A of Company X, Platoon Y, Squad Z.

The first week also saw recruits perform strenuous exercises and physical fitness training. There were constant calisthenics that included push-ups, pull-ups, jumping jacks, bends and reaches, sit-ups, squats, lunges, and more. Drill sergeants ordered them to run long distances, participate in obstacle courses, and go on long hikes. The thrust was to concentrate on military courtesy, physical fitness, discipline, first aid, sanitation, and map reading.

At the end of three weeks, Max had never been in better physical shape.

CHAPTER 46

As promised, Max took aptitude tests and was asked to choose and rank three different military occupational specialties, or MOS, for his advanced training. There was no guarantee the army would slot him where he'd chosen, but they encouraged him to pick something he was already familiar with; he'd have an easier time when he got to advanced training.

Max already knew he didn't want to be a mechanic. He wanted to be in combat, but not necessarily infantry. He recalled that Dudley, the Chicago recruiting officer, had mentioned a new intelligence program for which Dudley said Max would be well suited. He remembered how Jacob had labeled the work he'd done in Amsterdam "intelligence." To Max it was simply monitoring the news from Germany. Still, he'd been fascinated by the nuggets he reported and sometimes added his analysis of how the reported information or propaganda might help or hinder Hitler's plans to conquer Europe.

The manual he'd received when entering basic included a list of advanced training subjects. He scanned the possibilities described in

"Intelligence." Most were broadly described and included few details. The position of intelligence NCO, for example, was summarized as handling counterintelligence activities and the safeguarding of military information, but nothing more. Another position, an intercept operator-G, helped collect, evaluate, interpret, and distribute enemy intelligence. Still another job identified and intercepted German military radio signals by means of a radio receiver. Max remembered offering to set up a two-way radio operation for Jacob. That could be a possibility.

There was also the position of a scout, who "obtains information concerning strength, disposition, and probable intentions of enemy forces, route conditions, locations for bivouac, and terrain features in order to facilitate tactical moves."

Was the new program Dudley mentioned one of those? Or perhaps it wasn't mentioned at all.

CHAPTER 47

October–November 1942
Fort Sheridan, Illinois

A week into basic everyone in the platoon was issued a card with specific weapons printed on it. The weapons were kept in the armory, and once each recruit picked up one of the weapons on his card, they were taught how to load, unload, and clean it.

Most of the soldiers practiced stripping and reassembling their rifles whenever they could, including Max. They weren't allowed to keep them in the barracks, so they had to take them out to the field. Max's father had brought home his service revolver, a Luger semiautomatic pistol, that he used during the Great War. He'd taught Max how to shoot it. But Max had no experience with rifles, machine guns, shoulder-launched bazookas, or other ordnances, and he was determined to learn. He wanted to develop expertise in a variety of field weapons.

After the US economy pivoted to wartime status, the production of guns and other equipment for soldiers was a priority, and Fort Sheridan's prominence guaranteed they were sent the latest and best of everything. The men were able to practice with several rifles, even a model that wouldn't be officially released until December. Because weapons were constantly evolving, soldiers needed to adapt to whatever weapons became standard issue.

One afternoon before dinner, Max and two other men were timing each other to see who could fieldstrip and reassemble their rifle the fastest. Happily, the kid from the Ozarks had shipped out a few days after Max arrived, and he'd found some friendlier men to knock around with. Harry, a farm boy from Wisconsin who'd been shooting a long gun since he was twelve, was in the lead.

Harry was working with the Remington M1903 Springfield, officially the United States rifle. The M1903 was a nine-pound, five-round magazine-fed, bolt-action repeating rifle. The first time Max used it, the kick under his armpit almost knocked him off-balance. It was reliable and accurate, but both the front and rear sights weren't the best. A later model improved the rear sight. A sniper version of the rifle added a telescopic sight, but it was limited in long-range targeting and its scopes fogged up in heat or humidity.

Max had the faster-firing semiautomatic eight-round M1 Garand, also about nine pounds, which was fast replacing the M1903. It was the army's first standard-issue semiautomatic military rifle and gave the US an edge in firepower.

Danny, from Fort Wayne, Indiana, grabbed the stopwatch. "On your mark . . . get set . . . go!" He pressed start on the timer.

Max raced to strip down the M1 Garand. First he pulled the op-rod handle fully back and inspected the chamber. No ammo inside. He laid the rifle on its side and made sure the bolt was closed and the safety on. He pulled the trigger guard toward the end of the butt-stock, and lifted it out, and then the op-rod and spring, the gas cylinder, and front hand guard. He was two minutes into the drill, still working, when Danny yelled, "Time's up! Harry wins."

Max looked up. Harry had been working with the M1903 and was grinning from ear to ear.

"Wait a damn minute," Max grumbled. "Unfair! The M1903 is less complicated than the M1. No gas cylinder for starters. All you have to do is get the bolt out!"

"Wrong!" Harry jumped in. "I removed the striker, moved the firing pin, and relieved the tension."

"Hey, Steiner. Complaining won't keep you alive in combat," Danny said.

Max let out a breath, then said, "Okay. Let's do it again! But let's switch rifles. I want to see Farm Boy deal with the Garand." He smiled when he said it so Harry would know he wasn't too sore.

"You game?" Danny asked Harry.

"Sure as shit am."

They switched rifles and repeated the drill. This time Max won. Harry didn't even get as far as Max had.

"Everybody happy now?" Danny asked.

Max grinned and extended his hand to Harry. "You know I was just giving you shit." His language had coarsened since he joined up, but he didn't mind. It made him feel more—well—American.

Harry smiled back, and they shook. "You're right. That Garand might be more accurate with less kick than the M1903, but stripping it down is a Charlie Foxtrot."

Danny cut in. "Then you guys are gonna be real happy when the carbines arrive."

Max was looking forward to the M1 carbine. The army had commissioned it a few months before Max enlisted. Formally called the US Carbine, Caliber .30 M1, it was a lighter—by four pounds—and shorter long gun. Its superior accuracy and penetration over pistols and submachine guns made it attractive. However, it was not intended for front-line infantry. It was designed for officers, NCOs, and specialists who needed to carry radios or other gear as well. Tank crews, drivers, artillery crews, mortar crews, and other non-infantry soldiers already had requested it. "When will we get some to practice on?"

"I hear they'll be here in another week," Dan said.

"Roger that," Max said.

There were other weapons for Max's platoon to learn. Due to the high demand for pistols, the army reissued the M1917 Colt and Smith and Wesson .45 revolvers. In time revolvers were replaced by an automatic pistol. The army's new M3 submachine gun, known as the grease gun, would enter service in December. Produced by General Motors, the M3 was an automatic-only, blowback-operated weapon. Danny thought they'd get some in November to try out. They practiced with grenades, or pineapples, as GIs called them, as well as shoulder-launched bazookas. They also had to qualify with a rifle: Marksman, Sharpshooter, or Expert. Max missed Expert, but he was more than happy with Sharpshooter status.

As they became more comfortable with the guns, the content of their classes intensified. Their drill sergeant started talking about methods of attack. They were taught how to belly-crawl over the dirt with their rifles and other gear. They learned to rappel up and down walls and rock faces with rope rigging while carrying rifles and backpacks. How to advance with a team on the battlefield. How to cope with gas without a gas mask. The best techniques for hand-to-hand combat. How to pitch tents. How to attack an enemy from the front, the rear, and the side. By the end of the eight weeks, the drill sergeant pronounced them ready.

The month of November saw the end of basic training and graduation day. Max was now a private first class in the United States Army. He invited Willie and Rosa to his graduation ceremony, and they celebrated with a meal at a Highwood restaurant. The soldiers he trained with were already shipping out, and new recruits filled the barracks. But Max didn't receive his orders. He and one other guy from his platoon hung around Fort Sheridan, working out and practicing with the M1 carbines that arrived exactly when Danny said they would, although neither Danny or Harry was still around to experiment with them. Both had been sent to North Africa to help the British defeat the "Desert Fox," Field Marshal Erwin Rommel.

Thanksgiving came and went. Max took a week of leave and spent it with his relatives. When he returned to base in December, his orders had come in.

PART IV

CAMP RITCHIE, MARYLAND

1943

CHAPTER 48

December 1942
Camp Ritchie, Maryland

J ust south of the Pennsylvania and Maryland state line was an almost 650-acre tract that looked more like a summer resort than a military base. It was perched in a high valley with a view of Catoctin Mountain, part of the Blue Ridge and Appalachian mountain chain. The land, dubbed Pen-Mar Park, became a destination for well-to-do Baltimore and Washington, DC, dwellers hoping to escape the hot, muggy cities in the 1800s.

An industrialist built two lakes and founded the Buena Vista Ice Company. A railroad spur was added. Homes and mansions sprang up. Presidents visited, an amusement park was built, and summer tourists flocked to the area.

The stock market crash ended Pen-Mar Park. The Maryland National Guard, assisted by the Army Corps of Engineers, took over the land and built a summer training camp on the shores of the lakes. It was named for then governor Albert Cabell Ritchie. In 1942, the US Army acquired it and tasked Colonel Charles Banfield with the creation and administration of the first US Army intelligence program.

Max's interview with General Banfield continued.

"So, I assume you'd like to know about your classes." Banfield toked on his cigar but didn't wait for Max to reply. "We have built and assembled the best of the best in field intelligence. In short, we have reproduced, as accurately as we can, everything a soldier might confront in the field, whether Europe, North Africa, or the Pacific." He smiled. "In your case, for example, we have built a German 'village' that includes homes, businesses. Even a bell tower."

He leaned back. "Imagine, if you will, a German 'sniper' shooting down at you. We'll teach you how to defend yourself and neutralize the sniper. We also have built enemy nests deep in our forests that you will discover and defuse. We have Axis uniforms, weaponry, and vehicles, even bicycles that you'll get to know better than American bikes. You'll learn to read aerial maps, use Morse code, and, of course, your most important task: how to interrogate a prisoner."

Max tried to suppress his wonder. "How did you pull this together so fast? As I understand it, your program only started last June."

Banfield smiled. "The Brits have two years on us. They're helping. Your courses will be intense. Your training will be equivalent to an undergraduate college degree. In a fraction of the time."

Max smiled.

"What's so funny?" Banfield asked.

"I started to teach myself Morse code in Holland."

"Then you'll have a head start." Banfield waved his cigar. "Lieutenant Townsend will take you on a tour and show you your barracks. The rest of your schoolmates will show up over the next few days. Classes begin Monday. Now. For your first assignment. You're on KP until then."

Max's mouth opened. Mess duty? After working KP sixteen hours a day in basic? Wasn't he past that? He was puzzled but knew enough not to say anything.

Banfield watched his reaction. Max wondered what he saw. Then: "Gotta keep you men humble."

"Yes, sir."

He laughed more to himself than Max. "You have family here, soldier?"

"Cousins. In Chicago."

"What about your parents?"

Max shook his head. "Sobibor. A few months ago."

"I'm sorry, lad."

Max nodded.

Banfield was quiet for a moment. "You're dismissed. Now, get the hell out of here."

CHAPTER 49

December 1942
Camp Ritchie, Maryland

After the interview, Townsend took Max on a tour. The sun was
warming the outside. Max was wearing his army boots, but
frozen ridges of dirt on the ground and melting snow meant there
would be plenty of mud on those boots tonight.

"What are you building?" Max asked.

"Whatever we need. We're always in some phase of construction.
We have nearly a hundred buildings now."

Max whistled. "A hundred in six months?"

"Some were already here. But it'll probably be over a hundred
fifty by next year."

Max tried to step gingerly around one site, but the mud was
already relentless.

"You can't avoid it," Townsend said. "Don't even try." He unbut-
toned his jacket. "The guard had about three thousand soldiers in
tents when they were here. We're going to need space for six thousand." He pointed in different directions. "We already have a
finance office, a theater, a signal office building, and a training
supply building. Our gym is almost finished, and we broke ground

on a hospital. Should be operational"—he grinned at his own pun —"next year."

Max rubbed the back of his neck. "This is unbelievable. Real egg in your beer!"

Townsend laughed at Max's awkward use of military slang.

"Tell me something, Lieutenant," Max said.

"It's Bob, for Pete's sake," he joked.

"Most officers wouldn't meet with a new recruit, much less invite me into the head honcho's office. Why me? Why here?"

Bob smiled. "Because we're a 'different kind of animal.' We want to get to know our students. It will tell us whether you're suitable for the work we have in mind."

"Well," Max said, "am I?"

Bob laughed. "What do you think, Private?"

Max grinned. "I figure that's a 'yes.'"

They ambled over to a set of buildings close together. "Here's the village," Townsend said. "They told you about that, right? It's better than a Hollywood set."

Max looked around. It did look like a movie set. He focused on a "house" with a chimney. Next to it was another two-story house that was missing its front. Inside was a room, table, and chairs that could be used for interrogation. The first floor was constructed so that soldiers could "capture" whoever might be inside. Near the house were other buildings and some shops.

"You'll be spending a lot of time here," Townsend said.

They continued around the campus. Max saw tanks, both American and German, foxholes and trenches, a rifle range, and a theater. Townsend said the "sets" were used, in part, for fake Nazi rallies. "You'll practice interrogation techniques in tents that are over there." He pointed. "Classrooms are over here. When you're outside, you'll be practicing warfare. Inside you'll be studying." They walked past neat cottages with pitched roofs and windows in front that reminded Max of Fort Sheridan.

Finally, they reached the barracks. Like Fort Sheridan, the barracks at Camp Ritchie were made from wood. Dozens stretched behind the classroom buildings, across from which was a grassy field that turned out to be the parade ground.

"I'll take you to your quarters," Townsend said.

"It can wait. I've got a question for you."

"Shoot."

"Townsend isn't a Jewish name. How'd that happen? Are you Jewish on your mother's side?"

Townsend laughed. "When I graduated, I was supposed to go back to Europe. They took us to Hagerstown and got me expedited citizenship papers. But they strongly encouraged us to change our names. For two obvious reasons."

"Two?"

"Number one, if we weren't citizens, the Nazis would arrest us as traitors. And number two, they don't want any POWs or others to know we're Jewish."

Max's eyebrows arched. "I never thought of that."

"My real name is Avi Bernstein."

"No kidding?"

"Emes. But I rather like Bob Townsend."

Max smiled. "Why did they change their minds about sending you to Europe?"

"Since the program is only six months old, they've asked a few soldiers to stay to either teach or help run the camp. It happens that I'm married and my wife is pregnant. So . . ." He threw Max a look. "Banfield made me his administrative assistant."

"You're not sorry?"

"At first I was. I wanted to kill Nazis, you know?"

Max nodded eagerly.

"But now?" Townsend smiled. "We have younger, stronger men like you who'll do a better job than me." He paused. "And Banfield? Well, he fills the air with lots of bluster. But his heart's in the right place."

∾

During the next few days, men—and not so young men—officers and noncoms, converged on Camp Ritchie. Max was working KP during mess, and the conversations, chatter, and laughs seemed to get louder at every meal. English was the predominant language, followed by German. To his surprise, though, he also heard snippets of French, Italian, Polish, a language he thought was Russian, some Japanese, and even Dutch. Camp Ritchie seemed to recruit soldiers whose families came from every country touched by this war.

His barracks, too, resembled the Olympic games in miniature. About the size of a platoon, like Fort Sheridan, it housed thirty-five or so soldiers. They all spoke English, but there were at least ten German immigrants like Max, two Italians, and the rest ran the gamut of languages he'd heard in the mess hall. Some were university educated while others never finished high school. Which surprised Max until he realized some men were so eager to enlist that they lied about their age and got away with it. One or two weren't sure why they'd been assigned to Camp Ritchie until they were told it was due to their fluency in the language they spoke at home.

His bunkmate on one side was one of those. A second-generation Italian, Lorenzo, or Larry Rossi, from the Bronx, left high school before he graduated. He'd always had trouble with authority and was arrested once or twice, he said, for underage drinking, and once for stealing a car.

"My parents were sure I was headed for jail or the mob, so they made me enlist." Larry laughed. "I hated 'em for it but, you know, now I think they mighta' had the right idea."

"Why is that?" Max asked.

"I dunno," Larry said. "The more I hear about dese a-holes Mussolini and Hitler, the more I wanna see 'em rot in hell."

"You and me both, buddy," Max said. Larry, voluble and cheerful, reminded him of Jimmy Esposito, his pal from Chicago. Max wondered if Jimmy and Buddy had been drafted yet. When he made it back after the war, he'd make sure to look them up.

His bunkmate on the other side was an arrogant-sounding soldier from Virginia who spoke German with a southern American accent, if that was possible. Conrad Spitzer was American-born, the son of German Jewish immigrants from Berlin. Spitzer was drafted at the end of his freshman year at UVA. A scrawny blond fellow, he looked doubtful when Max told him he'd studied at the University of Chicago at night.

"Night school? Isn't that for people who aren't smart enough for day classes?"

Max took an immediate dislike to the man. "Not that I've noticed," he replied coolly. "It's for people who need to work during the day."

Spitzer stared at Max, then turned away as if he'd decided Max wasn't worthy of his time. The familiar bitterness bubbled up from Max's gut, but he suppressed it. Spitzer wasn't worth it.

CHAPTER 50

January 1943
Camp Ritchie, Maryland

Training began Monday morning after breakfast. There were about 250 soldiers total, not including a few men and even a woman or two who came to Camp Ritchie for advanced training in a specific subject. His first class was designed for German soldiers only, so there were only about thirty-five students in a large room.

Colonel George Davis, the director of training, and Major Theodore Gresham, who had created the program, tag-teamed each other in an introductory session. Davis said, "There's good news and bad news, men." He cleared his throat. "Right now we concentrate on several areas of study, which Major Gresham will explain. The bad news is there could be a brand-spanking-new class at any moment. As soon as we discover a need, we provide a solution. And because we report only to the War Department in Washington, we don't struggle with red tape. Our primary mission is to prepare you for war."

Davis went on to explain the first course would be German Army Organization. "You'll study the uniforms, medals, and other decorations on your enemy's clothing until you know what rank and the branch of the Wehrmacht they are and can call them out in your sleep. Then you'll examine German vehicles and weapons. That will help you assess a specific enemy unit's capability for battle when you're in the field."

They would also learn what's called the Order of Battle, which was the actual real-time structure of the German Army divisions including names of commanding officers. Davis emphasized that these were always changing, but that knowing whom they were fighting would give them an edge in interrogations.

Gresham took over. "You'll be required to learn Morse code and you'll be tested on sending, receiving, and transcribing before you graduate." He paused. "You'll study Terrain and Aerial Intelligence. You'll draw your own topographical map, and you'll interpret features of aerial photos. You'll study signal intelligence and counterintelligence and close hand-to-hand combat. German-speaking soldiers are also expected to study and read German documents."

They would also see live demonstrations showing the wrong and the right way to perform what they learned. In some cases the demonstrators would be fellow soldiers; in others, they could be professional actors. These demos would be held in the theater, the pseudo village, the parade ground, or the cut-out house.

"All these skills will come together at the end of your training, when you'll participate in an exercise outside camp. You may be required to interrogate enemy soldiers. You may be required to read maps, regardless of language, and make your way to a predetermined spot with only a compass for orientation. You will also be tested on fifty different uniform elements and weaponry scattered around the fields and meadows.

"Colonel Angus Rogers, our British ally who has pioneered a lot of these classes, will follow your progress every step of the way. He'll also step in as needed to teach. Let's give him a hand now."

The soldiers clapped for a tall, neat man in uniform, who stood up in the first row and gave the men a nod.

Gresham concluded the session. "He'll answer all your questions and set you straight." He looked at his watch. "You're free until lunch.

Then meet back here at thirteen hundred hours for your first class. By the way, most of your classes will be conducted in German."

Max was surprised but happy.

~

Max was eager to start the German Army Organization class. He figured he had a head start. His father had brought home his uniform from the Great War along with his Luger, and Max had asked his father lots of questions about his decals and patches. Plus, he'd seen plenty of Wehrmacht soldiers and SS men when he was still in Germany.

But he hadn't realized all the changes in German war uniforms over the months and years. Or the variations, depending on a soldier's assignment. The instructor, a man who looked about ten years older than Max and said to call him Kent, took them through some of the changes. The folks at Camp Ritchie had managed to get a couple of German uniforms from the North Africa campaign—Max didn't dare ask how—and one was being modeled at the front of the room.

"Those of you from Germany probably recognize the field-gray tunic, jackboots, and color patches on the tunic's collar that indicate a soldier's branch. As you can see, shoulder patches and colors display the soldier's regiment. White represents infantry." Kent pointed to the patches. "Since the war began, however, tunics have changed colors. Leather suspenders were added, and company numbers were removed from shoulder patches. But now suspenders are cloth, not leather. And helmet decals have been removed."

Astonished at the details the Americans had sussed out about German uniforms, Max took copious notes.

Kent looked out at the class. "Now, why am I telling you all this? Anyone want to take a guess?"

One soldier raised his hand. "So that we'll know who we're dealing with, even if the uniforms aren't identical?"

"Not a bad guess," Kent said. "Anyone else?"

Another soldier raised his hand. "So that if we ever have to impersonate a Krauthead, we'll know we have options?"

"Good answer, soldier. That's part of it." He waited.

Max had no idea, but he straightened up, keen to hear Kent's response.

Kent went on. "If you've been keeping up, you know that the North Africa campaign has been a seesaw between the Krauts and us. The Germans have been fighting there over three years, but the Allies, namely us Yanks, are fresh out of basic training. We've got better tanks, better rifles, better everything. Most of all, we have motivation and energy.

"Anecdotally, we hear the Germans are suffering from battle fatigue, and their uniforms indicate it. Supplies are tightening up and the materials they're using are cheaper. Some soldiers are wearing years-old tunics, helmets, and decals. Of course, it's not just their uniforms—it's their tanks and their weapons as well. Panzers are notorious for breaking down. In short, the Wehrmacht is exhausted. Even Rommel. That's great news for us. So be aware of that when you see Germans, even officers, whose uniforms aren't—'uniform.'" Kent grinned. "That's why."

He paused. "Speaking of officers, let's move on to their uniforms." He went through the Wehrmacht officer uniform, the black-and-gray uniform of the SS, and the black panzer uniform of German tank operators. Kent said they should be aware of the differences between Wehrmacht, Waffen-SS, and even local policemen's uniforms, all of whom wore black at one point or another.

"One other question for you." Kent held up an index finger. "It's not hard to see the difference between Wehrmacht and Waffen-SS men if they're wearing their tunics, correct? You look at the insignia on their collars. But what if their jackets are off? How would you tell?"

No one raised a hand.

Kent proceeded to tell them about the Waffen-SS blood group tattoo. "Most Waffen-SS have a tiny tattoo under their armpit with their blood type in case they are wounded and need a transfusion."

Max felt his eyes widen. That didn't show much confidence in their ability to fight.

"Of course, when you're in the middle of a skirmish and bullets are flying, don't look. Just shoot. Especially since the Waffen-SS are ruthless and fight to the death. In fact, let's all promise that you'll help them do just that." Kent smiled and looked up at the clock. "Okay, men. That's an eighty-six for now. Let's take a break."

CHAPTER 51

January 1943
Camp Ritchie, Maryland

After the break Kent plowed through the German Heer, the land-based army ranks. Max was familiar with German officer positions, which were roughly similar to the US Army's. Soldat—soldier. Korporal—corporal. Leutnant—lieutenant. Hauptmann—captain. Up to major, Oberst, and general.

However, Max grew frustrated when Kent said, "Keep in mind that when you figure in all the specialties, backgrounds, and importance to the war effort, there are over a hundred different Wehrmacht designations with unique insignias, decals, and colors, whether the soldier is a noncom or an officer. Even the Germans don't know all of them. And that doesn't include the Waffen-SS."

Max had been chatting with a German immigrant soldier from Alsace, Friedrich Hahn, who shared Max's barracks. Like Max, Freddy, as everyone called him, was blond with blue eyes. They were the same height as well. Freddy sometimes wore glasses, but Max thought he could have passed as an Aryan.

Max's mother's family came from Alsace, so when they first met, they played "Jewish geography" and stopped only when they discovered they knew one or two people in common. Those shared contacts endeared them to each other, and they became friends. Freddy told Max he'd wanted to join the Army Air Corps and fly planes. "But, you see, I flunked the physical." He pointed to his glasses.

"Tough break," Max said. "But maybe you'll find this will be more satisfying."

With their blond hair and light eyes, they looked so similar that they were often referred to as Frick and Frack, the Swiss ice-skating duo who immigrated to the US in 1937.

Now Freddy leaned over and whispered, "It's not easy, cramming all this knowledge into our tiny brains in eight weeks."

Max chuckled. "Do you think we have to learn every verdammt specialty?"

Freddy shrugged. "I have no idea."

Conrad Spitzer, who was sitting a row in front, turned around. "Den Mund halten." Shut up.

That evening Max and Freddy pored over the class materials, including mimeographed sketches, charts, and photos, which they'd spread out on Max's bunk.

Max said, "I think the Germans we'll be interrogating will probably come from the lower ranks. Infantry. Don't you?" He didn't wait for Freddy to answer. "Which means we'll need to learn as much as we can about those classifications."

"I'm not so sure," Freddy said. " I heard Kent say there could be officers too. He said we'll have some intel on an officer before we question him. It may be skimpy, but we won't be going in totally blind."

"Good to know. You were clearly listening more carefully than I. Did you hear him say something about a special designation for any German who's spent six years in the Heer?"

Freddy nodded. "Ja, but, Max, what sort of man spends six years in the army? He must have joined back in '37. Think about it. What were you doing then?"

In 1937 Max had been in Holland rescuing Annaliese from prostitution. It seemed like another lifetime. As if it had happened to a different Max. A Max who believed he could right any wrong, destroy any evil, and in so doing, change the course of history. Looking back, he wondered whether those efforts had begun because of the emptiness and shame he felt at being run out of Germany. If there was even a grain of truth to that, the opportunity he now had as a Ritchie Boy was better than a second chance. It could be his salvation.

"I was in Holland," Max said. "What about you?" Max asked.

"We'd just arrived in America. Philadelphia. My grandparents opened a bakery. We lived in an apartment above it. My father was a beer distributor."

Max noticed that Conrad Spitzer was pretending to read a novel on his bunk but hadn't turned a page in a while. Spitzer was eavesdropping. When Freddy said the words "beer distributor," Spitzer scowled and mumbled something that sounded like "Kartoffel," a derogatory term for Germans that meant "potato." He rolled to the other side of his bunk. Max was tired of Spitzer's crap. He wanted to punch him in the face.

The next morning the class met at the parade grounds to study German vehicles and weapons. The parade grounds normally housed a US tank, a seventy-five-millimeter Howitzer Motor Carriage M8. Overnight, though, an array of German weapons, both real and mocked-up, had appeared. A mock-up of a panzer, shoulder-fired missiles, a jeep, two motorcycles from a German platoon, and a bicycle that was used in smaller German units flanked the tanks.

Demonstration experts showed the men how a German panzer division would advance and what weapons the soldiers would carry. Others demonstrated the motorcycle platoon; still others, the armaments of a reconnaissance unit on bicycles. The idea was that the Ritchie men should brainstorm and visualize enemy units in all types of war situations. Through this process, it was hoped—in the field— they would better analyze the firepower, characteristics, and capabilities of German units and pass that information to Allied infantry commanders.

That afternoon introduced the class on Morse code, which Max had been looking forward to. For Max it felt like learning a new language. The dot-dash sequence for each letter of the alphabet came back to him, and he made it a point to slip into the code room after classes to practice. The folks at Camp Ritchie had the new X-35 radio and transmitter. It was smaller, portable, and much lighter than the bulky suitcases. Max practiced on it as much as he could.

His most difficult class was the German Order of Battle, or OB, which began the next day. Defined as "all known information about the enemy," the class was an encyclopedic description of the actual real-life divisions and units they might confront in Europe. This, Max thought, had to be the gold standard of intel every Allied unit needed. It was published in a thick pamphlet called "the Red Book."

The instructor, a former Ritchie Boy who'd become an expert on the German Army and now taught other Ritchie Boys, said, "Each of you will receive a copy, and you'll get an updated version once your team is in the field. Of course, the book is highly classified. You cannot, under any circumstances, take the Red Book into battle. If it falls into enemy hands, you'll have a real SNAFU. Which means you need to memorize parts of the book every time you change locations." He paused. "The other problem is that we constantly update the book. So we expect you to memorize all the updates too."

The instructor laughed at the groan that went up. "It's worth it. This info can be extremely helpful during POW interrogations. First off, you'll be able to ask more specific questions about the unit's tactical and strategic situation. But the real benefit is psychological. Showing a POW that you know his commanding officer's name, for example, can have an effect on a prisoner. The POW might think that if you already know *that*, what else do you already know? And why not spill more so at least he can get cigarettes or chocolate bars out of it?

"Believe me, gentlemen, that intel will save American lives."

CHAPTER 52

February 1943
Camp Ritchie, Maryland

Life at Camp Ritchie wasn't always serious. A poem, written by prior Ritchie Boys, was apparently circulated with every new class. Max found the first verse clever:

> *Vas you effer at Kamp Ritchie,*
> *Der very schönste Platz of all,*
> *Vere die sun comes up like Donner*
> *Mit recorded Bugle Call?*
> *Where the privates are professors,*
> *And the corporals write the books.*
> *And the PFCs scare captains*
> *With their supercilious looks?*
> *Where the sergeants all talk*
> *Hoch Deutsch, Hindustani, Czech, or Greek,*
> *And they all are intellectuals*
> *In whatever tongue they speak.*

Currently there were ten verses. Max suspected that every Ritchie class added a verse. He decided to round up some of the other German men to collaborate if no one wrote a new verse by the end of training.

Less funny but more dramatic were the presentations by men, and a few women, who were recruited to write or act in specific scenes meant to reinforce what Ritchie trainees learned. Max had only been at Ritchie a few days when he attended a "Nazi rally" in the Camp Ritchie theater. The players went to great lengths to make it realistic, with the appropriate uniforms, flags, signage, and actors, including a fake Hitler. The first time Max watched it, chills ran over his skin.

He'd been told by Ritchie Boy instructors that had been through the training that there would be more dramatic "playlets." At the end of the eight weeks, they'd see a longer play that described what soldiers should do to secure a German command post in France and interrogate French villagers. One or two of these dramas were even opened up to the public.

There were two courses Max would never forget. The first was how to interrogate POWs. If he passed that course he would be a member of the Army's Interrogation of Prisoners of War, the IPW team. He would have the power and authority to make decisions about a Nazi soldier's future—where he would be imprisoned, how long he would be there, and under what conditions. The chance to do to Nazis what they'd been doing to Jews like him for the last ten years became his raison d'être. He only had to learn how.

The next day Colonel Angus Rogers, one of the British officers on loan to Camp Ritchie, appeared to teach the interrogation class. As Max and Freddy entered the classroom, they spotted him at the blackboard and exchanged enthusiastic glances. He was well thought of and respected.

As the class got underway, Rogers said, "This class is the first of its kind. It was pioneered by an American who worked in marketing and persuasion for the ad industry."

Some of the students looked at one another, confused. Rogers paused. "Oh, yes. Did I forget to say he also worked as a British secret agent in the 1930s?" He looked around the room. "It turns out 'perception' is the most reliable motivator of behavior there is. We define 'perception' as what a person thinks of his situation, and how he believes it will drive his decisions. If we at Camp Ritchie do our jobs right, you, as interrogators, will have wide latitude in creating the perceptions the German POWs have of you in the field. We hope you will be perceived as friendly, trustworthy, but firm."

He went to the blackboard behind him, picked up a piece of chalk, and wrote the numbers 1 and 2 on the board. "But we'll get back to that. Let's start at the other end. There are two reasons why interrogation is critical to the Allied war effort. Can anyone tell me what they are?"

Max raised his hand.

"Yes, Private?"

"Tactical and strategic information."

"Very good." Rogers nodded. "What's the difference between them?"

Max went on. "Tactical intel is the current situation of a German unit. How many fighters, what kind of equipment. What is their morale? Who's in charge? Where were they before we picked them off? Where was the unit headed?"

"And strategic?"

"That would be broader information. How close is Hitler to producing an atom bomb?

What kinds of chemical warfare is he planning? What's the V1 rocket? The V2?"

"Excellent," Rogers said. "The truth is that most of you in this class were chosen to become interrogators because of your German roots. But not all of you will make it. It's not easy. You must persuade every POW you interview that his perceptions of you and the US

Army are more important than the prejudices he's been carrying around since he started fighting.

"In this class you'll learn by doing. We will only have two or three days of instruction. Everything else will be role-play and practice. In addition to the techniques you'll learn, you will need to use your imagination and wits. We'll try to expose you to as many different personality types as possible, but there will always be one German soldier who doesn't fit easily into any category. You'll have to improvise sometimes to be successful."

It was at that moment that Max fully understood why he was at Camp Ritchie. American soldiers like Conrad Spitzer might speak German fluently, but immigrants like Max, who grew up in Germany, understood the German soul. Whether Prussian, Bavarian, or even Austrian, Germans had a similar mind-set: formality, pride, and, most of all, order. They obeyed rules. They were law-abiding. Disciplined. Punctual. Generally well-mannered. The native-born Germans at Camp Ritchie knew this. Most of them were the same way. Plus they knew German history, culture, sports teams. They could draw on all those areas to quickly build a connection with a POW.

Max began to understand something else as well. When he focused on the similarities of German people, he realized that the Nazis were an aberration, not the norm, of German society. A massive sickness had infected his homeland: a sickness and moral degeneracy that turned German against German for no good reason. He could be part of the medicine that helped it recover.

But how? What would Germany be after the Nazis were gone? For the first time, it dawned on Max that in order to help break the fever, he might need to forgive the Germans who'd been infected by it. Who'd participated in the maelstrom but now wanted to return to their senses. He would need to forgive the Germans who'd destroyed his home, the people he loved, and his family. Was that even possible? He thought about the persecution he and his family had undergone. The spiteful behavior in others that changed his life. He shuddered. Hell, no. He didn't want to forgive.

CHAPTER 53

February 1943
Camp Ritchie, Maryland

The interrogation class boiled down to five key requirements. Max took detailed notes:

1. Show superior knowledge, especially about German military organization and individuals. (Review order of battle for specifics.) Make your first question one to which you already know the answer. If the POW doesn't reply, answer it yourself. Will make POW think there's no reason *not* to talk; interrogator already knows everything.

2. Act like a friend: Provide cigarettes, chocolates, possibly give POW special privileges.

3. Introduce a subject of common interest: music, culture, food, sports. Allow POW to volunteer his own subject; if not, you pick one to expand on.

4. Absolutely no physical contact, touching, torture, or violence. The

Germans don't honor that part of the Geneva Conventions, but the Allies do.

5. Take advantage of POW's anxiety, fear of prison, threat to families. POWs afraid their families will be taken away, imprisoned, or worse. Particularly afraid of Russian army retribution, Russian advances, Russian prison camps.

Above all, Rogers emphasized, the interrogator must look at the event from the POW's point of view, not his own. He should avoid thinking that every German was a Nazi. He should instead consider what the soldier already knew, what his needs were, what he was feeling. The soldier was undoubtedly afraid, stressed, and uncertain, no matter how he appeared. The interrogator should initially try to relieve some of that fear and stress.

However, that didn't mean the interrogator shouldn't use skilled interrogation techniques. He might want to start with some propaganda, citing the status of the North African campaign, where the Allies currently had the edge. Or the failed German invasion of Russia. He might want to pose paradoxes, such as "If the Germans are so powerful, why are you losing the war?" With the more difficult POWs, it was permissible to make them physically uncomfortable, such as forcing them to stand for long periods of time, not allowing a toilet break, or making the room too hot or too cold.

The *threat* but not the actual *use* of torture worked. Proclaiming that the POW would be turned over to the Russians was a powerful tool, especially among German enlisted men. Some Ritchie Boys smeared ketchup on another Ritchie Boy dressed in a German uniform, who screamed with "pain." Others bluntly promised the prisoner would be killed if he did not cooperate. One particularly successful ploy was to dramatically warn a prisoner he would be turned over to partisans or the Resistance if he didn't talk.

"So," Rogers concluded, "the difference between friendship and firmness is a thin line. Your skill as an interrogator will depend on when to use each."

With that Rogers called for a break. When the soldiers came back ten minutes later, five men had joined Rogers at the front of the room. Four were in German infantry uniforms; one was dressed as a Leutnant. Two chairs had been set up on opposite sides of a small table.

Rogers gazed out at the men.

Max swallowed. He had a feeling.

"You!" Rogers pointed at Max. "Give it a try. Since it's your first time, we'll be gentle."

A hearty laugh erupted from the class.

As Max made his way to the front, Rogers asked, "Name? Rank? Birthplace?"

"Steiner, Max. Private first class. Regensburg."

Rogers gestured to one of the soldiers. He sat in one chair. Max stood at the edge of the room. "Should I assume he is already in the room?"

"If you want."

Max nodded and took a breath. Then: "Good morning, soldier. I'm Max—um—Stone. Captain, US Army." He'd decided in advance to change his name, just like Bob Townsend had. And elevate his rank, since he saw the soldier was lower-level infantry. "Who are you?"

The "soldier" looked up at Max and cocked his head. "You speak German without an accent."

Max smiled. The guy had just given him a "tell." He might be ready to talk or he might not. For now, Max replied, "Thank you." He waited. "And you are?"

"Heinrich Brinkmann. Gefreiter Wehrmacht. Born fifteen nine 1920. Serial number KL-9826301."

"Brinkmann" had just satisfied the Geneva Conventions requirements. He didn't have to say another word if he didn't want to. Then Max realized that Brinkmann had given him another opening. They had the same birthday! Had Rogers arranged this in advance to test Max? Or was it just a coincidence? It didn't matter. Max decided to go with it. "You're not going to believe this, Heinrich, but we have the same birthday. September 15. Even the same year. Where did you grow up?"

"Berlin. What about you?"

Max avoided an answer. "Berlin is a beautiful city. My parents took me there when I turned eight."

"So you are native German." Max realized he had slipped. He'd admitted he was German, which wasn't a problem, but he'd told Brinkmann when he'd gone to Berlin. Which wasn't a good idea. What if Brinkmann thought about it? And realized Max had probably come to America because of Hitler? It wasn't a disaster, but he'd given away too much.

"It was many years ago," he lied, leaving open the possibility that they'd visited Berlin from the US, not another location inside Germany. "What's your favorite thing to do in Berlin?"

Brinkmann thought about it. "Go to the movies."

Another hit! Max loved movies. "Favorite actor?"

"Charlie Chaplin."

Max laughed. "Favorite actress?"

"Rita Hayworth."

"Good choice." He wondered if he'd done enough schmoozing with Brinkmann. "I like Charlie Chaplin too. Very smart man." He bit his lip. That was unnecessary. Brinkmann would think he was an intellectual snob. Or a Communist. Max cleared his throat.

"Would you like a cigarette?" He pretended to pull a pack out of his pocket.

"Ja. Danke." Brinkmann, pretending as well, took it eagerly. "We don't have them anymore."

Max struck a match and leaned over to put the flame on the cigarette. Brinkmann inhaled deeply and sat back. He looked totally relaxed. It was time. "Why is that?"

"Can't get supplies."

"Where?"

"We're holed up outside Tunisia but hemmed in."

Once Brinkmann shared that, Max was more confident. He *was* a talker. He asked him several more questions about the size of the unit, what the commanding officer was like, where they were headed, and what gear they had.

In the middle of Brinkmann's responses, Rogers called out. "Okay. That's it. Good job, both of you!"

Relief washed over Max. He'd been more tense than he'd expected. Second-guessing all his thoughts. Making decisions on the fly. Wondering if he'd made mistakes. It took its toll.

"So, Private 'Stone' . . . smart of you to change your name, by the way." Rogers explained why to the class. Then: "How did it go?"

Max let out a breath. "It was difficult. I kept second-guessing myself."

Rogers nodded.

"I think I made a mistake when I told him I went to Berlin when I was eight."

"And why was that a mistake?"

"Because if he thought about it too much, he'd figure out I left Germany after Hitler came to power and that I might be Jewish."

"Frankly, I think that's a stretch. But he does know you come from Germany. That's not a bad thing. I think you played it well. Especially the movie angle. Commonalities. And your birthday. Is that really the date?"

Max laughed. "It is."

"Well played. Anything else?"

"I should not have said Charlie Chaplin was a smart man. A lot of people think he's a Communist. If the soldier did as well, he could think I was one too. And a Jew. I should have said he was very funny and left it at that."

"Hmm . . ." Rogers's eyebrows furrowed. "I didn't catch that. But you're right. A soldier with above-average intelligence might have made that association." He turned to the class and explained how carefully they needed to parse their words and comments. He turned back to Max. "On the whole, though, well done, Private."

Max felt his cheeks redden with pleasure as he went back to his seat.

CHAPTER 54

February 1943
Camp Ritchie, Maryland

Two more role-plays followed. As he listened, it occurred to Max that the fundamentals of human behavior that he was now learning were what made the Nazis so good at persuasion. Goebbels, Hitler, Heydrich, and the others already knew how malleable German society was. They understood that people wanted to forget the disgrace of the Great War and the Depression, and reclaim their position as the most powerful European nation, as they once were when Prussia and the Hapsburgs were all-powerful states. If the Jews had understood that, perhaps they could have deflected and responded Nazi propaganda more successfully. He was grateful to the US Army for teaching him these life skills.

Finally, Rogers called up Conrad Spitzer. He strode confidently to the front, where a soldier sat at the table. Spitzer entered with a pad and pen, sat across from the soldier, and pretended to write. After a considerable silence, he looked up.

"Name. Rank. Serial Number," he barked.

The soldier responded.

"Would you like a cigarette?" The POW nodded.

Spitzer pretended to flip over the pack. "Take two."

The POW smiled.

So did Spitzer. He watched as the POW pretended to light it. "So, it's clear you Germans aren't as smart as you think you are."

The soldier frowned. So did Max.

"You're all stupid enough to get caught." Spitzer scoffed. "What was your mission?"

The soldier squirmed but didn't reply.

"I said, what was your plan, soldier?"

No comment from the prisoner.

"I see. You prefer the silent treatment?" Spitzer glanced at the POW, who met his eyes. Max was sure he saw scorn in them.

"Well, in that case, we have a place for you. In a Russian prisoner-of-war camp." He paused. "How would you feel about that, comrade?" He emphasized the word "comrade."

But the damage had been done. The prisoner remained silent.

Spitzer rose from the table and raised his voice. "Soldiers, come get this traitor. This man is going east." He strode away from the front of the room.

Max dared to exhale. Except for offering the man a cigarette, Spitzer had done everything he'd been taught not to do. Had he listened to Rogers at all?

Rogers paused before speaking. Then he said slowly, "Righto, men. Let's have a go about—what is your name, soldier?"

"Conrad Spitzer, sir." On his way back to his seat he threw Max an angry look, as if he knew what Max was thinking.

"Right." Rogers turned away and looked over the class. "Who's got a comment?"

Half a dozen hands shot up.

Max felt sorry for Spitzer. Almost.

In addition to interrogation, the other class that fascinated Max was Counterintelligence, taught jointly between the army and the

Office of Strategic Services. The OSS, which would later become the CIA, ran its own training camp less than ten miles from Camp Ritchie.

As a Ritchie Boy, Max's job was to provide intel about the German war machine, its progress, and its problems through interrogations of POWs. But counterintelligence was the act of destroying or compromising that very same war machine, and that was where Max wanted to be.

The OSS conducted missions behind enemy lines, provided weapons to resistance groups, and sabotaged infrastructure to stop German military advances. If Max was part of an OSS mission he could make a difference and see the effect right away.

The Counterintelligence class had previously been taught in Chicago. As usual, though, the Maryland instructors improved it through props, actual equipment, and military experience. The core of the class focused on reading and analyzing maps in several languages, but unusual scenes occasionally popped up on Camp Ritchie grounds. Ranks of men practicing German short-order functioning drills, a battery of German horse-drawn artillery clomping across the parade ground, or a Nazi rally in full swing gave soldiers the chance to participate in hypothetical missions.

The men studied maps, some in English, but many in German and French. Some were aerial photos, some topographical maps, some even hand-drawn. Max had trouble with aerial photos. The features were often blurry, and while he could make out basic contours, details were difficult to see. His most valuable tool was a compass. He learned the differences between grid north, magnetic north, and true north and which to use when.

Counterintelligence focused on identifying saboteurs and spies. If, for example, a POW answered that a minefield was to the left but gestured to the right, the interrogator had to make a split-second decision. Was the prisoner confused? Or was he lying? If he thought the POW was lying, he would observe, as one instructor said, "his Adam's apple, his eyes, his nostrils, his lips, the little arteries in his temples—all the places where a man might involuntarily betray himself." If any of those features shifted, the POW was probably lying.

Often interrogators had to trust their gut when something didn't seem right. If the details were vague, if the answers too short, if the POW started out talking slowly but sped up, the interrogator went on high alert.

Sometimes interrogators tried to trick a POW by telling them something they knew was untrue, hoping the prisoner would reveal the true response instead. In other cases, bluffing was an effective technique. Former Ritchie Boys recounted how they passed through German checkpoints by pretending they held a higher rank or dropping the name of one of Hitler's inner circle as a relative.

Every night Max went to bed exhausted and fell instantly asleep. Nothing penetrated. His nightmares became less frequent, and his memories of Annaliese were wrapped in a gauzy, surreal haze.

CHAPTER 55

March 1943
Camp Ritchie, Maryland

For most Ritchie Boys, their final mission was the most challenging. In early spring they were driven after dark to a thickly wooded part of Catoctin Mountain and dropped off miles from the camp. Each soldier had a compass and a map in French or some other language than English. They were told to meet at a spot on the map by midnight for a ride back to camp. If they missed it, they would need to hike more than twenty miles back. Usually they were paired with another soldier. Max sighed when he discovered his assigned partner was Conrad Spitzer.

Although it was nearly spring, a light snow that day had turned the earth into mud.

The snow had stopped, though, and it was clear. A silvery half-moon threw enough light to read the map. Max had the foresight to ask the driver to point out where they currently were on the map. The driver shrugged as if he had no idea. Max winced. No luck there.

He scanned the clearing they'd been dropped in for the brightest area and positioned himself in it. Clutching the map, he squatted on the ground. The map was an aerial photo, the map he least liked. He wished he'd been given a topographical map, but he had to make do. He looked up at Spitzer. "Hey, Conrad. Come on over. Let's figure out where we are."

Spitzer took his time walking over. His lips stretched into a thin grim line. Was he angry? Max wondered. Afraid? Offended? Max decided it didn't matter. They had to focus on the map.

"Take a look. Any thoughts? Aerial photos aren't my favorite."

"The mighty Steiner has a weak spot?"

Max's instinctive reaction was to lash out at Spitzer. Instead he controlled himself and gazed around, hoping to find some landmark that was represented on the aerial photo. But all he could see in the photo was a dense expanse of darkness. The pickup spot sat at the top of the photo and was marked by an X. A lighter stripe sliced through the darkness at the X, which meant the forest had been cleared, probably to build a road. Between the dark expanse they were in and the X were lighter areas that were murky and out of focus. They could represent landmarks, perhaps even buildings and homes, but Max wouldn't be sure until they got there. At the moment nothing jumped out at him.

"I see some lighter areas that could be landmarks, maybe even buildings, but right now we don't know." He handed the map to Spitzer. "It would help if we could figure out the distance to the pickup. What do you think?"

Spitzer studied it. "Well, that's obviously a road. At the top of the map. I think we should walk toward it."

Max nodded and took out his compass. "It's almost directly north." He paused. "But how far do you think it is? There's no scale on the map."

Spitzer shrugged as the driver had a few minutes earlier. "How should I know?" He huffed. "You're the expert."

Max struggled to keep his mouth shut.

Spitzer shifted. "We have to make a decision, Steiner."

Max looked at his watch. "It's only twenty hundred hours. We have four hours."

"Well then, let's start."

"Okay. Give me back the map."

Spitzer took a step back. "No. I think I'll keep it."

"Conrad, you know I can read the map."

"You said you didn't like aerial photo maps."

"You're right. But that doesn't mean I'm ignorant. I can figure out our terrain from the photo. And whether the land is dense forest or something else. For example, the lighter area could be a depression in the land, or a lake, or some other impediment, and we might have to figure out a way to avoid it."

Spitzer frowned. Then a steely look came over him. "Anyone can do that, Steiner. I'm keeping the map."

But Max had had enough. He rose and took three quick steps toward Spitzer. "Conrad, give it to me. Now. I do not want to get lost in the woods with you."

"That makes two of us."

Max extended his hand to grip Spitzer's arm. But Spitzer was ready. He whipped around and shoved Max back with a hard thrust to his chest. As Max staggered backward, he tripped on a barely visible tree root. He fell to the ground and landed on his buttocks. He immediately groaned and cried out.

"My ankle!" He sat up and tried to feel his left ankle, but the hurt of even a gentle touch was excruciating. "It twisted when I fell. I think it's broken!"

He bowed his head. Scheisse! What now?

"It's your own damn fault, Steiner," Spitzer said. "You shouldn't have lunged for the map. Give someone else a chance. Don't hog all the glory for yourself."

Max moaned again. He couldn't deal with Spitzer right now. How was he going to get back to camp? Waves of agony surged through his ankle. He couldn't walk. He couldn't even stand up.

"What's the problem, Steiner? Hurts a lot? I'm so sorry. I guess you're a weakling after all and you're going to fail this exercise, huh . . ."

"Spitzer, stop the bullshit, okay? We need—"

"No, Steiner. You stop. I'm going to the pickup spot. And I'm taking the map. Good luck." With that he whirled around and marched out of the clearing into the woods.

"Spitzer, come back. You don't know what you're doing."

There was no reply.

Max raised his voice. "Conrad, come back while you still can."

Nothing. He was alone.

Max blew out a breath. The first thing he did was tell himself not to panic. He could deal with this. He looked around. The evergreen tree whose root he'd slipped on was behind him. He forced himself to slide closer to it, using his hands and arms to propel his torso. Once his back was against the tree, he relaxed, closed his eyes, and tried to empty his mind of all the pain and anger muddying his thoughts.

He stayed in that position until an idea occurred to him. Was it possible? Could he do it with only one foot? There was no guarantee. But it was worth a try. Before he started, he contemplated removing his boot. Ultimately, he chose not to. He was afraid the ankle might swell more than it already had.

The pain was still throbbing when he awkwardly removed his knapsack. Inside were several items, including a pocketknife with multiple tools attached that was issued to American soldiers. It was produced by a Swiss company named Victorinox, and GIs started to call it a "Swiss Army knife" during the war. In addition to the blade was a bottle and can opener, a small chisel, a hard wire cutter, and a screwdriver. He fished in his knapsack, found an undershirt, and cut it into strips. Then he tied the strips around his ankle as a brace. It might not help, but it couldn't hurt.

Once Max was satisfied his ankle was protected, he used the tree trunk as leverage. He leaned his back into it and slowly tried to slide up to a standing position on one foot. The bark was rough and scraped through his shirt and grazed his skin. He cursed at the stinging pain but forced himself to keep going. He made it but his balance was off, and he mis-stepped, which made his left leg crumple. He saw stars and screamed, for once grateful that no one could hear him. He took a few ragged breaths and tried to stand completely still until the new pain ebbed.

When it did, he hopped around on his right leg and faced a low-hanging branch. Luckily it was a thin but healthy branch that extended about four meters, or twelve feet, from the trunk. He still thought in terms of European metrics. Using the blade of the pocketknife, he started to saw through the branch. Within minutes, despite the cold March night, he worked up a sweat. He stopped and checked his progress. He'd only cut through a couple of centimeters. The diameter was at least eight or nine centimeters, four inches. He checked the time. Almost twenty-one hundred hours. Would he make it to the pickup in time?

He kept sawing. Aside from the blade's scraping, the forest was silent. A cold breeze whispered through the trees and his jacket. Max started to shiver. On top of everything else, he ran the risk of frostbite. He'd hoped to saw through the branch in ten minutes, but it took him thirty minutes to wrest the branch from the tree. He took a long, relieved breath and leaned the branch vertically against the tree trunk, eyeing its length. If he made an additional cut, he would have two pieces that were roughly equal.

This time it went more smoothly, and he was done in twenty minutes, but his wrist and fingers ached from the cold and the effort. He shaved the ends of the pieces so they were more or less smooth and wouldn't catch on random leaves, roots, or stones on the ground. He packed up his equipment, took a long drink from his canteen, and hoisted the knapsack onto his back. Then he grasped the two pieces a few centimeters from the top of each one. Gingerly, he plunged them into the muddy dirt as if they were ski poles. They held, and slowly he shifted his weight onto both and hopped forward on his good leg, swinging the bad one behind. It worked. He tried it again. Then again. It seemed like he might have fashioned a solution. He took a moment to thank Hashem for the idea and pushed forward on his makeshift crutches.

CHAPTER 56

March 1943
Camp Ritchie, Maryland

The crutches that saved Max were only temporary. Wood was porous and the bottom of the branches were already taking on moisture. At the same time, he couldn't hurry. If he wasn't careful, the crutches might snag on something and he could fall again and end up in an even worse situation.

He stopped at a tiny clearing where the moonlight was strong enough to check his watch. Twenty-two hundred hours. He had two hours to make it to the pickup point. If he were still running track, he could cover eleven miles an hour. But he guessed he was barely doing half that on the crutches. He fished out his compass to make sure he was heading directly north. He would intersect the road eventually. He hoped the pickup was close to the spot from which he emerged.

He found a rhythm—plant crutches, hop, swing the bad leg—and was making steady progress, despite the woodsy terrain. The only sounds were the plop of his crutches and the swish of his clothing when he hopped. He began to feel cautiously optimistic. He might make it after all. He skirted around some boulders and was just beginning to think the woods were thinning when he heard a soft howl. It sounded like the loons he'd heard in Wisconsin when he and Buddy went up to fish one weekend. He stopped. There were no loons in Maryland. At least in the mountains.

There it was again. Max frowned. It almost sounded human. As if someone was crying.

"Is someone there?" There was no reply. In the silence that followed, Max figured it out. Spitzer.

"Spitzer. Is that you?"

Still no response. Max had been wondering what he would do when saw Spitzer again.

"Over here, Steiner." Spitzer's voice had a slight echo as though it was coming from a distance. If Max deviated from his path to find Spitzer, he might miss the pickup, and it would be impossible to hike back to camp. He should keep going.

True, he shouldn't have lunged at the man, but his unbearable nature infuriated Max. The fucking guy had broken his ankle. If they had been in a real war, Max would be dead by now. On the other hand, if Max didn't go back, and it had been a real battle, Spitzer would likely be dead. Max didn't like the son of a bitch, but they were supposed to be a team.

Max called out. "I'm coming, Spitzer."

Spitzer was leaning against a tree about a half mile west. When Max reached him, he could see, even in the dim moonlight, that his eyes were puffy and glazed. But his words were straightforward. "I got lost and I couldn't find my compass. I thought I was going to die."

Max took a breath. "Come on. Get up. I could use some help. If we hurry, we can still make the pickup."

"How did you find those?" Spitzer gazed in awe at the makeshift crutches.

"I made them."

"What? When? How?"

"I'll tell you on the ride back." He gestured awkwardly. "If you support me on this side, I'll only need one."

Spitzer nodded and flanked Max on the right. He took one of the crutches and fastened his left arm around Max's waist. "Lean on me, Max."

Max was surprised. "Thanks." He draped his right arm around Spitzer's shoulders.

They made the pickup spot with two minutes to spare. When the driver saw Max's makeshift crutches, his eyebrows shot up. "What happened?"

Max paused for a moment. "I broke my ankle."

The driver sat up straight. "And you two limped all the way back?"

Max glanced at Spitzer, who didn't say a word. "That's right," Max said.

"Well, you're one hell of a lucky SOB."

Max didn't reply. The driver went to the back of the bus and made sure Max was in a seat by himself with his foot up. Max was exhausted. He fell asleep.

~

When they got back to camp an hour later, the driver took Max to the infirmary. A sleepy doctor unwrapped the strips of cotton Max had tied around his ankle and slipped off his boot.

"I'll take an X-ray, but I can tell you right now that ankle is definitely broken. Look at the swelling."

"I kept my boot on. I was hoping to reduce it."

The doctor's eyes widened. "Christ. The pain must have been unbearable!"

"You could say that."

The doctor moved the portable X-ray machine to Max's bed and took a few pictures, then prepared to set the break and fashion a cast. Max lay back with his eyes closed, grateful he was inside, warm, and taken care of. The pain was still acute, but the doctor had given him some codeine and it was no longer excruciating. Meanwhile, Conrad Spitzer had disappeared. Max figured he'd gone back to the barracks. The doctor told Max he would be staying in the infirmary overnight. Max didn't argue.

CHAPTER 57

March 1943
Camp Ritchie, Maryland

By the next morning news of Max's accident had spread. Freddy was the first to arrive, with a bottle of whisky. Max wondered how he'd "appropriated" it so quickly. He was in the first of a dozen beds in the room where patients recuperated after they were patched up. Luckily, he was the only occupant. Freddy poured them both a couple of shots, which helped Max forget about the pain. He needed to. The codeine had worn off, and the pain had been getting worse since the doctor set his ankle.

"So, what happened, man?" Freddy asked, sitting on a straight-backed chair beside the bed. "When I heard you were down for the count, I got worried."

Max was about to tell him the story, but a few more soldiers from the class drifted in. They brought newspapers, chocolate bars, cigarettes, even a girlie magazine. Max was overwhelmed and grateful, although he did blush at the magazine.

Still no trace of Spitzer. "Where is he?" Max asked when he and Freddy were alone again.

"He was debriefed early this morning," Freddy said in a low voice. "No one's seen him since." He poured Max another shot.

"Who debriefed him?"

"Shipley Davis."

Max took a sip of whisky and raised his eyebrows. "Top brass." When Freddy nodded, Max asked, "Do you know what Spitzer said?"

Freddy leaned back in his chair. "No idea. He's probably FUBAR, I'd imagine."

"Do you think he went AWOL ?"

"Spitzer? He couldn't find his way out of a paper bag."

Freddy should only know, Max thought. He kept his mouth shut.

Freddy squeezed one eye closed. "Okay, Steiner. What really happened?"

Max shook his head. "I—I'll tell you after I'm debriefed."

Freddy opened his mouth to say something, but Colonel Shipley Davis suddenly appeared in the infirmary, smoking a cigar. The odor wafted over Max, a few feet away on the other side of the wall. The doctor asked the colonel to put it out.

A moment later, he entered the room where Max was resting. He was a burly man, with thinning hair turning gray on the sides of his head. He was in a uniform that needed laundering. "Good morning, soldier." His gravelly voice pegged him as a heavy smoker.

Freddy rose right away and saluted. "Please sit here, sir. Max, I'll come back later."

Max smiled and waved. Davis sat in the chair. "I'll have some of that booze," he said.

"What booze?"

"Steiner, you know how a cigar stinks up a room?" He didn't wait for Max's response. "Well, whisky is the same. It's fucking all over here."

Max felt himself redden. "It's under the bed. Along with the glasses."

"Not surprised you needed a few, after last night." Davis got up, bent down, and felt around the floor under Max's bed. "Ah, here we go." He brought up the now half-empty bottle and the glasses, poured two shots, and handed one to Max. "I debriefed Spitzer."

Max took the glass.

"*You* want to tell me what happened? Or should I just believe Spitzer?"

"No, sir. That's okay. I'll tell you what happened." Max summarized the events of the previous night. He wanted to leave out the part about the tussle between Spitzer and Max. And how Spitzer stranded Max and vanished after Max rescued him. But what if he went AWOL in a real battle? He would have jeopardized other soldiers' lives. He had to tell Davis. He tried to downplay Spitzer's flight but essentially told the truth. When Max finished, he took a large pull on the booze.

"Is that it?" Davis asked.

"Yes, sir." Max squinted at Davis. The hooch was having its effect. He was having trouble seeing. There were two Colonel Davises on the chair.

Davis ran his tongue around his lips, then tossed back the rest of his shot. He stared at the empty glass, rolling it in his hands. Davis took his time. Max had no idea what was coming. Then:

"Max, it's a shame the army doesn't give out badges for being a team player, because you're one of the best I've seen."

Confusion washed over Max. "I don't understand, Colonel."

Davis sighed. "When Spitzer and I began the debriefing, he was extremely, shall we say, contrite. He admitted he goaded you into grabbing the map so he could hurt you. When you tripped and twisted your ankle, he panicked and ran. But in his haste, he lost his compass. He followed what he thought was the right way, but he got hopelessly lost. He said he had given up and was sitting against a tree trunk crying when you found him. You rescued him, broken ankle and all. And said nothing about his deceit."

Davis picked up the whisky bottle. "Isn't that the way it went down, soldier?"

For the first time Conrad had been honest. Max was astonished. Maybe there was hope for him after all. His confession prompted

Max to say something he never imagined. "Spitzer had his reasons. I was pissed off at him for taking the map. He retaliated."

"Whatever. I don't know the man, son, but I took a look at his grades and the comments from the instructors. He's being transferred to an infantry company. He'll end up on the front." Davis put the bottle down. "But, you, Private Steiner, are a different kettle of fish."

"What do you mean?"

"Spitzer confessed that he was jealous of you. You performed well. On everything. He didn't. He hated you for that."

Max wasn't surprised. If Spitzer had grown up in Germany and hadn't been Jewish, he would have made a perfect Nazi. As soon as he thought that, Max rebuked himself. How could any Jew resemble a Nazi? And how could he accuse Spitzer of it? He was stereotyping Nazis the same way they stereotyped Jews.

He recalled his thoughts after his first interrogation class. When he acknowledged that in order to truly live a life of peace when the war was over, he might need to forgive—not the Nazis—never. But what about the people who made their rise to power possible? Who looked the other way when invidious laws came out? Or ignored the plight of the Jews, Catholics, and other enemies of the Reich?

In a way Spitzer fit into that category. Although he had grown up in America, his family was powerless to save their relatives back in Germany. They were powerless, as well, in the face of American anti-semitism, which, while not fatal, was subtly malignant. Powerless to shield themselves against encroaching evil. Was Spitzer's fear of that the reason why he was so guarded and selfish? Or was it the result of an unpredictable and malevolent era? To be fair, he should give Spitzer the benefit of the doubt. If he had been just a bit nicer, Max would have taught him everything he knew. But Spitzer couldn't get over himself.

Davis must have been reading his mind. "Some men can't see past their own nose, son. Spitzer never realized he was part of a much larger purpose. A life-and-death mission. To save our world and rid it of a monster." He sighed. "A shame, really. Playing the victim has consequences. Then there are men like you. A real team player.

That's what we hope every soldier becomes . . ." He let his words trail off. "Well, I'll let you get some rest now, soldier. You need it." He got to his feet, the whisky bottle in hand. With his other, he saluted Max.

Max let his mouth fall open, astonished yet again. "Tha—thank you, sir."

Davis chuckled. "I won't report you for drinking whisky on army time." He paused, then raised the fifth. "But I will take the rest of this bottle."

CHAPTER 58

April 1943
Camp Ritchie, Maryland

Max needed six weeks to recuperate from his ankle injury, including two weeks of dogged therapy. Classes ended, and soldiers took written exams and participated in live demonstrations. The live demos included a final interrogation of a trained staff member. Max spotted Lieutenant Bob Townsend among the German "POWs." He wasn't Max's subject but he did pass along a wink and a nod.

Only about twenty German Ritchie Boys graduated, down from the thirty-five who began in January. As had happened in basic training, once again Max was not assigned to any of the six-man teams. But other members of his class were sent to advanced training at various locations in the US and England. Freddy was on his way to England, and another Ritchie Boy class was underway.

In the middle of April Max was called to Camp Ritchie headquarters. When he arrived, he was directed into an office, empty save for a desk and two chairs. A tall bald man with a no-nonsense expression rose and introduced himself.

"I'm Colonel Bill Fitzhugh from the OSS." He extended his hand. "Please sit." He sat behind the desk. A folder was open, papers spread across the desktop.

Max shook and sat. He'd heard the stories about the OSS's founder, Fighting Bill Donovan. His wartime exploits had won him plenty of medals and accolades. With FDR's help, Donovan had built the OSS into America's first wartime espionage organization. More than ten thousand employees worked there now. A thrill of anticipation buzzed Max's nerves.

"How's that ankle?" Fitzhugh asked.

If he knew about his ankle, Max thought, he must know a lot more. "I'm pretty much one hundred percent, sir."

"Good." Fitzhugh appraised Max as if he was examining a new rifle or machine gun.

"You come highly recommended for your skills, quick thinking, and attitude. Tell me about yourself."

Max started with his childhood in Regensburg, his escape to Holland, and what he'd done for Jacob's resistance group. He told him about his escape to America, his two years of relative normalcy working on cars in Chicago, how and why he'd enlisted.

When he finished, Fitzhugh nodded as if he'd already known everything in Max's background and Max had passed an honesty test. "We need people like you. I assume you know what we do. Are you interested?"

Max didn't hesitate. "You bet I am, sir. But how would that work? Would I be officially transferred? Who would I report to? What would I do?"

Fitzhugh smiled. "I can give you a few answers. Others I don't know. You would be transferred from the army to the OSS. We are a different organization, but we're—cousins, let's say. We both report to the War Department. The OSS has small-team special operations as well as larger operational groups in European countries. Like I said, I don't know where you will fit in yet, but you will be assigned to carry out specific missions.

"Since we have a 'fluid' relationship with our cousins, you may well be transferred back to the army at some point. You may not. Depends what's needed when. As long as you're with *us*, though, you report through our chain of command." He flicked a finger against his nose. "There's one more benefit, soldier. We will get you early citizenship as a reward for your service."

Max sat up straighter. He'd already decided he wanted to live in America. This was—how did the Americans put it?—"the icing on the cake."

"There's one more thing, son."

"What's that?"

"In recognition of your exceptional service record, your natural leadership abilities, and your quick thinking, you're getting a promotion. To staff sergeant. You'll be able to teach other enlistees what you know. Congratulations, soldier."

Max's mouth fell open. "I'm honored, sir."

"You earned it."

Max smiled. "Thank you." He hadn't expected his behavior to be rewarded before he'd been battle-tested. It helped his self-confidence. But he didn't want to become too self-assured. He guessed there was a shortage of qualified NCOs and the powers that be were desperate to send men into the field. "So where do I go next? Will I need time to put my affairs in order?"

Fitzhugh's expression grew amused. He chuckled. "I don't think so. You're only going a few miles."

Max cocked his head.

"You'll do a few months of training at Camp Greentop, which is eight miles south of here. About a mile from FDR's wartime getaway." Fitzhugh chuckled again. "Okay with you?"

"Yes, sir."

Fitzhugh changed the subject. "I understand you speak German and Dutch, correct?" Max nodded.

"Anything else?"

"A bit of French."

Fitzhugh nodded. "Good. You might end up in any one or more of those countries."

Max's pulse sped up. "When do I start?"

"Get your belongings together, Sergeant. I'll give you a lift."

PART V

MARYLAND AND EUROPE

1943–1945

CHAPTER 59

April 1943
Camp Greentop, Maryland

T he objective of OSS training was to prepare recruits for missions of subterfuge and sabotage behind enemy lines. They were taught that nothing should be taken for granted, especially people or time. As if to prove the point, the evening Max arrived he was required to take hours-long IQ and psychological exams. He was also given a new name to use as an alias. Max Steiner was now Mark Everett from Indianapolis, Indiana.

The group of recruits was much smaller than Max's 250-member German Ritchie class. They spanned the ages from eighteen to fifty, and like the soldiers of Camp Ritchie, they came from all over the world. Camp Greentop was smaller than Ritchie. Concealed in the rugged part of Maryland's Catoctin Mountain, it had previously been a summer camp for handicapped children. The camp was so small that recruits shared Camp Ritchie facilities and instructors from time to time.

The training was rigorous, both mentally and physically. At Ritchie, physical activity had been less important than mental. But Camp Greentop was akin to being back in basic training and then some. Compared to Greentop, his final exercise in the woods with Spitzer was child's play.

Max went on punishing hikes, sometimes carrying a knapsack filled with forty pounds of rocks to simulate a radio set, and a Mason jar, which mimicked a vacuum tube. He and his team trekked up and down hills, climbed over walls, belly-crawled under fences, and forded streams with no bridge while machine-gun fire and explosives rained down and booby traps threatened. If the Mason jar was not broken by the end of the exercise—Max's wasn't— his "reward" was a two-day training in parachute jumping at Quantico Marine Base in Virginia, where, after five jumps, he managed to qualify.

Classroom instruction was more intense as well. While the content was familiar and a good review for Max, it quickly became a graduate course in counterintelligence. He was not only expected to master Morse code; it was anticipated he'd learn to recognize other types of coded telegraphy as well. He was expected to use a radio and transmitter setup, and it was assumed he'd master the new X-35, with which, fortunately, Max already had some experience. New courses taught Max how to use explosives, create disguises, handle poisons, pick locks, and work with miniature cameras like the Minox.

Their final assignments, too, were more complex than Camp Ritchie's. His team of recruits were told to conduct a night raid on a nearby dam, railway bridge, or industrial facility. They would need to elude police, FBI agents, or military guards who were policing the site. Finally they were to radio back their progress in taking control of the site on an X-35.

At the end of training, the number of men left in Max's OSS training class had shrunk from thirty-three to six. All six were taken to Hagerstown, Maryland, where they were sworn in as citizens of the United States of America.

CHAPTER 60

August 1943
Holland

The night sky was inky black. Backlit clouds concealed the moon and stars. That was both good news and bad, Max's teammate, a British paratrooper, reported. "It's good because the Germans won't see us coming," Stewie Humboldt said. "But it's bad because we can't see either, which means our landing could be a bitch."

Max was riding in the back of a C-47 bomber, a parachute strapped to his shoulders. He'd never expected to be here; his mission was to arrange and manage an arms drop to one of the resistance groups in Holland. He'd planned to stay in London while it happened.

Over the past three years the Resistance in Holland had finally become a viable force in the struggle to run the Nazis out of the Netherlands. Several groups operated, mostly autonomously. The fiercest was the CR, who were known not just for counterintelligence and sabotage, but also for assassinations. They'd begged the Brits and the Americans for weapons.

Max's mission was a cooperative effort between the OSS and

Britain's secret Special Operations Executive, the SOE. Members from the two organizations often worked on the same team. Max moved from the OSS office on Grosvenor Street to the SOE's station on Baker Street for the operation. The SOE's office wasn't far from Sherlock Holmes's fictional home, which had inevitably led to the SOE nickname "Baker Street Irregulars."

This was Max's first mission, and he'd carefully planned it with his SOE counterpart. The head of the Gestapo in Nazi Germany was Heinrich Mueller. The CS 6 Resistance knew that an official in his inner circle, Hans Baader, who had direct control over the Dutch Gestapo, would be visiting Amsterdam for two days, and they wanted to take him out. Plans were made, arms were collected, and the mission was given a green light. At the last minute, though, twelve hours before the drop, the resistance group had gone silent. No radio contact. Nothing.

Max, who was now using his alias, Staff Sergeant Mark Everett, was close to panic, but he tried not to show it. Many reasons could account for radio silence. The OSS equipment given the Resistance was not as dependable as the X-35; the heavy cloud cover could have hampered communication; the radio man might not know how to operate the equipment.

Or the Gestapo could have ambushed the CS 6 on a tip, taken them prisoners, and were lying in wait for the arms and the Allies who delivered them.

Given the situation, Archie Stimson, his SOE partner, wanted to cancel the drop. "It's only prudent," he claimed. He was right. But Max hesitated. Himmler's deputy would only be in Amsterdam two days. If the CS 6 didn't go after him now, that window would close, perhaps forever.

The Gestapo had snatched Max's father and sent him to Dachau. Later they rounded up his parents and sent them to their deaths. Max couldn't let the opportunity to avenge their deaths slip away. Given the chance, he'd take out the Gestapo officer himself. The only way to make that happen was to fly in with the paratrooper and figure out what was going on. Reckless? Perhaps. Potentially significant? Absolutely.

"You're daft, Everett," Archie said. "You think you're a cowboy, but you're going to be a dead cowboy if you go. You're not the Lone Ranger. The Indians will have your scalp."

Max was stubborn. "If that happens, I'll have died doing the right thing."

"Everett, think it through. You could be walking into a trap."

"I have thought it through." He glared at Archie. "You going to stop me?"

Archie threw up his hands. "I suppose the Dutch need our gifts."

"Then they'll get them."

"At least you're not going in on a flying coffin." Archie meant a glider, which some units used to ferry arms and soldiers behind enemy lines. Their visibility caused pilots to be shot down, and their lack of flexibility could result in a crash.

Max didn't tell Archie the other reason he wanted to parachute into Holland. He wanted to find out anything he could about Jacob and Carl Weber and if, by some miracle, they were still alive. He wasn't sanguine. The Germans had deported or killed more than half the Jews in Holland and were still at it. But the Webers were family. He had to know.

He and Archie checked the manifest one last time. They had assembled a combination of British and American weapons. Among them were British Stens, Bren machine guns, a cache of captured German and Italian weapons, and Max's favorite, the new American carbine rifles. There were American Beano grenades, other explosives that looked like pieces of coal, and limpet mines. Also in the package was the American FP-45 Liberator pistol. They had been intended precisely for resistance fighters but were vetoed at the last minute by the US military. However, they were already in production and some managed to slip into arms drops anyway. Finally, there were chocolate bars, English biscuits, Spam, and more.

∾

Which was how Staff Sergeant Mark Everett, US Army, found himself in an American C-47 bomber flying across the English Channel. Max had studied his Red Book, the latest order of battle he'd received, and knew there were no Wehrmacht units in the area. But he decided to wear the German Army uniform he'd put together at Camp Ritchie. If he was caught, he'd try to talk his way out of the situation by claiming he was on leave visiting family nearby.

Suddenly the plane made a sharp descent. Max's stomach leaped to his throat. "What's going on?" His voice cracked.

"No worries, mate. That's the signal to get ready. We'll jump soon."

Max clutched his seat anyway. "We've reached the proper coordinates?"

"Apparently." Stewie laughed. "Relax. I haven't had a bad jump yet. Too bad we don't have a Mustang escort."

"A Mustang? They're tiny."

"Yeah, but they light up like Christmas trees and point the bombardiers to the right target when it's dark. 'Course, then they fly like a bat out of hell to get away."

The C-47 dropped suddenly, at what Max thought was an excessive speed. The clouds followed them down, and the plane bounced. His stomach was in his mouth. Once they were at fifteen hundred feet, they'd jump.

"Open the door and throw out the packages," Stewie yelled, squinting as if he could see the ground. "Make sure no strings are caught on anything. Then get out. I'm right behind you. And say your prayers!"

Everything happened at once. Max opened the door to the plane, made one last check of the eight arms packages, which were encased in metal canisters attached to tiny parachutes, and threw them out. Then he made sure the static line was hooked in, jumped out the door, counted to three, and pulled the ripcord.

CHAPTER 61

August 1943
Holland

It was a hard landing, and Max felt pain in his left ankle. He hoped to hell it wasn't broken again. He gave himself ten seconds on the ground and then got to his feet. The ankle was tender but he could walk on it. He mentally thanked Hashem. He looked around. Shadows and shapes in various shades of black loomed in every direction. His hand automatically went for his Colt .45, and he waited for his eyes to adapt to the dark. It appeared as if they'd just brushed the trees at the edge of a forest. He didn't see Stewie.

He tried to fold up the parachute the best he could and dragged it into the forest. Along the way he spotted two of the arms canisters. Relief washed over him. He detached the parachutes and folded them into a giant bundle along with his own. As he got to the edge of the woods, he heard what he thought was an owl coming from deeper in the trees.

He echoed the call back. A moment later, Stewie showed up, limping. Another wave of relief washed over Max.

"Told you," Stewie whispered.

"You okay?" Max whispered back.

"I'll live."

"You ditch your chute?"

"Yeah." Stewie unholstered his pistol. "Now we wait. They'll be on their way. If they're coming. The C-47 made noise."

Five minutes later a light flashed on and off three times. It came from the other side of the field, well away from the forest.

"What do you think, Everett?" Stewie said.

"It could be our guys," Max said uncertainly. He dug into his pocket and pulled out a flashlight.

"Hold off." Stewie slipped his hand over Max's flashlight. "You sure?"

"No," Max replied. "Let's back up to the forest for cover."

Once they were under cover of the woods, Max took a breath. He wouldn't admit it to Stewie, but his pulse was racing, and his throat felt thick. One wrong move, they were both dead. He snapped on the flashlight and returned the signal. Then they waited.

It took ten minutes for five resistance members to reach them. Even then, Max made Stewie wait before they revealed themselves. He aimed the flashlight at the man in the lead, flicked it on, and hoped he was blinding the man with the glare. The man, whose white collar shaded his eyes, said in Dutch, "Thank God. We didn't know if you were coming. Turn that off now."

Max, still suspicious, snapped off the light. "What's the password?" Every SOE-OSS mission had a password, shared when planning an operation. It was used each time they communicated. Or else the Allies shot.

"Wooly mammoth."

For the third time Max felt relief. They emerged from the woods, Stewie aiming his gun at Whitecollar, who suddenly backed up, a startled expression on his face. He went for his gun. Max threw his hands in the air. "Don't shoot. I'm American. The Deutsch uniform is my cover." He pointed to Stewie. "He's a Brit."

Whitecollar and his men exchanged wary glances but didn't shoot.

Max said, "You have a truck? Or wagon? For your gifts?"

Whitecollar yanked his thumb. "Across the field. Off the road. Behind a barn."

Max nodded. "What happened to your comms last night?"

"Our safe house was raided. They smashed the place up. Including our radio."

"You know who?"

Whitecollar's lips thinned. "We think so. We'll deal with them tomorrow."

Max raised his eyebrows. "Them" implied more than one. Not good.

"Is that why you're here?" another man asked Max.

Max didn't answer. "There are eight canisters. I spotted two of them. Let's round them up."

The men found all eight and carried them across the field to a dirt road. Whitecollar was obviously the leader. He slipped beside a barn and the road and trotted around to the back. Max followed. A pickup truck was waiting, the engine running. The driver wore a face of impatience mixed with fear. "Let's go, let's go, let's go," he said under his breath.

The men hefted the canisters into the bed of the truck, and the man who'd asked Max if he was here because of the raid climbed into the cab and sat in front with the driver. The truck took off in a hurry.

Max, Stewie, and the other men headed back across the field. They were about halfway to the forest when a barrage of machine-gun fire erupted from the woods. Stewie and Whitecollar went down. Max dropped to the ground and tried to low-crawl away. But the spray of the weapons was too wide. Muzzles sparked, showering orange flashes for a fraction of a second. The bullets homed in on the remaining resistance members and Max.

Max heard the Gestapo shout, "We have you surrounded. Give yourselves up!"

Max knew they were lying. They had been in the woods, waiting to ambush them. But the field that led back to the road was clear. No enemy there. Max was torn. He wanted to grab Stewie, but when he looked over, the form that had been Stewie wasn't moving.

There was nothing Max could do for him. Or Whitecollar. He winced.

The three resistance men left were, like him, belly-crawling across the ground. Their only advantage was darkness. But it was temporary. The shooters might have had some kind of night-vision apparatus. But even if they didn't, the dark wouldn't last. The Gestapo would advance across the field with flashlights. When they saw Max in a German Wehrmacht uniform, they would shoot and ask questions afterward. If Max was going to save himself, it had to be now.

He got to his feet and sprinted toward the road. There was a momentary lull in the gunfire. Maybe the Gestapo were confused. Which adversaries should they target? The moving figure? Or the ones still on the ground? Someone had to give the order.

The machine-gun fire started up again, sputtering and spitting in Max's direction. Thankfully, he was out of range. He ran full bore to the dirt road and kept going.

CHAPTER 62

August 1943
Holland

Max ran as fast as he could for as long as he could, grateful he'd been a runner in his youth. The dirt road was studded with rocks, and he was concerned about twisting his ankle again, but it held. The landing spot was in the middle of rural Holland, and he ran past sturdy farms and orderly fields of wheat and maize, but he didn't pass any landmarks. He checked his compass and discovered he was heading east. If he kept going, he would eventually reach the ocean.

Sweat poured off him and his clothing was damp, but the night air was cool and a breeze made it tolerable. After a few miles, his fear began to ebb, and he slowed his pace to consider his options.

He didn't know whether the arms drop had succeeded. Two resistance members had taken off in the truck with the stash of weapons, but they might have been collaborators working with whoever raided the safe house. If so, the Gestapo had scored a significant win. By now they would know about the plan to take out Mueller's deputy in Amsterdam. They'd also know the weapons had come from London.

The assassination of Baader would be aborted once London learned about the ambush.

So much for the success of his first mission. He should have listened to Archie and canceled the drop when they lost communication. But he'd been too eager or arrogant to heed the warning. Archie was more experienced. He'd known the risks. But Max wanted to prove himself, to play the hero. Now two men, maybe more, were dead. His first mission had failed. An ache that would become all too familiar each time good soldiers died spread through his gut.

Two hours later, according to his watch, he was not tired as much as he was thirsty. He'd emptied his canteen an hour ago. He figured a farm would have a pump, and the thought of clear, cold water made his mouth even more parched. But the squeaks and clanks of using one in the middle of the night would wake the farm's owners before a drop crossed his lips, and someone would run outside with a shotgun aimed at his chest.

The clouds were finally clearing, and Max could see the next farm about a mile away. The adrenaline that had fueled him began to subside. He was exhausted. He needed to rest. He would hide in the next barn for a couple of hours. Pull straw over him and get some sleep. They'd had a pickup by boat arranged on the coast, but the boat's skipper was long gone by now. He'd figure out how to get back to London in the morning.

When he reached the farm, he slowed to a walk. A barn or milking shed stood about fifty meters from the farmhouse. Between the two buildings was a pump. He felt almost dizzy with thirst. A bucket lay beside the pump. When Max peered into it, he was overcome with joy. It was half-filled with water. He was so thirsty he didn't care how long the water had been there. He quietly picked up the bucket and drank. It tasted like heaven. Again Max thanked Hashem.

Noiselessly he approached the barn and saw the door was slightly ajar. He pushed it open just enough to squeeze through. He was in a milking shed. A dozen cows stirred and stomped when he entered. One of them mooed.

Scheisse. To be betrayed by a cow? After the night he'd had? "Quiet," he whispered. For some reason, the cow went quiet. He climbed a wooden ladder to the hayloft, went to the corner farthest from the ladder, and sat on the floor. He scattered as much loose hay as he could on top of himself. Using his knapsack as a pillow, he lay down. Within seconds he was asleep.

CHAPTER 63

A perfect rosy dawn made the old saying that beauty follows darkness seem like fact, Max thought the next morning. An early sun poured through the window in the hayloft, shooting sparkles of light everywhere as it filtered through the glass. Max lay back appreciating the beauty before he remembered what had woken him.

The door to the barn or, more accurately, the milking shed, squeaked open and he heard footsteps below. Someone was inside. He lay still and listened. The scratch of something being pulled or pushed across the floor, the sigh of someone releasing their breath—sitting down, perhaps—and then a voice. A female voice.

"Good morning, Stella. You're going to be first this morning." She chuckled.

A cow mooed.

"Yes, and then I'll come to you, Veronica."

A higher-pitched moo. Must be a different cow. She's got the cows talking to her, Max thought. That's why the cow that lowed last night stopped on command. Remarkable. He heard spurts of milk hit a tin bucket. Max was curious about how she'd trained the cows to respond to her. He wished he could take a peek. But that would be a huge risk. He forced himself to think about his own plight rather than the cows. If he could lie still and didn't cough or sneeze, he could slip out when she was done.

It seemed like hours until she finished milking the twelve cows in the shed, but eventually she opened their stalls and herded them out to a meadow. He could see her through the hayloft window. She was older than he'd expected, with gray hair and a round body. She picked up two buckets and headed back into the house. He waited another five minutes to make sure no one else was about, gathered his knapsack, and climbed down the stairs. He brushed off as much straw as he could, but his uniform was badly wrinkled, and it smelled like manure. Max crept back to the road. Despite his sloppy appearance, his visit had been a pleasant diversion.

A signpost just east of the farm indicated that he was two miles outside Tilburg. He picked up his pace, hoping to find a café; he was famished and needed coffee. Compared to Amsterdam or Chicago, Tilburg was a small city, but it boasted a good university and a national park and was only an hour's train ride from Amsterdam.

He found a café, which, at this early hour of the morning, was bustling with customers who all seemed to know one another. He tried to ignore their disapproving glances and whispers as he wolfed down breakfast and an entire pot of coffee. Still wearing his German uniform, he must look like he'd slept in a—well—a hayloft. Not an auspicious look for a proud soldier of the Reich.

Tilburg had three railway stations, all with hourly trains for Amsterdam. By now the OSS would know something had gone wrong with the mission. Archie would be worried. Max needed to contact him, and he needed to clean up at an OSS safe house. Most of all, he needed to find someone trustworthy.

After paying for breakfast, he walked to the closest station and boarded a train.

~

Max arrived in Amsterdam before nine in the morning. It was an uneventful journey. No one stopped or seemed to notice him. Just another soldier on leave. As he stepped off the train at Central Station and walked outside, the city seemed weary and bedraggled, like a house in need of a fresh coat of paint. The Dutch, in Amsterdam at least, appeared to have lost their will to keep up the cheerful cleanliness Max remembered. After four years of occupation, who could blame them?

Even so the city brought back memories. He'd spent more than four years in Holland, the most "normal" years of his life. It was here he grew from a child to a man, known the comfort of close friends, the ecstasy of love. It was also here that he'd felt the unspeakable horror of death. From here that he'd fled for his life. Learned that evil never dies. It lies hidden away, waiting for the right time to swoop in and destroy.

Max couldn't go back to the Jewish Quarter—if it still existed. None of his friends were there. They were either dead or in hiding. And while there was only a small chance he would be recognized, it would be fatal if he was. He had no idea what to do.

Then it occurred to him that there was one person who might help.

As Max climbed the stairs to Annaliese's apartment, more memories came alive. The scent of cabbage simmering in oil. The slight musty odor in the hall. He didn't know if Kaarina, her mother, still lived there with the younger children. Or if she did, whether she would allow him inside. Four years was a long time. He wouldn't be surprised if she blamed him for her daughter's death. Even though it was Heinrich Wagner's Nazi thugs who'd precipitated the violence.

He took a breath and tapped on the door.

Kaarina opened the door with impatience. She wore a light sweater on top of her dress and carried a bag he knew was for food. She looked at Max without any sign she knew him, scanned his messy German uniform, then peered at his face. "Whoever you are," she snapped, "you have the wrong apartment. I'm on my way to market."

As soon as she said the words, though, recognition dawned, and her mouth dropped open. "Max? Is that you?"

He raised a finger to his lips and nodded. "May I come in?" he whispered.

A bewildered look came across her face, but she opened the door wide and ushered him in. She locked the door when he was inside.

"Thank you." He looked her over. She was still as he recalled: an older version of Annaliese, slim and graceful. But her blond hair was cut short in a bob, and he thought he saw new worry lines on her forehead. She'd always worn her fear on her face.

She gazed at him too, seeming to take in his messy appearance, his fatigue, and his anxiety. She opened her arms, and he went into them, hugging her close. His throat thickened, and he saw she was blinking back tears.

When they broke apart, she said, "What are you doing here? In a German uniform? Did anyone see you come in? Are you hungry?"

Max sat on her sofa. "I'll tell you what I can. May I have some water, please?"

She went to the kitchen, filled a tall glass from a spigot, brought it out, and sat across from him. Max told her he'd escaped to the US but left his parents behind. When he heard they'd been slaughtered in Sobibor, he enlisted and was sent to a special camp for other German émigrés.

"For what purpose?" she asked.

He hesitated. "I'm not at liberty to say."

"Ahh," was all she said. She looked thoughtful, as though she was putting pieces together. "I suppose that has something to do with your uniform."

He didn't reply. After a long pause, he asked, "The little ones are in school?"

She nodded.

"Would you mind if I bathed? I've been sleeping with cows in a hayloft, among other things."

"Of course," she said. She looked him over once more. "I assume you don't have any other clothing."

"No."

"Wait here." She got up and went into her bedroom. When she came back, she was carrying a man's shirt and pants. "Try these. After you clean up." She didn't say where they came from, and Max didn't ask. "And, though I loathe them, let me try to get that German uniform into shape."

Max felt almost human after he showered and dressed in the clothes Kaarina gave him.

He sat in the same spot as when he'd come to dinner years earlier and the children barraged him with questions. "There isn't a day that goes by that I don't think of her," he said.

Kaarina let out a breath. "It is the same for me." She was quiet for a moment. "But I think she would be proud of us."

"Why?"

"It appears as if we are both involved in avenging her death." She added, "Among other things."

Max cocked his head. "What does that mean, Kaarina? What are you doing?"

"I trust you, Max," she said. "I know how much you loved Annaliese."

"I treasured her."

She offered him a sad smile. "I hope you will trust me. Do you know of the Naamloze Vennootschap?"

Max stiffened. "The NV?" When she nodded, he said, "You are taking Jewish children into hiding?"

"Not anymore, sadly. There aren't many left. But that's how I started."

"You never went to the farm Jacob arranged?"

"We didn't need to. When Annaliese was killed, I was no longer a threat to anyone."

Max bit his lip. He should have realized that.

"You know, most of the resistance groups know each other. I now help the Landelijke Knokploeg occasionally. Mostly with radio transmissions. You know. Morse code."

Max leaned forward. "The LKP? You know people in the 'Brawl Crew'?"

"It's one of the largest, you know."

"I do." Max raised a hand to his forehead and massaged his temples. An idea was materializing. The LKP, along with the CS 6, were the only Dutch resistance groups actively involved in sabotage and counterintelligence. With luck, perhaps the LKP could do what the CS 6 couldn't: put a mission together tomorrow night, when Hans Baader was scheduled to fly back to Berlin. But could he trust Kaarina to be his emissary? She'd started the conversation by saying she trusted him and hoped he would trust her. He mulled it over.

"Kaarina. I have an idea. Let's talk."

CHAPTER 64

August 1943
Amsterdam

An hour later Max and Kaarina parked their bicycles—Max borrowed her son's—in back of a house in an affluent neighborhood of Amsterdam. It wasn't far from the ballet studio Max had visited as one of the Four Musketeers years earlier. Kaarina knocked on a door with stained-glass panes at the top. The door was opened by a young woman.

"Kaarina! I was hoping you'd come today." She gazed at Max with alarm. "Who is this?"

Kaarina explained. The woman said, "Wait here," and disappeared. She returned with a man a moment later. "Tell him."

Kaarina went through it again. She referred to Max as "my friend." The man looked to be about Max's age, blond, but not tall. He kept his eyes on Max.

When Kaarina finished, the man said, "SOE or OSS?"

Max answered. "A joint mission. It went sideways. I'm hoping you can help. But I need to contact my people. May I have your permission?"

The man pursed his lips, thinking it over. A strange habit, Max thought. He expected a negative reply. But the man surprised him. "You may call me Eric. And you?"

"I am Sergeant Mark Everett from America."

"Come in, Sergeant, and tell me what you want."

An hour later in an upstairs bedroom, Kaarina helped Max compose a brief coded message to Archie Stimson in London. She went through the procedure. "Because of Nazi interception efforts, we only transmit in emergencies, and never more than once every two hours. Messages are sixty seconds at most."

"Thank you," Max said. His message was brief. "Mission SNAFU. Casualties. Trying again. Need extraction twenty-three hours."

The rest of the afternoon Max turned into an observer. Eric went upstairs to a second bedroom, this one at the front of the house, and raised the window shades. An hour after that, three men and another woman knocked at the back door.

Eric explained the situation. They nodded at Max but didn't interact with him. Two hours later Kaarina and Max went back upstairs to the radio and opened the transmitter/receiver. It wasn't an X-35 but seemed functional.

Archie had replied. "Relieved. Go. Rotterdam pier 17."

Max told Eric, who smiled. "Good. But now you need to leave it to us. We have a plan. It's safer if you don't know it. Go back to London. If all goes well, the mission will be over before Baader flies back to Berlin."

"You'll let me know?"

"You will know."

Max extended his hand. "I am grateful."

Eric canted his head and shook. "Victory is ours."

Max and Kaarina rode the bicycles back to her apartment. She was starting to cook dinner when the little ones arrived home from school. They weren't so little any more. They didn't remember Max, but they'd matured enough to be shy around him, no longer boisterous. Max, feeling nostalgic, missed their energy.

Kaarina had washed his German uniform and hung it up to dry. He changed back into it.

"You have gone far beyond my expectations, Kaarina. I am in your debt."

"You have as well," she said. "But now you must go. Keep the clothes. You may need to sleep in another hayloft."

Max laughed. "Before I leave, do you have any updates about Jacob Weber? What happened to him? And his family?"

She turned away from the soup simmering on the stove. "You don't know?"

"The last time I saw him he was trying to arrange a ride to Rotterdam for me."

"He never returned to the bookstore. It had been destroyed anyway. He went underground to work with the Jewish Resistance. I do not recall the name."

"DJRL."

"Yes. That's it. We heard later he was shot last summer, in July. By the Gestapo. But I think perhaps his son and family are still in hiding."

Max wasn't surprised. He squeezed his eyes shut. They were wet when he flicked them open. His mentor and surrogate father was gone. He swallowed, trying to think of the right words.

Kaarina put her finger on his lips. "This is war. There is nothing more to say. Godspeed, Max. You are a fine man. I know Annaliese is smiling at the work we have done together."

～

Max was back in London the next day when he heard about the tragic explosion of Hans Baader's plane after it took off from Amsterdam's Schiphol Airport.

CHAPTER 65

November 1943
Occupied France

Over the next few days Max felt lighter, as if he'd paid a long-standing debt, although it was Kaarina who'd made it possible. Annaliese's mother hadn't hesitated to suggest that the LKP finish Max's mission. Had she always been so determined? Or was it the result of her daughter's murder by Nazi thugs? In the chronicles of life, however, it didn't matter. War brought out both the best and the worst in people, but often they had to hit bottom first. He thought about Annaliese; she took after her mother in so many ways. Would she have had the same strength of her convictions? He never had the chance to find out.

As for the mission, Max's higher-ups at the OSS showered him with praise. Because of his initiative and quick thinking, they said, he'd been able to salvage a disaster and turn it into a success. The assassination of Gestapo leader Hans Baader was a turning point for Holland. And not just for Dutch morale. It was, in addition to the Battle of Stalingrad, proof that Nazis were not invincible. They nominated him for a Silver Star.

Max insisted that he had very little to do with the mission's success. It was due, he said, to the commitment and courage of a woman with more balls than most men. That didn't stop the praise, though, and Max grew embarrassed. It hadn't been his skill. Or his initiative. He'd run from the ambush rather than fight, and he'd lucked out with Kaarina. In fact, he was anxious to get back in the field to prove his worth. If only to himself.

He got his chance in November.

～

He was in the London OSS headquarters waiting for a radio transmission from an agent in Belgium when the door to his office opened, and his buddy from Camp Ritchie, Freddy Hahn, strolled in.

"Hiya, Frick," Freddy said with a grin.

Max was already out of his chair. He hurried over to his friend, and they embraced.

"What the hell are you doing here?"

"Heard you needed a tennis partner," Freddy said.

Billy Hanover, with whom Max shared an office, looked up from the report he'd been writing. He studied Freddy, then Max. "I see why they call you Frick and Frack."

"Oh, you got that," Freddy said with heavy sarcasm. "It couldn't be because we're both the same height, blond with light eyes . . ."

"Give him a break, Freddy." Max laughed. "He's from Montana."

"And you two are the famous Swiss ice-skating heroes." Billy gave as good as he got.

"Seriously, Freddy, what brings you here?"

"They haven't told you about your new mission?"

Max shook his head.

"Well, let me educate you," Freddy said.

～

According to Freddy, the French Resistance in Occupied France had discovered several huge munitions factories in Saint-Étienne, a midsize industrial city in east-central France, some thirty-three miles southwest of Lyon.

"The city is known for manufacturing firearms and other armaments, as well as coal mining and textiles," Freddy said. "In fact, a machine gun used during the Great War was called the Saint-Étienne."

"I knew I'd heard 'Saint-Étienne' before," Max said.

"It was famous but unreliable. Now, though, Saint-Étienne supplies firearms to the Wehrmacht," Freddy explained. "The Allies want to bomb the factories that produce the weapons and the railways that deliver them to Germany, but they need accurate locations for their targets."

"And that's where we come in," Max said.

"Correct. When I learned you were in London, I was able to request that you join the team." Freddy grinned. "Based on your expertise with maps."

"Clever." Max smiled too. "But Spitzer stole it, remember?"

"And got hopelessly lost."

Max laughed. "Which makes me the expert?"

"Hey. I trust you, soldier. We'll survey the possible targets and prepare precise coordinates."

"You said 'team.' Who else is on it?"

"Not sure yet."

Max tipped his head sideways. "Why not?"

"There may be a problem traveling across Occupied France."

"I breezed through Holland in a German infantry uniform."

"The problem isn't us. It's the head of the Lyon Gestapo, Klaus Barbie."

"The Butcher of Lyon?" Max stiffened. "You know he was instrumental in the invasion of Holland. He worked with Eichmann to torture, deport, and murder Dutch Jews. He's a monster."

Freddy nodded. "He's a crafty bastard, too. When he's not torturing and murdering, he's got spies and informants scouring the entire region for traitors. He wants to destroy the Resistance. Saint-Étienne is part of his region. If he gets us, that's all she wrote."

"So our mission is to stay out of his clutches while we pin down the locations."

"Among other things."

"What other things?"

Freddy yanked a thumb in Billy's direction. Then he held up a finger. Billy didn't see either gesture.

Freddy and Max walked to a busy Soho pub. Max had recommended they leave the neighborhood; there were too many eager ears around Grosvenor Street.

"So what's the real mission?" Max asked once they started their pints.

"It's off book. And highly confidential. My direct superior is the only one who knows. And he thinks I'm insane."

Max shot Freddy a doubtful look. "Off book? That's not like you, Freddy."

"It has to be."

Max took a gulp of ale. "I'm listening."

Freddy cleared his throat. "One of the resistance leaders in the region told me about an orphanage for about thirty Jewish children. It's in a secluded part of the French Alps. Well, the foothills. Practically hidden if you don't know it's there. About ten miles from Saint-Étienne. Surrounded by forest."

Max blinked.

"Apparently, an informer—a truck driver, I'm told—happened on it by chance yesterday and told the Gestapo in Lyon what he saw. Barbie's planning to seize the children. Imminently. Do you have any idea what he will do to them? And the people caring for them?"

"I might. Did you hear about the French Resistance member who said her father was beaten and his skin torn? His head was dunked in a Benwayet of ammonia and cold water. He couldn't sit or stand. He died three days later. All thanks to Klaus Barbie." Anger tightened Max's throat. "So yes, I do have an idea of what he might do. Barbie's the one who's insane." He paused. "So we're going there to do what? Rescue the children? Get them to Spain or Switzerland?"

"We're not going to rescue the children."

"What do you mean? How are they going to get out?"

"There are four or five groups that rescue Jewish orphans. The Resistance says the children are already leaving the place with two of those groups. They'll all be gone by tonight."

"How did they organize so quickly? The Resistance, I mean?" Max asked.

"We are all in close contact with each other."

"No, I mean, how did they find out Barbie's men are coming to seize the children?"

Freddy leaned back in his chair. "They have a high-level source in Lyon. Who is on Barbie's staff."

"That's some source."

"I was also told that Barbie himself is coming to 'supervise' the event," Freddy said. "Sometime tomorrow. He wants photographs."

Max leaned forward. He templed his hands on the table and stared at Freddy. "Are you saying what I think you are?"

"If we can set it up . . . say . . . with enough explosives to level the house when he goes inside . . ."

"Jesus Christ, Freddy!" Max heard the wonder in his own voice. "We're going to take out Klaus Barbie!"

"I figured you might want in."

Max bit his lip. "I'd say so. But why is this off book?"

"Because the higher-ups think there's too many unknowns. And uncertainties. If we fail, they don't want the blame."

Max winced. "So we take it on the chin. If we make it out alive."

"Exactly." He looked at his watch. "I have a C-47 waiting for us. And the coordinates. We'll parachute in tonight. The third man is George Kaiser. He's an expert with explosives. He can prang an ant from a mile away. We'll set everything up. Then wait for Barbie to show up tomorrow."

"I don't know, Freddy. Sounds too easy. What did your boss say?"

"He said if I'm crazy enough to risk my life—knowing the chances

of success are slim to none—he'd give me seventy-two hours' leave."
Freddy took a long pull on his pint. "He said, 'What you do on your
own time is your business. I can't stop you.'" And then he ran down a
list of all the things Barbie would do to me if I was caught."

"Scheisse, Freddy. Just scheisse."

"So, are you in?"

"The thought of getting Barbie off this earth is tempting. He
doesn't deserve to breathe the same air as us. But . . ." Max rubbed the
back of his neck. ". . . I hate to say it. Your boss is right. There are too
many unknowns. The chances of us getting caught are enormous. It's
a suicide mission." Max tossed back the rest of his pint. "Still, I can't
let you do this alone." He sighed. "I'll inform my direct supervisor,
who will tell me I'm as crazy as you, but he won't stop me either.
What time do we take off?"

"Wings up at twenty-one hundred hours."

"So, the firearms factories and railway stations were our cover?"

"Actually, no. But we can do them next week." Freddy grinned.
"See you later."

CHAPTER 66

November 1943
Occupied France

Three men parachuted into the foothills of the French Alps late that night, their explosives carefully packed in canisters with five tiny chutes dropping ahead of them. The terrain was carved out of rock, with cliffs and valleys that were densely wooded. They reminded Max of Catoctin Mountain in Maryland. They spent more than an hour searching for the canisters. Three were on the ground; two swung from nearby overhanging trees.

Once the explosives were secured, they hiked three miles to the place where the orphans had lived. It wasn't a house, more like a secluded hunting lodge with a campsite that had grown with the number of occupants. Three small wooden cabins were slapped together twenty yards from the lodge, which contained a schoolroom, kitchen, and dining area. Each cabin held four bunk-bed frames and one chest of drawers. There had been an attempt to build a playground in between the lodge and cabins, with swings and a slide. The lodge could be accessed from a dirt road, the origin of which was out of view. It widened into a sandy parking area at the entrance. Behind the cabins were the woods.

Kaiser went to work inside the lodge. They had requisitioned general-purpose explosives with both demolition and fragmentation components and a few incendiary devices. Most of the components were TNT combined with barium nitrate or aluminum powder. Kaiser wired two small "packages" downstairs, and another two in the cabins, since they didn't know where Barbie would first step foot. Each set of packages had a wired plunger that could be detonated at the appropriate time. They decided to stake out in the woods behind the cabins, so they buried all the visible wiring in the dirt, making sure to gently tamp down the earth so it looked natural. In addition, all three men carried rifles, pistols, and grenades.

The sky was lightening from black to gray when Max heard a birdcall coming from deeper in the woods.

"*Rit-rit-rit-rit-ritseeyu.*" A cardinal's call. Except the cardinal was an American bird. There were none in Europe. Freddy, who must have taught the Resistance the birdcall, returned it but unholstered his pistol. Max did too.

Two male partisans emerged from the woods behind them. Freddy snapped on the flashlight. Their clothing was tattered and rifles were strapped to their shoulders.

"Password?" Freddy said in a low voice.

"Ted Williams," said one of the men, with such a thick accent the poor baseball star's name was practically undecipherable.

Max smiled.

Freddy holstered his pistol. In perfect French, albeit with an Alsace accent, Freddy said, "Happy to see you. We have questions."

"We are here to answer them," the lead man said. He wore a beret that had seen better days.

"When will Barbie arrive?"

"We do not know. Only that it is on his schedule for today. It could be any minute. Could be tonight. But I suspect not. He will want to see the children. Perhaps dispose of them right away."

"Are you sure he doesn't know the children are gone?"

"We are not sure of anything. But our informant said it would be a modest motorcade. Barbie wants to surprise the caretakers. I am sure he thinks they are part of the Resistance, and destroying us is his primary goal."

"How many men will he bring?"

"Again, we have no way of knowing. But he never travels with less than six. They typically make a three car motorcade."

Max said, "He rode in a chauffeured Mercedes-Benz in Holland. Is that still the case?"

"Yes," the second partisan said.

"Where will they be while he goes inside?"

The second man shrugged. "Most are bodyguards. They will go inside with him. As you might know, he is everyone's favorite target." He laughed. "Very popular."

The first partisan said, "With your permission, may I reach into my backpack?"

Freddy nodded. The man released his pack, rummaged inside, and pulled out a thermos and two baguettes. "They just came out of the oven. My wife. And strong café."

"Merci," Max said.

"Vous parlez français?"

"Un peu."

"Ahh. What else do you need to know?"

"At what point can we assume Barbie decided not to come? Or that the mission might have been compromised?"

The two partisans looked at each other and shook their heads. "We do not know."

Max began to realize why their superiors thought they were crazy. There *were* too many unknowns. The situation was unpredictable and highly volatile. He ran a hand through his hair. This had been— what did the Americans say?—a "harebrained" scheme. They had no business trusting Resistance members who could be making up answers. Telling Max and Freddy what they thought they wanted to hear.

"You're sure all the children are accounted for?"

"Oui. The OSE, L'*Oeuvre de Secours aux Enfants*, and Le Chambon were here last night. I watched them lift the children into trucks."

"What is the safest way for us to get out of here afterward?" Freddy asked.

"Behind the cabins into the woods. In about two miles you will emerge into a valley with peaks in the distance. Head east toward the tallest peak. We will find you and make sure you get to the railway station. You escape by boat?"

Freddy didn't answer. Good move, Max thought.

CHAPTER 67

November 1943
Occupied France

D awn broke into a dull gray overcast with fitful clouds and a bone-chilling wind. None of them had slept. After two cups of coffee Max was wired and his hands shook. He ate half a baguette hoping it would settle him. Freddy was quiet, and Kaiser, who had hardly said a word since they arrived, ate the other half of the bread. They washed up at the pump in front of the cabins, then resumed their positions in the woods.

The next three hours seemed endless, and Max was filled with trepidation. What if Klaus Barbie didn't go into the lodge? Or the cabins? What if he sent his bodyguards instead? What if someone spotted the wired explosives or they didn't ignite? He knew he was allowing fear to overcome reality. Klaus Barbie deserved death. Ultimately, he had been responsible for killing his parents. If Max had a chance, he would return the favor.

Max looked over at Freddy. From his expression, he suspected the same doubts were plaguing him. Only Kaiser looked half-asleep, as if a nap was the most important event of his day. Max tried taking slow, deep breaths.

Finally, at what would be considered lunchtime, Max heard the crunch of tires on the dirt road. He went on high alert, tightening every muscle in his body. A moment later three black Mercedes-Benz sedans rolled up to the lodge. Each car sported a fluttering swastika on the front hood.

Max sucked in a breath. It looked like there were two people in each auto. But no one inside moved. Did they figure out the lodge was abandoned? Would they turn around and leave without getting out? Max and Freddy exchanged a glance. This would happen one way or the other in the next few minutes.

The driver's door of the lead Benz opened, and the driver poked his head out. Sensing no response, he slowly climbed out of the car. He wore an SS uniform. Corporal, Max deduced from the decals and patches. The driver glanced in every direction, including behind him. His gaze swept across their hidden nest in the woods but didn't stop. For the moment, they were safe. Max let out his breath.

The SS man approached the lodge but didn't go inside. As he had done when exiting the Benz, he opened the door and stuck his head in. Twenty seconds later he turned around and shook his head at the other cars. The door to the second Benz opened. Two soldiers, both in SS uniforms, got out and walked toward the lodge. The driver of the third Benz got out and opened the rear door.

A man in a snappy civilian suit emerged from the back seat. Klaus Barbie. For years when living in Holland, Max had wanted to see him in the flesh. Barbie wore an overcoat, but it wasn't buttoned. Max was surprised at how short he was, perhaps only five foot five. Photographs made him seem taller. His hair was brown and his eyes dark.

A buzz skimmed Max's nerves. He felt hot and cold at the same time. He pulled out his carbine, sighted down the barrel, and focused on Barbie. Max had him. He could easily make the shot. He started to shake again, and beads of sweat broke out on his forehead. He wasn't sure he could wait. Freddy looked over and saw Max on the precipice. He grabbed Max's rifle, pointed the front end up in the air, and vehemently shook his head.

Max knew what Freddy was doing. If he shot Barbie now, he'd kill him, Max knew. But the mission could become a bloodbath, and there was a good chance they'd never leave Occupied France alive. He swallowed, took a breath, and nodded.

Freddy kept his hand on Max's carbine until he was sure Max wouldn't do something crazy. He let go of the rifle slowly, and Max laid it down. His thoughts turned to the plunger and the subsequent explosions that would decimate Barbie and shred him into a thousand pieces.

Barbie waited for his bodyguards to surround him, then slowly walked up to the lodge. At the same time a shout came from one of the other men. It sounded like it was coming from the second floor of the lodge. Max craned his neck and gazed up at a window. One of the SS men had opened it and yelled down, "Come up! There is a child! Hurry!"

Barbie stayed where he was but motioned to one of his bodyguards to go up. Max, who had grabbed the plunger when the shouting started, went rigid. "Go inside, Barbie. Go. Now!" he muttered. But Barbie stayed where he was. "No. No. Inside," Max said. Freddy threw him a look that said, "Shut up!"

A moment later, the SS man came downstairs and appeared at the door of the lodge. In his arms was a small child. A little girl. Not more than three years old, Max guessed. Where had she been? How had they missed her? She wasn't crying, but she clutched the SS officer's jacket as if her life depended on it. Max and Freddy exchanged horrified glances. How could they blow up the lodge now? An innocent child would be killed. An innocent Jewish child.

Riveted, Max stared at the scene. Maybe, just maybe, the child would end up outside and Barbie inside. Or maybe Max could somehow rescue her. Deep in his heart, however, he knew neither situation would happen. He knew, too, that the child would probably not survive the day. Barbie or one of his men would see to it. Given that reality, he considered pushing the plunger down anyway. If her death was imminent, what did it matter?

The thought was so overpowering that again, Max could practically taste it. Despite all the unknowns and uncertainties, they had made it this far. They were seconds away from success. They could eliminate a heartless monstrosity from the world. And potentially save hundreds of lives. Was the life of one little girl worth giving up all that?

~

It was. In the end Max couldn't do it. He couldn't live with the blood of an innocent child on his hands. Freddy clearly felt the same way. His hand had gripped the other plunger, but after a long minute, he let go. All three men exchanged glances, silent glances that seemed to approve of the others' decision. Barbie had one of the SS men take a photo of him with the little girl in his arms. Max considered it an atrocity.

They waited for Barbie and the SS men to pile back into the Mercedes and start their engines. They slept until dark and made their way back through the woods. When they reached the valley, two new Resistance members met them and led them to the railway station.

Twenty-four hours later they were back in London, where they got stinking drunk. Max and Freddy never discovered who the little girl was, or why she'd been left behind. They guessed she panicked at the noise and disruption caused by the rescue groups who'd come the previous night and hidden. Their last sight of the little girl was in the back seat of Barbie's car, sitting next to the Butcher of Lyon. Tears welled up in Max's eyes. The image of the little girl, happily chatting with the monster, on her way to her death, would be seared into Max's memory forever.

~

As time passed Max felt relief that the mission had failed. Klaus Barbie was a subhuman bastard. But if Max had played a part in his assassination, he would have had a connection, albeit tenuous, to

Barbie for the rest of his life. Whenever he reflected on his OSS days, Barbie's evil specter would darken Max's mind and remind him that Max, too, had chosen to brutally murder a human being. That connection would have dragged Max down to the same sewer Barbie occupied. The enormity of it would have been too much to bear.

CHAPTER 68

April–June 1944
England

R umors of an Allied invasion of Europe began soon after Max returned from Occupied France. In December 1943, FDR appointed General Dwight D. Eisenhower Supreme Allied Commander in the European Theater of Operations. Operation Overlord wasn't exactly a secret; Ike's remit from the Combined Chiefs of Staff said, in part, "You will enter the continent of Europe and in conjunction with other Allied nations, undertake operations aimed at the heart of Germany and the destruction of her armed forces..."

The specifics of the invasion, however, did remain secret to all but a few high-ranking military officers. In April Max received a top secret telegram saying he would lead a POW interrogation team attached to a military unit once the Allies had established a beach-head in France. Which military unit, his team members, and where he would go ashore were still undetermined. Since he had jumped a few times in the past, he wondered whether he might be assigned to an airborne unit. Both the 101st Airborne Division and the 82nd had been training in England since the previous summer.

Sure enough, in May, Max received his orders. He was to report to Westbury, a village in Wiltshire, where he would be billeted for a month and would train with the 101st. He would fly along with 8,400 other soldiers in the 101st one night in early June. The invasion would begin the next morning. He and his unit would be dropped behind enemy lines at the western area adjacent to Utah Beach. They were to proceed into the Cherbourg Peninsula to head off any eastern German advance.

Two other Ritchie Boys had been assigned to Max's team. Both were from different classes than Max. Usually the Ritchie teams included six men led by an officer; however, so many army units required interrogation teams during the invasion that not every unit had the requisite six. They were told not to take prisoners until they were sure the invasion had succeeded and there'd been time to build fences and prisoner cages. Because Max and his team would be behind enemy lines, they'd need to depend on radio transmissions to find out whether the Allies had established a beachhead.

The weather on June 4 brought hard rain, high winds, and storms. Visibility was dire, so Eisenhower decided to delay the invasion for one night. Twenty-four hours later, on June 5, thousands of paratroopers were trucked to Portland Bill on the English coast, where both the 101st and 82nd US Airborne Divisions would take off for France. The weather was improving, but heavy fog and rain still obscured the skies. Nevertheless, the invasion would proceed.

At midnight on the fifth the soldiers boarded C-47s with all their gear. Max had jumped, but never with so many others at the same time. He'd never carried so much gear before either. The extra seventy pounds of equipment, weapons, and incidentals reminded him of the rocks they put in his knapsack at Camp Greentop when he was training with the OSS.

He sat on one of two facing rows of metal seats running down the sides of the C-47 and eyed the other soldiers. The thunderous noise level inside the plane would discourage conversation, but fear and anxiety churned Max's gut. There would be no second chances in the upcoming battle. Or rescue effort if they failed.

The paratroopers listened to a taped message from Ike before they took off. He called the invasion a crusade and proclaimed the upcoming battles would not be easy. "The enemy will fight savagely," he said. "But I have full confidence in your courage, devotion to duty, and skill in battle."

More than eight hundred planes with thirteen thousand paratroopers took to the skies that night and early the next morning. The flight to the French coast was approximately thirty minutes, and the first half was manageable. As they neared the coast, though, a heavy fog descended. The pilots were flying in at a low altitude—one thousand feet—and the armada was detected by the Germans. Heavy gunfire erupted from the French coast.

Max's C-47 took evasive action. The lumbering bomber rocked, dipped, rose, and fell, sending Max's stomach skyward. The plane in front of them was targeted by German artillery, and after thirty seconds of sustained gunfire, it exploded. A few seconds later, they heard a series of metallic thumps hit the plane's belly. Max and the soldier next to him exchanged glances. They'd been hit. Max's pulse started to race. He'd jumped before, even in bad weather. But he'd never been shot at the same time.

The guy next to him pulled out a rosary and started to pray. Max recited the Sh'ma. The plane abruptly ascended five hundred feet. Max was on the verge of panic. What was happening? Had they been shot at again? No. The unit leader made circular gestures with his arms, signaling that the jumps would begin. He struggled to pull open the plane's door.

Max, sandwiched about halfway down the row of paratroopers, would be about the tenth soldier to jump. He tried to breathe evenly to calm himself, but it didn't work. When it was his turn, he almost forgot to check that there were no loose straps or cables. But he remembered, then made sure his static line was connected, and hurled himself into the night.

CHAPTER 69

June 1944
France

Once he descended below the fog, Max saw dozens of whitish canopies dotting a black sky. Some looked so far away they might land in Belgium; others were closer, but not by much. He wondered why. Curiously, the gunfire from the coast hadn't followed them inland, and his landing would have been uneventful, except that the wind blew him off target. He was trying to steer the chute away from a forest but didn't quite make it. His canopy caught in the branches of an oak tree, and the sudden stop jerked Max up and then down.

He was about thirty feet from the ground, too far to jump unaided. Luckily, he wasn't far from the tree trunk. If he started swinging toward the trunk, eventually he'd be able to grab on to it and release himself from the chute. He bent his knees and brought his legs up as far as he could, making himself into a ball, and started to swing. The chute's fabric tore. He thought he'd made a huge mistake and that the chute would drop to the ground with him Benwayled inside it.

He froze. Despite ominous ripping sounds from the canopy, it held. Max cautiously started to swing again. On his fourth attempt he was able to grab the trunk of the tree. He released his chute and shinnied down. Once on the ground, he pulled on the chute, which finally dislodged. He folded it up the best he could and hid it under a thick bush.

Max had no idea where he was. It was the middle of the night, and he couldn't hear or see any other paratroopers. He stayed under the cover of trees and fished out his compass. The Cherbourg Peninsula was northwest of Utah Beach, where most of the 101st would land. The assembly point for the paratroopers was northwest of Sainte-Mère-Église, a midsize town directly west of Utah Beach. If he headed west to the town, and then cut northwest, he'd eventually reach one or the other—assuming he was fairly close to Utah Beach.

Max counted himself lucky a second time when the path west led straight through the forest. He would have ample cover if any German soldiers materialized. He wanted to pull out his map and study it, but that would require a flashlight. Too risky. So he crept quietly through the woods hoping to get his bearings at a crossroads or signpost.

Dawn was just breaking when the forest gradually cleared and Max found himself walking down a road flanked by farmland. He guessed he'd walked almost ten miles overnight. By now he should have come across Sainte-Mère-Église. Something was wrong. He stopped and pulled out the map. His directions were correct, if, and "if" was becoming more significant, he'd been dropped near Utah Beach. He needed to find out. But he was exhausted and hungry and footsore. First he needed to rest. He looked for a barn in which to hide.

Max woke up a few hours later when the door to the barn he'd found squeaked. No cows or animals here. No hayloft either. Just a collection of farm equipment, rusted barrels, and moldy blankets. He'd chosen a spot in a corner and moved an empty barrel in front of him.

He craned his neck as the door opened. A young woman entered. She came in and, not noticing Max, searched through the tools. Max didn't want to frighten her. In fact, he was reluctant to make contact with her. What if she was pro-Nazi? Or her husband was? Unfortunately, he didn't have a choice.

"Excusez-moi, madame," Max said softly in badly accented French.

Startled, the woman literally jerked away from his voice and cried out. He realized he now knew what it looked like to "jump out of one's skin."

"Qui est-ce?" she demanded in a shaky but urgent voice.

"Je suis Americain. Please do not be afraid."

"Yankee?" Her mouth fell open, but she didn't run away.

"Oui, madame."

"You are really American?" she asked in French. She was very attractive, Max noted. Long, pale blond hair, dark eyes, slim figure. She reminded him of Annaliese.

"How did you get here?"

"Parlez-vous anglais?"

She shook her head. Max tried to explain, using his limited French and lots of hand gestures.

She seemed to understand. "On a entendu les coups de feu hier soir." *We heard the gunfire last night.*

"Oui," he said.

"Where are you trying to go?" Her fear seemed to be developing into curiosity. Was that good or bad?

He yanked his thumb in the air. "Cherbourg."

She pressed her hands together in a silent clap. "C'est formidable! Nous serons libres!"

Max relaxed. She was on their side. "Yes. Soon you will be free. Where am I?" He asked. "What town, what area? How far is Sainte-Mère-Église?"

Her eyes widened. "You are in Amfreville. We are west of Sainte-Mère-Église."

"The town is east of here?" Max was baffled. If that was true, he must have been west of the town when he jumped. So much for the pilot dropping them on precise coordinates, gunfire or not. The pilot had been twisting and turning to avoid a hit. He hadn't succeeded, but the C-47 was obviously sturdy enough to keep flying.

Max let out a sigh. All that hiking for nothing. "If you please, may I have some water?" He handed her his canteen.

"Bien sûr." She smiled and took it. "You must be hungry."

"I am."

She placed her finger on her lips. "Wait here."

A few minutes later she returned with a full canteen. She was also carrying a dish towel tied at the top. "Voilà."

She handed it to Max. Inside was a fresh baguette, ham, an orange, and coffee.

Max ate everything. "Merci. I'm grateful for your kindness. I have one more request, if that's possible."

"Of course," she said.

"May I stay here until dark? I don't want to run into any Germans in daylight."

"Je vous en prie. I will bring you dejeuner."

"Please, no. I am already in your debt."

She gave him a dismissive wave. "It would be my honor."

"What is your name, mademoiselle?"

"Eloïse."

"I am Max. Thank you, Eloïse."

She extended her hand and Max took it. They shook. Her cheeks reddened. "I will return at lunch."

Max retreated to the corner for a nap. He felt a smile on his face.

Max woke up when Eloïse returned. This time an older woman came with her, carrying a tray with a hearty lunch of cassoulet, fresh bread, and vegetables. The woman had the same pale blond hair and dark eyes, but her face was creased with lines, the result of the anguish of war. Her mother. She smiled, set the tray down, and gave him a big hug.

"We were hoping every day you Americans would come," she said in French. She raised her fist. "Victory is ours!" She turned to her daughter. "Eloïse, does he know about the other soldiers?"

Before Eloïse could reply, Max cut in. "What other soldiers? Americans?"

"Oui," Eloïse's mother said. "My friend saw two of them last night near the café. They were going through la poubelle."

Max frowned. "La poubelle?"

"The garbage. The barrels."

"The garbage cans?" Max perked up. "Did they talk to your friend?"

"No. She pretended not to see them. But they were American. Like you." Her smile faded. "Alas, the Germans are here, too. At the café. You must be careful."

"Do you know where I can find them? The Americans?"

"I do not. But peut-être my friend does."

Max was reluctant. He didn't know her friends. To be honest, he didn't know her, either. Or her daughter. "No, merci. I will find them myself. Tonight."

When it was dark, Eloïse returned. Max cleaned himself off and shouldered his knapsack.

"Attendez," Eloïse said with a shy smile. She handed over another package wrapped in a dish towel. "Dîner."

Max didn't know what to say. He could tell she wanted more from him, and as she continued to stare at him with a small smile on her face, he considered it. It was tempting. He even felt a stirring, the first time since Annaliese he'd felt something for a woman. But this wasn't the right time or place. He had a job to do.

CHAPTER 70

Max had to make a decision. He could head into the small town of Amfreville and hope that the two American soldiers who'd been seen at the café would show up. Or he could begin to hike east through the forest to Sainte-Mère-Église. Three soldiers were better than one, especially behind German lines, so he struck out to the café. He would lurk near the garbage cans.

The café was little more than a small rickety shack that looked like it was built in a hurry. An expanse of dirt stretched from the front door—he couldn't call it an entrance—to the road. One light bulb shone above the door. There were four small windows, but they were so grimy he didn't think anyone could see through them. The garbage area, which announced itself by its rancid odor, was in the back. If the Americans had been ferreting through the garbage, they must be starving. Had they lost their rations? He decided not to eat the dinner Eloïse had prepared.

He crouched down close to the garbage cans and waited. An hour passed, then another. He was about to give up and start his trek east when he heard what sounded like a jeep pull up to the front. He stealthily moved to the side of the building and watched three uniformed soldiers jump out and hurry inside.

Max went rigid. His heart thumped in his chest. It wasn't an

American jeep. It was the German version, a Kübelwagen, and they were German soldiers. Max scuttled back to the garbage cans and picked up his gear. Peals of laughter, men's and women's, streamed out from inside. Time to go back into the forest.

He moved slowly away from the café, trying not to attract any attention, in case anyone was peering out the window. When he was fifty yards away, he started to jog and kept going until he reached the forest.

The woods seemed more menacing this time. Probably because he'd spotted some Germans back at the café. Max tried to walk silently, but all his gear made it impossible. He thought about ditching some of it but didn't want to waste time going through it.

He'd hiked about a mile when he felt rather than heard himself drawing closer to a presence. He slowed his gait as he advanced. He heard whispers. A rustle or two. Then movement. He took a few steps. Everything stopped. No more sounds. He unholstered his Colt. This would be close quarters. He tried to keep his breathing even but his stomach was turning somersaults. Time passed in an unknown measurement that could have been a few seconds or an hour. Finally a whisper.

"All clear?" English! With no accent. Had he found the Americans?

More rustles. "Let's hightail it out of here!"

Max called out right away. "Sergeant Mark Everett here. Attached to the 101st. Who are you?"

A hush came over the woods. Then two loud clicks as pistols were cocked. The faces of two men, smeared with grease or soot, emerged from opposite sides of a bush. "Hands up!"

Max raised his hands. "Don't shoot. I'm from Chicago."

The men held their ground. The taller one was closest to Max. "Well, bless my boots, Chicago." The man had a Texas twang. He holstered his pistol. "What kind of SNAFU brings you to these woods?"

Max had to grin. "Probably the same one that put you here."

"I'm PFC Tex Martin, he said. "You can lower your hands. And yes, I'm from Brownsville."

The other soldier chimed in too. "PFC Harry Preston. Columbus, Ohio." From what Max could tell in admittedly just the light from the moon, he was dark and swarthy. "And yeah. They call me Hairy Harry."

"Wait a minute," Tex said, suspicion in his voice. "Where's your Screaming Eagle?" Tex shrugged his shoulder to show off his. "You said you were with the 101st."

"I'm attached to your division on special assignment. I was dropped way off course. Couldn't be helped. Our C-47 was hit. I'm supposed to be north of Sainte-Mère-Église heading to Cherbourg. Were you the guys going through the garbage cans at the café?"

"How'd you know?"

"You were seen. Which means the Germans saw you, too. I barely avoided them myself. I was waiting in the back to see if you'd come back."

"We decided we wouldn't go to the same place twice. Meanwhile, we think our assembly point is east of here. Fucking maps."

"Not maps," Max said. "The pilots. They were dodging bullets. We probably have the same meet-up place. I'll bet there are other men scattered all over the peninsula. Because of the pilots' evasive action. Actually it's a miracle we're still alive. We watched a couple planes explode. One of them was in front of ours. We got hit but stayed up."

"Us too."

"Hey, you guys must be starving." Max handed over the dinner Eloïse had given him.

Tex grabbed the food and gave Max a broad smile. "This'll hit the spot."

He sat on the ground and untied the dish towel. Harry sat down too. In between stuffing baguettes in their mouths, Harry asked, "How'd you end up here, Sergeant?"

"Two women helped me out. A mother and daughter. They were very kind. I spent a night in their barn. They were grateful Americans were coming."

"I'll bet." Harry grinned.

Tex changed the subject. "How come you got an accent?"

"I'm originally from Germany."

"Wait . . . I heard about you guys. Aren't you're the ones interrogating POWs?"

"Exactly."

"Well, let's go round us up some fer you to interrogate."

Max liked Tex. If they could avoid German soldiers, they might even make it.

Twenty minutes later they were heading east. It was a warm, humid night. Tex wrapped the dish towel around his head. Max worked up a sweat but kept his helmet on. Harry did the same. Max checked his compass and kept them going east. At some point they'd have to hit the two-lane blacktop, the French version of a highway, leading to Sainte-Mère-Église. For two hours, they made good progress. Max checked his watch. Almost midnight.

Max could smell his own body odor as well as the others'. He couldn't recall the last time he'd showered. A vision of a cool fresh stream tucked away in a sheltered part of the woods came across his mind. He was watching Eloïse strip off her clothes and drop into the water.

A snap made him freeze mid-vision. Someone had stepped on a twig. Not loud, but distinct. Close by too. Not more than fifty feet away by the sound of it. He gestured for Tex and Harry to stop. They went still. The snap wasn't natural. They waited. A voice suddenly rang out in German.

"Achtung! Who goes there?"

Max didn't answer. How many were there? What weapons did

they carry? Were they on patrol? Or were they tasked to do something like bury land mines?

"Identify yourself. Or we shoot."

Max slipped his rifle off his shoulder and threw himself down on the ground. Tex and Harry followed. Max tried to sight, but in the dark he saw nothing but the outlines of trees, leafy branches, and bushes.

A spray of machine-gun fire shot through the bushes.

Scheisse. The Germans could very well keep this up indefinitely. Max and the two men were in deep trouble. He had to do something. He stretched his arm down to his waist and pulled out a pineapple grenade from his belt. But he'd need to stand up to aim it accurately. That would be a problem. If they saw him, he'd be dead in an instant.

He raised his free hand to his lips, signaling Tex and Harry to be quiet. Then he belly-crawled over to the nearest tree. A new round of machine-gun fire sputtered through the trees. Max tried to push his chin into the dirt but ended up with a mouthful of mud and leaves. He couldn't spit it out. He would cough and that would make noise. How far away was the damn tree? This was the closest he'd come to death since he'd joined the army. Out in the open without any cover. If only he had a foxhole.

Finally he felt the roots of the tree poke through his shirt. He scrambled to his knees but couldn't see anything but brush and bushes. He'd have to stand upright. If he did, though, would they have a visual of him? He guessed the Germans had identified them from what they'd heard, not what they'd seen. But he couldn't be sure. He moved around to the back of the tree, sucked in a breath, and stood up. On the other side of the underbrush and bushes was a clearing about thirty feet away. He thought he could make out dark forms in attack positions. It looked like more than one German had a machine gun. But they were looking ten yards in front of where he now was. They hadn't caught sight of him. Yet. Max pulled the pin and lobbed the grenade into the clearing. Then he threw himself back down on the forest floor.

The noise was so deafening his ears started ringing. The ground shook and shifted beneath him. He smelled cordite. Saw smoke and then heard and saw the crackles from fire. He thought he heard screams as well, but his ears were still ringing. The machine guns went silent.

Max waited until the air cleared; it must have been five minutes. Max worried that more Germans were on the way. Then what? Had he wiped out the enemy nest? Or were there one or two still alive? As the highest-ranking American soldier, he was in charge. They needed to move. Now. He beckoned Tex and Harry to get up and pumped his fists so they'd know to run. He took the lead; Harry was in the middle, Tex in the rear. He started to jog. The others followed suit. But as Max picked up speed, a machine gun stuttered. Max whipped around just in time to see Tex fall.

Scheisse. Tex wasn't moving. Max winced. He whispered for Harry to cover him, crawled over to Tex, and grabbed his dog tags. He and Harry had to get away. To make any kind of stand meant they would die. Max crawled about twenty yards in the opposite direction from Tex, praying that would put them out of the enemy's machine-gun range. Then he stood, Harry behind him, and they jogged south as fast as their gear would let them. They kept their mouths shut. Max felt like a failure. He hadn't been able to protect his team. He glanced over at Harry, who was scowling.

"I'm so sorry," Max whispered when he knew they were safe.

Harry glanced at Max. "It wasn't your fault." He sighed. "We're fighting a war. But Brownsville Tex was a character, wasn't he?"

"I'll take your word for it. I wish I could have known him better." Max tightened his lips. The familiar ache of losing another good soul began. "I know how much you'll miss him."

Max cut east. There were no further altercations with Germans. The sky began to lighten. By sunrise, they'd intersected the road that led to Sainte-Mère-Église. Without the cushion of forest, they could hear far-off artillery and bombers and see B-17s and 24s taking off from the direction of the invasion landing zones. Max took that as a sign the Allies had made a beachhead. He and Harry hugged the edge of the forest and headed up the road toward their original assembly point. When they heard or saw German trucks on the road, they ducked into the forest and hid. With luck the Germans would find the road blocked at the assembly point by thousands of American paratroopers.

When they reached Sainte-Mère-Église there was good news. The 82nd Airborne had taken the city. It was the first French city to be liberated by the Allies. Max was proud to have played a tiny role. He and Harry shook hands and embraced. Max hoped Eloïse and her mother were celebrating.

CHAPTER 71

June 1944
France

The next day Max and the other Ritchie Boys attached to the
82nd began to interrogate captured POWs. When the Germans
realized they were on the losing side, at least at Sainte-Mère-Église,
they became friendlier. Most seemed relieved and willingly gave up
intel. Max had his Red Book and knew the German soldiers
defending Cherbourg hailed from the 3rd Battalion and 4th Battery
of the Grenadier-Regiment. An antiair Wehrmacht division, the 30th
Flak, was also stationed in Sainte-Mère-Église.

Max had the names of the commanding officers and started each
interview with this knowledge. It usually worked, and he followed up
by offering the German a cigarette after the soldier gave him some
intel of value. He found out how many soldiers were in a POWs
platoon, where they'd planted land mines, or how many panzers
they had.

Only one POW gave him a hard time. A captain, or Hauptmann,
the officer kept his mouth shut after stating his rank and serial
number, which was all the Geneva Conventions required. Max tried
to loosen him up by talking about Germany's winning soccer team,

but the man refused to talk. Max wheedled, taunted, and threatened in turn, but nothing worked. He finally gave up.

An hour later, he had an idea.

~

Ritchie Boy Horst Keller, a corporal, was attached to the 82nd. He and Max hadn't crossed paths in Maryland, but they met that morning when the POW interrogations began. Max tracked him down in a nearby tent and waited until Keller had finished interviewing a German infantry soldier.

"Guten Tag, Horst," Max said. Keller wasn't tall, but he was built like a brick, with thick muscular arms and legs that Max suspected were as powerful as a truck.

"Hey, Steiner," Keller replied. "I'm out of cigarettes. You know where I can get some?"

"I'll give you mine." Max dug in his pocket, extracted half a pack of Luckys, and handed them over.

"Thanks, buddy."

"Horst, I need your help."

Horst's eyebrows arched. "Sure. What gives?"

Max explained the situation. "What I'm hoping is that you can impersonate a German officer—you came over in 'forty-one, right?" When Horst nodded, Max went on. "Good. We'll get you an officer's uniform and put you in the same pen as my holdout. He's a captain in the Wehrmacht antiaircraft unit, so he'll be in the A yard. You'll play the role of a 'fellow officer' who's been captured. You'll be sympathetic to the captain and hostile to interrogators like me."

Horst lit a cigarette. He grinned. "Got it. What intel are you looking for?"

"After you've ingratiated yourself with the guy, we want to know everything about their antiaircraft plans. Where they're heading next. How many troops are in the division. What about reinforcements? And anything else about their weapons and antiaircraft strategy."

"Got it. Where am I gonna be from?"

"Since he's with the 30th Flak, it'll have to be one of the Grenadier-Regiment units."

"I can just make up shit, right?"

"Pretty much. As long as it sounds truthful. Here's the thing, though. We need to do this ASAP. Things are moving pretty fast, and you know how a situation can change on a dime. The bombers need your intel."

"You want me to stay with him overnight?"

"No. I'll figure something out. Maybe we'll call you in for additional screening tonight. Give you a chance to get some shut-eye, and then watch him fall apart tomorrow morning when he realizes he's been had."

"Well, this sounds like a good job, for once. It's hard making small talk with a Kraut who probably gave permission to kill Jews."

"I know the feeling," Max said. "Good luck."

Max disguised himself for the "drama in the pen" as they jokingly called it after the fact. He donned a dark-haired wig and glasses and wore a lieutenant's uniform. But he tried to stay inconspicuous, passing the pen where the German officer was imprisoned only a few times. From what he saw, Keller did a remarkable job. He impersonated a captain in the 4th Battery of the Grenadier-Regiment. Over the course of the day, he gained the officer's trust and returned with 90 percent of the information they needed. He brought back the coordinates for their mobile antiaircraft guns as well as German ammunition and fuel dumps. These were passed on through the appropriate Allied radio channels, and, as a result of this information, American naval guns successfully destroyed them all.

Best of all, when Keller showed up the next morning in his crisp, clean US Army uniform, the German captain's face turned bright red, then white. Max and Keller exchanged satisfied smiles. Max sent the captain to a POW camp in south Texas.

Still, it took most of the month of June before the Allies took

Cherbourg, which, because it was indispensable for resupplying the campaign in Western Europe, was considered the most important harbor in the world. American troops from the 79th Infantry Division managed to seize the city on June 26.

Max had been attached to the 101st Airborne, but he hadn't worked with them at all on D-Day and its aftermath. He'd been flexible, though, and was proud of it. He was ready when they called him back to England at the end of the month. He was trucked back to Omaha Beach to board a boat that would take him back across the Channel.

The destruction, body parts, uniforms, and smells of death that other soldiers who'd landed at Omaha Beach described were gone. Now the beach was filled with large barbed wire cages occupied by hundreds of German POWs waiting for passage out of Normandy. Max had two minds about German POWs. He'd interrogated enough Wehrmacht soldiers to know most were just doing their job. What they'd been ordered to do. But there were always a few who were committed Nazis. They were getting off lightly. American prison camps were too good for them.

CHAPTER 72

September 1944
England

Operation Market Garden was supposed to be the last great battle of the war. British general Bernard Montgomery persuaded Eisenhower to stage a massive airborne invasion of the Netherlands and the Ruhr, Germany's heavily populated industrial heartland. Monty's plan was to capture the Rhine River crossings that would pave the way into the heart of Germany. The 101st and 82nd Airborne Divisions, plus the 1st British Airborne, and even a Polish unit, were consolidated into the 1st Allied Airborne Army. Together they would seize nine important bridges. The British 30 Corps would follow up on the ground to safeguard the bridges and destroy Germany's Siegfried Line, a well-defended track that stretched from the border of the Netherlands to Switzerland. The Allies would then cross into Northern Germany.

Max was teaching advanced interrogation and counterintelligence techniques to Ritchie Boys and OSS agents in England all summer and fall. He was crushed when he wasn't deployed to Operation Market Garden, which would be largely fought on familiar turf in the Netherlands.

It didn't take long for the operation to run into trouble. The Allies were able to take some of the bridges, and the city of Eindhoven was liberated. However, their most important objective, capturing the bridge over the Rhine at Arnhem, failed. That failure revealed several problems. First, airborne troops were dropped seven miles from the bridge, and only one division was able to reach it. Second, German defenses were much more robust than expected. Allied intelligence had failed to pick up the presence of two panzer divisions, as well as a veteran infantry division of the German 9th. Allied airborne troops did not have the heavy weapons necessary to withstand those tanks.

Third, the terrain was unexpected. There was only one highway for ground troops to reach the bridge, and marshes, narrow roads, drainage ditches, and dikes slowed their advance. Heavy equipment bogged down and got stuck. In addition, the thickly wooded Arnhem forest cut off most communications between units, and those that went through were spotty. Rain and low clouds further slowed resupply and ground forces.

The 1st Airborne Division, which couldn't take the bridge, lost eight thousand men out of a twelve thousand complement. To make matters worse, once they withdrew, there weren't enough boats to bring all the men back across the Rhine. The Germans rounded up even more Allied soldiers.

In the midst of the FUBAR events, Max and several other Ritchie Boys who were also teaching in Wiltshire gathered at a pub in the village. Outside London in the countryside lay the England Max had heard so much about. Summer skies stayed bright until ten or eleven at night; sheep and goats crossing the roads often caused traffic jams; people spoke with such thick accents that Max often asked them politely to repeat what they'd said.

The village pub, too, had none of the sophistication of a Chelsea or Mayfair bar. It was a one-story building with low ceilings and an uneven floor. Max, who was carrying three pints from the bar to a table in the adjacent room, had to bow his head in order to squeeze through. A sign at the top of a wall reminded him to "Mind Your Head."

He set the pints down on the table. "A sign back there said to 'Mind my head,'" he said. "I'd like to ask Monty what happened to his."

One of the soldiers at the table laughed. "This was clearly not a well-thought-out plan." He swigged a mouthful of beer.

"I can't believe Ike approved it," a second man said.

"And let Monty run the whole thing." Max shook his head.

"Can you believe they didn't have the right intel on the enemy?" Harvey, the first soldier said.

"I'll say one thing about Patton," Max said. "He reads everything that comes in. All our reports. I wonder if Monty even asked for them."

"You think that's the problem?" the second man, Bruce, asked.

"I don't know. Were there any Ritchie Boys attached to their divisions?"

The other two shrugged.

"If they didn't have any Ritchie Boys, or OSS help, it would be a shonda." Max found himself becoming irritated. "Think about it." Max held up his index finger. "One, they didn't know how many enemy troops were in the area, what equipment they had, or where they were concentrated." He held up a second finger. "Two, they had no idea what the terrain would be like. And three"—he held up a third finger—"what kind of battle strategy calls for twelve thousand troops but only one road for them to advance on?" He swilled down more beer.

"All the conditions could have been addressed if commanders had known about them. And knowledge of those conditions is our primary responsibility. I have to assume we had teams assigned to the airborne and ground troops." He gulped down a mouthful of beer. "So what happened? Did our teams fuck up? Was the intel somehow sabotaged? Or . . ." Max paused. "Did we provide the intel to battle commanders who then proceeded to ignore or dismiss it?"

The more he talked, the more his irritation grew. "In which case why are we risking our lives to get this information if it's not going to be used?" He flipped up his palms. "You fellows have any thoughts?"

"Well," Harvey said, "we can't force them to read it. Sometimes, when you're at the top, you don't think the little guys have anything worthwhile to say. You know? You don't appreciate them."

Bruce said, "I sure don't appreciate the guys at the top losing eight thousand men. And then not be able to get the others back across the river. What were they supposed to do? Swim?"

"I'm sure some of them did," Max said. He shook his head again. "Let's hope the SNAFU was just—as the Brits say—a 'one-off.'"

CHAPTER 73

December 1944
Ardennes, Belgium

It was never supposed to be much of a fight. Italy had been conquered and switched sides. Mussolini was in hiding. Paris was now a free city, as were swaths of the Netherlands and Belgium. The Allies stretched from southern Italy to the Netherlands and were heading east. The Russians had stopped Hitler on the eastern front and were now marching west. Hitler would soon be surrounded.

At the end of November Max and a new team of Ritchie Boys had been deployed to Belgium near the Ardennes Forest. Was it a reaction to the failure of Market Garden two months earlier? No one said so, but Max suspected it. He was attached to a mobile field intelligence unit, which was exactly what its name described. He and his team members patrolled their turf, did reconnaissance behind German lines, and interviewed POWs as well as civilians in nearby villages. And, if a little sabotage was in order, they would take care of that, too.

Max was heartened by the assignment. Someone was paying attention. There would be no Market Garden this time.

On an overcast gray afternoon in early December, Max and David Bender, a German-born Ritchie Boy from Freiburg, took their jeep and stopped in at a tavern in Celles, a small village in the Ardennes. A fire was roaring at one end of the room, and someone had thrown in some herbs. Between the fire, the aroma of the herbs, and the thought of a pint, Max could have stayed there all day.

Two elderly men were drinking port, deep in conversation at a nearby table. When Max heard the word "panzer" he nudged Bender, who spoke fluent French, and told him to eavesdrop. Bender strolled up to the bar but remained within earshot of the men.

When the owner came up to Bender for his order, Bender had heard enough to buy the men a bottle of port and take it to their table. The men seemed surprised but thanked Bender, who bent his head and asked them a question. The men looked up, noticed Max, and slowly nodded. Bender gestured for Max to join them. After he sat down, Bender said, "They're telling me they've been seeing a massive German buildup," Bender said. "Troops, trucks, even panzers. Something is going on."

Max arched his brows at the men. "Vous êtes sûr?" The latest intel from command headquarters reported a lethargic German presence, with too little equipment, ammunition, and low morale.

One of the old men whispered angrily, "Of course I'm sure. Do you think I'm a liar?"

Max raised his hands defensively. "I trust you. Where exactly is this buildup?"

"In the Ardennes. You may not see it because the forest is so thick. But if you climb out of the valleys, you will see a line of tanks. There are bottlenecks where the tanks are stalled."

"We should find them," Max said to Bender.

"You must go now. They move at night," the old man said.

"Where exactly can we see them?"

"The valley next to the hill with the castle."

"Merci beaucoup, monsieur." Max stood up as he spoke and grabbed his jacket. He practically ran to the jeep.

~

The castle was perched on a hilltop in Celles. As a little boy Max had seen drawings of the castle in fairy-tale books. With its turrets, towers, and gardens, now bare, it was picture-perfect for children's bedtime stories. Now he and Bender climbed up and looked for a spot to observe the nightmare below. An icy wind whipped around them, and Max's eyes teared with the cold. A thick forest was an excellent cover for massing troops, but level ground offered a smoother surface for tanks.

He removed his binoculars from his pocket and took off his gloves. Lifting the glasses, he focused the lenses with his fingers, already bitter cold. He started a slow pan of the hillside down to the road through the valley below. Then he panned over to the next valley. He stopped and focused the glasses.

"Scheisse!" he croaked. His lips were chapped. The old man was right. The one-lane main road intersecting the valley was filled with a line of panzers. Max couldn't see the beginning or the end of the line. All he could see was that they weren't moving. He passed the glasses to Bender.

"Oh my God," Bender cried.

"It's Hitler's revenge for D-Day," Max said. "He's going to launch a surprise attack through the Ardennes!"

They hurried to the jeep and raced back to their unit. Max wrote a quick report and sent it up the chain of command. Then he marked it "URGENT" and "CONFIDENTIAL" and sent it to the attention of the battlefield commanders. The Allies had to prepare. Max already knew that the two American divisions defending the line, the US 99th and the 106th, were fresh out of training and had no war experience. The battle-seasoned 28th Infantry Division was also there for recuperation. But if a surprise attack was imminent, they had to be warned. Reinforcements needed to be mobilized.

Over the next few days Ritchie Boys from other units in Belgium filed reports as well. Some saw as many as three divisions of panzers and armored vehicles. Nearly three hundred thousand troops and two thousand artillery pieces. Reports of a German paratrooper drop surfaced as well. Max prayed the commanding generals were acting on their intel.

CHAPTER 74

December 1944
Ardennes, Belgium

On the morning of December 16, the Nazis attacked, advancing through the forest. Despite the warnings, the Allies seemed to be caught by surprise. The mostly American forces had been lightly defending the Ardennes, and that hadn't changed. Their attitude seemed to be *Who would launch a surprise attack in winter through a forested terrain covered with snow?*

The result was almost a rout. The 6th Panzer Division and its artillery barrage spanned an eighty-mile area. They hit command posts, troop camps, and communications centers. They were followed by their infantry with shoot-to-kill orders. The attack cut a swath through the untested American soldiers, particularly the 106th Infantry. Many cut and ran. Thousands more were killed.

Heavy snowstorms kept Allied airpower grounded and slowed Allied tank progress. The Germans, who'd already seized the advantage of the roads, advanced. Their immediate goal was Bastogne, a way station on the road to Antwerp, the Belgian port on the English Channel. If Hitler could take Antwerp, he could force concessions from the Allies. All the roads through the Ardennes Forest led to

Bastogne. Control of those roads would give Germany a head start toward Antwerp.

"It's a bold plan," Max said. He, Bender, and the rest of his six-man Ritchie team were billeted with the mobile unit in the church of a medieval-looking village called Houyet. As the senior army official on the Ritchie team, Max was analyzing the intel his men had ferreted out from the interrogations they'd conducted so far.

"Hitler has been shrewd," he told the others. "Because we cracked Enigma and some other communications codes, he's maintaining radio silence and sending orders by courier. And he's moving men and materials at night."

"But we're stuck," Bender added. "The weather is Hitler's friend. Our bombers can't fly in fog or snowstorms."

"Sergeant Everett," Corporal Miller, one of the other team members, asked, "what happened to the warnings you sent up through channels? Didn't you tell them about the German buildup?"

Max felt a ripple of irritation. Of course he had. Twice. "Yes. More than once," he said evenly. "And something did get through. Whether it was our intel or not, I don't know." He explained that their mobile unit commander told him that once SHAEF, the Supreme Headquarters Allied Expeditionary Force, was informed, Eisenhower mobilized quickly.

"As you know, British general Montgomery is in charge of American forces already on the ground. Including us," Max said. "But Ike ordered Patton's 3rd Army to head north from France toward Bastogne. He also deployed the 101st to Bastogne to defend it, hopefully before the Germans get there."

"But you sent your intel weeks ago, didn't you?" the soldier said.

Max nodded. "Back at the beginning of December. When we first arrived."

The soldier scowled. "The Germans attacked on the sixteenth. What happened during those two weeks? Was all that time wasted?"

"I don't know, Miller. I'm as frustrated as you," Max said. "Frankly, no one's told me if Monty reads—or is informed about—our reports."

"What? Are you shitting me?" another soldier asked. "If that's true, it's the second time he's ignored our intel. Didn't he do that at Market Garden?"

"We don't know that," Max said.

"Why are we risking our lives to get intel? If he fucks us over, I'll—"

"Look, men," Max said. "I know we're all upset, but blaming the commanders is not—"

"Christ, Max." Bender cut in. "You said yourself Patton might be crazy as a loon, but at least he reads our intel."

Max almost smiled at that but kept a straight face.

"I just don't know about Monty," Miller added huffily. "Or the Brits. I almost expect to see lines of Redcoats gearing up to fight the Krauts like they did two hundred years ago. The Jerries'll kick their asses, just like we did."

"That's not fair," Max said. "The Brits were the ones who taught us what we know about intel and counterintelligence. They wrote the books we're using. They've been doing this longer."

"Well then, Monty must not know how to read."

"It could be his lieutenants," Max said. "But until we know for sure, keep up the great work you're doing."

Over the next few days the battle seesawed back and forth. The weather remained bad. The Americans were able to delay the German advance toward Bastogne, and the 101st reached Bastogne before the Germans. By December 21, though, the Germans had caught up and cut off all highways leading to Bastogne. They laid siege to the city.

American soldiers were outnumbered five to one. They lacked cold-weather gear, ammunition, food, and medical supplies. Resupplies by air were grounded, and there was no tactical air support. The picture was bleak.

Max's men also picked up reports of a massacre of American soldiers at Malmedy, a village near a road that led to Antwerp.

Rumors surfaced of German paratroopers behind Allied lines. So did stories of English-speaking German soldiers disguised as Americans, who captured critical bridges, cut Allied communications lines, and changed signposts so American troops would get lost.

On December 22 the German commander, General von Lüttwitz, sent a message to his American counterpart, Brigadier General Anthony McAuliffe, demanding the Allied forces in Bastogne surrender. His message said the Germans would annihilate American troops if they didn't.

McAuliffe's reply was short and to the point.

To the German Commander.
NUTS!
The American Commander

In retrospect, unbeknownst to McAuliffe, that reply was the turning point of the battle. On the very next day, December 23, the weather cleared. Within an hour the skies filled with Allied C-47 bombers resupplying US forces and bombing Nazi supply lines. Patton's army fought the panzers around Bastogne and by the twenty-sixth of December broke through. The siege of Bastogne was over.

By the end of December Patton's army was deep into Belgium, and continued good weather allowed the Allies to bomb new German supply lines and fuel depots. The German advance slowed. The Allies gained ground. By the new year, the German advance had stopped altogether. The fighting continued for a few more weeks, but the final outcome was never in doubt.

The German advance had been able to create a "bulge" in the Allied line in the Ardennes, from which the battle got its name. By the end of January, though, that bulge was completely closed and the Allies were poised to advance into Germany itself. The Battle of the Bulge had been the costliest and most brutal battle of the war. More than one hundred thousand Americans lost their lives, and fifty thousand became POWS. German casualties were roughly the same, but the Allies were able to replace their troops and equipment. Germany could not. Hitler had lost his last chance to force the Allies into peace negotiations.

Afterward Max sometimes wondered whether the Allied victory was due to luck more than skill. American troops held their own, but the Germans fought a fierce ground battle. It was the superior airpower of the Allies that won the battle, and that was due to a lucky change in the weather. He decided to keep his theory to himself.

CHAPTER 75

December 1944
Ardennes, Belgium

Max and his interrogation team were one of dozens attached to Allied divisions, battalions, airborne, and infantry after the battle—the number of captured Germans was in the tens of thousands.

Most of the Germans Max interrogated were cold, exhausted, and hungry. Once their immediate needs were satisfied, their attitude was one of defeat. They knew this had been Hitler's last chance to win the war, but most didn't seem too upset that he'd lost.

Only once during an interrogation did Max lose his composure. A German Korporal was giving him details about the massacre at Malmedy, which happened on December 17, the second day of the Battle of the Bulge. Waffen-SS officer Joachim Peiper had killed eighty-four US soldiers who surrendered after a brief skirmish. The Nazis corralled the men into a field and mowed them down with machine guns. The few who survived were promptly executed by a shot to the head. Max learned this same unit went on to commit additional crimes afterward.

Max began his interrogation as he did them all, determined to convey humanity and, if possible, compassion. However, after he introduced himself and sat across the table from the Korporal, Max didn't search for a safe topic about which they could chat. The massacre was so reprehensible, the slaughter so primal, he needed to understand how the young man he was facing could have taken part in it. He must have known the wholesale murder of American troops was a war crime, not simply the result of a hard-fought battle.

Max shook out a cigarette from the pack he kept in his jacket pocket. The soldier eyed it eagerly and relished his first drag once Max lit it for him.

"So"—Max scanned the name of the soldier from his list—"Korporal Eric Schmidt. Tell me about the Waffen-SS. How did you get deployed to them?"

Schmidt took another long drag and nodded. "Your German is quite good, Sergeant Everett."

Max had learned simply to say thank you. "Danke."

"In order to be accepted into the Waffen-SS, you must be a loyal Nazi," Schmidt began.

"And you were?" Max asked.

"I still am."

"I see." Max pressed his lips together and scratched his cheek.

"I was a member of the SS before the war," Schmidt said proudly. "In Frankfurt. You know, of course, I am pure Aryan."

Max's anger grew. He tried to suppress it. "Yes, but how did you get attached to Joachim Peiper? He was a personal assistant to Himmler, was he not?"

"Very good, Sergeant. You've done your homework."

Why was this low-level Korporal patronizing Max? Was every SS member this arrogant? Did this kid—Max had to be three or four years older than he was—have connections?

"How did you come under his command?" Max repeated.

"It was a special deployment."

Max fisted his hands below the surface of the table. "Perhaps your families knew each other?"

Schmidt glared at Max. Bull's-eye. Max felt better. "How could you condone the murder, and it was murder, make no mistake . . . a serious war crime, in fact, of American soldiers?"

"Because it is war. Terrible things happen," Schmidt said. He looked unconcerned.

"And you just let this happen. Why?"

The soldier looked at him as if Max were crazy. "You know."

"I want to hear your opinion."

"I would have been shot in the field along with your soldiers if I'd objected."

Max folded his arms. "So you didn't. And here you are. Without a scratch on your body. Was it worth it?"

"I'm alive," the soldier said.

My family isn't, Max thought. Neither are my friends or the woman I loved. Because of people like you.

"Sergeant," Schmidt went on. "This is the Waffen-SS we're talking about. I had no choice."

Especially when your father and Peiper know each other. Max found it difficult to restrain his rage. The Waffen-SS didn't just instigate atrocities against civilians and Jews in the occupied countries. They were now doing the same thing to Hitler's military enemies. Their adherence to Nazi ideology went far above the norm. It was intolerable.

"You are a member of a cult," Max's voice was laced with fury. "But your cult has lost the war. And you will face consequences for murdering Americans. I see a long prison term in your future."

Schmidt's expression didn't change.

"But I think I'll send you to a Russian POW camp instead."

Schmidt's face went white. The threat of being sent to a Russian camp, where conditions were barely tolerable, and there was no guarantee of survival, was a German soldier's biggest fear.

"Now, get the fuck out of my sight."

Schmidt hurried out of the interrogation tent as fast as he could. Max recalled Spitzer using the same threat in training. They'd been told to use it if a POW wasn't cooperating. Schmidt clearly was not.

David Bender came into the tent an hour later. Max was still angry about the Malmedy massacre.

"What happened?" he asked Max.

Max told him.

"Well, I have something that might make you feel better. One of the POWs I interrogated gave me details about a couple of German soldiers who are impersonating American soldiers."

Max looked over. "And?"

"They're not far away. They're with the 6th Panzer Army in a battle group that's near the Celles and Foy-Notre-Dame area. You think we could flush them out?"

"Only two soldiers?"

"That's right."

"We need a plan."

"Let me work on it."

"Bender, let's keep this quiet for now."

"Yes, sir."

Two days later David explained his plan. They would go drinking at a tavern near the 6th Panzer Army's position. Maybe even the one they'd gone to before the battle. They would be loud and boisterous. Obnoxious Americans. An informer in the tavern would pass the information to the soldiers impersonating the Americans. They would hurry to the tavern in their disguises and pretend they were buddies. Max and Bender would take them before they had a chance to do the same to them.

"Who's the informer?" Max asked.

"I went back and talked to the old man who told us about the panzers. He says it's the tavern owner. If we come in, he'll pass word to the Germans."

"Nice work, Bender," Max said. "But you're not done yet."

"What do you mean?"

"You're relying too much on chance. The Germans might not come inside at all. If they do, why waste time pretending to be our buddies? It would be smarter for them to ambush us when we leave. The plan would be stronger if something or someone lured the soldiers to the tavern and *we* ambushed *them*. What would it take? Free beer and cigarettes? Women? Some intel they can't afford to pass up? That would permit us to lie in wait and take *them* before they go inside."

"I get it," Bender said. "Let me figure it out."

"Okay." Max wasn't thrilled with the plan. "Another thing. I think we'll need a third person. As a lookout, if nothing else."

Two mornings later, Bender said he was ready to go that night. He'd talked to the old man, and the old man claimed he'd talked the owner into opening a few bottles of a good German wine for the men to drink on the house. The fighting around them was light, so Max agreed. Bender chose a third Ritchie Boy to join them. Jan Steyer was new to battle, having just finished his advanced training in England.

During the day, however, a senior field commander, Major John Driscoll, ordered Max to distribute maps of where they'd placed land mines over the previous two days. Max had drawn up the map, covering part of the northern sector of the Bulge. Driscoll wanted everyone in the field to have the map. Which meant Max had to distribute the maps to as many units as he could after dark, driving the jeep on back roads to avoid Germans. He wouldn't be able to participate in Bender's mission. He ordered Bender to cancel it. It wasn't worth the risk.

Max didn't get back to the church in Houyet until well after dawn and was eager to sleep. Instead, he found a note to see the mobile unit commander ASAP. Max found him at a makeshift desk in the apse of the church.

"You wanted to see me, sir?"

"Two of your men were killed last night, Sergeant," he said.

Max gasped. "Who? What happened?"

"Bender and the new guy. Steyer or something."

Max blinked. He kept his mouth shut.

"You don't seem surprised."

Max explained it was an off-book counterintelligence mission designed to capture Wehrmacht soldiers who were impersonating Americans. And that he'd ordered Bender to cancel it.

"Looks like he didn't follow your orders. The Germans ambushed them when they showed up at the tavern. They didn't have a chance in hell."

Max rubbed his hand across his forehead. "Shit. They didn't deserve to die."

"None of us do, son." The commander was quiet for a moment. "Who was Bender? Out for glory? Someone who wanted to be a big wheel?"

"I didn't think so," Max said softly. "Maybe I should have."

"Sergeant, there's no way you can psychoanalyze every GI you come in contact with. Not in the middle of a war. I don't want you to take any blame for this. You told him not to go. He went anyway. It got FUBAR'd real bad." The commander sighed. "It's too bad about the new kid. I'll write the letters."

Max slowly left the church and went to his bunk. What he hadn't told the commander was that he'd still been pissed off about Schmidt and the Waffen-SS's massacre when Bender first suggested the plan. If Max hadn't been so wrapped up in his own rage, maybe he would have put the kibosh on the mission earlier. He did blame himself. He should have been more concerned about his men.

By the end of the battle, Max was ready to quit fighting. It wasn't just because people he worked with and had come to care for were dead. The apparent absence of the Ritchie Boys' intel at the highest level of battlefield commanders nagged at him. So many setbacks could have been avoided. He missed the independence of the OSS compared to the über-organized, compartmentalized army.

He was upset with himself as well. He'd been trying to forgive the German people. At least to accept that they'd been coerced, bullied, and threatened into supporting the Nazis. But Schmidt had triggered his rage. Would he ever know peace? Would he ever have a life and home he could find joy in? He didn't know.

CHAPTER 76

May 1945
England

The Germans surrendered unconditionally on May 8, 1945. When Max arrived back in England he was asked if he would consider returning to Regensburg—it was in the American sector—to help denazify the local government before he was discharged from the army.

"The United States and our Allies believe our key objective is to get Germany functioning again. Nazi-free. We must rid every element of German and Austrian society from the Nazis and their beliefs. That means removing any Nazi or SS member from positions of power. Disbanding and exterminating any organization that condones or associates with Nazis. And, of course, we will prosecute and try prominent Nazis for war crimes at Nuremberg."

"What will my role be?"

"To be honest, it won't be much different than interrogating POWs," the official said. "You'll decide whether an individual is prepared to renounce Nazism. They will fill in a questionnaire, a Fragebogen, about their activities and memberships during Nazi rule. You will discuss those activities with them, and then classify the individual in one of five categories: Major Offenders, Offenders, Lesser Offenders, Followers, Exonerated Persons."

"What if I decide they cannot renounce their Nazi affiliations? Or that they're trying to hide it?"

"They will be barred from public office and restricted to manual labor."

"How long will this assignment last?"

"A few months at least. Current employees who work for the local government will be required to make appointments with you. Citizens who want to work for the government as well. You will have a staff to do the clerical work, but you will report to the army."

"Where will I stay?"

"Wherever you can find a billet. A hotel is fine."

Max wasn't at all sure he wanted to return to Regensburg. Strangers were likely living in his home. They would be Gentiles, of course. But what if they were Nazis? A Nazi living in his childhood home would be a hard hit to his gut. Why put himself through more anguish? Especially since Jews were not permitted to take their homes back. It would be easier if he never knew what happened to his home, his friends, his city. Perhaps he should ask to be assigned to a different town.

The official seemed to sense his reluctance. "Sergeant Steiner, if you don't want to go, it's okay. You wouldn't be the first soldier to choose not to go home. I can find another assignment for you."

Regensburg was no longer "home." But if not Regensburg, what *was*? Amsterdam? Chicago? England? Or had the past thirteen years forever poisoned the idea of home? Like the hordes of refugees liberated from concentration camps and now in displaced-persons camps, Max was technically homeless.

There was another problem as well. Why should Max pass judgment on people he'd known in his past? People who turned away from him because he was Jewish? Forced him to leave school? Sent his father to Dachau? Stole his father's business? His personal history was inextricably bound up in what the army was asking him to do. How could he separate his past from the decisions he was being asked to make? Whatever he decided, the individual under consideration would consider his decision either revenge or favoritism. How would that help denazify Germany?

It would be awkward to interview a Nazi supporter from his past. He understood he wasn't the one who should feel awkward—he'd been the victim; it was the Regensburg citizen who should squirm. But Max would internalize their shame and humiliation anyway. It would be like slipping on a second skin that no longer fit. Five years ago it would have given him satisfaction, a sense of retribution, even justice, to pronounce judgment on the Nazis who persecuted him. It no longer did. Klaus Barbie had taught him that.

"Well, Steiner?"

Max gazed at the official. Max should decline the offer. But then another thought occurred to him. If not me, who? Who else could be objective or dispassionate enough to make informed decisions? He was the one with his roots here. His Ritchie Boy training had taught him that he understood the people of Regensburg better than most soldiers. He could put them at ease or not—depending on their history—with a shared memory of a time, place, or event. From the army's point of view, he was the perfect candidate to interrogate civilians. Even the persecution, oppression, and shame he'd faced could be turned into a positive. Yes, he'd suffered in Regensburg, but he'd found a way to turn it into a strength by emigrating to the US, fighting in a just war, and making informed judgments about German individuals.

Max straightened up. "I'll do it."

"You sure?"

"Yes."

CHAPTER 77

June 1945
Regensburg

Max set up his office inside the Regensburg district court building, an imposing four-story structure in the heart of downtown. His staff would consist of three women who worked in the court system and could access citizen records. There were several applicants. He would make a final decision after interviewing them. He wanted to know how they were selected, what their specific jobs had been, and what their connections were to and with the Nazi Party.

The first thing that Ingrid Richter, a middle-aged woman with gray hair and a steely expression, told Max was that her husband had been a Nazi Party member. "We could not work or earn a suitable salary unless we joined the party," she said. "And anyone who tells you otherwise is a liar." She folded her hands in her lap. "If that disqualifies me from this job, I will understand."

Max smiled. "I appreciate your candor, Ingrid. If you are always this truthful with me, I will not have a problem with your past." He paused. "As long as it is your past. Not the present."

She pressed her clasped hands together. Her knuckles turned white.

"What is it, Ingrid?"

"My two sons were killed, one in North Africa, the other in Belgium. My husband died of a heart attack when our second boy died. I *have* no present, other than work."

"I am so sorry. I hope you can forgive Germany's erstwhile enemies."

She nodded.

"Are you prepared to identify and help apprehend other party members, particularly those who may still be closeted?"

"I do not blame the Allies for my sons' deaths. I blame Hitler. And the Nazi Party. Arrogant pigs."

Max accepted her as his administrative assistant.

Beatrix Kuhn, a thirtyish woman with black-framed spectacles and her hair in a tight bun, had much the same to say. Her husband had been killed last winter in the Ardennes. "Imagine, Herr Steiner. He made it through the entire war without a scratch. Only to die at the last major battle of this verdammt war!"

She, too, had been forced to join the party, she said. But now? She made a dismissive gesture with her hand and mirrored it with a contemptuous exhalation. "I have two small children to raise. I had to move back in with my parents across the river. I don't give a fuck about the party. What did they ever do for me?"

Max hired her as well.

Elsa Sommer, somewhere in her twenties, was attractive. As she walked into his office, a cloud of perfume moved with her, like an invisible but aromatic web. Her face was heavily made-up, and her clothing a little too revealing. She sat across his desk and folded one thigh over the other. Her skirt stopped above her knee.

"Miss Sommer. How do you do?" Max said politely. "Can you tell me what your job was in the court system?"

She swung her leg back and forth. "I was secretary to the chief judge."

"I see. And what were your duties?"

She shrugged. "Whatever he asked." She shot him a seductive smile. "But he wasn't half as handsome as you."

Max knew she was offering herself to him, but it was more about her needs than his. She must be desperate, to throw herself at a complete stranger. Then again, that's what prostitutes did, wasn't it? Except for Annaliese. She'd made him come to her all those years ago at Der Wallen. Made him so crazy with desire he couldn't stay away. And then she'd kept him at a distance until she was sure he loved her.

He would need to interview someone else. He would tell Miss Sommer he didn't think she was a good fit for the job. But he found the fact that he was noticing women again, after so many years of denial, surprising.

He learned from the first two women that the army had requested government applicants a few hours after the end to the fighting in Europe was announced. Within forty-eight hours, a skeleton German government in Berlin was ready to operate. Who were those bureaucrats? According to the women in Regensburg, they were the same people who had done the job the day earlier. And a month before that. And the previous year.

It was clear that in order to run a complicated bureaucracy, the more experienced employees would, of necessity, have been party members. The new "Nazi-free" government needed experienced personnel. If those employees renounced the Nazis, at least publicly, they would likely keep their jobs.

But there would never be a "clean slate." Max would still interact with people who were anti-Semites, harbored authoritarian leanings, and would never change. He'd already heard rumors of Operation Paperclip, through which rocket scientist Wernher von Braun and 150 of his scientific colleagues would be emigrating to America. Other rumors focused on the disappearance of high-ranking Nazi officials, some of whom eventually popped up in South America. To "fight" Communism.

Like Klaus Barbie, for one. He, and other former Nazi officers, would have needed help to escape Germany. Was America now embracing the evil they had so zealously fought against the past five years? Or were the Americans simply pragmatists, cherry-picking the best talent for the country, no matter where they came from? Max understood that "the enemy of your enemy is your friend." Now, though, apparently, so was the enemy itself.

CHAPTER 78

August 1945
Regensburg

In August President Truman dropped the atom bomb on Hiroshima and Nagasaki. The emperor surrendered on August 15. Finally, the world was at peace. Until the next war. The Allies were already talking about dangerous Communists in the Soviet Union. But the next war would begin without Max. He wanted to make peace. He was trying to begin in Regensburg.

He had plenty of time to reacquaint himself with the city. Its medieval influence was still evident. The market, city hall, and the Gothic cathedral, all built during the Middle Ages, had miraculously survived. The Old Stone Bridge was still in use and had been repaired, as were thousand-year-old monasteries and churches.

In fact, Regensburg was one of the few large German cities that had not been significantly damaged by Allied bombs. A Messerschmitt factory was destroyed in 1943, but it was in the suburbs. The only part of the city that had entirely disappeared was the Jewish Quarter.

Now that he was seeing the city with adult eyes, Max realized how cloistered he had been as a youth. Regensburg's downtown was bigger and more dynamic than he'd realized. Because his life had been focused on school, sports, and the Jewish community, he'd missed the international fame accorded to the city. He vaguely knew Regensburg had been a center for trade through the centuries, but he didn't know—or he forgot—it had started out as a free city in Bavaria, occupied by the Romans, the Swedes, then the French, and then passed back to Bavaria. With so many cultures stamping their mark on the city, of course it would be sophisticated in its markets and wares.

Although Regensburg seemed to have survived the war intact, it did have a black mark. For one month, from March to April 1945, a satellite camp of the Flossenbürg concentration camp was set up at the city Colosseum. By the time Max arrived back in Regensburg, it had been closed. Max wondered if the city fathers were embarrassed by their association with Nazi ideology. He'd heard more than forty people had died while it was open.

Perhaps it was the city's reputation as an international center, or perhaps it was just coincidence, but Regensburg became the site of a displaced-persons camp in 1945. Refugees from Nazi-occupied countries, former concentration camp inmates, and Jews who spent the war in hiding poured in during 1946 and 1947, making it the largest DP camp in the country. Built in the workers' district of Ganghofer Siedlung on the edge of the city, the camp housed more than six thousand people. A large percentage were Ukrainian. The size of a small village, the camp even organized its own postal service.

Max had wandered through the camp a few times, hoping against hope he'd see a cousin or friend or neighbor who had somehow survived, but he never ran into anyone he knew. He tried to track down his mother's cousins from Alsace, knowing his uncle Leo Bendheim in New York would want to know. He discovered through the camp that Leo's cousin, and Mutti's too, had stayed in Germany. They had been sent to Theresienstadt, where they were transported to Auschwitz and gassed. Uncle Leo would be devastated.

It was this paradox—the earnest efforts of some Germans, particularly in Regensburg, to prove they had cleansed themselves of the

Nazis' evil, coupled with the deaths of so many Jewish families—that convinced Max he could never make Germany his home. He would go back to Chicago when the army discharged him.

～

Near the end of August Max got a letter from Freddy Hahn, who, fortunately, had survived the Ardennes. Max had written to let him know he was temporarily in Regensburg. In the letter, Max raised the issue of their interrogation intel and that it seemed not to have reached the desks of military leaders.

Dear Max:

I am thrilled that you are well and still sane almost a year after our "adventure" in France. I wish the results had been different, but I will always be grateful for your assistance. There is no one in the world I'd rather have with me in a tight situation. Although I do question your sanity for volunteering to return to Regensburg.

I am in Lyon interrogating French citizens, who now proclaim that the dirtiest word in the French language is "collaborator." You would not believe how many are eager to tell me that their neighbor, employer, landlord, doctor, even their best friend, were cooperating with the Nazis. Not them, of course. They supported a Free France from the beginning. Ahh . . . the Froggies. Not even a world war can change their charming personalities.

Now that we'll always (once again) have Paris, I hope you and I can get together before we're discharged. I've only spent a few days there—have you spent any time in gay Paree? Perhaps Christmas? We must trade stories of our weeks in the Ardennes. They're now calling it "The Battle of the Bulge," but I keep thinking of a man whose belly flops over his belt.

Seriously, though, I spent most of my time in Bastogne and then was attached to Patton as he zoomed across Europe. I have never traveled so quickly or so far with so few casualties. At least George was reading our intel.

Which brings me to the point of this letter. I hope you saw the article in the Paris Herald Tribune last year on December 28. The article claimed that the initial German breakthrough was "universally considered a catastrophic failure of American intelligence." You and I know the real story. How could this have happened with so many Camp Ritchie–trained officers on the ground?

The answer that I'm hearing through the military grapevine is that it didn't. Other factors were to blame. Namely, the generals at the highest level did not consider our work credible or actionable. They were convinced that Germany had been so severely crippled from massive bombings, and were on the run from battleground defeats, that they could not mount an attack. (I always knew I disliked Monty.)

But it's not just Montgomery. I believe even Ike and SHAEF decided to ignore the warnings of their trained intelligence officers on the ground—most of it collected by Ritchie Boys—that the Germans were mounting a huge attack. I also believe the absence of this timely intel caused the decimation of the 106th Infantry Division. And the lives of at least twenty thousand men who could have been saved. Only General Omar Bradley honestly admitted, "In the face of this astonishing German build-up, I had greatly underestimated the enemy's offensive capabilities."

We warned SHAEF. They chose to ignore us. This was the biggest blunder of the war. Perhaps you and I can discuss the best way to make sure there will not be blunders of this nature in the future.

In Pax Semper,

Freddy

Max was relieved and reassured by Freddy's opinion, which mirrored his own. Why did they risk their lives in the first place, if not to pass information through channels that would safeguard troops and defeat the Germans? He'd been told that the Ritchie Boys were responsible for collecting more than 60 percent of the intel on German troop movements. The thought that his work, and that of his Ritchie Boy brothers, had been ignored sat like a stone in the pit of his gut.

CHAPTER 79

September 1945
Regensburg

It took Max until the middle of September to visit what used to be the Jewish Quarter. First he walked to Stadtamhof, the residential neighborhood on the other side of the Old Stone Bridge. His house looked smaller than he remembered, but it wore the same attractive blue-gray stone tiles and gray mansard roof. Curtains covered the windows but the lights were on inside. Who lived there now? He walked around to the back. The stable had been torn down. He wasn't surprised. He remembered the rides he and Klara had taken around the city when he was young.

Max tried to be stoic about the house. It was just property. Although he did wonder what had happened to the furniture and clothing they'd left behind. He had an urge to ring the doorbell to ask. He was wearing his uniform. When the new occupants opened the door, they might be taken aback. Perhaps frightened of whatever business the occupying power had with them.

He supposed he could force them to come down for an interview. He could classify them. Then he wondered why he was bothering.

Furniture and clothes didn't matter. In fact, it was possible the current occupants didn't know who lived there before they moved in.

He walked around the block in Stadtamhof and realized he was only a few houses from Renée's house. It had been months since he'd thought of her. They'd lost contact—her last letter had told him she was engaged. She would be married now, living the high life in Shanghai or some other exotic city. He should check out her house and write her what he'd seen. She would appreciate it. If the letter reached her.

When he got to her house, it was dark inside, and the windows were covered with paper. A huge half-timbered home, it now looked isolated and lonely. Had no one lived in it since the Herskowitz family left? That was hard to imagine. It had been nearly a decade.

Max climbed the steps to her front door. The memory of her cinnamon vanilla cookies washed over him with an aroma so powerful he had to stand still until he realized he'd imagined it. Those wonderful cookies were more than cookies. At the time they gave him the reassurance that something in the world was still sweet. And good. Despite the fact his life was coming apart. He sat on the stoop. He still had her copy of *Huckleberry Finn* somewhere among his possessions. He let out a breath. They had lost so much.

After a long while he rose and started back to his hotel. He decided to skip the area that had housed the Jewish Quarter. It was no longer there, anyway.

CHAPTER 80

September 1945
Regensburg

One morning near the end of September, Max was looking over his upcoming interview at ten o'clock. He liked to familiarize himself with the individual who was applying for a government position. The official who told him his job wouldn't be much different than interrogating a POW had been right. By preparing himself with the name, age, and background of the applicant before the appointment, Max could begin the conversation with a known fact about the person, which, hopefully, would elicit deference and respect from same applicant.

With this particular individual, though, Max was concerned. His name was Johann Schröder. When Max read his CV, he realized the man was Max's former public school teacher, who had chosen to personally humiliate and persecute Max during the Nazis' rise to power.

Memories of that period came flooding back. Schröder had made him stand and read aloud excerpts from the antisemitic screed *The Protocols of the Elders of Zion* in front of Max's fellow students. He'd defaced Max's desk with swastikas, photos, and insulting sketches of

Jews. He'd threatened Max's family with deportation to a camp, and he'd lied to the school principal about what he'd said and done. Max never forgot. Now he would be deciding the man's fate.

Max sat at his desk and went through the application. It was unclear exactly what Schröder had done in the war; it was clear from the absence of information about his company, division, and rank that he had not been a soldier. There was something about writing articles and speeches. But for whom? And why? At least he wasn't torturing other Jewish students.

Max vowed to be fair. He wouldn't prejudge, and he would listen. He did have an advantage, though. Schröder didn't know Max was the person who would be interviewing him. Max had another idea as well. Just in case. He called downstairs. Afterward he told Ingrid what he'd done and what he wanted her to do.

Ingrid called Max at five minutes before ten. Schröder was early. "Do you want him to wait, Sergeant Steiner?"

Through the phone Max could hear Schröder ask in a surprised voice, "What was that name?"

"Sergeant Max Steiner," Ingrid replied. "United States Army."

A beat of silence. Then: "I'm afraid I must go. I have a very important appointment. More consequential than this."

Oh no, Max thought. He's not getting off that easy. He quickly strode to the door of his office and opened it wide.

"Good morning, Herr Schröder. It is time for your appointment. Come in."

Schröder gaped at Max. His expression registered fear. "I'm afraid I must go."

Max stared at Schröder. He was older now, with gray hair at his temples and the sides of his head. His clothes were ill-fitting, and he now had a belly. "Of course you may leave. But if you do, you won't be coming back. The US government offers only one opportunity for

German citizens to rehabilitate themselves. I suggest you take advantage of it." Max signaled to the open door of his office.

Schröder didn't say anything, but after a moment, he turned and walked into Max's office. Max guessed Schröder thought Max didn't recognize him. That would be like him, Max thought. To think he could, as the Americans said, "put one over" on Max. Max decided to play along and see where it went.

He sat at his desk and gestured for Schröder to take the chair across from him. "I'm glad you decided to stay. How long have you been in Regensburg?"

"I came here in 1930. From Frankfurt."

"Frankfurt is a big city. Why here?"

"The stock market crash. A lot of jobs were wiped out."

"But you are a teacher, are you not? Everyone needs teachers, crash or no crash."

"Not the schools in Frankfurt, apparently."

"I see. So you got a position here"—Max paused while he pretended to skim his application—"as a social studies teacher at a public school in Regensburg."

"That is correct."

"But you didn't stay past . . . let me see . . . 1936. Why not?"

"I was given a better opportunity."

"Please. Elaborate."

"I'm afraid I can't."

Max frowned. Where was Schröder going with this? "There's something about writing articles and speeches. For whom? When? Did it pay better than teaching?"

Schröder nodded and shot Max a smile. Max thought he looked smug. At least insincere. "It was, as you Yankees say, 'top secret.'"

What game was Schröder playing? If he really thought Max didn't recognize him, wouldn't he be more candid about his past? Didn't he understand the importance of this interrogation? Max would give it one more try. "I will need to know more about the nature of this work. Was it propaganda for the Nazi Party? The Communist Party? If so, local or national? Who else was involved? How long were you doing it? Why were you not conscripted?"

Schröder folded his hands in his lap. The smile remained. "I will take it up with your superior officer. You look much too young to handle matters of this nature."

Max decided to stop playing games. Schröder was clearly playing his. "Matters that you called 'inconsequential' when you arrived?"

Schröder arched his eyebrows as if to say, *What are you going to do about it?*

Max's irritation boiled over. He had interrogated plenty of arrogant Nazis during the war. But there was something about Schröder —he wasn't sure what—that made him want to lash out and belt the man, just as he'd done a decade earlier. Was it the fact that Max knew Schröder was trying to make him lose his composure? Was it that the man didn't have a dollop of compassion or empathy? This was a man who should never be in a responsible position, public or private.

It occurred to Max that Schröder had become a teacher because he'd failed to impress or manipulate adults. Students were the only people with whom he could flex his perceived power. Young minds, like Max, whose emotions often overruled their behavior. Adults wouldn't stand for it. That made Schröder the worst kind of Nazi, cruel and abusive. He searched for a soft spot in his victims so he could disparage, insult, and persecute them. He had done those things to Max. He'd enjoyed them. He was doing them now.

It was time to end the charade.

"Schröder, do you really think I don't recognize you? Or that I forgot what you did to me twelve years ago? I remember everything. My only regret is that I didn't permanently disable you. You will never work in a government institution. I am classifying you as a Major Offender, and you will be sent to a reeducation camp."

"I don't think so," Schröder said. He rose and slipped a revolver out of his pocket.

Max tensed. He'd expected something like this, but it was a dangerous situation just the same. Max reached for his own revolver and unholstered it from his belt.

"And do you think I didn't know who you were before I walked in here this morning?"

Max knew Schröder was lying. There was no way Schröder could have known in advance he would be interrogated by Max.

Schröder continued with a counterfeit smile. "This is a simple matter of an arrogant, unforgiving Jew who never understood he has no place in Aryan society. Because of your actions I am compelled to act in self-defense."

Before Schröder fired, the door to Max's office burst open, and the two MPs Max had requested when he realized whom he would be interrogating grabbed the man. Surprise and fear flashed across Schröder's face.

"You can't do this," Schröder said. "You don't have the authority."

It was Max's turn to smile. He raised his own gun and pointed it at the man. "Schröder, you are under arrest. You will be held in our military prison, and I will be submitting a case to the Nuremburg prosecutors." Max knew it probably wouldn't go that far, but Schröder didn't. "Adieu, Schröder. How fortuitous to have run into you."

Schröder's gaze darted from Max to the MPs and back. He looked like a rat who'd been trapped in a maze.

Max walked out of his office to thank Ingrid.

CHAPTER 81

October 1945
Regensburg

Max finished his last interview of the day, a doctor who seemed quite remorseful. Max reassured the doctor he would not be stripped of his license to practice medicine. Afterward he thought about going to a café for a beer. He wasn't much of a drinker, but German beer was the best in the world. At least it used to be, and many of the cafés and taverns were touting free beer at their Oktoberfests. He was reaching for his jacket when Ingrid buzzed him.

"Yes, Ingrid?"

"Someone would like to see you."

"I'm finished with the interviews for the day."

"I don't think that's what she's here for," Ingrid said. "What was your name again, miss?"

"I'm a friend from his childhood," Max heard the woman say. The voice was familiar, but he couldn't quite place it.

"Send her in." Max thought it might be another job applicant. He hadn't hired a third assistant. The door opened, and a tall, slim, fashionably dressed young woman stood at the entrance. She had curly dark hair piled in an attractive arrangement on her head, pale white skin, and eyes that were an astonishing blue.

She smiled shyly. "Hello, Max. I've been looking for you everywhere."

The eyes. The voice. The smile. "Renée?"

Her eyes shone.

Max's mouth gaped open. "How? When? Where?"

She came to him. "First, we must share a proper hello." She opened her arms.

Max opened his and pulled her toward him. "I can't believe it!"

"Neither can I." She blinked several times. Were her eyes wet?

They remained in each other's arms for a long minute. Max pulled away. She was a married woman. "So, you've been looking for me?"

"I have." She brushed a hand across her forehead. "I even wrote to the army to find out where you were."

"Did they tell you?"

"They did! I can't believe you are here."

"It's just temporary. A few months or so."

"That's what they said."

"But what about you? Why did you come back to Regensburg?"

"I told you part of it in my last letter," she said. "May I sit down?"

"I have a better idea."

After they were seated at a café and had drinks, beer for Max, wine for Renée, Max said, "What letter?"

"I wrote you a long letter about six months ago. You never got it?" She frowned.

"I did not. But I was moving around quite a bit."

"Oh, dear." She let out a breath. "So you don't know anything—wait. That means the last letter you received, I had just become engaged to Tomas."

"Yes."

"Tomas was executed by the Japanese a year ago for espionage and treason."

Max swallowed. Anything he said would trivialize yet another horrifying event.

She bit her lip. "Thank you for not saying how sorry you are."

He nodded.

"I think I hinted at our activities in one of my letters. As you know, the Japanese occupied Shanghai in 1937. For the most part, they left the Jews alone. But after the Americans entered the war, things changed. They forced us to move into the ghetto in Hongkou, which is a horrid slum. They also treated the Chinese—well—as badly as the Nazis treated Jews. They had big plans. They thought they would conquer the world. Tomas wanted to know exactly what those plans were. I helped him research and choose surveillance targets." She paused. "They caught Tomas breaking into the Japanese consul general's home in the middle of the night when we thought he was away. They arrested him and shot him two days later."

Max was quiet for a long moment. "Do you think our lives will ever be normal again?"

"What's normal?" she asked.

He shrugged. "I think you know."

A sad smile flitted across Renée's face. She changed the subject. "What are you going to do when this is over?"

"I'll go back to Chicago. Finish school. Attend college. Then, I don't know. You?"

"Sell my parents' house. After that, I don't know either."

"I was going to write you about your house. I walked by it last week. It looks as if it hasn't been lived in at all."

"That's what our neighbors told us in their letters. I don't under-stand it. My father told me he sold it, but since he passed I—"

"Oh no."

"He developed pneumonia in the ghetto. Mercifully, it was fast."

"I respected him. I'll never forget how you brought him over when Papa was in Dachau," Max said. "I thought of him when I got to Amsterdam. I almost applied for a job at a diamond dealer." He was quiet for a moment, surprised at how easily they were able to talk to each other.

"Papa would have loved that." She cocked her head and smiled. "So Max, about Amsterdam. There is one thing you never mentioned in your letters. I know you haven't been celibate these past ten years. You're so smart and handsome I'm sure plenty of women threw themselves at you."

"Let's take a walk," he said. He helped her out of her chair, paid the bill, and they went back outside. "I wish Klara was waiting for us."

"That would be perfect, wouldn't it?"

As they walked, Max told her the story about Annaliese. How she had been a prostitute, how he fell passionately in love with her, how talented a fashion designer she was, how he rescued her and found her a job.

When he finished Renée was quiet. Then: "She sounds like a courageous woman, Max."

He swallowed. The words came out slowly. "She would have liked you, Renée." Why had he felt so constrained from putting it down on paper? Was he afraid of hurting her? She'd told him about her Tomas. She'd been nothing but honest. But Max hadn't told her the whole truth. "But I was responsible for her death."

"What? How could that be? You loved her."

He winced. "I need to tell you the end." He explained how she'd been blackmailed by a former client. How Max had tried to avenge her honor, and how it ultimately led to her death. "I've never looked at another woman since."

"Because you were consumed with guilt."

He nodded. They approached a marble ledge protruding from the front of an apartment building. "Come," she said. "Let's sit."

They both sat down. "Now I will tell you the part of my story *I* haven't told anyone else." She hesitated. "I was the one who suggested Tomas break into the Japanese consul's office. He wasn't in favor of it, but I persisted. I was sure he would find some letter, some telegram, some document that revealed what monsters the Japanese were." She let out a long breath. "He listened to me and ultimately agreed to do it. He didn't find a thing, but he didn't have time to look. He was caught right away and they executed him two days later."

Max looked over. Tears filled her eyes. He took her hand.

"So, you see, I have always thought I caused *his* death. Had I not pushed him . . . had I realized it was a foolhardy idea . . . he would still be alive."

"Oh, Renée."

"Don't say it. I've punished myself enough. For both of us." She squeezed his hand. "As have you, dear Max. But we were at war. We thought we were making the best decision we could at the time. We need to forgive ourselves just like we're trying to forgive our enemies."

Max's throat felt suddenly parched. His breathing grew irregular. A tear started to edge down his cheek. He tried to blink it away, but another took its place. Soon they fell more freely. He bent his head and hunched over. A sob escaped. Then another.

Max could not remember weeping as a child. Now he couldn't stop. The sorrow, regret, guilt . . . and forgiveness that he'd forced himself to keep at bay all these years had found a crack and were spilling out. Renée sat beside him and held him while he cried. And cried.

Max had no idea how much time passed, but gradually, his sobs grew farther apart. The tears slowed. Renée released him but kept one hand on his arm. When he was through, he turned to her, about to say something, but she spoke first.

"Max, I'm so sorry you had to face everything alone. In America. Without your family or friends from Amsterdam. I wish I could have been there. At least when Tomas died, I had my mother."

What more was there to say? They'd both survived. They both had scars, but they weren't the only ones. It would take years for them . . . and other Jewish survivors to feel normal. Whole. If they ever could.

But Max didn't want to think about that now. He was grateful that Renée had been the one to whom he confessed. And she to him.

He wiped his nose on his sleeve. "Is she well? Your mother?"

Renée smiled. "When I decide where to live, she'll join me."

"What about Wolf?"

"He married a Chinese woman. They have a son. They are planning to move to Hong Kong."

"Wolf? The little menace?"

She giggled. "Not so little anymore. But you should see his son, Chaim. He's very much like his father."

Max smiled, too. They rose and walked a block in silence holding hands. Then: "Renée, do you remember when you first told me about Tomas in a letter?"

"I do," she said solemnly.

"I should have told you about Annaliese then."

Her expression softened. She moved closer to him. "Life got— quite complicated—between us, didn't it? But I never stopped loving you, Max."

She looked up at him. He gazed at her. In the space of an hour, the twelve years they'd been apart seemed like only twelve minutes. Had it always been this easy? Of course, they'd only skimmed the surface, but for the first time in years Max felt safe. No one understood him like Renée. Even when they weren't talking, there was a sense of trust. Forgiveness. Perhaps even peace. She knew him. He knew her. How could he have thought otherwise?

He disentangled his hand from hers and brushed his fingers down her cheek. She smiled, lifted her hand, and twined his fingers with her own. She moved their joined fingers to her lips and kissed the back of his hand. It was the perfect gesture.

They continued to stroll down the streets of Regensburg, hand in hand, taking in the city, sometimes talking, sometimes allowing a comfortable silence to envelop them. With Renée by his side, it occurred to Max that his war was over at last. He might—just might —have come home.

ACKNOWLEDGMENTS AND AUTHOR'S NOTE

I now understand why World War II is such an inexhaustible subject of literary fiction. It is impossible to cover its breadth and depth in one story—or a thousand. I used to say that World War II was the last war where good and evil were so clearly defined. But now that I've researched *Max's War* I realize that isn't much of an explanation. The fact is so many nations, so many events, so many people, lived through it—each with their own unique story—that it truly is a fool's errand to make any kind of generalization.

This is the first novel I've written where 90 percent of the plot emerged organically from my research. That research included Hitler's rise to power, the Ritchie Boys' history, Jewish persecution, Holland before and after the occupation, missions and battles, and my late in-laws' history. Still, it required enormous paring, shaping, cutting, and streamlining to create a cohesive whole. I barely touched the Pacific theater, with the exception of Shanghai where many European Jews took refuge, the Battle of Stalingrad, or the invasion of Italy.

I did move a few events to better fit the chronology of the story. For example, the resistance movements in the Netherlands did not begin as early as they do in *Max's War*. Neither did Klaus Barbie's children's orphanage event in occupied France, which was based on the action in Izieu that occurred a year later. I also changed the names of Camp Ritchie officers and instructors.

My major source for Ritchie Boy history and class materials was the excellent and detailed *Ritchie Boy Secrets* (2021) by Beverley D. Eddy. It became my bible for weeks. Much of her information ended up in "Max's" fictional instruction. Also integral to my research was *Sons and Soldiers* (2017) by Bruce Henderson. Both are now dog-eared but proud additions to my library. I liberally borrowed Guy Stern's interrogation techniques, as reported by Ms. Eddy, for Max.

Not much fiction has been written about the Ritchie Boys (yet). I read *An Immigrant Soldier* by K. Lang Slattery and *A Ritchie Boy* by Linda Kass. Both were eloquent, enjoyable novels based on both authors' relatives who became Ritchie Boys.

Among the experts who helped guide me were Don Whiteman, whose knowledge about World War II radio is extensive; former Army Lieutenant and Bombardier Robert Crowe, who flew missions during the Battle of the Bulge; Barbara Alter, whose knowledge of Hyde Park during the 1940s helped me create Max's neighborhood; and Michael Black, a former US Army soldier. Mary Ellen Kazimer, a WW2 expert herself, fact-checked the manuscript. Any mistakes are mine alone.

Still other sources included *Before Auschwitz: Jewish Prisoners in the Prewar Concentration Camps* by Kim Wunschmann (2015); *The Diary Keepers: World War II in the Netherlands* by Nina Siegal; German Propaganda Archives, including a Calvin University collection of *Das Reich* articles and speeches by Joseph Goebbels: 1933-1945; a host of academic articles indexed by JSTOR (available on request); films about Jewish immigration to Shanghai and other online Holocaust historical events.

Max's jacket on the cover of this book is deliberately unadorned. It was difficult to find the proper decals and badges he would have worn. And, as you might suspect, Max preferred to be anonymous. I also changed some of the spellings to modern versions of the originals.

In conclusion, I am grateful for the careful reading of the manuscript by my writing group, Tim Chapman and Diane Piron Gelman. I also owe a debt of gratitude to Kent Krueger and Jodie Renner for their "sit on your hands" read-throughs. And Eileen Chetti for her always thorough and accurate copy editing.

They say word-of-mouth is the best sales tool in the world. If you liked *Max's War*, would you please leave a short review on the site where you bought the book? I would be grateful.